'Following

On 20th February 2001 a case of Foot and Mouth Disease was confirmed at an abattoir in England. In the weeks and months that followed, the outbreak progressed to become the most devastating and costly epidemic of FMD the world has ever seen. Whilst newspaper articles attempt to look at the human stories behind the misery, and official reports to document the 'facts' as they are presented, neither can do justice to the full extent of human involvement: the 'life-changing' actions, emotions, and personal anguish of the vets, farmers, and support staff directly affected.

Following Orders is an attempt to rectify this. It should be read by anyone who has an interest in the way we are governed. There is a danger that policies made by people remote from the consequences of their implementation can have undesired outcomes. This book may help us all to understand how things can snowball and quite simply 'get out of hand'.

Following Orders is a work of fiction. Inevitably some people will try to see beyond the fiction to real, live people. But all the places, characters and conversations in this book are fictitious, and any resemblance to actual places or persons, living or dead, is purely coincidental.

Following Orders

James Drew

Bluebell Publishing

First Published in Great Britain by

Bluebell Publishing
Sandford
Strathaven
Lanarkshire
ML10 6PN

e-mail: books@gobluebell.fsnet.co.uk

ISBN: 0-9538220-0-1

Printed and bound in Great Britain by
Cox and Wyman Ltd, Reading, Berkshire

Designed by: david@thedesignkit.com

To all the people and animals of the world that
have suffered through the abuse of power

With love and thanks to my wife and children

Glossary of Abbreviations

GVS   Government Veterinary Service.

AHO   Animal Health Officer. A technician employed by the Ministry of Rural Affairs whose job includes blood sampling, supervision of cleansing and disinfection, logistical support, etc.

VO   Veterinary Officer. A vet who is permanently employed by the Ministry of Rural Affairs.

TVI   Temporary Veterinary Inspector. A vet who is temporarily employed by the Ministry of Rural Affairs.

DVA   Divisional Veterinary Administrator. A vet who is in charge of the local Animal Heath Office of the Ministry of Rural Affairs.

RVA   Regional Veterinary Administrator A vet who is in charge of a particular region of the country.

PVO   Principal Veterinary Officer who is in overall charge of the Government Veterinary Service and answerable to Ministers.

IP   An infected premises where disease has been confirmed.

DC   Dangerous Contact. A premises that because of its contacts with an IP is considered likely to develop disease.

Acknowledgements

My wife and children for being there.

Lindsay, Stuart, Sue, Sarah, Alasdair, Mary, Margaret, Celia, Dave, and Carol, for reading the manuscript.

David for putting it all together.

Prologue

It was two thirty in the morning and he lay in his bed at The King's Head hotel, surrounded by dead and dying animals. The mattress and sheets were damp and clinging, not with the sweat of love but with the sweat of fear and disgust. He tried to think of other things. Of puppies and kittens. Of white sand beaches with turquoise seas. His mother and father, brothers and sisters; friends and past lovers. Good food and wine; parties and happy laughter.

But always it returned. The long neat row of dead day old lambs stretched out before him; growing longer as he laid each tiny body gently on the straw, arranging each in turn with love, so it seemed that it was only sleeping. He hoped he had reached the end but the supply grew bigger. The faster he slipped the sharp, shiny needle between the ribs and into the heart to inject the lethal dose of barbiturate, the faster another lamb was brought to him.

On some farms he had seen dead lambs slung on top of each other in heaps but felt it too disrespectful of life to do the same. So he lay each one down as tenderly as he could; each touching the other for warmth and comfort and in a pose that brought order out of chaos, and love out of brutality. And all the time ringing in his ears was the bleating of the ewes and the click, click, click of the captive bolt and the coarse exclamations of the slaughtermen as they went about their work with neither pleasure nor distaste, just a purposeful detachment from a job to be done for which they were well paid. He felt tears in his eyes, the sharpness of the salt on his tongue; black and purple flooded his mind, confusion and disbelief. He could not understand. Did not know what to do. He wanted not to feel the way he did. There was no future. Not for him; not for the lambs; not for humanity.

He lay in the dark, silent, the events of the last weeks teasing and taunting him. He thought of the Jews in Auschwitz and the Bosnian Moslems at Srebrenica and of the people who had killed them. 'Just following orders' they said; obeying a few simple instructions without understanding or considering what it was they were doing. History forgotten. Responsibility betrayed.

The long line of lambs turned into Jews and he continued injecting them one after the other as they were brought to him, silent and unresisting, exposing their breast to him in an act of submission of their body, their consciousness proud and unbowed. Then the Bosnian Moslems arrived and he made a fresh line of them and all the time

1

the click, click, click of the captive bolts sounded in his head, and his body felt cold and clammy with the sweat. Babies and young children came next and he continued, unstopping; unthinking; he had to have the job done by the end of the day so that the reports could be sent and a new day's work planned.

More black and purple washed around his head. The lambs were wakening, lifting their heads and bleating plaintively for their mothers. Babies too began to stir and wail and hot fired panic seized him as he saw that his bottle of barbiturate was nearly empty. Everything was waking and the line of sheep and people to be killed was growing longer, longer. He heard the curses of the slaughtermen, their captive bolts jammed, melted with the heat of overuse. The job, the job, it could not be finished; there would be consequences.

Relief and joy, he saw a pile of gleaming machetes stacked in the corner of the barn. He ran to them and handed them out to the cheering slaughterers and led the way as they cut and slashed amongst the bleeding animals and people. The bleats and screams grew louder and he was in the jungles of Rwanda with the Tutsis fleeing in fear or crowded in dignified prayer in the village church as the Hutu warriors cut their way through them and then set them on fire.

Faster and faster they worked and harder and more frenzied they cut and thrust and he began to laugh and to sing and the slaughterers joined in. Slowly the cries of the people subsided and he walked amongst them, arrogant and triumphant. He found a young girl lying alive and half buried beneath the twisted corpses, blood stained and pleading to him with eyes and outstretched arms. He killed her with a savage blow. Coils of slowly moving intestines skidded under his feet, dark red blood congealed in the sun and thick black clouds of flies buzzed and landed to feed and lay their eggs. He was hungry now and he was disgusted. Disgusted at the filth on his hands and clothes. He washed them under a stream of clear cool water and unwrapped his sandwiches, eating with relish. He thought of his friends and family at home; wondered how they were; hoped he would see them soon.

He looked around at the carnage he had created. They would soon be stinking he thought. He thanked God he didn't have to clean up the mess. Thanked God his orders didn't stretch to that. A job well done, completed ahead of schedule. Good work he told himself.

The black and purple swirled in his head, disappeared on the horizon, and he knew he was awake. His body dripped with sweat, his head burning with fear and pain. He glanced at the clock through the blackness, it was 3.00 am. He quickly got out of bed and felt his way to the bathroom, finding the light switch just in time.

His stomach churned and he threw up into the toilet bowl, retching and retching until his stomach bled. Bile and stomach acid burnt his throat; he had gone to bed without eating. The acid taste of the bile mixed with the salt of the tears that flowed down his face. Tears of pain and bitterness; tears of shame; and tears of enlightenment too. Now he understood clearly how the atrocities of the world came to pass. The process was the same. The power of corporate action and diffused responsibility where no one was accountable. Policies and demands passing down a long command chain that with each step distanced the individual from their actions. And he understood too the ability of people to do, without question, exactly as they were told.

He looked in the mirror and saw the blood stained eyes and the snot on his top lip. Only this time he had the self respect to wipe it away. He washed his hands and face and turned on the shower. He stepped into it and washed his hair and lathered soap all over his body. Then he rinsed away the foam and the sweat and with them every bad thing he had done in the last few weeks; done out of ignorance because he didn't know what else to do. He watched with satisfaction as the froth disappeared down the plug hole.

He dried himself and dressed, pulling back the sheets to air the bed. He settled himself in a chair with 'For Whom the Bell Tolls', the third Hemmingway he'd read since the whole damn ghastly business began. He sat until nearly 7.00 a.m. and then switched on Sky News.

42 cases of Foot and Mouth Disease had been confirmed the previous day. The fields and barns of Northern England and Devon were full of rotting and stinking animal carcasses; the air thick and black with the clinging smell of burning flesh. The Government Principal Scientist and the Minister for Rural Affairs stressed the need to increase the rate and extent of the killing. Those with voices of dissent were derided as misguided, subversive.

At 7.30 a.m. he made his way down to the dining room and ate a huge fried breakfast. A weight had been lifted from his shoulders and he ate with the joy of a condemned man spared. It was not an easy decision and it would have life changing consequences, but the terrors of the night had concentrated his mind such that amidst all the mayhem and confusion, he now knew what he had to do.

PART ONE

The Warning

Chapter 1

Veterinary Officer Steve Turner switched on his computer and waited for the e-mails to download. He had been skiing in Chile for two weeks and the messages popped on the screen one after the other, solid black titles, urgent replies requested. He laughed to himself and closed his eyes imagining he were back in Chile. Sharp rigid peaks, the might of the Andes sprawling into the clouds. Mile after mile of grey and white in every direction; an aching blue sky; the lemon milky sun of a Southern Hemisphere winter, the icy cold on his nose and lips, and in his eyes.

Crisp chilling snow. The clear air like crystal focusing the depth of his view. The musty smell of fresh roasted lamb; the taste of blackcurrant rich Cabernet. The taste and smell of Chilean women, aromatic and spiced with vanilla and musk. South American Indian mixed with European blood; high cheekbones with shining black or deepest brown hair. Isabella and Marianna, practicing their English with giggles and blinking eyes. Beautiful, friendly girls. He sighed out loud.

The high pitched 'pop' from the PC told Steve that the e-mails were safely in his in-tray; fifty eight of them. There were FINs (Field Information Notes), EIs (Emergency Instructions), ANs (Action Notes), and a heap of memos from his boss. And there were WANCs (World Animal News Circulars). Steve liked WANCs the best. He liked them because he knew that the guy who invented the acronym had no idea of what he'd done. That was the irony that was their Head Office in Sage Street.

He opened and read the first few and then deleted them all. It was all shite, he thought. Not just shite, a load of fucking shite. He sighed with irritation. In the space of ten minutes, the stress relief and relaxation achieved from two weeks and two thousand pounds spent in Chile had gone, melted away like frost in the sun.

Along the corridor he could hear the voice of his boss, Divisional Veterinary Administrator (DVA), Herbert Bluster, talking on the phone to Ron Steady, the Principal Veterinary Officer (PVO). Herbert wore a self-satisfied expression on his face whilst Ron was expressing his thanks for all the hard work that Herbert had recently put in on the National Emergency Review of Disease-free Status (NERDS) committee. With only a year to go to retirement Herbert was still hoping for recognition on the Civil List for his life's devotion to The Service and his achievements.

Herbert Bluster had joined the Ministry of Rural Affairs Government Veterinary Service (GVS), over thirty five years ago and cut his teeth on outbreaks of good old Foot and Mouth Disease; Swine Vesicular Disease; and Brucellosis eradication. He looked back with untold fondness to the great Foot and Mouth epidemic of 1967 and never tired of repeating the story of his part in its eradication to anyone prepared to listen or who had no polite means of escape.

The words, 'Back in '67' became a signal for those with more than a passing acquaintance with his ways, to smile, nod their heads at appropriate points in the ensuing monologue, and let their mind wander. Wander to planning that next exotic holiday in the sun, or to just what they'd like to do with that new girl in admin with the tight bum and perfect breasts who was more provocatively dressed each time they set eyes on her. Herbert, taking encouragement from their smile, would drone on with passion about the funeral pyres that were built and just exactly how many tons of coal it took to properly burn a cow, a sheep or a pig.

To his credit, Herbert was a hard working man. Anxious to please his superiors he said 'Yes' many more times than he said 'No'. He did not fight his corner or that of his staff if it meant conflict with those above him. But he did not shirk responsibility either, his shoulders were squarer metaphorically than in reality. Indeed he would willingly shoulder, even volunteer for, more responsibility if by so doing he ingratiated himself to those with more power. Even at his age the procurement and attainment of 'Brownie' points was a powerful motivating force.

Steve Turner did not care for 'Brownie' points. His only ambition was to survive the GVS, though he suspected this was not something to include in his Personal Development Plan of SMART aims and objectives. He nurtured no dislike of Herbert and tolerated him as best he could but he did not respect him. Herbert lacked judgement which made him vulnerable to ridicule, and though Steve ridiculed him not infrequently it left in his mouth the bitter taste of dishonesty that was hard to explain. After all, Herbert frequently ridiculed those beneath him with undisguised pleasure.

No, strangely, Steve felt only a benevolent pity which he assumed Herbert would find condescending. There was a boringly predictable conventionality about Herbert's nice upper middle class existence. He was a pillar of the community and proud of it. The middle of the range family saloon car. The detached house in one of the posher parts of town. The obvious pleasure in the free tickets to the local shows and bowls matches. The bed, breakfast and evening meal holiday packages at traditionally run family hotels. The two or three pint limit at conference get-togethers.

What Steve wanted to say to Herbert was 'Get a life pal. Do something extraordinary for a change. Drink ten pints and throw up over the PVO, then we'll see how fucking sincere his thanks are.'

Staff meetings were the stage on which Herbert performed. A stage he delighted in, projecting himself in the most influential and glowing light. There were liberal references to his chats with the PVO concerning advice that had been solicited from Herbert and duly supplied. Ron it seemed was always impressed with the speed and quality of his response. Herbert's contacts with local MPs, Chief's of Police and Consultants in Public Health Medicine were sprinkled on the agenda like dung on a bed of roses.

The importance of good, accurate paperwork, the need to get the monthly and quarterly returns in on time was paramount. Work recording codes and which code should be used for each piece of trivia were matters that made Herbert's eyes shine with an inward passion. Senior Management needed these (works of fiction), on which to base their most telling management decisions, he said. And so it was inevitable that at one such meeting, after Herbert held the floor for an hour or more about the Business Plan, then Personal Development Plans, before eventually grinding on to Modernising Government, that Steve suddenly thought enough was enough.

'Quite frankly this is getting on my nerves Herbert,' he said. 'Why can't we just get on and do our work to the best of our ability without being weighed down by all this crap? We all know it's a load of bloody bollocks! We're being ruled by administrators. In twenty years time people are going to look back on this and say "What a load of bloody tossers they were. They just stood and let themselves be shafted without a whimper." I'm sick of it Herbert. I'm overwhelmed with initiatives and reporting, audits and bloody quality checks. I've had enough. I'm worn out by it: I just want to do my job,' he added, withering like an erect penis at the sound of children's feet on the landing.

9

He felt his face and neck flush hot; felt the slight tremor in his speech. He knew he'd gone too far, but it was genuine emotion, pure and simple; a gut reaction. Honesty, with no hidden agenda.

Many of those present looked shocked and Herbert's face contorted with a rictus that appeared out of control. Veterinary Officer (VO), Sammy McLeod had an admiring and amused look on her face. And Willie McDonald, an Animal Health Officer (AHO), assumed a look of mock offence and horror.

After much struggling Herbert regained his composure and strangely appeared to be smiling.

'Let's not get over-excited Mr Turner,' he said with an uncharacteristic fatherly air. He started to drone on again but by now Steve was not listening, his mind in tune to the pain he had relived constantly for the last fifteen years.

He was thinking of Rachel. He was thinking of his wife.

Chapter 2

Sammy McLeod was only a few years from retiring and single by choice. There had been no lack of past suitors but all had failed to live up to her expectations. She was hard working; crushingly honest; and with a big heart and big sense of humour that endeared her to all her close colleagues. She did not though suffer fools gladly and to her, Herbert Bluster was a fool.

It seems likely that Herbert sensed this because, as Sammy delighted in telling, he had only to arrive in the car park and glance across to her office window for his nervous twitch to run rampant.

'It was so bad the other week,' she recounted at coffee one morning, 'that I honestly thought he was having a fit'.

Willie McDonald laughed out loud. Capable and able to cut through the bullshit he had been with the Ministry for twelve years. He had spent time on detached duty in Devon burning mad cow carcasses and helping out with TB control, and had seen a lot of ways of working and almost as many ways of not. He was as Scottish as it is generally considered sensible to be. His wife Morag was an angel and they had six children, four boys and two girls, from fifteen down to four years old. Morag fed and clothed them on Willie's salary and could hunt out bargains at all the National high street names like

Oxfam and Marie Curie. There was no spare money but there was plenty of love, and time and patience too.

Most Fridays Steve dropped in to the McDonald house on his way home and had a beer or two with Willie, and more often than not stayed for supper. He liked the kids and read to the young ones and joked with the older ones like contemporaries. Sometimes he had more than one or two beers and then Morag ran him home.

She was very protective of Steve. She didn't think it right that someone like him should be alone. He should have a partner she thought. Someone he loved and who loved him. It didn't suit him to be living alone, he should have a heap of kids like Willie and her. Sure he had a lot of freedom and there was no shortage of money, or women either. But they weren't the right sort of women; nothing to offer him other than their undoubtedly beautiful bodies. They were never around for long, a few weeks, a couple of months if they were lucky, and then up popped another one and the previous name was spoken no more. Morag was sad and told Willie so, but he just laughed and teased her that he wished he was in Steve's shoes.

In truth Steve envied Willie. But he had vowed that he would never again put himself in the position he'd once been in. Never, never, ever. He had plenty of money now and he enjoyed it. He rented a small farm cottage, no mortgage round his neck. The years he spent working in The Emirates had given him a secure financial future, he had savings plans and government bonds in droves. And he liked spending money now. Good food and wine, the twice yearly exotic holidays and the high maintenance women. Without his government salary the investments would soon dwindle to nothing and he was not prepared to start again. Not for a third time.

Only two months ago he'd bought himself a 1963 three litre Austin Healey. It was outrageous by Ministry standards where most people drove entry level models of mass produced tat. It was the car he had dreamed of owning; he hadn't driven a soft-top since leaving university, and that seemed like a million years ago.

Back then it was a white 1275 cc twin SU carbed Mark IV Austin Healey Sprite. For a student it was a car in a million. A car to kill for, a car to die for. Impossible to drive it fast enough; to throw it round the corners hard enough. Impossible not to make the tyres scream and smoke on every journey he made. He thought of the summer he drove down to Devon with Rachel in the passenger seat, hood down and sun shining and he felt like a fucking hero on a galloping white horse with his damsel and her hair blowing in the wind.

And then a few months later at that party in Bridgewater. The rejection, the sucker punch, the knockout blow. He remembered creeping out of the house at first light, a morning of pure brilliance and light with milk fed sun and a faint haze of heat hanging over the still sleeping town. He felt the bitter furtive taste of testosterone in his mouth, daring and adventurous as he carefully unpopped the tonneau cover and noiselessly opened the car door. He clicked off the handbrake and pushed the car down the hill past the stone built houses, so that no one would hear the roar from the engine and the bark from the exhaust, jump starting it fifty or sixty yards from the house. Then with tears streaming down his face and the sort of thoughts that only a jilted twenty one year old can feel, he stamped on the throttle and in a screech of tyres and the smell of burning rubber he was off on another adventure, galloping across the wide expanse of Somerset towards his friend's house in Devon and shouting out loud, 'Fuck you bitch. Fuck you.'

Never a day passed that he did not think of all that had gone since then. But he told no one and it sat inside, at his centre, like a piece of rotting meat, tainting everything he did and thought. At times he fought against it but in the right mood he loved to recollect and nurture the pain. And use it to excuse him for everything he had failed to do since. He controlled it, keeping it manageable and tame. But he would not let it go. Could not let it go, because he fed off the memory and it kept him from making the same mistake again.

Sammy knew there was something. Something in his past that had left a mark, a scar; a memory that held him back. She saw it in his cynicism and flippancy. And she sympathised. Because in spite of her energy, Sammy too was tiring of the job. She was the product of an age where the only target was to have the work done to the best of her ability by the end of the day. This modern talk of objectives and business plans, well, … she didn't understand it. But she knew that her work and efforts were not enough for her managers and went unappreciated.

There was too much change going on, change for changes sake, much of it for the worse in her view. There was no longer stability. At her age and stage of career she didn't want to progress, didn't want to develop any further. She wanted very much the same as Steve. To get on and do her job. She had trained as a vet and ̶ she wanted to do. Her career had embraced many discipl̶ practice; two years in Bolivia with Voluntary Service ̶ lecturing; Veterinary Adviser to a multinational drug compa̶ finally joining the Ministry of Rural Affairs.

She and Steve were soul mates. Their common bond was their lack of ambition and they shared the knowledge that with no ambition their boss had no power over them. There was no purpose in brown-nosing, the greasy pole was left untouched, and threats from above were as hollow as fish bones boiled and sucked dry. It was fun to be on the sidelines, to sit back and watch the jostling for position with an interest born only of entertainment rather than self-promotion. So long as the job was well done, all unnecessary pressing of the flesh could be left to those who wanted to progress. They could say what they thought, speak as they found, and not tow the party line.

They giggled about it together with glee, like naughty children rather than the mature professionals they were supposed to be. It made them exclusive. Members of a tiny and prestigious club not accessible to all.

And Herbert Bluster knew. To him a lack of ambition to progress within The Service was the equivalent of witchcraft, sorcery and heresy. If Investors in People had permitted burning at the stake, then he would have concurred with enthusiasm and self-satisfaction. The Modernising Government doctrine of 'valuing diversity' did not sit easily with his thirty five years of Ministry experience. He valued a rigid dogma and unquestioning obedience and was disappointed that his own career progression had apparently come to a halt. In truth he felt slighted, but took comfort in the assumption that he had the ear of the PVO and was highly regarded and respected by his peers.

Yet in spite of his underlying disappointment, there was, deep inside, a part of Herbert where a passion still burned. A passion that made him tremble at the knees and which tugged at his heart with, these days it seemed, an ever increasing pain and sense of loss. He often thought back to those far off days and felt the butterflies fluttering deep in his stomach like someone experiencing new love. He could hardly believe himself that he had once felt like that. Big, jowly, plain faced Herbert, surely an impossible dream. But he knew it had been true and he wanted to feel it again.

He rocked back in his chair, closed his eyes and let his mind drift. Yes he could remember it all fresh and clear as though it were yesterday. He remembered the passion, the ecstasy, the unpredictability and the spontaneity; the late nights away from his wife over bottles of fine wine in the intimate atmosphere of some romantic country inn. Yes, he wanted to experience it again, just one last time, surely that wasn't too much to ask for? He leant back further and sighed, speaking it quietly like a mantra under his breath as if he needed to reassure himself.

'If only,... if only. Foot and Mouth epidemic 1967.' Now those really were the days he thought.

Chapter 3

The George Stevenson that designed 'The Rocket' was a wholly different sort of man to the one that shared his name and owned a specialist pig veterinary practice in the east of England. The original George Stevenson was intelligent, well educated, a risk taker who followed his dreams and became forever remembered in history. Our George had no dreams. No sparkling fire that burned with passion. Just a mild interest in pigs and the myriad diseases of production that sprung up with depressing regularity the minute your guard was down.

He had been into pigs since he was a boy. His father farmed them in traditional back yard style, the pigs in sties and fed on swill collected from schools, hospitals, restaurants and hotels, carefully boiled and poured into the troughs twice a day. In those days a forty sow unit was a good size, big enough at least to ensure that young George always smelt of a mix of pigs and overcooked school dinners; an all pervasive smell that a bath (when he bothered to take one), tempered rather than removed.

The kids at school called him 'Piggy' Stevenson or 'Porky', and he became not displeased with the name and the fame and recognition it bestowed. He was a studious boy and passed exams with ease, deciding that instead of a life of feeding and mucking out pigs he would train as a vet and treat sick ones instead. He could not know how the pig industry was set to change because industry it truly became. Intensive, fast turnover; an accountant's dream or nightmare depending on which part of the pig economic cycle was current. When pig meat prices rose, farmers with the right facilities (and often those without them), piled into pigs and some made their fortunes. When the price fell, and it always did, some fortunes were lost; many went out of business, and others clung on to be first in the queue when the good times returned.

George had seen this cycle many times since leaving the Royal Veterinary College in London and, wisely as it happens, set up a specialist pig practice in a market town in East Anglia. It was good pig country. A surfeit of cheap grain grown close by to feed the pigs, and plenty of well drained arable land on which to spread the increasing quantities of manure and liquid slurry. Pig herds had become bigger. Five hundred sow units were now commonplace and one thousand sow units increasingly so. Intensity of production had risen too. The number of piglets born and reared per litter; the number of litters per sow per year; the weight of feed consumed for each kilo of body weight; all became critical factors in the drive to make an enterprise profitable. A small change in any one of them or in one of a host of other factors could mean the difference between riches or insolvency.

With the increase in numbers, individual pigs became worthless in the context of the enterprise and George's work changed from that of animal doctor to animal disease controller and production adviser. Routine visits to large pig units became the norm. Visits where the production records would first be analysed, and only then be followed by an inspection of the pigs and a discussion as to how faults could be rectified and profitability increased. A change of stocking density perhaps in the dry sow house; a change of temperature in the flat-deck weaning house, or the addition of antibiotic to the feed in the growing pens.

Pig production became concentrated in the hands of a few, huge, integrated pig companies. The companies that owned the pigs had them contract bred and reared by dozens, even hundreds of individual farmers. Throughout the production chain the parent company fieldsman kept a check on progress through weekly visits and inspections. Those farms constantly at the bottom of the ladder for poor food conversion rates or high piglet mortality were ruthlessly pruned from the enterprise. It was in their interests not to remain at the bottom for too long and there were ways, some of them illegal, to ensure it did not happen.

George was employed as a consultant to one such production company, Farm Fresh Pigs, UK, Ltd. And today he was concerned. Very concerned. For eight months the company had been beset with problems. Two new syndromes, Porcine Dermatitis Nephropathy Syndrome (PDNS), and Post Weaning Multisystemic Wasting Syndrome (PMWS), had emerged from nowhere. They were recognised too in the States and continental Europe but no one knew where they'd come from or even what caused them. There were some viruses implicated but they were not the whole story and in some respects the cause was irrelevant. What did matter were the huge losses that the two diseases caused amongst post-weaning piglets with up to 40% deaths.

Church Farm where George now stood was an eight hundred sow breeding unit that reared and fattened about half the piglets it produced. The others were sent out to seven or eight different farms for rearing. The owner of Church Farm had a contract with Farm Fresh Pigs and the rearing farms were under their control too. The last three years had been dire for the pig industry with widespread losses and redundancies. Investment in infrastructure had been non-existent and many pig farms were dilapidated and in filthy condition. Now though the price of finished pigs was rising and had passed the break even point, heading rapidly into profit. PDNS and PMWS removed some of the cream but pig industry accountants were beginning to smile again and visit new car showrooms. The future was rosy.

Weaned pigs at Church Farm had suffered with both PDNS and PMWS. George was familiar with this from his previous monthly visits but today he had been called in specially by the farm owner, Dave Cox, because the disease had 'jumped' from the piglets to the sows. Four sows dead in the last three days and another ten sick. Many of their piglets dead too.

As soon as George climbed into the pen he saw that things were bad. Sick sows lay flat on their sides breathing hard, unmoved by the presence of a stranger. Some had a red and purple discolouration of their ears, snout and legs, while others had a diffuse red rash all over their body. One was paralysed in its back legs, dragging itself hopelessly around the pen, and two more were shaking and trembling. George took out a thermometer and checked the rectal temperature of four of them. Instead of

16

the normal 101 Fahrenheit, they were all above 105. George pursed his lips.

'Where's the sow that died today?' he asked.

Donning rubber gloves and taking a curved post-mortem knife he deftly cut through the sow's skin, slicing through the muscles on the inside of both hind legs right into the hip joints and then through the muscles that attached the front legs to the rib cage. Next he forced all four legs flat against the ground where they acted as stabilisers propping the carcass on its back. More sweeping cuts through the skin, fat and muscle on either side of the lower jaws exposed the submandibular lymph glands which were red and swollen. He sliced into them and they oozed blood, rich and haemorrhagic like ripe blood oranges. George gasped involuntarily, droplets of sweat coalesced on his face and ran down his nose to splash onto the torn carcass.

Another swift knife cut and the sow's belly was opened from pelvis to breastbone. Thick fat bulged through the skin and a thin, blood stained fluid flowed out and onto the straw. Two more cuts through the abdominal muscles perpendicular to the long axis of her body allowed the abdominal wall to be folded to one side exposing the coiled mass of intestines, bright pink, far pinker than they should have been, the blood vessels supplying them engorged and inflamed. The mesenteric lymph glands that drained the lymph from the intestines were hard and swollen red, splashes of blood glistening as the light played on them.

George rummaged deep inside the body for the kidneys, red and enlarged with tiny spots of blood peppering their surface. He cut into them and blood flowed freely. Almost as an afterthought he pulled out a piece of the colon and with a pair of scissors opened it out about a foot along its length. The raised, circular, button-like ulcers on the inner surface gave a cheery wave.

'Absolutely classic,' he murmured. 'Classic,' he repeated, 'I don't think there's any doubt.'

'Doubt about what?' asked Dave. 'What is it? PDNS? The sows don't usually get that do they?'

George shook his head. 'No, the sows don't get PDNS,' he said slowly. 'It's not PDNS Dave. I can't be certain but,' he hesitated, 'I'm convinced this is Classical Swine Fever; Hog Cholera; call it what you like.'

'But we don't have that here,' said Dave reassuringly. 'Whatever it is, it can't be that.' He was adamant and agitated. 'What do we have to do?' he continued. 'Get these dead ones into the pit and mix some antibiotic into the feed for the rest of them? That should do the trick shouldn't it?'

George didn't reply. He was thinking. Thinking of what he had to do next.

'I need to phone the Ministry,' he said finally. 'Phone the Animal Health Office and get them to come and take a look. If it is Swine Fever then the shit really hits the fan. They'll close this place down, slaughter the whole damn lot. It's a bloody nightmare.'

'I'll phone Farm Fresh Pigs and let them know what's going on,' said Dave thinking quickly. 'They'll pay compensation I suppose? It might even be to our advantage.' He spoke his thoughts out loud and regretted it.

Veterinary Officer Sarah Fowler was at her desk in Broadwich Animal Health Office reading some of the less interesting instructions on her computer screen when the Duty vet came into her room with a look on his face that suggested something bad had, or was about to happen.

'Suspect Swine Fever at Church Farm,' he said excitedly. 'Can you go?'

'Who reported it?' she asked, unmoved. 'Dave or old George? It's probably George panicking over a bad dose of PDNS,' she added.

'George sounded pretty worried,' said Bill, calming himself down at Sarah's lack of concern.

'Yes, I'll go and hold his hand and make it all better for him,' she teased. 'I'll just check I've got all the right gear in the car and I'll take a copy of the Swine Fever Instruction Manual with me. I haven't done one of these for years…. probably won't need to today either,' she mused.

She finished her cup of tea, checked her forms folder, post-mortem and sampling kit and drove the twenty three miles to Church Farm in intense sunshine and heat, her car windows open and Bruce Springsteen sounding from the speakers. She ran through the signs of Classical and African Swine Fever, as she drove. They were caused by two different and unrelated viruses but were clinically indistinguishable from each other. Both could cause acute disease with rapid death, and a more chronic disease that was clinically more difficult to diagnose. CSF was still present in parts of Europe associated with wild boar and the last serious outbreak in domestic pigs had started in Holland in 1997 and grumbled on for a year or more before it was finally brought under control. An epidemic in Britain would have serious financial and trade implications for the pig industry.

On the way to Church Farm she passed field upon field of outdoor pigs; great white sows rooting around in the earth or lying huddled together in communal nests of golden straw, their sleeping arks abandoned because of the stifling heat. There were a lot of pigs in the area and the number of outdoor herds had increased in the last few years. If one of the Swine Fevers were to be confirmed thought Sarah, well it would be a severe test of the Vet Service's resources with staffing levels so low. The up side was that it might just be the shot in the arm that was needed to bring those in charge to their senses and make them realise that the cost cutting had to stop. It could be that an outbreak of Swine Fever was just what was needed to remove the complacency that existed at Sage Street. It was a pity that it would just be PDNS, she thought.

Chapter 4

She felt her heart banging away against the inner surface of her breasts, the saliva dried in her mouth and her skin lifted tingling from the flesh beneath. George had greeted her at the gate, sheepishly, almost apologetic, like a boy caught smoking at school.

'I hope I'm not wasting your time,' he said.

You are, thought Sarah, but she smiled sweetly anyway.

'Not at all,' she said, and now, having examined the sick sows and the remains of George's post mortem she had come to the conclusion that dull old George was probably right. Dave was adamant that no pigs had come onto the farm for several months and that none of the farm workers had been near pigs on other farms. No swill was fed to the pigs; no semen brought on for artificial insemination. It seemed impossible for it to be Swine Fever but the clinical picture was textbook stuff.

She looked at George with more respect than previously. 'I think you're right George. It looks like Swine Fever unless PDNS has become more virulent and is attacking adults too. It's possible I suppose. Either way I'm going to phone Sage Street and tell them I suspect Swine Fever.'

George breathed a sigh and relaxed. The fear of being mocked, even belittled had been real enough. Now the relief flowed easily, his shoulders relaxed, the hollow feeling in his stomach gone. Responsibility passed like an electric current from him to the Ministry. He had played his part and not been found wanting.

'We'd better go to my office,' said Dave, the skin of his face the colour of uncooked filleted fish.

'Can you put me through to the Veterinary Adviser, Exotic Diseases Section please?' Sarah asked the telephonist as she sat in Dave's pig shit stained and fly blown office.

The person who came on the phone had been at Sage Street for only a couple of months. Recently separated from his wife, the opportunity to get away from her on a temporary minor promotion had come at just the right time. An enhanced salary, accommodation allowances, and the chance to immerse himself in his work and meet new and interesting (?) people. A lifeline to a drowning man.

Sarah had never spoken to the guy before but formed the opinion that he was at least pragmatic if somewhat uncertain as to what he should be advising her to do. At first he was not persuaded by her diagnosis but with the benefit of self-confidence and long experience, she stood her ground and convinced him that all necessary procedures should be brought into play. At last he agreed to the service of Form A restrictions, prohibiting the movement from Church Farm of all pigs and other livestock, farm machinery, and all fomites like manure, feed, and protective clothing. After that she would take the necessary diagnostic samples and it would be a question of wait and see. He thanked her jokingly for ruining his day and left her to get on with it.

When she came off the phone, Sarah flicked through the instruction manual to the section on sampling. Up to four post mortems needed to be done on recently dead or euthanased sick animals, and paired samples of clotted and whole blood were to be taken from ten sick pigs for antibody and virus isolation tests at the Government Veterinary Laboratory (GVL) in Surrey, and the Exotic Viruses Research Institute (EVRI) close by.

She phoned her own Animal Health Office to tell Bill what was happening.

'Can you get one of the Animal Health Officers to organise the lab submission forms, cool boxes for the samples, and then take them to the labs as soon as I get back?' she asked. 'And Bill, could you phone the labs please and tell them they're coming so that they can process them tonight without waiting around till tomorrow? This is hot Bill. Very hot,' she added, keeping her voice cool and steady but with a tone of urgency that could not be ignored.

Bill admired her attitude. There was no hint of panic. No melodrama or overreaction. Just a clear statement of what she wanted and expected.

Sarah prepared herself mentally for what she needed to do. Take the necessary samples as quickly as possible; prevent the spread of disease from the farm; and make an assessment of where the disease might have come from and have already spread to. While she toyed with all this in her mind she hastily wrote out a Form A restriction notice and gave it to Dave Cox, explaining that nothing that could possibly be infected was to leave the farm. Equipment, machinery, the lot.

'Please explain that to all your workers,' she said.

'We're in the middle of harvest,' said Dave. 'We've got to take the combines and tractors and trailers up to the neighbouring farm. The grain's ready, and if the weather breaks it'll all be ruined. Farming's in a bad way. If we lose money on that too we'll be out of business.'

He was sweating, hackles raised, ready to fight. Sarah thought quickly.

'Where's the grain store in relation to the pigs? And do you use the same tractors for harvesting as you use in the pig unit?' she asked.

'I'll get a map,' he said rummaging around in a filing cabinet. He unfolded it on the desk; it was worn and held together with sellotape, smears of dried dung and dust stuck to its surface.

'This is where we're harvesting and these are the grain sheds.' He ran his finger over the map. 'They're a good hundred yards from the pig pens and there's a separate entrance to them up the lane. The tractors we use for scraping out the pigs are different to those we use on the arable land. So are the men. We've got to keep the harvest going.' He was pleading with her as he traced out his words on the crumpled paper.

Sarah studied the map quickly.

'Right,' she said. 'Can I draw on this?'

'Go ahead,' replied Dave.

In blue biro she drew an outline from the roadway up the track into the yard and around the grain sheds.

'The harvesting machinery can only enter this area,' she pointed. 'It mustn't go any nearer to the pigs. Neither must the tractor drivers. And the pigmen mustn't go near the grain shed. If you can to stick to that I'll specify that area as being outside Form A restrictions. Does that help?'

'Thanks,' said Dave. 'We'll stick to it.'

She smiled. 'Now, I want to take some samples from the dead pig and from two of those sick sows. I'll need to slaughter them though I'm not sure how. I don't know what the story is about compensation, but I think they're going to die anyway so you'll not be losing anything extra.'

'Kill what you need,' said Dave. 'In fact I can kill them for you. I've got a shotgun that I use if we get a sow with a broken leg or something. I'll fetch it and meet you in the yard.'

'Can you spare a couple of the men to hold sows for blood sampling? The sooner we get all this done the sooner we can get a result one way or the other. And George, can you stay and give me a hand please? You can't go onto any more pig farms until you've had a shower and changed your clothes, and I suggest you wait a couple of days anyway.'

'Of course I'll help,' said George smiling. He was enjoying himself now. Even above the pigs she smelt sweet.

They returned to the half mutilated pig carcass and whilst George held and labelled the screw top plastic universal containers, Sarah quickly took two sets of samples; submandibular lymph gland; mesenteric lymph gland; spleen; kidney; and a single sample of ileo-caecal junction.

'Now for the bloody tonsil,' she said, knowing it was a while since she'd looked for one and hoping it would be easy to find.

Cutting down hard through the skin over the lower jaw she peeled it away from the jawbones on either side to reveal the underside of the tongue. She inserted the knife to the side of the tongue hard against the inner surface of the left lower jaw and cut down and through all the soft tissues, repeating the process on the other side. With prodding and pushing she grabbed the tongue and pulled it backwards and out of the space between the jaws, pulling and cutting to either side as she went, pulling the tongue in the direction of the sow's swollen and fat laden neck.

With a final heave the soft palate at the back of the mouth came into view revealing the pale stippled tonsillar area on either side.

'There it is,' she cried excitedly and, motioning to George to take hold of the tongue, she took forceps and a sharp scalpel and quickly dissected out the tonsillar tissue, dividing it between the two pots that George offered her.

'Label each of those with "Sow 1" please George,' she said, 'and write on each pot what the tissue is inside. Then we'll go and pick the two sickest sows to slaughter.'

It was not a difficult choice. One old sow, already the mother of seven litters, was paralysed in her hind legs and did not try to rise when they checked her temperature. They moved the other pigs into a neighbouring pen and Dave levelled the muzzle of a 12 bore shotgun six inches from her skull above her eyes. Aiming slightly upwards he pulled the trigger. A circular hole the diameter of a shotgun cartridge appeared in the skull, blood poured as though from a spring, and the sow kicked and paddled involuntarily. Death had been instant and kind.

With a chain round a hind leg she was dragged into the yard with a tractor whilst another sow in the neighbouring pen was slaughtered in the same way. Then Sarah post mortemed the two of them, taking from each the same tissue samples as before, along with blood into red topped clotted blood tubes and purple topped whole blood tubes. 'For antibody and virus isolation respectively,' she said to George.

Dave looked with admiration. In the past he'd been suspicious of female vets. His conversion was complete.

'Right, let's get some blood samples from the other sick sows and those that are in the same pen,' Sarah said. 'I've got a couple of snares so if you two strong guys can catch,' she pointed to the two pigmen that had been roped in, 'and hold them nice and still; I can take the blood.' She said it with confidence.

The pigmen looked doubtful. 'I've never used a snare,' one of them said finally.

'That's alright,' she replied. 'I'll show you how to do it.'

The snare was a running loop of braided wire with a T shaped metal handle at one end reminiscent of an instrument of torture.

Sarah opened the loop with one hand and dangled it in front of one of the sows who inquisitively and obligingly explored it with her mouth. Deftly the loop was pulled backwards along the top jaw and upwards to tighten it behind the upper canine teeth. The sow pulled backwards tightening it further and began to squeal, a continuous high pitched squeal of rage and frustration. A 250 kilogram tub of pork and lard pulling in the opposite direction was not worth fighting with and Sarah quickly passed the metal handle to a wide-eyed pigman who dug in his heels and kept the sow still.

'Lift the snare to keep her head up and nice and straight in line with her back,' Sarah shouted above the squealing, and, taking two red and two purple topped tubes she handed them to George for safe keeping.

She attached a two-inch long double ended hypodermic needle to a plastic holder and carefully slid one of the red topped tubes partially onto the needle inside the holder. She stood on the right hand side of the sow, level with the right foreleg, and placed her left hand on the sow's back between the shoulder blades. She looked along the length of the underside of the neck until she recognised the tiny indentation a few inches from where the neck joined with the pig's chest. Then, aiming upwards in the direction of her left hand, she plunged the two inch long needle through the skin up to the hilt. The squealing continued but the sow did not move. Using sleight of hand Sarah pressed the tube home onto the other end of the needle and the vacuum sucked a rapid stream of deep red blood into the tube, filling it in seconds. She swapped the tube with George for another red one, quickly followed by the two purple tops.

'Okay,' she said a few seconds later, 'you can let her go.'

The snare was slackened off, the sow shook her head and the squealing stopped.

'One down, nine to go,' she said cheerfully.

By the time all the samples were in the bag, heads were banging to the beat of shrieking pigs and Sarah wished she'd remembered to bring ear defenders. It was also four thirty in the afternoon.

'Right,' she said. 'Dave, you understand the Form A restrictions yeah? Nothing must go off the farm that has had any contact with the pigs or with where pigs have been. Overalls, boots, the lot. And no one must come on without a licence either. Put a chain up and a notice at the farm entrance. I'll leave you some disinfectant to make up a footbath.

'George and I can splash some disinfectant over our own cars' wheels now. When's your next feed delivery due?'

'Tomorrow,' said Dave. 'It's the company's own lorry. All bulk feed.'

'Good. Here's a licence for that. Phone them and tell them to deliver here last of the day and you can disinfect the wheels as the lorry leaves. Give the driver plastic overshoes to wear, make sure he leaves them here, and don't let him anywhere near the pigs. I'll phone them as well. I'm pretty sure the virus wouldn't last long on the wheels of a vehicle anyway.'

She fetched a bucket of water and measured in a volume of disinfectant and set about scrubbing her boots with a stiff brush. She didn't bother with her waterproof overalls.

'I'll leave these here and collect them if it turns out to be negative,' she said. 'If it's positive it will be paper suits from now on.' She winced at the thought.

George smiled at her.

'Thanks for coming so quickly,' he said.

'I'll get these samples back to the office now and someone can take them to the lab tonight. It'll probably be a couple of days before we get a result. In the meantime Dave I want you to prepare a list of all the pig movements onto and off the farm in the last say, three months; plus all the visits you've had from people who might go to other pig units. You know; feed deliveries; fieldsman; knackermen; anybody like that you can think of. We need a list so that if the shit really hits the fan we can start following all these things up. No harm in getting prepared for the worst. I'll phone you first thing tomorrow to get the most recent movements and we'll get someone straight out to those farms.' She scrubbed the wheels of her car, washed her hands and got in.

'I'll leave you the rest of this disinfectant. That should get you started. Any more questions? No? Good. I'll phone you tomorrow Dave. Thanks for your help all of you, I must fly,' and she was gone.

'She's some woman, isn't she?' said Dave, turning to George with a smile.

George thought of his own dull wife at home and, somewhat wistfully it seemed to Dave, he slowly nodded.

Chapter 5

On the drive back to Broadwich Sarah tingled with excitement, tiny adrenalin rushes fluttering her stomach like on a first date. This was what she was paid for. Not for reading all the other crap about business plans and the rest. She was a vet not a bloody administrator. That was why the Ministry of Rural Affairs employed her, wasn't it? For her veterinary skills. Sometimes she wondered.

She looked at the pigs she passed with new interest. Were there pigs out there in the fields flashing by, incubating Swine Fever in front of her eyes? Imagination running wild, she thought. It might be nothing.

Bill had everything prepared. Good reliable type Bill. Forms all filled out as far as he could; an Animal Health Officer all geared up to deliver the samples.

'What do you think? Really think?' he stressed.

'I'd say it was. I've never seen anything like it. It makes things more exciting anyway.'

'Peter wants to see you. I've filled him in on everything so far but I think he'd like to hear it first hand.'

Sarah went through to see Peter her boss. Dull old Peter but she supposed it was a requirement for the job. Unless it was the job that turned otherwise interesting folk into dullards. She suspected the former to be the case.

'I hear we may have problems,' said Peter as she entered his lair. 'How likely do you think it is to be positive?'

'I'll be amazed if it's not.' And she went through everything she'd seen and done.

'You should have gone through the movement records today,' he said when she'd finished. 'We need to visit the farms where pigs have moved to straight away and see if there's any evidence of disease there. It's a pity you didn't do that,' he added.

She felt her excitement evaporate like a splash of water on a hot stove. No, 'Well done,' or, 'It's been a long day.' She didn't want praise, just a friendly word of comfort, reassurance that she'd done a decent job. A feeling of anticlimax, an empty space, growing and spreading. And then like an almost beaten boxer she shook her head and came straight back, attacking with strength and courage.

'I've arranged to get that information first thing in the morning,' she said calmly. 'I felt the most important thing was to get the samples taken, back here and despatched to the labs. If it is Swine Fever it will have been around for a few weeks. Another 18 hours isn't going to affect the outcome and the farmer had had enough for one day. He agreed to go through all the movement records tonight and give them to me first thing tomorrow. We've not lost any time. And if that's all for now I'm going home for a shower. I stink of pigs and I've got the gym booked for seven tonight. I'll see you tomorrow.'

Without letting Peter answer she turned and left, quietly satisfied that she hadn't let him push her around. Should have got the movement records all sorted out today. Stuff it up your arse, she thought. Sometimes their managers didn't seem to be on the same planet. When was Peter bloody Timms last on a pig farm, or any farm come to that? He wouldn't recognise a bloody sow if one grabbed him by the balls. If he still had any, she thought.

It was this sort of thing that really pissed her off. Always some smart arse in a position of relative seniority who would have done things differently if they'd been there. And of course they never bloody were there; always too busy pouring over the Business Plan or working out their pathetic little budgets and how they could possibly meet their bloody targets. Or dissecting their Veterinary Officer's travel claims and querying why 27 miles had been claimed from the office to some abattoir or other when by their own reckoning it was only 26.

She smiled to herself. Peter had tried to push her around once or twice in the past and she had firmly put him in his place on those occasions too. He wouldn't try again for a while. He was a weak kind of guy; a bully who liked to flex his puny muscles. The office staff bore the brunt of it. Too young and timid to stick up for themselves. They didn't hang around long, six months, a year; no more. And Peter always moaning that just when he'd got someone trained up they were off. Never realising that it was because of him; his indifference; his lack of warmth and appreciation.

Sarah lived a few miles from the office in a small farm cottage she had bought ten years previously. She had a cat and a horse. She was unmarried and she assumed, likely to remain so. Lost loves from the past had always foundered on the final hurdle, children. She passionately and adamantly wanted none. Her partners had without exception had a desire to populate the world single handed, needing only the complicity of a woman of childbearing age to achieve their aim. She always resisted and as one relationship after another ended, a successor became increasingly difficult to find. She was now over forty and fast approaching that stage in a woman's life when her most likely admirers would be middle aged widowers and divorcees; most of them desperate for female company and the cooking, washing and ironing that went with it. She was not that desperate. She would prefer to be alone than in the sort of relationship she despised. She would have a partnership of equals or none at all.

Horse riding and the thrice weekly sessions at the gym kept her fit, her muscles toned. She knew the route of physical idleness led to a flabby body and with it a flabby mind. Acquired wisdom had shown her the link between mind and body but she was not a fanatic. No strange dietary fads or colonic irrigations for her (the very thought was enough to send her scuttling to the loo). Eating sensibly meant a chicken or seafood salad and a glass of dry white wine. At five foot six inches tall and never over eight and a half stones, her body was smooth, taught and supple with well defined but not exaggerated leg and arm muscles. Pale blue eyes set in a gently contoured face the colour of ripe corn, and straight, shoulder length, clean brown hair. She was not beautiful but there was a pleasant self confidence in her looks that men found attractive and she suspected scared many of them away.

In the gym that evening she pounded out a beat on the running machine and in spite of the shower she'd taken the smell of pigs oozed out of every pore. She arrived home again at twenty past eight. A bright sunlit evening with hot sultry air pressing down on her like a Latin lover. She took another shower, the aroma of pigs hovering on the surface of her skin above the droplets of sweat that bathed her bared arms. She put on shorts and a T-shirt and taking a plate of wild rocket salad and smoked salmon with a glass of ice chilled Australian Chardonnay into the back garden, settled herself down with 'The Field' and prepared to enjoy a relaxing hour to herself.

The sound of a combine at work several fields away was a welcome reminder that peace reigned. The harvest was late, July wet and cold, but now with August came sun and heat, rushing in unstoppable and with it the grain had ripened and everyone had been hard at work for a week. Everywhere you looked were orange fields of corn, some standing tall waiting for the combine's knife, others of prickly stubble, huge round bales of straw littering the landscape.

Wood pigeons, crows and rooks scoured the stubble for spilt grain and grubs exposed by the cutting of the corn. In the late evening and early morning hares could be seen gambolling and playing, hunting foxes too, drawn in by the abundance of naïve and fat young pheasant poults recently released from their rearing pens.

The once common corncrake long since gone, the grey partridge badly depleted by pesticide sprays and the lack of hedgerows and headland cover. The hedgerow birds too in decline, their source of food and nest sites eroded with every hedgerow that was pulled out and destroyed. A yellowhammer perched in the hedge at the bottom of Sarah's garden and chirped a mournful song. As dusk slowly settled around her, the bats came out from their daytime roosts and flitted across the garden in their hunt for moths and other insects.

In spite of the warmth of the evening she felt a chill. Blowing from inside her, toying with her peace and well-being. A chill to warn her that all was not as she thought, that she was not immune to its touch. She shifted in her chair, shivered and glanced round as though she sensed an evil presence but she shrugged it off without a lasting thought. Sitting there alone in the heat and softly falling gloom, Sarah Fowler could have no idea of what had been unleashed that day. In the months ahead lay a chain of events that were to change her life and that of many others too, beyond all comprehension and recognition.

Chapter 6

The following day, six farms that had received weaned pigs from Church Farm during the previous month were visited by one of Sarah's colleagues and all were found to have pigs with signs suspicious of Swine Fever. Sarah Fowler felt vindicated in her actions and the manner in which she had taken them.

Rumours began to find their way down the communication channels; by landline; mobile phone; e-mail and simple word of mouth. A buzz in Animal Health Offices throughout the land, a buzz and talk of what would happen if Swine Fever were confirmed. How many vets and Animal Health Officers would be needed on detached duty and for how long?

Steve Turner was Duty vet at the Animal Health Office when his e-mail popped. He opened it immediately.

'Classical Swine Fever confirmed on a farm in Norfolk,' it read. 'A disease control centre is being set up in the Animal Health Office at Broadwich and VOs and AHOs are needed to staff it with immediate effect. All volunteers should be co-ordinated through their own Regional Veterinary Manager (RVM).'

Steve considered for a moment, turning the pros and cons over in his mind. Something interesting for sure; something to get stuck into; a proper veterinary job for a change; could only be good fun; plenty of 'Après Swine Fever'; lots of new faces; a great chance to show off the Healey; and most of all, a chance to get away from Bluster for a while. Yes, he thought, he was most definitely up for it. He would speak to Willie and Sammy and present it to Bluster as a complete package.

Willie was soon on board, Morag could cope on her own for a few weeks. Sammy jumped at the idea too so Steve bounced along the corridor to Bluster's office and put their names forward.

Bluster raised his eyes slightly at the proposal, the office would be badly depleted but at least all the troublemakers would be out of his way. Within an hour it was settled and Bluster gave Steve the news that all three of them were to leave first thing the next day, initially for three weeks.

They left in convoy at first light, a crisp, clear, dewy morning that promised heat and sun to come. Steve put the hood of the Healey down and there was a holiday atmosphere as they crossed from west to east along the A66 to Scotch Corner and then down the A1, stopping for lunch and a laugh on the way.

'This could be awful,' said Willie.

'Yeah, and shit stinks,' replied Steve.

'You young boys,' said Sammy. 'What's an old lady like me to do in such company?'

The journey took nine hours and it was late afternoon when Steve drove into the car park at Broadwich Animal Health Office. A crowd of forty or fifty people were milling about, many of them on mobile phones shouting to be heard above the general din. There were the familiar faces of vets he'd met on courses and a few heads turned as he eased past them and into a parking slot.

'It's bloody chaos,' he heard a voice. 'There's no one in charge or anybody who knows what we should be doing. I've been here for four hours and I haven't even got somewhere to stay yet. It's another typical bloody Ministry cock-up.'

'The phones are all down,' giggled another. 'Apparently there were so many incoming and outgoing calls the whole system just crashed. Welcome to the 21st century. It's like son of millennium bug in there,' he motioned to the main office building with its big square windows and peeling paintwork.

'I've heard the DVA is hiding in his office whilst the clerical staff ring round all the hotels in the area trying to get accommodation for us. There's a race meeting on at Newmarket this coming weekend and all the hotels are full.'

'What's happening in the field?' said another voice. 'Is it true they're slaughtering out one of the Infected Premises (IPs) today; four and a half thousand pigs or something? How are they getting rid of the carcasses? Burial? Burning? Anyone know? Anyone care?' he laughed.

'I've heard they're going to be loaded into leak-proof lorries and be trucked under licence to a renderer in the Midlands. Someone will be making a fortune out of it as usual.'

'The hotel bills are being paid centrally so at least we don't have to fork out the money and claim it back. Bed and breakfast paid for and another twenty one pounds a day on top to cover other meals. There's no money to be made on expenses these days... removes the incentive for doing detached duty as far as I'm concerned.'

'When are the portacabins arriving? It's so crowded in there you can hardly move.'

'Who's running the show in Sage Street? I heard the PVO's been called back from his meeting in Brussels to take charge; or is it from holiday? I can't remember.'

Sammy looked at Steve and giggled.

'What a shambles,' she said.

'Everybody's just doing their best,' said Willie. 'The fact that no one has a fucking clue about what to do is just, well,.. unfortunate. I know I'm only an Animal Health Officer and haven't been to university but it looks as though we're lacking a bit of organisation here. What do you think Mr Turner?'

'Who do we have to report to when we arrive?' Steve asked a tall bloke in his early fifties who appeared unperturbed, even relaxed.

'God knows,' came the reply. 'Probably some poor junior admin

31

clerk who's been in The Service a couple of months and even as we speak is being set-up to take the blame for everything that went wrong once The Inquiry into the great Swine Fever outbreak of 2000 pens its report.'

Cheerful bloke, thought Steve. But probably fairly near the mark.

'I have it on good authority,' he continued somewhat more helpfully, 'that there is to be a briefing at 5.30 in the canteen. So, in approximately twenty minutes, all may be revealed. And I love your car. Mark II or III?'

'Mark III.'

'Nice to see someone else with something a bit different from all those lease hire Vauxhalls that everyone else seems to drive now. I've got an Alfa T-spark myself. Pokey machine and wonderful going round corners.'

As five thirty approached everyone made their way up to the canteen. It was standing room only as men and women of all shapes, sizes, and ages crowded in, jostling and talking amid an atmosphere of barely restrained anticipation. For most of them it was the first time that anything like this had happened and they were unsure of what to expect. The air inside was warm and muggy, windows flung open; a strong smell of rancid sweat hung and wafted from one or two of the less hygienic persons present, not all of them men.

Biblically there came a parting of the crowd, starting at the door and rippling along the front to the middle of the room. An entourage of three persons was the cause, a silver haired man followed by Peter the DVA and somebody in a suit who could only be from Sage Street. Slowly the talking died away.

'Who's the grey haired bloke?' hissed Steve to the girl standing next to him, at the same time marvelling at the size of her thighs and how she could possibly have stuffed them into the tight khaki cargo pants she was wearing.

'Alan Todd, the Regional Veterinary Administrator.' Her respect shone through in the sugary sweet tone and dew moist look in her eyes.

'A wanker then,' Steve smiled back. He caught Willie's eye and made a gesture with his hand. Willie smirked.

The man with the grey hair began by sincerely thanking everyone for their speedy response to the request for assistance. Steve groaned to himself. It was like a virus spreading insidiously through the management structure; with every training course, management meeting, and assessment, the virus became more virulent and infective.

'There are now seven IPs,' he went on, 'with the first one at Church Farm, believed to be the primary or index case. The other six premises have all received weaners from it during the preceding month. One of those six has been slaughtered out today. All the carcasses have been loaded into watertight lorries and are at present en route to a rendering plant north of Birmingham. They're being closely followed by an Animal Health Officer to ensure they don't deviate from the agreed route. Over the next two or three days the other IPs will be slaughtered out and in order to try and get a hold on how long Church Farm has been infected, every pig on the place over six weeks of age is to be blood sampled.'

A murmuring and sighing went around the room. Many of those present, Steve and Sammy included, had never bled a pig in their life. It was not a welcome prospect.

'We're hoping to get the samples immediately after slaughter by cutting the tails off and catching the blood in an open tube. Someone is away now buying half a dozen pairs of secateurs from the local B & Q so that we're properly equipped.' He was smug, as though he had thought of everything.

Steve whispered to the girl with the large thighs. 'Excuse me madam but are these secateurs suitable for cutting off pig's tails? I wouldn't want to waste my money on them if not.'

She looked at him as if he were a maniac, contempt in her eyes, and edged carefully aware. The smell of stale sweat diminished noticeably.

Steve glanced across at Sammy. She was giggling and she turned away to avoid looking at him.

'How is slaughter being carried out?' someone asked.

'We have the local knackerman contracted to do it. He'll use a shotgun for adult sows and boars, and a .22 rifle for fatteners. All head shots. The small pigs will be a job for vets using intra-cardiac Euthatal.

'Valuations of the pigs have been carried out today and will continue tomorrow. The plan is to all meet back here at eight thirty tomorrow morning when the Allocations team, led by Raymond,' he looked around. 'Where are you Raymond? Over there.' He pointed.

'The Allocations team will assign each of you to a team and a task.

'We've also set up an epidemiology unit in the building. Their job is to try and find out where the disease has come from and where it might have spread to. They'll be looking at all the pig and personnel movements; you all know the score I don't need to go into detail. They'll provide the Allocations team with a list of the most urgent jobs that need doing. I don't need to remind you of the importance of good disinfection procedures on and off the farm but I'm going to anyway. We have to demonstrate that we are not responsible for continuing to spread the disease.

'Accommodation for all of you is being arranged by the office staff and a spreadsheet will be going up on the wall here at six thirty tonight showing where each of you is staying and for how long. It's not been easy to get rooms so you'll have to bear with it if you need to swop hotels every few days.

'There are four portacabins on order which will be put in the car park to increase office space and there is work going on as we speak to upgrade the phone and computer links to enable us to really get to grips with this thing.

'Swine Fever Declaratory Orders have been put in place defining infected areas around the infected farms. The movement of pigs into, out of, and within these areas is completely prohibited. There is a complete standstill on.

'I'm sorry to be brief but I've got a video conference with Sage Street in ten minutes time. We'll see you all at 8.30 tomorrow morning.'

Chapter 7

'This is the best hotel I've ever stayed in,' said Willie as they sat in the bar that evening drinking beer.

He was in 'The Fat Goose' with Steve, Sammy, and about fifteen others, with other staff dispersed over half a dozen more hotels, some in Broadwich, the rest five or ten miles out of town.

The Fat Goose was four stars, a recently refurbished group of sixteenth century houses knocked through to each other on the High Street of one of the more expensive outlying villages, seven miles from Broadwich. Exposed wooden beams and rough plastered walls throughout, furniture from the period in the halls and corridors, and all the mod-cons in the rooms that you could need; CD player, satellite TV, steaming baths and showers, and a price tag of over £100 per night bed and breakfast.

'It's also the most I've ever paid for a pint of beer,' he added. 'Twenty quid won't go far in a place like this.'

Steve had grabbed a room with a double bed. He was now a man with a mission and had scanned the packed room at the earlier briefing to pick out a likely candidate. To his disappointment many had made the girl with the huge thighs and no sense of humour appear vaguely attractive. He consoled himself with the thought that there would be others.

'The price of a meal here is outrageous too,' said Sammy sipping a gin and tonic. 'Secateurs to cut their tails off. Who thought up that bloody idea? I nearly choked when I saw you laughing Steve, you bastard.'

'I think it was the guy in the suit's idea. Who was he anyway? He never opened his mouth, just hung on Alan Todd's every word. Brown noser or what? I bet I know who he's sharing a room with tonight.'

'That's rather a strong inference to be making in a public place Mr Turner,' said Willie with feigned seriousness. 'I expect he is a very decent and hard working bloke who sincerely appreciates our diversity and professionalism.'

'Shut up,' laughed Sammy, who nevertheless agreed with Steve. 'He was from Sage Street. A Veterinary Adviser. A high flyer I'm told.'

More men and women from The Ministry drifted into the bar with the inevitable introductions and brief life histories exchanged. A few had arrived the day before and discovered a pub up the road with excellent cheap food and beer, so in twos and threes they made their way up the street to The White Lion. Inside there was a restaurant area and a small bar. Steve's gang of three seated themselves in the bar, ordered a meal and got stuck into the drinks. Through in the restaurant they could see Alan Todd and the brown noser in animated conversation, each with a half pint of best bitter on the table in front of them.

'It wouldn't do to overdo it,' said Steve, slinging down his fourth pint of the evening and signalling to Willie that a refill was urgently needed. The food appeared and a plate of smoked chicken salad with skinned and sliced avocados was place in front of him. A knife, sharp and bright pierced his chest and the pain surprised him.

The last time Steve had seen avocados sliced that way the temperature was 30 degrees Centigrade and it was Christmas. Christmas 1980. They parked their car on a campsite in a coconut grove on the shores of the Yucatan peninsula, looking out to a Caribbean of aquamarine beyond a white sand beach undisturbed by human footprints. Above them, a powder blue sky lit by gleaming sun filled with screaming Frigate birds that soared with deeply forked tails higher and higher until they became swallows in the mind.

He and Rachel had left the USA five weeks previously, driving down the west coast of Mexico through deserts with cacti ten feet tall and through dusty towns with dusty children on the streets and pale dogs lying in the dirt, and limping and scratching their skin raw where the mange annoyed them. Fat women with straight black hair and sun red skin swept the pavements and hung washing out to dry amidst the rubbish and blowing polythene bags caught in fences.

They always knew when a town was up ahead by the rubbish dumped along the highway; rusting tin cans, paper and polythene. Rotting slowly if at all, a developing nation incapable of disposing of the inventions of its revered and powerful neighbour to the north.

They lived in shorts and flip flops and cheese cloth shirts and Rachel's skin was the colour of deep baked honey flecked with dust and sweat, the taste of salt and sea breezes. Nine months married and all the home they knew packed inside their old Pontiac that had taken them from New York across the USA and Canada like a big blue barge, cruising the black top rivers and the dirt chip roads in the mountains and forests of the Rockies; and they slept and consummated their love on the wide back seat behind the purple flowered curtains, and in the heat of Utah's deserts and the cold of British Columbia's nights.

The Mexican Border guards with stubble faces and hungry eyes held out their hands for bribes and licked their lips and wiped their chins at the golden haired curls and the blue eyes that sparkled with life and laughter. A warming glow of passionate pride, a storm with heat and fire, an aching of the soul with fear of future loss. Indian villages, with markets where the coiled intestines of pig and sheep hung and swelled in the sun, the colour of green and purple, coiling and moving with gas as serpents, a cloud of flies feeding and buzzing, the smell of putrefaction, the sound of a butcher's cleaver on a wooden block.

Red mounds of tomatoes, green interwoven, piled high on wooden benches with limes and peaches and thick warty cucumbers and the

36

shiny skinned avocados, a kilo for a few pennies, and children sitting in their mother's laps and watching from black eyes beneath black hair and pointing and laughing with joy.

The warmth of white sand, serrated rustling of coconut palms, cries of Frigate birds, underwater rainbows with gills and spines in shoals of twinkling light, and salads overflowing with sliced avocado and warm moist crusty bread topped with slices of pale salty butter. The taste of Rachel, cayenne pepper and olive oil washed down with iced tequila and a twist of lime.

'Is there something wrong with your salad?' Sammy said. 'You haven't started it.'

'No. Nothing. It looks wonderful. Just thinking; reminiscing; old times and happy days; you know the thing.' Fuck you bitch, he thought. Fuck you Rachel.

The door to the bar opened and three young girls came in. Half drunk, giggling. The smooth skin and tight clothes of youth; early twenties, lines and wrinkles unimagined.

'You've no chance pal,' Willie said, seeing the flame ignite in Steve's eyes. 'Not in a million fucking years.'

'You just watch me. Watch and learn. Ladies, come and join us,' he said pulling a couple of chairs over to the table. 'I saw you in the office at Broadwich today didn't I? Are you up here for the Swine Fever too?'

They giggled in reply but took the offer of a seat.

'Drinks everyone? It's my round. Same again Sammy? How about you there? I don't know your names. I'm Steve and this is Willie and Sammy, we're from Scotland. Introductions complete he made his way to the bar. He ordered them three dry white wines.

'Large or small glasses?' said the barman.

'Large please.' He was emphatic. And on the pull.

And Catherine was his prey. The one he wanted. Blonde with good bones and an upright stance; narrow waist and tiny hips, curiously boy like. Fine, heavy looking, well rounded breasts, not overlarge, there was something ugly and off-putting about huge breasts, he thought. He preferred small breasts to large ones. Large ones were a diversion, a salesman's pitch like a saying a car had a large boot. A large boot didn't make a good car. A good car always had a boot. Boots and breasts, they were all the same to him.

37

Catherine was in Information Technology and twenty four years old. She had a degree in computing and was helping set up spread sheets for epidemiology. Most importantly she was staying in The Fat Goose. She had come for a month, a new experience and the chance of overtime. A chance to save money to travel she said. She'd always wanted to travel. Who hadn't, thought Steve. But how many bothered. A huge leap from the desire to the reality. He told her about Mexico and Central America but not about Rachel. That time had passed. The time when he would tell strangers about her and repeat himself to friends until they shunned his company. Not now. Not anymore. He told no one now. It had dried up inside him like a hidden seed, dead and spent.

Sammy looked on amused, with the faint whiff of envy brushing against her. She had never seen him like this before; in action. Prickles of unease; an old friend she thought she knew.

By closing time another handful of glasses of wine had disappeared and the 'kill' was in his sights. Catherine whispered in his ear, the warmth of her breath on his neck stirring sensations of Christmas and birthdays and summer holidays with lazy days of food and drink and love and laughter. He looked around the bar at the smiling faces, the noise of harmless chatter, reflected smiles and smoke filled eyes. He placed his hand on her knee, patted it twice and let it rest, butterfly-like, the softest touch, gentle and ready to move if it were disturbed. He felt her hand rest on his, small and dry and warm, soft and smooth, the nails sharp but stayed, like cats' claws sheathed. A gentle pressure, securing his hand against her knee, the faintest touch of her bare thigh against his own, denim clad.

He winked at Willie. And they all rose and went out into the balmy night, the Saxon church opposite glowing with the lights reflecting off its flint made walls. Middle England at its best, thought Steve, and a pretty girl to boot. They ambled down the street towards The Fat Goose, Steve's arm around Catherine's waist felt her relax, her legs flexed with the drunkenness of inhibitions lost.

'You must see my Austin Healey,' tomorrow he whispered.

'I saw a blue one in the car park today. Is that yours?' she simpered.

'You smooth bastard,' hissed Sammy in his free ear.

They stumbled through the front door and Steve collected his room keys from reception. Catherine did not even ask for hers and the desk clerk registered no emotion born of a discretion long since learnt.

'Goodnight Sammy,' Steve said.

'Goodnight. And don't say anything you might regret later,' she added maternally.

'You don't need to worry about that,' Steve called back over his shoulder. 'Because, and you can take it from me, I never, ever do.'

Chapter 8

Raymond Johnson stood at the front, a confident and dapper figure in cavalry style twills and carefully pressed cotton shirt. He was ex-military and his careful, clear and straightforward manner were a rare treat.

From a master list he read out the teams, some comprising a vet and a couple of AHOs, others with two of each. Each team had a task and some tasks had more than one team allocated to them. It took five minutes to read through the list: Steve's name was linked to Willie's, plus Sarah Fowler and another AHO from Wales. They and two other teams were going to Church Farm to supervise and assist with the slaughter, and blood sample the pigs.

'So what sort of night did you have Mr Turner?' Sammy enquired innocently. 'I didn't see you at breakfast.'

'Very pleasant,' replied Steve with the smile of a naughty boy. 'We had breakfast in my room.'

'Very romantic I'm sure. And is it true love? Do I hear the sound of wedding bells already?'

'I don't think so, do you?' Steve said. 'Just two adults coming together in the joining of their bodies for mutual pleasure.'

'Very philosophical,' teased Sammy. 'But will that suit the lady?'

'How are you doing you big English poof?' said Willie. 'Looks like we've got an exciting day ahead of us. Who's this Sarah wifey?'

'I am,' said Sarah from directly behind him and he turned to find the well honed body of Sarah Fowler only a few feet away.

'I'm Willie,' he said. 'Very pleased to meet you,' he continued, grabbing her hand. 'I'm from Scotland.'

'I would never have guessed,' she replied sarcastically.

'I'm Steve. I work in the same office as Willie here.'

'That must be nice for you.' The note of sarcasm the same. 'All the kit we need was made up last night so if we load it into two or three cars we can head off. I've arranged to meet Horace Carey the knackerman on the farm at 10.00 am. We've got a long day ahead of us and it's going to get hot. The sooner we get going the better.'

Sarah rounded up the other teams and in a convoy of four cars, Steve with the roof down in the hope that the fresh air would clear his hangover, they headed for Church Farm.

'She seems a bit nippy,' said Willie once they were on their way. 'Scary lady.'

'Oh I don't think so,' Steve smiled back.

Horace Carey was waiting for them at the farm with an accomplice. The smile on his face and cheery manner did not seem in keeping with a man who was just about to lead the destruction of something approaching five thousand pigs. As he unloaded shotgun cartridges and .22 rifle ammunition rounds he whistled to himself with the unconcerned air of a man taking everything in his stride. In his mind the longer Swine Fever went on the better, just so long as he could keep the contract for slaughter. He'd be able to retire at the end of it if he was lucky.

'What's the score then?' asked a VO from Wales. 'How are we going to co-ordinate all this?'

Sarah took control and explained what she wanted.

The dry sows were in straw pens in groups of about fifty. George was going to enter a pen and shoot one sow at a time with a shotgun. The team with George would sample the sow by cutting off its tails with the secateurs which Sarah produced and waved in front of them, the B & Q price tag still attached.

Steve suppressed a giggle.

Horace would shoot another sow and, like so, it would progress until the whole pen was finished. The contractors from a waste disposal company would load the dead sows into the leak proof lorries already lined up in the yard and George and his merry band would move on to the next group.

Sows in farrowing crates either with piglets or heavy in-pig could then be moved from the farrowing house to a vacated pen. Dave the farm manager would organise that and another team would set about slaughtering the unweaned piglets by injecting a concentrated solution of barbiturate anaesthetic into their hearts. Once the vet in charge was satisfied that all piglets were dead they would be loaded into a handbarrow and wheeled round to the disposal lorries for loading and counting.

Horace's pal Wayne was the .22 rifle man and his job was to kill the fatteners. He had a fine array of tattoos down both arms, a lip and nose stud, and a two inch long piece of bicycle chain hanging from his left ear. His hair was cropped, shaved would not be too strong a description, and this revealed the upside down 'This way up' tattoo on the back of his head.

Wayne swung his rifle around in a manner that implied personal safety and the safety of those around him were not at the top of his list of priorities. He wore camouflage trousers with an obscene number of pockets and a camouflage jacket with the sleeves torn off so that it resembled a waistcoat. The pockets had spread to this garment too, and as they watched, he crammed and stuffed cartridge after cartridge into every opening until his body bulged and you wondered that he could move with the weight. The only thing missing to complete the picture was the word psychopath tattooed on his forehead.

Nice bloke, thought Steve. Just the sort you'd like to go for a drink with in the evening.

'H-H-Has anyone d-d-done a health and sa-sa-safety audit on to-t-t-today's procedures?' stuttered Kevin, a vet with large glasses who looked as though he had emerged from the set of 'International Rescue': one of the back room boys rather than a Thunderbird pilot himself.

'There was no one qualified to do it,' replied Sarah, 'and not the time either. It's a case of using caution and common sense.'

'You don't need to worry,' said Wayne. 'Safety is my first concern,' he added as he fed live bullets into the rifle magazine and waved the weapon around like a conductor waved his baton, his trigger finger extended outwards in a gesture of due care and attention, the safety catch switched to the primed position.

'I'm not working with that fucking maniac,' Steve muttered to Willie. 'Let's make sure we're with fat Horace or putting the little piglets down.'

'You're right,' Willie whispered back. 'Err, Sarah. Steve and I and Rhian here will go with Horace then shall we?' and Sarah, having no objection, nodded.

'Thank Christ for that,' said Rhian in a sweet Welsh voice. 'That Wayne bloke ought to be a mercenary. He's a dangerous looking cunt isn't he?'

Steve and Willie nearly choked. They had never before heard the word uttered with such delicious intonation.

'Kevin,' said Sarah. 'You take your team with Wayne and get started on the fatteners, and the team over there…, yes that's you; you can have a go at the weaners. By the time you've finished them they'll hopefully be a dry sow yard that's empty and Dave can start moving the sows out of the farrowing house. Dave, can we have one of your men to each team please to help out with catching, fetch and carry, you know the sort of thing. And don't forget to label all the bloods with the pen of origin and make sure the pigs are completely dead before loading them. It's not a very pleasant job for anybody,' (apart from Wayne), she thought, 'but it wants doing properly and humanely. Right, let's get going.'

Willie, Steve and Rhian followed Horace to the first pen of sows carrying boxes of blood tubes, labels, forms, pig snares, and a couple of pairs of gleaming secateurs.

'What's the best way of doing this Horace?' asked Steve. 'You shoot a sow, we'll cut the tail off, get the blood, and then you shoot another one? We'll have a go at that and see if we can get a decent system going. And please be careful. We don't want anybody hurt, least of all me,' he added with a smile.

'Rhian, do you want to start by labelling the tubes that Willie gives you and writing up submission forms? You can swop over after a while. Willie, you chop the tails off and collect the blood.'

'And what are you going to do?' asked Willie sarcastically.

'I'm going to supervise and check that the sows are dead,' Steve replied with an air of self-importance but with a tongue-firmly-in-cheek smile on his face.

Killing the sows was easy. Their inquisitive nature meant they approached close to Horace, head held at the right height for him to point the shotgun at their brain and pull the trigger. The noise of the gun and the paddling of the fallen sow had no effect on the others; no mass stampede or panic, contrary to all the tales from the vegetarian lobby that animals quaked in fear at the smell of blood at the abattoir.

Willie dived in with the secateurs crunching through skin and bone but the tail remained stubbornly attached by a few stringy tendons and the blood oozed rather than flowed into the tube. It took several minutes to half fill a tube by which time a pint or more had poured from the gaping hole in the sow's head to form a rich crimson pool on the golden straw. Horace huffed with frustration and the desire to get on with the next kill.

'Plan B I think,' said Steve. 'Get the blood from that fucking great hole in the skull in future, and give those things to Morag for Christmas for pruning her roses.'

Horace downed another sow and would happily have unleashed a barrage of shots to take out five or six if Steve hadn't restrained him.

'We've got to get blood from every one,' Steve was firm, 'and we've got to do it safely. One at a time Horace, one at a time.'

The morning progressed and on the rare occasions that blood didn't flow, a quick stab incision with the post mortem knife into the thoracic inlet never failed. There was plenty of clean straw to throw down and absorb the blood but even so the floor of the pen became slippery and the sun beat down on their backs and the sweat dripped down inside their paper boiler suits and into their rubber boots and they were soon sloshing around like on the deck of a pitching yacht. But with the exception of a couple of sows which moved their heads at the last moment and needed a second shot to finish them off, everything was killed instantly and Steve felt comfortable and pleased with the way it was all going. When the last sow fell he checked round the pen that nothing was still breathing and then gave the go ahead to the disposal gang to move in with their chains, tractors and telescopic loadalls to begin the task of dragging the carcasses to the trucks and piling them in.

'Forty seven,' said Rhian, and they moved on to the next pen.

Around the corner in the flat deck weaner house the squealing of pigs split the air like the pierce of a train whistle. Two farm workers were catching, two AHOs were loading Euthatal into syringes and two vets were injecting the piglets. If the injection hit the heart then death was immediate but if the heart was missed it took several minutes for the piglet to wobble around and slowly sink into a deep sleep from which it would not recover. Missing the heart was annoying but in the great scheme of things a minor distraction in a job that was unpleasant to all. Though everyone knew that slaughter was the ultimate fate of all the pigs, it was the 'waste' that went against their traditional beliefs. Killing baby animals and throwing their bodies into a heap rubbed against the grain; against an innate sensibility that this was outwith the natural order of things.

At one o'clock Dave's wife brought out filled rolls and ice cold cans of coke for everyone. The coke washed the dust from their mouths and into their stomachs and revived them like a cold shower. Never had anything without alcohol been so willingly consumed by Willie McDonald. He stripped off his paper suit and all his clothes down to his underpants. They were wringing wet and steamed in the heat of the sun.

'W-w-w we must bring bottles of water in future,' said Kevin. 'K-k-kidney st-stones could be a p-p-problem in this heat if we d-d-don't keep our fluid intake up.'

'I tend to take all mine on board in the evening,' said Willie flippantly and winking at Steve. 'How's Wayne behaving himself?'

'You mean J-J-J-John Wayne. M-m-maniac is far t-t-oo kind a word,' stuttered Kevin. 'I've spoken to him a d-d-dozen or more times about not p-p-pointing that rifle around at anyone but whether he's d-d-deaf or stupid, or both, I don't know. He's scared me a few times today I can tell you. I-I-I'll be glad when it's a-a-all over.'

The afternoon dragged on in a haze of blood, sweat, the crashing of guns, the buzzing of flies, and squealing pigs. Steve called up Sammy on her mobile to see how she was getting on.

'No problem,' she answered, 'we're just getting cleaned up now. No sign of Swine Fever and we've got all the bloods. The AHO here is some guy when it comes to bleeding pigs. In and out, quick as a flash.'

Steve let it pass.

'Mad fucking Max here is the worst thing. Plus of course the heat.'

'I'm stripped off to my underwear as we speak,' returned Sammy.

'What a vision of loveliness,' Steve said and he heard her laugh out loud.

'Right, better go,' he added. 'Oh Christ what's happened to Kevin?'

Sammy heard the screams down her mobile, 'I-I-I've b-b-been shot, h-h-help me. I'm sh-sh-shot.'

'What's happened?' she shouted into her phone but Steve ignored her.

'I'll call you later,' he said and rang off.

Kevin was staggering around clutching at the side of his head screaming, and with blood oozing out from between his fingers.

'I've b-b-been shot. The b-b-bastard's shot me. Help me someone. H-h-help me.'

Steve ran to him and sat him down on a bale of straw.

'Stop shouting. You're alright. Sit down. Stay still. Rhian, there's an unopened pack of cotton wool in my car and a First Aid kit under the passenger seat. Get them quickly, the car's not locked. And bring some pairs of plastic gloves back with you,' he shouted after her.

Kevin sobbed and shook, holding the side of his head.

'D-d-don't let me d-d-d-die. Please don't l-l-let me die.'

Steve didn't think he looked much like a man that was dying but he dare not prise Kevin's hands away from where they were clutching his head for fear of increasing the flow of blood.

'You're going to be fine,' he said. 'Don't worry, we'll sort it all out for you. It'll be something to impress your kids with when you go home. Shot in the line of duty.'

Kevin managed a weak smile. He looked pale but Steve guessed it was the first stage of shock rather than the result of blood loss. After all, there was no big puddle of the stuff on the floor yet.

Rhian arrived back with the cotton wool and First Aid kit just as Wayne came around the corner, a sly smirk on his face, the rifle still waving around.

'It's just a graze isn't it?' he said as though speaking to a kid who had taken a tumble from his bike.

'Put that fucking thing away,' shouted Rhian and Steve glanced at Willie who returned his 'raised eyebrows' look in kind. The way she said 'fucking' was exquisite.

Steve put on some gloves and took a piece of gauze and a big wad of cotton wool.

'Right Kevin old lad,' he said. 'I want you to take your hand away so that I can see what's happened here.'

A chill made him shiver, like the first frosts of winter on a grey early morning, and sweat prickled his skin and ran into his eyes at the thought of Kevin's brains spilling out onto the yard like spaghetti from a tin.

The blood flow increased with the release of pressure but Steve could see immediately what had happened. The bullet had passed through the base of his ear, partially severing it and missing his skull by a few millimetres. With a rich blood supply it was bleeding like the pigs they had stuck earlier.

'Don't worry, you're going to live,' said Steve as kindly as he could. 'Hold on though 'cause this is going to hurt a bit. I'm going to put a pressure bandage on to stop the bleeding.'

He placed a large wad of sterile gauze over the damaged ear and pressed it back into a normal position against the side of Kevin's head.

'Once they've finished stitching this up,' he said jovially, 'you'll be wanting the other one done as well to stop it sticking out so much. Rather a drastic means of getting cosmetic surgery on the National Health but effective enough I suppose.'

Kevin smiled again, relieved he was not about to die, but he winced as Steve put a large pad of cotton wool over the gauze and began to bandage it tightly against his head. Bandaging skills, once learnt were like riding a bike, and he prided himself on being able to make a leg bandage on a dog or cat look like a work of art.

Rachel respected his veterinary skills, particularly his surgical technique; a gentleness and care with handling the tissues that was unexpected in one so brash, outspoken, some would say uncouth. He winced, remembering the look of disgust on her face, not even pity or compassion, a vengeful malicious sneer; the smile over his shoulder, focusing on something that was hers alone. And he, defeated, broken and dispirited but still fighting.

'Very neat,' said Rhian admiringly and Steve, looking in her face, felt a warm flush of sexual interest pass across him and disappear somewhere at the bottom of his soggy Wellington boots. He heard Sarah speaking urgently and sternly with Wayne and saw her writing in her notebook.

Steve turned to one of the others in Kevin's team. 'Will you take Kevin to the hospital in Broadwich please. Find out from Sarah where it is. Leave all your dirty overalls and boots and stuff and we'll sort them out for you. Just get your hands and arms well scrubbed. We'll catch up with you later.

'You'll be fine now Kev,' Steve said, patting him gently on the shoulder. 'You'll be a fucking hero.'

'What happened?' said Steve aggressively to Wayne as he and Sarah approached.

'It was a ricochet,' said Sarah. 'Kevin was bending over a dead pig getting blood and Wayne shot another one, far too close as it happens, and the bullet just came out of the pig's skull and hit poor old Kevin. It's damn lucky he didn't loose an eye. Or worse.' She shuddered.

'From now on there will be no shooting until the vet in charge of each group gives the word and everyone.., and I mean everyone, is behind the shooter. Whoever it is may not be so lucky next time.'

They regrouped and set to work again. By seven thirty that evening it was finished, with the dead pigs loaded and on their way to the rendering plant. The total tally was 789 sows, 1034 unweaned piglets, 1276 weaners and 1743 fatteners. Everyone was shagged out and stinking of pigs and there was an eerie silence about the farm. It took another half an hour to disinfect and pack the cars.

'God I need a cold beer,' said Steve and Willie grunted in reply.

'I'm bloody starving too,' said Willie. 'How about going straight to The White Lion to eat? I'll phone Sammy and get her to order us something. How does that sound?'

'Marvellous,' said Steve. 'Are you going to join us Rhian?' He was expectant.

'Thanks but no. I'll go back to my hotel and have a nice long shower followed by a long hot bath. Then I'm going to phone my boyfriend.'

'Bad luck,' Willie hissed smugly but Steve's disappointment was short-lived as he remembered Catherine. He started the engine and span the wheels ever so slightly as he pulled away.

'Twat,' said Willie unimpressed.

They phoned Sammy as they bypassed Broadwich and asked her to order a repeat of the smoked chicken salad for Steve and steak and kidney pie and chips for Willie.

'Going for the healthy option then,' teased Steve.

'Oh aye,' grunted Willie.

A cheer greeted them as they entered the bar.

'Two pints of lager please pal,' said Willie and both he and Steve sank them in one and ordered another.

'Right, tell us what happened,' said Sammy.

'Any news on Kevin?' Steve asked. 'Is he still in hospital?'

'I've heard he's back at his hotel,' she said. 'Thirty something stitches but he'll mend. Now for God's sake tell us what happened.'

So Steve and Willie related the day's events and warned of the dangers of working with a gun loving lunatic. The bar was silent when they got to the bit about Kevin; 'There but for the grace of God...' running through their minds.

More drinks were put in front of them and nobody commented on the smell of pigs that drifted from their bodies into the sultry atmosphere. When they'd finished they were clapped on the back and laughter and banter flew round the room like a flock of birds.

'Well done,' Sammy said, 'and now I've got some news for you that might not be quite to your liking.' She waited, enjoying the effect and looked around at them with a shiny eyed grin on her handsome face.

'Bluster's coming,' she said simply. 'For all I know he might already have arrived. And the story, as far as I can make out, is that he's coming down here to take charge.'

Chapter 9

'Oh fuck, not Bluster,' Steve shouted it. 'You come all this way at the drop of a hat to get shot of the stupid twat and within a couple of days he follows you down. The arsehole. The stupid fucking arsehole.'

'I take it you're not particularly happy with that piece of news then?' said Willie. 'I'd have thought that once Mr Bluster's incisive mind is brought to bear on the matter that the organisation is bound to improve.'

'It is a mess at the moment,' said Sammy.

'Well I think I'll leave you to talk shop,' said Steve, 'because I see Catherine over there and duty calls.'

He made his way over to where she stood drinking with the same two friends as the previous night.

'Hi,' he said, 'how are you?'

A tiny flush of pink over the cheek bones and she smiled sheepishly. 'Fine,' she replied. 'I was worried you might have been shot.'

'It would have made things simpler if you had been,' said one of her friends and Catherine frowned.

'Can I talk to you? Privately,' she said.

They went outside and walked up the street towards the church.

48

'I'm not sorry about last night,' she said eventually.

'But?' Steve prompted gently.

'I didn't tell you the truth,' she went on. 'I'm engaged. I'm getting married in three months. I love him and I don't know why I did what I did last night. The wine and the..., the whole situation I suppose. You're a nice bloke; attractive; intelligent;.. and an Austin Healey.' She was teasing.

'Keep going,' laughed Steve.

'It's just that last night was last night, and that's it as far as I'm concerned. I don't regret it, not really,' she said. 'But I love my boyfriend and I don't want to ruin everything that he and I have planned together.'

'What does he do?' asked Steve. Genuinely curious, and not particularly upset by the news.

'He sells mobile phones,' she enthused. 'For one of the big companies. The prospects are excellent. If he sticks at it for a few years he could become an area manager, and after that the sky's the limit.'

Steve chuckled to himself. Bloody mobile phone salesman, he thought. He knew the type; boring as fuck; all haircut, mouth and trousers. Poor Catherine, she deserved better, much better, but it was her life and there was no future for her with him. He looked her carefully full in the eyes, saw them moisten, and then he kissed her tenderly on the lips.

'I enjoyed last night,' he said, 'thank you. Now in we go and no hard feelings either way. Let's enjoy the rest of our stay here. Your boyfriend's a lucky man,' he added, and he was partly telling the truth.

'You're not mad at me?' asked Catherine.

'Mad at you? Of course not. You've done nothing wrong. A little fib perhaps but it's what I wanted to hear. No I'm not mad, I'm very happy for you. Come on, I'll buy you a drink.'

They went back into the bar, Steve saw Sammy watching him carefully, trying to read the body language and see what it was all about. He bought Catherine a drink, kissed her on the neck and whispered something that brought the colour to her cheeks again and made her giggle. Then he left her and sat back down next to Sammy.

'Well?' she said, an inquisitorial look on her face. 'What did you say to the lady that made her giggle and blush?'

'Trade secret,' said Steve. 'Mind you, thinking back' he added, 'I don't think anybody had ever done that to her before.'

'And why is she not here now by your side?'

Sammy was sharp thought Steve. No wonder Bluster was scared of her.

'Catherine is not by my side,' he replied in a theatrical voice, 'because we have decided to call a halt to our relationship and remain just good friends. That is as she wishes and since I have no objections myself, it seems an eminently sensible option, leaving me, I might add, in the enviable position, of being able to enjoy what other fruits may be placed before me in a totally guiltless fashion and with the clearest of consciences.'

'And why the sudden change of heart on Catherine's part?' persisted Sammy.

Steve looked her straight in the eyes, they didn't moisten, but he thought he saw a flickering flame of love and concern somewhere deep inside the glowing blue; a love and concern that alarmed him as to why it was there at all. He continued to stare at her.

'I am going to let you into a very intimate and secret, secret,' he whispered. 'The reason,' he glanced around and bent closer to Sammy, 'the reason that Catherine is no longer by my side,' he paused again waiting for the tension to build, 'is that she can't stand the fucking smell of pigs,' and he pissed himself with his own wit and shouted to Willie to get him another pint.

Sammy slapped him on the arm and she was laughing too and called out to a tall, dark haired bloke standing a few feet away.

'Fernando, come over here, I want you to meet Steve.

'Steve this is Fernando, one of our Spanish VOs from the Midlands. He arrived today.'

'Hi Fernando,' Steve shook his hand warmly. 'Como está?'

'You speak Spanish?' said Fernando smiling.

'Just a little bit. I've travelled in Mexico and Central America and I was in Chile just a few weeks ago.'

Their car broke down on the Yucatan peninsula and they were towed by two English lads in a big Chevy Stationwagon. A Mexican police patrol stopped them, and when the problem was explained escorted them with lights flashing through the streets of Chetumal, across rights of way and through red lights to the General Motors Garage on the edge of town.

It was Saturday and the garage was closed. A watchman lived next door and they set up camp on the garage forecourt and there was a customer toilet outside that the watchman said they could use. The watchman's house was a wooden shack with a tin roof and earth floor and he lived there with his wife and three children. He had a bicycle and that evening they waved him off as he cycled into town, his wife dressed in all her finery borne proudly on the crossbar clutching the youngest child in her lap.

On Sunday they were invited in to share a meal; lettuce and tomato salad, flour tortillas, and Steve and Rachel provided the beer. When the first bottle was finished the watchman threw it over his shoulder into the bushes where the sound of breaking glass bore witness to the huge pile already lying there. Steve and Rachel followed his lead, and the children laughed and pointed and foraged around in the dirt.

The shack had three rooms, a kitchen with a TV, and two bedrooms; one with two hammocks stretched across, and the other with three. Making love in a hammock was something that Steve had not yet tried but he lived in hope.

On Monday morning the starter motor was replaced and they waved farewell, giving Rosanna a Silver Jubilee Crown that she hid in her skirt before scuttling off to show her husband. They knew they would never see them again.

They headed due east and then due south to Guatemala where the change from Mexico was as great as it had been from the USA. Instead of handguns in holsters the border guards carried automatic M16 rifles, carelessly slung round their necks or caressed across their hips like lovers. Some of the guards looked no more than fifteen years old, deep brown skins that betrayed the mixing of the blood of the Spanish with the native Indians and some black African thrown in.

There were three desks to visit. Three desks meant three bribes; two dollars, three dollars and two again. Rachel's sun-bleached hair and tanned skin in denim shorts and T-shirt were a dangerous attraction, the same hungry looks on the guards' faces; the same feeling of helplessness in Steve's head and heart as to how he could protect her. Two anonymous foreigners travelling in an anonymous region, torn apart by civil war in Nicaragua and El Salvador with Guatemala perhaps not far behind. Government atrocities and rebel guerrilla bands were frequently in the news and realisation crept over Steve like mist; realisation that their safety was in the hands of the personal morals and philosophies of the people they met along their way. His own responsibility to protect Rachel a heavy burden; their misunderstanding of the language and of simple instructions could be construed as disrespect, arrogance, or open defiance. Without alarming Rachel he tried to create around them an air of humble co-operation mixed with self-assured confidence. To have documents and dollars at the ready, to be calm and good-natured in everything they did.

The Guatemalan guards opened their car boot and with excited fingers pulled out some of their possessions, delighting in the discovery of a large plastic bag of pale green dried oregano. They called to one of the older, more mature men, rapid voices with hands on rifles.

'They think it's dope,' Steve whispered to Rachel.

'Para cocinar,' he said to the guards but they ignored him.

The older guard took a little of the oregano in his fingers and smelt and tasted it.

'Para cocinar,' Steve repeated in a friendly manner.

Rachel pretended to smoke and then shook her head and repeated 'No, No,' with a friendly smile on her bronzed and dust streaked face.

The older guard laughed and said something to his younger companions and soon they were all laughing and smiling and the boot was repacked, the barrier lifted and they were on their way to Guatemala City via Chichicastanango and the Guatemalan Highlands.

'We'll throw that away at the next town,' said Steve. 'We might not be so lucky next time.'

They drove on past fields of ripening maize, a land of tiny shacks of wood or mud, sometimes with a roof of tin, and at others of thatch. Chickens, small pigs, dogs and children mingled in the dust and dirt around the shacks, the older generation seated in patriarchal status on wooden chairs in the shade noted their passing with toothy grins that flashed gold.

This was the Pan-American Highway, a paved road with sudden deep and terrifying potholes; sometimes with whole sections of road torn away without warning. They were grateful for the wide chunky tyres and the air shock absorbers which withstood the bumps and bounces and kept them in a straight line. Once following behind a lorry, a whole litter of half grown spotted pigs ran across the road. The last one disappeared beneath the racing juggernaut and they saw it bounce and twist against the chassis and rear axle before it was flung to the side of the road broken and dead. Ragged children and their parents rushed to where it lay, wide eyed excited voices, pork for dinner that evening.

'I have spent some time in Mexico too,' said Fernando. 'A wonderful place, very friendly people.'

Steve agreed and bought him a drink.

Further across the room another group of people were arguing good naturedly about their day's work.

'You're not much of a pig bleeder, that's for sure,' said someone laughing. 'And you should have seen this vet I was with today. I showed him how to do it and he just kept on and on poking the bloody pig in the neck with his finger where he thought he should get the blood from.'

'Yes,' chimed in another, 'just leave the pig alone and stick the fucking needle in.'

Laughter erupted, joyful and spontaneous and Steve laughed too. What a bloody hoot, he thought. Wine, women; all they needed was the song. He stared around the bar at all the happy, pissed faces and took a long swig from his own glass. Fantastic. What a good crowd of people, and how it beat being stuck in the office shuffling bits of paper around. This, he thought to himself, is like being back at college. This is as good as it gets.

Chapter 10

At briefing the next morning, Herbert Bluster waxed lyrical. The outbreak was his stage and the room full of people his audience. A hush fell over them as he prepared to speak. He drew himself up to his full height; took off his glasses; hitched up his trousers to somewhere between his waist and his chest; screwed his face into one of confident concern, and began.

'Early on during the Foot and Mouth epidemic of 1967...,' Steve groaned and sought out Sammy and Willie. They were both smirking. '...the then PVO, David Chesterfield, took me to one side and said, "Herbert, this epidemic will either make or break the Veterinary Service."

"What do you mean Dave?" I asked.'

Steve cringed.

"'If we get this thing under control, I can ask the Minister for anything. If we don't,..."' he paused waiting for the unspoken consequences to sink in.

'Well I was talking to the PVO this morning, and Ron said to me…' he paused again, … '"this outbreak will either make or break the Veterinary Service."'

Herbert stood waiting for the gasps of astonishment at history, of which he was a central part, repeating itself.

'It must be a standard phrase that all PVOs use when they don't know what the fuck to do but want to give the impression of welcoming the challenge,' Steve whispered to the girl on his right.

She edged away from him and Steve recognised 'old fat thighs'. He was making a bad impression on her. Not to worry, she was pig ugly; in fact if she weren't careful she'd find someone slipping a snare on her fat face and trying to bleed her. He gave her another friendly smile which appeared to confirm her opinion that he was completely fucking mad.

'Do keep your diaries up to date,' Herbert went on, 'you'll need them to support your mileage claims, particularly if you're claiming for extra passengers or equipment supplement. All claims will be coming through me and I won't sign anything I'm not happy with. Any questions?'

'If paperwork would but defeat the disease we'd already be on our way home,' said Sammy philosophically.

'Do we know where the disease has come from and how it got here?' asked a keen looking chap from Northern England.

'I think I'd better put you on to the epidemiologists,' said Herbert, balking at the thought of some real veterinary work. 'Graham, can you answer that?'

Graham Thompson, stepped forward with a gentle humility that was in stark contrast to Herbert's bumptious cocksureness.

'Well, good morning everyone,' he smiled carefully. 'It's good to see so many keen fresh faces. This is what we've all trained for, it's an important job and one that you don't get the opportunity to do very often. Make the most of it; get as much experience as you can in every facet of the work; slaughter; cleansing and disinfection; tracings; on-farm investigations and inspections. There's no better training ground than an epidemic itself, don't waste the opportunity. Foot and Mouth could be the next thing.

'Having said all that,' he smiled again, more openly this time, 'enjoy the evenings too. Though having seen some of you in action last night, I don't think you need a lot of encouragement in that area.

'Well, in epidemiology we've been looking at various possibilities and although it's early days yet we can rule out most things and make an educated guess at what may have happened. The Government vet lab have typed the virus as one that has been circulating in the Pacific rim countries for a number of years and we can say for certain that it's not the virus that caused the big outbreak in Holland in 1997.

'So, if it came from Asia, how did it get here? The answer is that we don't yet know. We've checked all the movement records onto and off the farm and no pigs have been brought on since April of this year. All pigs moved on in the last ten years have been British bred. No semen from outside is used either so we can rule out both of these sources of infection.

'That leaves us with entry through fomites such as faecally contaminated clothing, wellie boots, feed utensils, equipment and all the rest, you know the score. Then there's wildlife; foxes carrying dead piglets or part of an infected carcass from one farm to another; and of course, infected meat products.

'None of the farm workers admit to having been anywhere near other pigs for over a year, but since that is a condition of their contract of employment, they're hardly likely to admit it, are they?'

A gentle snigger went round the room. At least someone was talking sense now.

'No visitors are allowed other than the company fieldsman and vet. Feed is delivered by bulk tanker from Farm Fresh Pig's own mill and blown into the silos. The driver isn't allowed to leave the concrete apron where he parks and is certainly not allowed anywhere near the pigs. So disease security is pretty good. And of course no swill is fed and the farm workers are well aware of the dangers of giving the remains of their lunch to the pigs. There are plenty of other pig farms in the area but we've already had patrol visits to the contiguous ones and there's been no sign of infection or increased mortality on any them.

'There is one other possibility. It's a long shot, but in this game you've got to keep an open mind. Three months ago there was a fire in one of the dry sow houses such that they had to find alternative accommodation for 100 dry sows. Since they had some old pig arks already on the farm and as the weather was good, they put up some electric fencing round a twenty acre piece of fallow land and the sows were put out for a three week period whilst the building was repaired. This land borders a very popular footpath down one side; it's used by fishermen, schoolchildren, local walkers; you name it, they use it. Apparently people were often seen "talking" to the pigs and you all know how inquisitive pigs are. So it's quite possible they could have been fed some infected pork product out of ignorance.'

'Were the sick sows at the start of this incident in the group of pigs that were outside?' someone asked.

'Thank you for that question because it leads on to what I was going to say next. No they weren't the same, but interestingly, about one week after the sows were rehoused on June 10th, one of them became extremely sick with a high temperature and skin blotches which everyone assumed to be erysipelas, especially when she appeared to respond to penicillin. She was moved to a hospital pen, improved for a couple of days, and then developed diarrhoea and a discharge from the eyes and nose. She died about a week later from what the pigman thought was secondary infection. The hospital pen was in the house where Sarah examined the sick pigs and there have been sows going sick in that house for several weeks now. So it may be, and I stress may be, that this sow was the index case and she had ample opportunity to infect neighbouring pigs through nose to nose contact or through faecal contamination of the neighbouring pen.

'What we do know is that this Asian strain of virus is not particularly virulent or fast spreading when it first enters a herd. It's only after it's passed through pigs a couple of times that it starts to go rampant, so that too would tie in nicely with the infection entering the herd about the beginning of June.'

'Any refuse tips close by where foxes or seagulls could have picked up some infected meat?' someone asked.

'It's a fair point but the nearest tip is fifteen miles away with everything land-filled with topsoil on a daily basis. So we think we can rule that out. Now, before I finish I would like to say that we may need some recruits for epidemiology from time to time, so if there is anybody out there with a burning desire to get involved, please let me know. And likewise, if anybody has another theory, however unlikely it may seem, let me have it. It's all too easy to get bogged down on one particular line of thought and become blinkered. So let us have your theories and we'll try to disprove them,' he smiled.

'Herbert, a practical point.'

At the sound of Sammy's voice Herbert Bluster's face went into a spasm which culminated in him twitching and throwing his left hand over his right shoulder. This sudden unprovoked onset of activity alarmed those standing closest to him and they drew back, and then relaxed again as Herbert regained control, hitched up his trousers, and replied in a voice tinged with hysteria.'

'Yes Ms McLeod. What can we do for you?'

'It's a question of laundry Herbert. We need to change all our clothes every day for disease control purposes and because they stink of pigs. I've put them into the hotel laundry service and it's going to be about seven pounds a day. Can you assure us that we can claim this money back?'

Herbert's twitch set off on another uncontrolled journey but he reined it in, the look of a hunted animal in his beady eyes.

'That'll have to come out of your twenty one pounds a day living expenses,' he blustered. 'That's designed to cover everything other than bed and breakfast which will be paid centrally. There's no money in the kitty for anything else.'

Graham Thompson looked doubtful and a murmur of disquiet spread around the room.

'I don't think that's right is it?' persisted Sammy. 'The twenty one pounds is for lunch and evening meal and you could soon get through that eating out down here.'

Herbert fumed and his face coloured a purple brown with dark rings around his eyes. Graham Thompson intervened.

'It's a good point,' he said. 'I think this is something we should take up with Resource Section at Sage Street. In the meantime, keep all your receipts for laundry in case you need to present them. Now, Raymond, do you want to go through today's allocations. Good luck everybody.'

He left the room with Herbert trailing after him like a big sloppy dog, jowls bouncing up and down.

'She has a point Herbert,' he said once they were out of earshot. 'It's a huge amount out of the allowance and the conditions people are working under are appalling what with the heat and the smell.'

'That's as maybe,' Herbert replied, 'but the allowance is to cover all normal costs. They'll be wanting money for beer and hangover remedies next.'

'That's a little different,' Graham replied calmly. 'Don't forget we need to keep the goodwill of the troops. The service has been cut to the bone, beyond danger levels in my opinion. We don't want an insurrection on our hands on top of everything else. We're going to be asking these people to work 12, sometimes 14 hour days, seven days a week for several weeks at a time. There's little enough incentive what with the cap on overtime for VOs. Morale is everything. Lose that and we lose the fight. Leave it to me, I'll speak to Human Resources about it.'

Herbert grunted grudgingly. The trouble nowadays, he thought, was that people were too bloody soft, uncommitted, not prepared for self-sacrifice. Why, back in '67, people had worked twelve hour days for the love of doing it and the self-satisfaction of a job well done.

Chapter 11

Saturday night and by 7.00 p.m. most people were in from the field, their blood samples packaged, and ready for a shower and something to eat. Steve phoned Willie on his mobile.

'What's happening this evening?' he asked.

'There's a karaoke at the Fox and Hounds in Broadwich. Plenty of people going. What do you think?' said Willie.

'Sounds good to me. I've never been to one but I'll give it a go. Who's driving?'

'Och, we'll find someone. Meet you in the bar at The Fat Goose at quarter to eight. I'm nearly there now.'

'Okay, I'm leaving the office now. See you soon.'

The evening was warm, swifts soaring and screeching overhead. Steve pulled out onto the main road and almost immediately into a petrol station. His head was dizzy, light headed, he was finding it hard to concentrate. Knackered, he thought. He'd been there ten days and worked 115 hours. No day off, late nights in the bar and too much booze. Age getting to you he thought. Maybe he would have an early night.

He filled the car with petrol and watched the traffic pass, car after car stuffed with humanity out for a good time in the heat of summer on a Saturday night. Loud music with a heavy beat, girls squealing with laughter, arms thrown from open windows, the scent of summer and long ago memories. He paid for his petrol, climbed behind the wheel and eased the Healey across the pavement and into a gap in the traffic. He drove slowly to The Fat Goose, apologised to the receptionist for the tenth time about the stink of pigs, went to his room and took a boiling hot shower followed by an ice cold one which revived his spirits and tempered his desire for an early night.

Fuck it's Saturday, he thought. Got to get out on the town: on the pull. He'd show her who was fucking boring he thought bitterly. Bitter that he was catching and bleeding fucking pigs for a living when he should have been out looking at his prize sheep and cattle in the clean Pennine air. 'I'll show you who's fucking boring,' he said aloud, shocked that it was still so raw and hot, like a slice of onion on the tip of his tongue. He had to let it go after fifteen years. Half a fucking lifetime, no, twice a lifetime. So vivid still. So real. He could close his eyes and see her. See them, together, on the steps of the farmhouse looking out to the eastern sky. He had to shake it off, get rid of it. So that he could begin his life again. He knew it and wanted it. But he did not know how.

He dressed and went down to the bar.

'And where have you been today Mr Turner?' Sammy purred as Steve accepted gratefully the pint pushed into his hand by Willie.

'Bleeding fucking pigs of course,' he replied flippantly.

'Better than fucking bleeding pigs,' I suppose said Willie.

'You're very sharp tonight,' said Sammy.

'I'll tell you what though,' Steve went on. 'I've decided that I'm a bit scared of the bloody sows you know. I was in a pen today with about ninety of them all just lying asleep so I was shouting and slapping them to get them moving and every now and then one would sit up on her fat arse and sort of woof at me, like a dog. And threatening too.

'And then one of the old bitches came up and nibbled at my boot and took hold of it so I shook her off and walked away and she started following me, purposefully, her mouth open and her old ears flapping away. And the faster I went, the faster she went and I tried to dodge round other pigs but she just kept on coming at me and I suddenly felt really vulnerable and I ran to the gate and climbed over. And do you know what? She just came and stood by the gate and looked at me as though she wanted to eat me. I was bloody scared of her.'

'That's because you're a big English poof,' said Willie, 'and err, my glass is empty…see,' he continued to point at it.

'Do you fancy driving in to Broadwich tonight Sammy?' Steve asked as they waited for the pints to be pulled. 'Meet at the The Swallow at …shit we'd better get going if we don't want to miss everyone,' he added looking at his watch.

'I suppose so,' said Sammy. 'Who else wants a lift?' she looked round the bar. 'Pizza Express and then karaoke isn't it?'

Three cars with eleven occupants set off through the warm Norfolk air and found Broadwich buzzing with the life of youth on a Saturday night. They found The Swallow, a big old-fashioned building looking out onto the town square.

'Anyone know what this place is like' Steve asked. 'I'm moving here on Monday; The Fat Goose is full apparently.'

'I've stayed and it's good,' said an admin bloke. 'Great cooked breakfast, a buffet. You can eat as much as you like.'

Inside, the bar was packed with Ministry staff. Fernando was sitting at a table with two girls.

'Steve,' he called, 'these are some Spanish colleagues of mine.'

Steve looked at them. One was tall with fleshless bones, long black hair in thick waves to below her shoulder blades. Smiling. Not a pretty face but attractive. Yes wonderfully attractive in a sensual and confident way. The other was short, black haired too and a kind, cheery smile. A Tomboy. Yes, a Spanish Tomboy thought Steve.

'Hi,' he said and shook a long elegant hand followed by a short stumpy one. 'A drink?' he offered.

'We are ready to go I think,' said the elegant girl, her accent like warm treacle.

Steve sensed a rival in Fernando. A rival so much younger than himself; too good looking by far. Great fashion; a kind caring manner; at ease in the presence of women; and an accent to die for. A rival? There was no contest.

'Are you coming with us?' Fernando smiled. He always smiled. 'Everyone is leaving now I think.'

The bar emptied in shuffling, jostling groups of three and four and six and seven. They moved along the shop windows in the crowded streets and came to the Pizza house, lit up in white and metallic purple, with waiters and waitresses young enough to be his kids. Except he didn't have any.

There were thirty five of them and the manager scurried round, rearranging things to make two long tables side by side and they settled themselves around them and Steve sat next to Fernando. He followed his lead in choosing a goat's cheese salad with Italian bread, crisp dry white wine on Fernando's recommendation; the boy was mature beyond his years and very kind. In an instant all thought of rivalry disappeared. This was a man Steve liked and they talked of Mexico and Central America.

A name like Chichicastanango sticks in the mind. A typical Indian market town set in the Highlands of Guatemala and peopled by high cheek boned red skinned peasants who carried bundles and baskets of vegetables and fruit to and from the market stalls. Or sat on the pavement with a brightly coloured shawl spread on the floor in front of them on which were placed a few handfuls of beans, maize cobs, avocados, or tangerines. Whilst they sat they hand spun a bundle of wool, gently teasing it out and winding it onto a spinning stick, a wool of natural greys and browns with beauty in its simplicity and connection to their culture. It was always women that attended the stalls, the men engaged in more worthwhile tasks, or not.

Above all Steve remembered their patience. They sat, sometimes in silence, sometimes chattering animatedly to their neighbours, always smiling, and always with no evident desire to be anywhere else. They were content. No, more than content. Fulfilled. Fulfilled to be there as part of the whole and with the prospect of selling something to put a little money in their pocket.

'The worst thing you can do,' someone told him, 'is to buy all their produce the minute they arrive. What would they do for the rest of the day if they had nothing left to sell?'

It made sense because it enabled them to make sense of their lives.

The children sat with their mothers and Steve never heard a baby or infant cry. Constant contact with their mothers, wrapped either in a shawl on her lap, or bouncing on her knee, they were always happy.

He and Rachel bought avocados that they mashed and mixed with chopped tomato and onion to make guacamole which they spread on warm flour tortillas and sprinkled with fresh ground black pepper. They washed it down with cheap bottles of Guatemalan beer kept chilled in their portable fridge that sat between them on the front seat plugged into the cigarette lighter. It cost 150 $ US, a huge chunk of their money and he was reluctant to buy it but Rachel insisted. Now with the feel of ice cold beer in his throat he had to admit that she was right and he was wrong.

Their skin was brown from their Christmas on the beach in the Yucatan, topped up now by their wandering the markets in shorts and T-shirts in a blazing, tropical sun. But in the Highlands the nights were cold and they cuddled close together for warmth and love and it was a wonderful dream.

Guatemala now seemed a long way off both in distance and time. Nearly twenty years he thought yet it was vivid and clear still. Which was no surprise. He had thought it through a thousand times since. Every last word and action respoken and relived, trying to grasp the truth, a clue, the reason for it all.

'Boring. Boring. Boring. Boring,' she said.
The word went in and twisted itself deeper, cutting and bruising, ripping and tearing.

'Steve, do you like the wine?' Fernando repeated a little louder.
'Beautiful,' he said and as he glanced around his eyes flickered on a handsome girl a few years younger than himself sat facing him on the next table. She looked up and their eyes danced the dance of mutual attraction. He smiled, she smiled back and then looked away. A surge of adrenaline hit his stomach and the back of his throat and left him trembling with memories and anticipation. God she was like Rachel, he thought.

He threw back another mouthful of wine, refilled his glass and offered the bottle around.

'Another bottle?' he called.
'Okay. Yes,' said Fernando.
'Yes I will take some more,' agreed the elegant Spanish girl. 'You have seen someone you know?' she asked.

'Someone who reminds me of someone I used to know,' he grinned. 'Someone I used to know very well, or at least thought I did,' he murmured to himself.

He looked up to see the girl's eyes on him again.
Play it cool, he thought to himself. Just play it cool.

He ate his salad, drank more wine and did not look at her again. He laughed and joked with Fernando and his consorts but all the time his mind was on her and what he would say to her and what he would do. He could not wait to start; could not wait to leave the

Pizza house and head up the road to the karaoke. The quarry had been spotted, she was fair game and he was up for it. The hunt was on.

Chapter 12

A noisy and happy crowd made their way up the street to the Fox and Hounds and Steve had the fire of alcohol in his blood.

'And who is the lucky girl tonight?' asked Sammy as she fell into step beside him and slipped her arm through his. He kissed her on the side of the head just above her ear.

'In another life Sammy it would be you,' he whispered.

He was teasing her, she knew that and she cherished that relationship with him. She liked him, and she loved him. Not platonically or lustfully. Loved him for being who he was and she wanted to see him happy. It was a steady undemanding love and she suspected that he loved her the same. And he did.

'I've seen a girl, a woman really Sammy. That one up ahead. Do you know her?'

She peered ahead and nodded.

'It's a vet I met yesterday. She's been taken on because of the outbreak. She's been doing locums in London the last few months. Apparently done a lot of travelling. Now there's a coincidence Mr Turner. You at least have something in common. Good luck,' she added as they turned in past the bouncer in his ill fitting black suit and bow tie into a world of flashing lights, video screens and harsh penetrating sound.

'Do you want a pint?' Willie shouted but Steve was the only one who heard above the din.

'Yeah, a pint of weak shandy mate.'

'You bloody English pervert, get a pint of lager down you,' he said thrusting one into Steve's hand. 'This is fucking brilliant isn't it?'

Steve knew what he meant. It was brilliant. Working hard and playing harder. He accepted the pint and inched his way through the crowd towards her just as someone started to sing.

'Hi I'm Steve,' he had to shout. 'Have you got a drink?'

'Yes. Thanks. I'm Julie. Julie Parker. And why were you smiling like that at me in the pizza house?'

Steve smiled.

'You're doing it again.'

'I can't help it,' he shouted. 'I like your face.'

She didn't blush. 'That's a start at least,' she replied.

The singer came to an abrupt end before the record but the crowd clapped and cheered regardless.

'How long are you here for on Swine Fever?' Steve asked.

'As long as it lasts,' she said. 'I'm doing locums and this seemed a good opportunity to get some regular work that's well enough paid. And have some fun?' Her voice rose as if it were a question.

'It's what you make of it,' Steve shouted again. A new singer was blasting out Blondie's 'I want that man', but she lacked the looks and sex appeal of Debbie Harry.

'Who's your lady friend?' asked Willie pushing his way in.

'Julie, this is Willie,'

'Very pleased to meet you,' said Willie. 'I am a fucking shit hot pig bleeder,' he said pointing to himself with his thumb.

'That's an original opening line,' she laughed.

'He also has a wife and six kids,' Steve said. 'So he's making the most of his new found and very temporary freedom.'

'And how many children do you have Steve?' asked Julie.

It was a strange question, direct and to the point and it took him unawares. He knew why she'd asked but it was, well,.. it was too intrusive, so early on.

'Er, none,' said Steve. 'Never wanted any, never had the opportunity.' He surprised himself at the mess he'd made of saying it and how uneasy he felt about it. As though not in control, not of his choice, something that had been imposed on him. It shocked him and he struggled to prevent the shock from showing.

Rachel had never wanted children, she was not that type. Her dogs and horse were all she needed. Those and him. Not quite true as it turned out. But kids? Hey get a life. He fell in with it; happily and willingly he thought. His life was too busy, too tied up and committed to need that sort of demand on his time and ambitions. Too many other things to do. To farm and to enjoy life. It surprised him how much it stung now.

'Me neither,' she said and was proud and content. 'Are you going to sing?' she added.

'I've never been to a karaoke,' Steve smiled, regaining his spirits and composure.

'But are you going to sing?'

'I will if you will,' said Willie to Steve.

Someone cheered and Fernando standing nearby cheered too.

Steve said nothing but accepted the offer of a pint from Julie.

'Who's the guy over by the bar? The one that looks like a stalker?' Steve asked Willie.

Willie looked across to where the hunched and ferret faced figure of a man sat perched on a bar stool like a malnourished bird of prey, his pint of black liquid cradled in the crook of his wrist. He was watching from the sidelines, detached, not participating.

'I don't know,' said Willie. 'I've seen him around at the office. He is a bit of a stalker though isn't he?'

Some people began to dance and the noise reached a level where conversation became impossible. The applause, shouting and cheering at the end of each performance increased with every pint drunk and Steve was firing on alcohol, inhibitions thrown aside. He was on the stage, microphone in hand, a seething mass of people moving before his eyes, cheering and laughing. He heard Willie's voice call out, Sammy's too and then they disappeared into a black hole of nostalgia as the music of Rod Stewart's 'I don't want to talk about it' came through the speakers. The words flashed up on the video screen but he didn't look, he knew them backwards, forwards, inside out and upside down. A huge cheer went up when he missed his cue and then he was singing the song, his mind transported back through the pain and sorrow of the last fifteen years.

He was driving along in his car, heading south, all the possessions he owned crammed into two black bin bags on the back seat. He was twenty eight and he could hardly see the road through his tears; his eyes red, blood streaked, painful as fuck. The tears ran down his nose, he risked a look in the mirror, snot hung from his left nostril and spilled off his top lip onto his chin and he left it there.

His stomach ached with hunger, nothing but tea and coffee had passed his lips for forty eight hours. The thought of eating made him want to vomit. Physical pain wracked his body, a dull aching pain that came wave after pounding wave, starting deep in his abdomen and spreading up through his chest and shoulders and down into his pelvis. A pain he could not defeat; it passed and then came again stronger and more persistent.

He didn't believe; couldn't believe; denial easier than acceptance. If he accepted he couldn't continue. Hope meant survival; plus the support of his family and friends. His dreams lay ruined; trampled and spat on as worthless garbage.

Deathly quiet surrounded him. The song had finished and he could feel tears running down his face. Quickly he wiped them away, he saw the surprised and worried faces amongst the crowd. He put his hands in the air above his head in a victory salute and laughed. There was a cheer and he walked back over to the bar.

Sammy was there immediately slipping her arm round him.

'Are you alright Steve?' she said, her voice concerned and comforting.

'Of course he is,' said Willie slapping him on the back. 'He just came over a bit emotional like. He needs a fucking pint,' he said and slapped him on the back again.

Steve laughed and wiped his eyes.

'You sang it not bad,' said Julie. 'It's a lovely song. But very sad?'

'Yeah, kind of,' he said. 'Who's round is it? Let's get pissed.'

'You have a very nice voice,' said the elegant Spaniard. 'Do you often sing?'

'No. Never,' said Steve. He felt foolish; vulnerable; as though he'd bared more than was good for him.

Fernando's phone rang.

'It is my mother in Spain,' he said. 'She is always ringing me. Holá. I will go outside to speak.'

'He is very close to his mother,' said the Tomboy 'A good Spanish son.'

Two rounds later Willie and a Scots girl hit the stage with The Proclaimers' 'Letter from America.' Willie stood, pint in hand, huge beer stain on his shirt, incapable of reading the words or following the tune. He joined in whenever the title phrase 'Letter from America' flashed onto the screen, punched the air and shouted it at the top of his voice so that the whole bar could hear. It was party, holiday, celebration all in one and Steve, sat on a barstool, found Julie leaning against him with her hand on his leg.

God she's like Rachel; scared at the thought, but excited too. He winked at Sammy.

Willie took his applause. 'That was fucking brilliant,' he slurred as he came back to the bar.

His companion, sober and more realistic said 'That was fucking terrible.'

'Where are you staying?' Steve asked Julie.

'The Swallow,' she replied.

'I'm moving in there Monday night.'

'Time to go if you want a lift,' said Sammy. 'It's gone midnight and we're all working again this morning even though it's Sunday. Steve?'

'I'm right with you,' he said. He took Julie's head gently in his hands and kissed her on the forehead. 'I'll see you tomorrow.'

'I'd like that,' she said.

As he turned to leave he saw, out of the corner of his eye, the stalker, pint of black liquid in his hand. He was watching them with a haunted malevolent look on his gaunt, angular face.

Chapter 13

It was Sunday and Steve, with a head like an axe split log, was working on a nine thousand pig breeder/rearer unit with an AHO from London. They had wasted the whole morning trying to find a farm to inspect and blood test one pig. By the time they arrived at the place the knackerman had beaten them to it by a couple of hours and the pig was already slaughtered and buried under three foot of soil 'In a bloody great hole.'

They returned to Broadwich just after midday and for the first time had been around when the sandwiches were delivered, great platefuls that arrived twice daily at 12.30 and 4.00 p.m. to keep the 'troops' fed and morale high.

There were fifteen or twenty people in the canteen. Some were new arrivals, others writing reports from the previous day's visit, yet more preparing to head out on fresh assignments. Some were still moaning about what had happened at that morning's briefing. Herbert Bluster had lain down the law in response to requests to clarify the instructions and resorted to barking out that it was up to vets to use their veterinary judgement because that was what they were paid for.

Steve had pointed out that they were all happy to use their judgement just so long as senior managers didn't complain if they failed to agree with the decisions the vets made. He also suggested with some glee that senior managers were paid to issue clear instructions to their staff which caused a few sniggers around the room and set Bluster off on one of his mini fits. Steve knew that Bluster would get his own back at annual reporting time but frankly he didn't give a toss.

Replete with prawn sandwiches he sauntered down to Allocations, hoping to meet Julie. He hadn't seen her at morning briefing and now he found she was out on another job. He called in at epidemiology to say hello to an old mate from college and find out if they were any closer to finding the original source of infection.

'How's it going Trevor?' he asked.

'Bloody hell, Steve Turner, you've been roped into this as well have you?' he drawled in a slow London accent.

'How's life treating you old boy?' Steve said.

'Well alright, except that I can't find out where this fucking disease has come from in the first place and now there's some smart-arsed epidemiologist at Sage Street who has her own ideas and they don't fit in with ours so it's all a bit complicated really. Plus Sage Street are getting the blood test results from all the surveillance zone bleeds and not bothering to pass them on to us so farmers are phoning up to get the results and surprise, surprise, we don't know them. Some of them are getting rather irate about it and starting to shout down the phone at me and I just have to tell them that I'm doing my best and that I can't do any more.

'Of course if we could find a discarded wrapper with "Ham sandwich, Best before June 2000" written on it in Taiwanese, then we could be pretty sure that's how the disease came here. The trouble is no one here would be able to read it and I don't think it's very likely to happen anyway, do you?'

Steve laughed. Trevor's attitude hadn't changed in more than twenty years. It was a refreshing revelation. He went down the corridor to Allocations and Raymond Jackson pounced.

'Steve, I've got a post-mortem report here from the local Veterinary Investigation Centre. Two pig carcasses they had brought in have had Salmonella isolated from them but the report says they can't rule out Swine Fever. I've spoken to epidemiology and they want someone to go out and serve Form A and carry out a full Swine Fever investigation. Can you and Jason do it? We need someone with experience, especially as it's already the afternoon.

Steve sighed. Frankly he was shagged out and more frankly he could have done with pissing off early for a long hot bath and an ice cold beer. That was what he had planned.

'No problem,' he said. 'We're on our way.'

And now, as he made his way round the unit in the heat and the dust, the smell and the flies; (God he never realised that these units could have so many fucking flies); he wished that he and Jason had buggered off to the hotel before lunch. Luckily the farm manager was helpful, and went along with Steve's plans to go through with the whole procedure, tongue firmly in his cheek.

Steve knew it wasn't Swine Fever. It looked a typical case of PDNS. 35% mortality in the post weaning piglets for the last three months, with diarrhoea, skin blotches, and a lot of weak, fading and ultimately dead pigs.

They had discussed the problem in the pub a few nights previously. Bluster had instructed that any farm with PDNS was to have a Form A served on it with a full Swine Fever investigation. It seemed the vets' clinical judgement was being usurped. What was the point of sending vets to farms with sick pigs if the outcome was already decided? They could just as easily send out a trained monkey instead. 'Or failing that,' said Willie, 'an Animal Health Officer.'

But instructions were instructions and Bluster was Bluster, so after inspecting all 9000 pigs on the place Steve post mortemed two dead ones and a couple of sick ones that he slaughtered, and Jason took bloods from another ten sick pigs. It was gone 7.30 p.m. when they left the farm and Jason drove at high speed. Steve phoned the Animal Health Office and arranged for a cool box and freezer packs to be left outside the lab door. They could leave the samples in Jason's car overnight and get them packaged up and couriered to the labs the next morning.

It was already dark when they drew into the Animal Health Office car park. There were three cars there and the lights in the building were off. They found the cool box and packed their samples carefully inside, taping the lid shut.

'God I'm fucked,' said Steve. 'How much longer are you here for Jason?'

'Another three days. How about you?'

'I think I'll just hang around for the duration. No wife or kids to worry about and the social life's alright here. If my liver can stand it,' he laughed. 'I'll meet you at The White Lion, Sammy's ordering grub for us.'

Steve jumped into his Healey and started the engine. It barked comfortingly. A movement in the shadows of the building from the orange streetlights caught his attention. The hunched and stooping outline of the stalker making his way between the portacabins was unmistakable.

'What's he up to?' Steve said to himself, a cold shiver from his childhood, of walking home from Cubs alone, with rustling trees and bushes and dark alleyways and the urge to run. He laughed and told himself not to be so suspicious and set off after Jason.

The White Lion was packed. He knew he stank and he wished he could see Julie. He had thought of her all day. The dancing, fluttering in his stomach. 'Play it cool,' he said out loud. 'Don't rush. Savour the moment.'

He sat down at a table with Sammy. He could hear a sensuous Spanish voice telling how a sow had bitten her forcibly on the buttock as she bent to change a needle. Raucous offers from the men to check it for her and Willie whispered to Steve that it had only done what everyone there would like to have done but were too shy to ask.

Now Fernando was recounting how he'd been leaning against a wall when suddenly a huge boar had reared up on the other side and 'woofed' in his ear.

'It's mouth was like a whale's,' he said excitedly, the whites of his eyes growing larger, 'with big curled husks just a few inches from my face.'

'Tusks,' said Steve, and Fernando laughed.

'I thought it was going to eat me. It was completely massive and it was attacking the bars of the gate whilst we were there. Herbert was saying we were to bleed all the boars and when I told the farmer he just laughed at me. He said it was impossible to touch this boar; if I wanted to bleed it I was welcome to try and where did I want him to send my belongings. So I left it. What could I do?'

'Quite right,' Steve said. 'There's no point getting hurt. Those tusks could rip your leg to shreds or have your guts spilling out into the pen with a flick of his head if you weren't careful.'

'It's all very well for Bluster,' said Sammy. 'He hasn't got a clue what it's like on the farm squatting down to bleed pigs whilst others are coming up from behind and chewing away at your boots or worse. It won't be long before someone's badly hurt.'

'Who is that stalker bloke?' Steve asked. 'I saw him outside the office tonight all by himself. He's bloody creepy looking.'

'I know the one you mean,' someone said. 'He's from Sage Street. Admin bloke. He's staying at The Swallow. Always has a pint of stout and cider with him and always the last to leave the bar but never seems pissed. Conrad his name.'

'Are there many here from The Swallow tonight?' Steve asked.

'Two car loads. Most of them went next door.'

'Any particular interest?' asked Sammy with motherly amusement.

'Just friendly curiosity,' said Steve and he stuck his tongue out.

He stood up on the pretext of going to the bar and looked through to the other room. He spotted Julie instantly. Julie in tight white T-shirt, bare armed and hip hugging jeans and talking easily to a pack of dogs, tongues hanging out, drooling, Herbert Bluster amongst them.

He was back at college, a Friday night and there was Rachel, same tight white T-shirt and figure hugging jeans, her hand on his knee, her eyes sparkling with life and love and lust for him. And there she was again, bathing in the icy waters of a rushing Peruvian river, washing away the dried mud, the clear soft water bringing up the goose pimples on her tanned skin and turning her wavy hair into a mass of wet streaked ringlets.

He dried her and handed her a plate of pancakes that he'd cooked on their petrol stove, covered with melted butter and golden syrup and with a cup of steaming coffee. They ate their breakfast looking up at the snow covered Andean peaks on the road to Cajamarca where they would buy food and rest a while.

The previous night they had looked for a place to stay; a place out of sight from the road where they would be undisturbed. It had rained all day, the road a mass of puddles and pot holes, and they turned off on a narrow track that wound its way up the side of a mountain with water and mud flowing down, a brown sticky river. The cloud began to descend, the slopes of the mountain forested to the edge of the track and there was nowhere to stop.

And then round a bend they came upon a mudslide stretched across the road. They ploughed through, lost their grip and then on again, laughing and joking to keep their spirits high. Onwards and upwards and round another bend, the road now nothing more than a ledge perched on the side of the mountain, hundreds of feet dropping down suddenly into a gorge on their left hand side. Another mudslide, deeper still.

Rachel got out of the car on Steve's insistence.

'I'll take a run at it and that should get us through,' he said.

The front wheels and bumper pushed through the mud and gravel, the old Pontiac slowed. Steve pressed the accelerator and the back wheels with their chunky mud and snow tyres began to spin, sending mud and gravel into the air, digging in but keeping the car moving forwards; and sideways; the rear slewing to the left; sideways faster, faster towards the edge. He was determined, more accelerator, turning the front wheels into the skid and the edge always coming closer.

'Stop Steve. Stop. Stop. Steve. Stop.' Rachel screamed it out into the swirling mist. Screamed for the whole world to hear; screamed with a love and fire and passion that he still clung to.

He took his foot from the accelerator and the sliding car came to rest a few feet from oblivion. In a moment Rachel was at the rain soaked window, tears streamed down her mud spattered face, her eyes shone and flashed with pain and indignation that he could even risk leaving her to face the world without him. He wound the window down and she thrust her face towards him, kissing him savagely on the lips.

'Don't ever leave me,' she cried. 'Don't ever do anything that will let me lose you,' she pleaded.

'Fuck you bitch,' he said under his breath, shaking his head slowly.

'What? Are you talking to me?' he heard Julie say. She was by his side, her hand on his forearm like she had never been away all those years.

'No. Of course not,' said Steve. 'I was miles away. Thinking. No of course I wasn't talking to you. How are you? What have you been up to today?'

'God you stink of pigs,' she said, and she kissed him passionately and enthusiastically full on the mouth.

Chapter 14

It was three weeks since they'd arrived at Broadwich and Sammy and Willie were heading home. There had been no outbreaks since the initial seven and senior management puffed out their chests and made rash statements concerning how soon restrictions would be lifted.

Bluster summed up the mood at briefing one morning when he said how lucky all those present had been to be in at the start; during the exciting phase when everything was new and fresh.

'From now on,' he said, 'it will become mundane; clearing up; surveillance bleeding; clinical inspections and field patrols to root out unregistered pigs. You've seen the best of it.'

He was confident, his trousers hitched up to make contact with his armpits.

On her last night Sammy threw back red wine and danced barefoot and laughing on the tables in the bar.

'So is this the real thing? Julie I mean.' Sammy asked him when she sat back down at Steve's side.

'Don't be so bloody daft,' he said. True love no longer had meaning. He remembered a time when it did. And the hurt. A hurt so bad that he never wanted to go there again.

From Guatemala they crossed into Honduras; El Salvador torn and ruined by civil war with killings and atrocities commonplace. Honduras was still peaceful, a rich green, luscious land of Brahman cattle and bananas, and, like the rest of the region, filled with machete wielding peasants.

They stopped by the side of the road one evening a little way from a village and cooked dinner on the stove perched on the bonnet of the car. The mosquitoes were a nagging sore and they pulled the mosquito net over the car and sat inside with the windows down as the cloud of insects settled on the outside of the netting, their probosci probing the tight knit mesh in their search for blood.

All was peace; a warm, humid, heavy scented evening of tropical skies and tropical rains; the damp earth; fragrant blooms; and the sweat of their bodies formed a thick layer of grease and dust on their skin. As they waited for their meal to cook a great group of machete carrying men appeared, heading back to the village from their work in the surrounding fields. They stopped and surrounded the car, smiling and laughing brown faces, inquisitive it seemed, but as each minute passed they showed no signs of moving, intent on outstaying their welcome.

Steve smiled and tried to answer their questions in his broken Spanish but the heat and the sweat on them caused unease and concern in Rachel's eyes. Still smiling he got out of the car, switched off the stove and packed it in the boot with the saucepan of half cooked food. They did not try to stop him but they were pressing in closer and their talk was high pitched and excitable, a pack of hyenas surrounding their prey, teasing and mobbing it, each waiting for another member of the pack to make the first move.

Fear bubbled through his body but outwardly he remained calm, years of playground training had instilled in him the knowledge of when to run and when to confidently stand his ground. He talked about the weather, the beautiful car, the village; anything to show that he was not frightened and running away.

He pulled the net from the car towards him as he stood by the driver's door, gathering it up in his arms, smiling and chatting all the while. He gently opened the door and threw it in then eased himself into the driver's seat. The keys were in the ignition, he prayed it would start first time. When the six litre engine burst into life he kept the revs low.

They crowded round now, touched the car, called excitedly to one another, stood in the way, eyes moving backwards and forwards between the car and each other, voices raised in pitch and volume. He released the handbrake, put the automatic transition in drive and with the tiniest pressure from his right foot the great blue barge moved forwards through the mass of men that momentarily drew back to reveal the tall grass which moved gently in the warm evening breeze, between him and the road. He smiled and gave the gentlest of waves and as more clear space loomed ahead he accelerated carefully so that the car bounced around on the rutted, uneven earth and the grass caught in the bumper and under the wheel arches with a swishing and crackling.

Then the men knew he was running and like a pack of mad dogs they chased after the car, shouting and screaming, machetes raised above their heads with excitement. The game was up, he stamped on the throttle, too much, the rear wheels spun in the dry earth and then in a cloud of dust and flying grass they bounced onto the welcome tarmac of the Pan American Highway and in a few seconds had left their pursuers far behind.

'Thank fuck,' he said to Rachel. He was shaking and the steering wheel

wobbled. Rachel was white faced save for a darkness around her eyes
that he had never seen. He put his hand out to her and she lay her head
on his shoulder with moist startled eyes and laughing lips and held tight
round his waist.

'*I love you Sunshine,' she said.*

Julie came over and rested her hand conspicuously and possessively on Steve's knee. In spite of Sammy's age Julie resented her relationship with Steve; it was more than just good friends if not overtly sexual. There was mental sex as well as physical sex; more meaningful if less passionate; grown out of understanding, familiarity, trust and respect. Yes, she thought, Steve and Sammy respected each other, their barrier to a physical relationship was their age, time and fate. How weird she thought. How weird that love and pleasure were so mortal. So linked to time and fate that they could not be separated from it.

'Off home tomorrow Sammy?' she said, and the note of relief in her voice was undisguised.

'Yes, off back to my own house for a few weeks and the drudgery of cooking and ironing.'

'Have you ever spoken to that guy?' Steve asked, changing the subject abruptly and nodding at the stalker sitting at the bar with a glass of black fluid in his hand.

'He's bloody weird,' said Sammy. 'I've never seen him without a glass in his hand. He just sits there, watching, taking everything in; but saying nothing. Do you know what I mean?'

'He's scary looking' said Julie. 'Dr Death I call him. He's always skulking around in the office with that sort of twisted grin on his face.'

'Mr Turner, why are you without a pint in front of you? Because you may have noticed that my glass is in need of refilling.'

'What is it? Lager?'

'Aye, go on then,' Willie slurred. 'I'm off home tomorrow to the lovely Morag and all the little McDonalds and that will be the end of my pig bleeding career. You Mr Turner on the other hand will have the opportunity to try and bleed at least one pig by hitting the vein first time. But being the crap vet that you are, you'll probably never manage it.'

'He's away,' said Sammy smiling. And suddenly she was sad; sad that she was leaving Steve and concerned for him too. She had grown to know him more in the last three weeks and understood more than ever how important he was to her. Suddenly she realised she wanted to see him settled and married with a good woman, not rushing from one casual relationship to another. She wanted him happy; happy inside and not just on the surface.

Fernando and his entourage came over to join them. Always surrounded by women, thought Steve, young and not so young ones; but all hanging on his next word or smile. A Latin gentleman, attractive to women and attracted to them, neither predatory nor shy of them, simply treating them like good friends.

'Steve,' he said, 'this is Sonia. She has been to Latin America too. And Africa, Australia, the Far East. All over the world,' he added smiling.

'Hi,' said Steve looking at her. 'When did you arrive?'

'Today,' she said. 'This outbreak came just at the right time for me. I've been doing meat inspection for the last few months, since I got back in May. But it's so boring. I'm getting some money together to head off abroad again. This is regular work, all expenses paid so it suits me fine.'

Another confident bloody woman, thought Steve. Where did the vet profession find them all? Weren't there any quiet, modest types around anymore? Were there ever? he thought.

He looked closely at her, a discerning eye. The tan was either fake or the sort that came after years of exposure to the sun, deep and ingrained like a piece of stained antique pine; the colour matured, intense, and thick like syrup. Her hair streaked blonde and mouse, sun or bottle, he could not tell; eyes intense with pride and something else too, a mysticism or preoccupation. She was drinking white wine, held delicately in fingers that were young and fresh, not yet knarled and swollen like those of so many women of her age.

Julie saw it all too and her instinct told her to beware. The injustice stung her. Just as she was to get rid of Sammy this horny bitch turns up, she thought. It wasn't easy being a single woman of her age. It was a biological and sexist fact that with every passing year the number of eligible men that would look at her decreased exponentially. Competition was becoming more difficult to handle, things did not always work out in her favour. She squeezed Steve's thigh more tightly, her knuckles whitening. He hardly seemed to notice.

'Where are you planning for your next trip?' asked Steve.

'Singapore, Malaysia, Thailand, Vietnam,' she replied matter-of-factly. 'I was in Australia and New Zealand all last year,' she said, 'and I stopped off on the way back for a couple of weeks in Vietnam, just long enough to get hooked on the place. I want to see South East Asia before it's completely ruined by tourism, while there's still some adventure left in the place. Have you ever fancied going there yourself?' she asked teasingly.

'I'd love to,' said Steve.

'What's stopping you?' the teasing continued.

He was about to give some sensible, boring answer about his job, his pension, security, peace of mind and then stopped. Stopped as though someone had driven a sword into his heart and twisted it; twisted it, pushing and twisting so that he writhed and squirmed and his stomach felt like a painful, hard, knotted rope, that was dried taut and swollen with grief.

'You're too boring,' Rachel said. 'Patrick would drive fifty miles just to get a hamburger if he wanted one.'

Steve looked at her with disbelief. Fifty miles to get a fucking hamburger. What a fucking hero. What a fucking Jack-the-lad. Fifty fucking miles to get a fucking hamburger.

He felt tears come into his eyes that he struggled to control and he pretended to choke on his beer, convincing everyone but Sammy. You fucking bitch he thought. You stupid fucking bitch. I would have driven a million miles for the sight of your smile; the touch of your hand. Was that worth nothing to you?

'There's nothing stopping me,' he suddenly blurted out. 'Nothing at all. I might even be persuaded to come with you,' he added.

Julie gripped his thigh tighter making him jump. Fernando was listening to Willie, trying to understand his slurred words, and the others were chatting about farms they'd been to earlier that day. Sonia and Steve stared at each other. Neither wanted to make the next move. Julie felt her hackles rise like a lioness protecting her kill and Sammy looked on with a quizzical expression of mild surprise mixed with extreme concern and interest. Meanwhile at the bar, the stalker sipped his stout and cider with the same lop-sided smirk on his face as he calmly and thoroughly took everything in.

Chapter 15

Sammy and Willie were gone but Steve had Julie. Life at Broadwich was hard work but simple. He hadn't looked at a computer screen since he'd arrived. Bluster, he could largely ignore. He teamed up with Christopher, a big bear of an AHO from the south west. A steady kind of guy; straightforward, honest, hard working; young and keen to progress; nothing was too much trouble.

Steve had been like that once too. The thought hurt. He was still hard working, a case of pride and ethics. But he had no ambition. He joked with Sammy that his only ambition in the veterinary service was to leave as soon as possible. He was a cynic and he wasn't sure he liked himself for that. He thought cynicism was bad for his soul. If he had a soul he thought. He hadn't always been like that. He was once open and kind and thought the best of people. He had believed in true love, in honesty and in loyalty. He still believed in honesty and loyalty. But true love? Naaah. And he knew too that his own feet were made of clay.

He sat in the canteen one Tuesday afternoon drinking coffee and eating prawn sandwiches. Everything was under control and the talk was of the whole thing being wound up within a couple of weeks. And then a murmur and buzz of excitement crept into the building and spread along the corridors and into the side rooms until it arrived at the canteen. There had been a report case from a farm close to one of the IPs. The farmer's vet had phoned to report several sows and gilts suddenly sick with two already dead. He didn't like the look of it.

The effect was immediate. From a sense of jogging along at their own pace, everyone became charged with adrenaline induced excitement. People talked hurriedly to each other with earnest concern; DVAs moved along the corridors with renewed purpose and dark looks on their faces. And Angus MacSporran, a vet from Allocations, burst into the canteen and spoke with self-effusive authority.

'I need two experienced vets and their Animal Health Officers to go down to Lower Wood Farm near Marshton. It's a report case, very suspicious. In fact it's hot, the hottest thing we've had in two weeks.'

He looked around with an expectancy that almost, but not quite, invited applause.

Without knowing why, Steve offered to go. He surprised himself.

It was late in the afternoon and normally he would have slipped quietly into the background, let the youngsters take it on. Maybe Christopher's enthusiasm was rubbing off on him. He hoped not. His life plan, or lack of it, did not have room for enthusiasm at work.

'I need another,' said MacSporran, 'there's five thousand pigs and it'll be dark in a few hours.'

Another vet rose from his chair. 'I'll go,' he said.

Steve had seen him around but never spoken to him. He looked in his late twenties; his clothes could only have been those of a vet; moleskin trousers; chequered shirt; polished brown shoes. He would have looked at home in any racehorse yard or consulting in an up-market small animal clinic in the Home Counties.

He strode across to Steve and shook his hand.

'Paul Smythe,' he beamed. 'Sounds exciting doesn't it?' He stopped short of slapping Steve on the back.

'Steve. Steve Turner,' he replied. God he wished he'd kept his mouth shut. Still, too late now. 'Have you got an Animal Health Officer?' he asked.

'Yes, fine chap. Great pig bleeder. Mind you I'm pretty good myself but it's fine to have someone to fall back on isn't it? How about you? Is this your man?' he nodded at Christopher.

Steve giggled. The thought of Christopher being 'his man' was something from a bygone age. Despite his youth Paul Smythe was old school; landed gentry; house in the country; horses and hounds; servants even.

Christopher took it in good part. His interest was in getting plenty of overtime under his belt and making a name for himself as a reliable, conscientious worker. He'd been with the Ministry for just a year but could already see a long and fruitful career stretching out in front of him; thirty five years; progressing to senior Animal Health Officer and perhaps to an admin job beyond that. He was getting married next year, looking for a house with his fiancé. Nothing pretentious, something modern on a nice estate. The extra money would be a blessing. He liked Steve but didn't understand him. Didn't understand his cynicism or his resentment. Christopher was a straight up and down man. Steve seemed more complicated.

Steve knew what Christopher thought. He felt responsible and tempered what he said to him. He didn't want to over influence him, to poison his mind against The Establishment. Let Christopher make his own way and find his own truths; he might be spared the more painful ones.

'I'll check my car has all the gear,' said Christopher.

'Show us where this farm is MacSporran,' said Steve.

'Right here,' he said, pointing to the map on the wall. 'Not far from IP 5. This is hot. The PVO has been informed and he wants everything done by the book. No short cuts. Form A when you arrive; full clinical examination, post mortems and sampling; clinical inspection of the rest of the stock. I'll line up a courier to get the samples away first thing tomorrow morning, you'll not be back till late. Now, get to it.'

Fuck off MacSporran, thought Steve but he just said, 'Okay.'

It was early evening as they drove along the main trunk road to Ipswich. Harvest was just about over, field on field of golden stubble lined the road, and every now and then a field of outdoor pigs; great fat sows covered in a thick layer of dried mud where they had been wallowing to cool off. They lay in open nests of straw or inside their tin shelters, the mud protecting their hairless skin from the heat.

'At least thank God it's not Foot and Mouth,' Steve said to Christopher. 'That would be a different ball game. We couldn't cope with that. We wouldn't cope with that,' he corrected.

'Why not?' asked Christopher innocently.

'It's different to Swine Fever. Much more infectious for a start and pigs produce massive quantities of virus. It can spread on the wind. You imagine an intensive pig unit with five thousand animals. If only a few hundred of them were infected the volume of virus put out would be enormous. It travels in a plume of air, the way smoke from a bonfire does. It'll go for tens of miles under the right conditions. It'd be a bloody disaster.'

'It won't come here though, will it?' Christopher said. 'I mean, how could it get here?'

'Just be thankful that the ham sandwich had Swine Fever virus in it and not Foot and Mouth. It just as easily might have had. Then we'd have seen what the PVO was made of,' he said.

'When this is all over,' said Christopher, 'I'm going to take my fiancé away for a weekend. Somewhere in the Cotswolds. Somewhere with beams and horse brasses on the wall and those old fashioned lamps and with a restaurant that does good steaks and mixed grills. En suite bathroom and telly in the room. She'd like that. So would I.'

'Sounds good,' smiled Steve, and closed his eyes.

That wasn't his and Rachel's style. Though looking back perhaps it was more Rachel's. Perhaps that was what she had needed, a bit of pampering instead of the hardship and penny pinching they'd grown used to. Tears came from behind closed eyes and he took out his hanky to wipe them from his nose.

They were travelling through Nicaragua and stopped late one afternoon not far from an army training camp. Half a dozen young soldiers walked up to them, brown skinned mixed race with short black hair. They carried M16 automatic rifles slung round their necks like chains of office, their hands resting on the barrel and butt simultaneously. Black metal and brown wood forged together. Young boys of 15 or 16. Had they fired their guns in anger? Even killed with them? wondered Steve. Their khaki shirts were sweat soaked; drops of sweat streaked their faces and stuck their straight black hair to their foreheads and temples.

Two of them were drunk. Even in Spanish Steve could tell their words were slurred, and their eyes had the pink tinged glow of drunkenness, slightly closed, unfocusing. A sweet sickly smell of alcohol with garlic on their breath and one of them spat repeatedly, too close for comfort. Sometimes the spit caught on the boy's lip and dribbled down his chin, and he unknowing or uncaring. Steve was frightened by the way he looked at Rachel and the way he gently touched her arm as he spoke, pretending to illustrate a point.

The rifle hanging from his neck swung carelessly, pointing up and down, sometimes at Steve and sometimes at Rachel, sometimes at the boy's comrades. These were the Sandinistas, freshly in power from their Revolution the previous year and there was no one in charge to restrain them. Like before with the machete wielding men they knew that they should leave; slowly and with dignity.

They drove further on the Pan American Highway and stopped a hundred yards from a small farmhouse. A girl on a horse passed by as they cooked supper and made it clear that they should move to the yard by the farmhouse.

'Peligro, peligro,' she repeated. 'Danger, danger.'

They followed her in their car and she tried to entice them into the fenced compound around the house but they were foolishly suspicious of her motives. They smiled and waved and parked at the entrance, she smiled back and beckoned them in but they could not be tempted.

In the dead of night they were woken by men shouting and lorry doors slamming, lights flashing, excited voices, the sound of heavy boots running on tarmac. Then hammering on the car window.

'Abra, abra,' a man's voice shouted. Urgent, demanding to be obeyed. Steve, naked and Rachel almost so, pulled back the curtains and a powerful torch shone in at them.

'Who are you? What are you doing?' Steve thought the man said in Spanish. He replied in his own broken Spanish that the lady in the house said that they could park there for the night. He waited, the taste of metal in his mouth. Metal tinged with rancid fat, his palms damp and cold; his heart jogging fast, ever faster, his brain imagining a row of guns somewhere out there, a few feet away, pointing at him, nervous fingers on the trigger.

'Turistas?' bellowed the man.

'Si.' Steve replied.

'Perdon,' he snapped his heels to attention. He may have saluted.

The sound of guns being uncocked and stood down; of boots on tarmac road; truck doors slamming and the engine accelerated away and the lights grew dimmer.

'Thank fuck,' was all that Steve could say. 'Thank fuck,' and he buried his face in Rachel's neck.

Their trip ended in Peru. The Pontiac began to make a noise from the rear differential and they took it to a garage in Lima where the owner was confident of a repair. But first they had to wait in a queue. A queue of beaten up old cars and trucks imported from the USA, ten, twenty, even thirty years ago. Big engines and big interiors, the body work distorted by dents and scratches, but hardly touched by the ravages of rust in the warm, dry climate.

They stayed in a small hotel. A respectable but basic hotel with one toilet with no seat shared between five rooms. The toilet didn't flush well and was poorly cleaned and overflowed onto the floor. It smelt of sewage and there were always peas or sweet corn floating in it and the used toilet paper was thrown in a bucket in one corner from where it spilled out and rustled with cockroaches that grew sleek and fat on the rich pickings.

The first night in Lima they had risked sleeping in the car to save their fast dwindling cash. They drove round the town in the heat and noise of a South American capital city; motor horns, police whistles and sirens; the rattling of bodywork breaking free from its welds; Latin American music screaming from every shop and café and restaurant.

They parked at the side of the road where there was grass and trees and where a regular procession of Peruvian lovers arrived, stopped for half and hour and then went on their way. Steve was uneasy, and as night fell and they drew the curtains and settled down to sleep, the eyes of all Peru were on them as each passing headlight scanned the inside of the Pontiac, a moving shadow across the roof and across his mind with slow monotonous thoroughness.

The lights came and went in the car and in his head and the two of them slept until the knocking at the window came again and it was the same voice shouting at him only this time it was a Peruvian policeman instead of a Sandinista soldier but he was demanding the same thing. It was all blurred now, one into the other and he could not remember what he had said only that they were left in peace again.

And now the car was in the garage and they were in a hotel and with each day their money grew less and he supposed their appetite for the journey ahead dwindled too. They spent each day sitting on the bonnet of their car in the garage compound, surrounded by Peruvian mechanics and broken wrecks, scavenged and pillaged for the spare parts that they offered. The mechanics worked away on the taxis and trucks, grease covered overalls open to the waist exposing taut brown bodies; grease streaked faces and hands with creases and finger nails etched in black oil.

They hoped by sitting to engender a sense of urgency to their plight and the desire to be on their way but they misjudged the Latin spirit which sees sitting as a respectable pastime, not a sign of sloth or impatience. The men worked steadily, laughing and joking with each other, and sometimes about them Steve was sure, and more often about Rachel. But it was good natured, they did not feel threatened and they had the use of a filthy toilet which flushed at least, a practical consideration but important nonetheless.

They bought bread from a tiny bakery for lunch and cheese and ham and the thick green cucumbers and huge red tomatoes, a healthy if monotonous diet. They sat there for four days and returned to their hotel each night and the spirit of adventure slowly left them as life leaves a newly dead corpse.

And Rachel became uneasy, bored and reluctant to compromise. She wanted some fun, to eat at a fine restaurant; to see a film or a play; to go dancing. The conflict grew as each evening Steve contemplated the dwindling wad of money, now below $500 US. Little enough to take *them on their way to Cuzco and Machu Pitchu; to La Paz; back to Chile and then across Argentina to Brazil. That was their dream when they spent $1000 US to ship their car from Panama to Guayaquil in Ecuador. And now the dream was gone.*

At lunchtime on the fifth day Rachel said that she wanted to go to a restaurant. Not wanted to but needed to. He should have acquiesced, he knew that now. But back then it was $25; five days food on the road; a tank of petrol and three hundred miles travelled; three nights in the hotel. How could you swop any of them for an hour and a half in a restaurant when you were not hungry.

He would not agree, would not submit and then she jumped from the car bonnet and ran out of the garage yard and down the street. Not jogging but running; running fast with purpose and intent.

Steve ran after her. He sprinted to keep her in sight as she dodged through the people on the street who turned and stared after her, laughing and shaking their heads. Steve remembered the thrill and terror, snakes in his mind, crashing planes, a bullet in his guts, a tearing in his chest; she sprinted across a main road, car horns honking, brakes and tyres squealing; police whistles. He followed as best he could, shrugging his shoulders at the drivers who threw their hands up off the steering wheel; crazy gringos!

And finally he caught her, grabbed her by the arm.

'Let me go. Get off me,' she screamed at him.

People stared. Red faced and soaked with sweat, wide eyed and hair bursting out like a firework he let her go as she span round to face him. Tears covered her face, her eyes glistening blue and red lined. The tears mixed with the sweat and the dust from the street, a street urchin from Lima save for the blonde hair that curled in loose ringlets over her ears down to her brown, exposed shoulders.

'I should never have married,' she shouted. 'Never, never.'

The words had power. No knife or gun could have wounded him more cruelly. No sword or machete, pike or billhook, pierced him so painfully. A pain so acute and intense, deep somewhere in the pit of his stomach that expanded and spread, weakening his breath and his muscles, his voice, his thoughts and his spirit. Weakening his spirit. He felt it flowing out of him like blood from a gaping wound.

'I should never have married.'

She might as well have said 'I should never have married you.'

Then it came to him that what he had could be lost. Never had it occurred before. Now his world was no longer as he had perceived it. That which happened to others could happen to him. They had been married but nine months and already she would throw in the towel. The pavement at his feet turned red with his spilt blood.

He knew by the fierce passion in her eyes that she was not joking. She was serious and earnest. Serious and in spite of the tears enjoying the effect. Cruel and satisfying in the knowledge of her power.

And then the tension was gone, like the passing of a storm. He held her to him and she sobbed on his shoulder and she said that it was nothing and that it would pass.

'We'll go to a restaurant now,' he said but had been grateful when she declined.

'I'm just being silly,' she said, and the warning went unheeded and forgotten.

'Here we are,' said Christopher, parking his car on the grass at the entrance to Lower Wood Farm.

'And here we go again,' said Steve cheerfully. He was thinking of Julie. And Sonia too. An enviable position to be in he thought as he pulled on wellies over his paper boiler suit. The farmer greeted him, and he switched back to Veterinary Officer Steve Turner.

By the time he and Paul finished at Lower Wood Farm it was clear to both of them that this was another case of Swine Fever. The symptoms in the live pigs and the lesions in the ones they post mortemed were classic. Paul, in spite of his Sloane Ranger manner had proved an able operator; confident, thorough, and with a good rapport with the farmer. Steve was impressed and warmed to him, particularly when he'd shown so much enthusiasm to hear about his Austin Healey.

With all the samples taken and disinfection complete, Steve phoned MacSporran to report back.

'I wouldn't bet my life on it but I'd bet a month's salary on it being Swine Fever,' he told MacSporran, who insisted on knowing exactly what had happened and what samples had been taken. Insisted, not once, but twice.

'And you took some for African Swine Fever too?' he asked. 'Current instructions are that we must continue to test samples for that too.'

Steve frowned. Who did MacSporran think he was?

'Yes MacSporran, don't worry, I've got everything we need. You can rely on me and Paul.' He pulled a face and Paul laughed.

'Yes, I've got a key to the lab door now so everyone can bugger off home. I'll put the samples straight in the fridge when I get back and they can go off by courier first thing tomorrow.... Yes, I'll label them correctly. Anyway I'll be in first thing tomorrow to oversee it all... No of course we don't want any cock ups.'

'Well I'm off home now that I know what's happening,' said MacSporran. 'Oh, and Sonia's here. She says to let you know that there's still room for one more on the South East Asia trip, whatever that means. Bye for now.' He hung up.

'Does she now,' murmured Steve, and a prickling heat stung him inside.

It was long dark by the time they reached the Animal Health Office. The car park was empty save for one or two cars randomly spaced. Car parks at night were always sad, he thought. A lot of empty spaces waiting to be filled. Like himself, he thought.

'You go and get the pints in,' he said to Christopher as he got out of the car. 'I'll put the samples in the fridge and I'll be right behind you.

'I'll sort this stuff out,' he shouted across the car park to Paul. 'You can shove off.'

The light outside the lab door was still on for which he was grateful. He didn't feel at home in the dark and Rachel had laughed at him. And now alone outside this huge building with dim light and the shadowy shapes of overalls drying on the line and shifting gently in the warm late summer breeze the sensation of being watched brushed his skin like early morning mist. A dryness in his throat, the urge to get in his car and drive away. Irrational thoughts he told himself.

He glanced around and the shock, hot and sharp hit him as he saw someone advancing from the gloom, then back away. He relaxed, a boiler suit hanging on a washing line, inflated and moved by a puff of wind, a headless and harmless monster. Grow up, he thought. You're not a kid running from the dark.

He took out his key and unlocked the door, he couldn't stop himself peering over his shoulder, his mind feeding on the anxiety. He found the light switch quicker than he'd hoped. He felt happier now everywhere was bathed in fluorescent rays but he locked the door behind him for good measure anyway. The lab was a series of rooms and corridors below the main offices with a stairway leading up from them through a set of swing doors. He scanned the room he'd entered, clean and tidy, wellies and overalls hung up neatly ready for use the next day.

He made his way down a short corridor and into the first room on the left, putting more lights on as he went. He opened the fridge door, it was empty. Good, he thought, no chance of mixing the samples up and he placed the polystyrene box he was carrying on the top shelf. As he shut the door he thought he heard the familiar noise of the swing doors. He shivered and went out into the corridor.

'Hello,' he called. 'Hello?'

There was no answer and the doors were still and silent. And then he heard the sound again, only further away; at the top of the stairs he guessed.

'Hello?' he called again but no answer came. The dryness returned to his throat and he felt cold in spite of the late August heat. He looked at his watch, twenty minutes to ten. Time to go, he thought and with difficulty controlled the urge to run. He turned the lights off behind him, quickening his step, walking faster, silently and quickly now, almost running, glancing from left to right and back over his shoulder like a startled animal.

He flicked off the last light, went through the outer door and locked it. He was breathing fast and his heart was thudding in his ears and the burnt metal taste of fear in his mouth. The overalls danced and the boughs of a low growing tree rustled against the lab wall. It was nothing he told himself. He'd imagined the noise. He stared up at the outside of the building. His heart quickened again, a sharp burst of fear hit him in the stomach and his legs flexed involuntarily. The light in the upstairs corridor was on, he knew he hadn't seen it when he went in. He stood staring, breathing in short, shallow bursts. It'll be a cleaner, he thought. Don't be paranoid. Perhaps they had been on all the time, someone forgotten to turn them off. What would anybody be doing snooping around at this hour? This is middle England in the new millennium, not Moscow in the sixties. He looked again just to make sure. The light still glowed.

He began to walk to his car. Slowly at first but the clammy and prickly sensation over his skin increased as the sense of being watched grew. He spun round and looked up at the windows. Nothing. He quickened his pace as the urge came to run; there was nothing to fear he told himself but he took the last few steps to his car at a jog.

He was shocked to find himself fumbling with his car keys and he dropped them on the floor with a clatter. He had played this game many times before as a child when he was scared. He had only so long to get his keys out and open the car door and get in and start the engine before the psychopath got him. It was only a game but the feelings were real. Only if he lost it didn't matter because there never was a psychopath following him. He played it again now. Ten seconds to pick up his keys, get in and start the engine.

He ducked down, grasped the door key and rammed it into the lock. Twist key, pull door handle and open. Still counting, 'four, five,' and he was in, loosing a split second as a finger caught in the key ring and as the key went home in the ignition he hit eight. Clutch depressed automatically, gear lever to neutral, 'nine' he murmured and turned the key to crank the engine and that familiar, reassuring roar from the exhaust.

'Yes,' he said to himself and slamming the lever into first he shot forward. 'No psychopath,' he said out loud and laughing and drove through the car park to the exit. A movement in the shadows of the portacabins attracted him and he eased off the accelerator to get a better view. There was a man there, trying the door of a portacabin and then moving on to the next. He appeared not to notice Steve because he carried on down the whole line trying each one in turn and then moved off round the corner of the main building.

What he was doing Steve had no idea but he didn't like it, didn't like it at all. Was he the cause of the noise in the corridor by the lab and the lights on upstairs? The hairs on his neck prickled at the thought and he glanced in the rear view mirror expecting to see someone staring through the back window at him. This time he couldn't control the feeling and instinctively he stamped on the throttle and with a screech of tyres leapt out of the car park causing another car to swerve around him. He ignored the unorthodox but easily interpreted hand signals of the other driver and tried to relax. His pulse was drumming in his head, his hands and knees were shaking and he glanced frequently at his mirror in anticipation of being followed. He didn't know what the man was up to or why he was there that late at night but he did, without a shadow of doubt, recognise him. The man he had seen skulking in the shadows and trying the door handles was Conrad. Conrad the stalker.

Chapter 16

Julie convinced Steve that he had everything out of proportion. They were in the bar and Conrad arrived around eleven o'clock, ordered his usual stout and cider and sat on his usual stool at the bar. If there was guilt on his conscience it did not show.

Steve looked in his direction time after time but saw nothing save the smug smirk that was always there. He went over it in his mind. He was good at that to the point of compulsion and it had annoyed Rachel. The way he worked everything around, turning it inside out, sucking every little bit of juice from the bones. It was the only way he knew how. Dissect and analyse so that all the possible outcomes were exposed. Only then could he understand.

Even things long since past he relived in his mind. Conversations repeated until he knew them by heart. Passages of books read as a boy he could still recite; the names of dogs from adventure stories thirty five years ago. In the last fifteen years half his life had been spent going over old events until it had driven him mad. He reached some low points in that time. Low points retrieved with the love and help of family and friends.

The suspicious new outbreak had brought a buzz to the bar that night with people affected in different ways. Some were enlivened, stimulated by the prospect of real action instead of the routine work of surveillance and pig bleeding. Others were battle weary after twelve or fourteen hour days in the heat and stench of pig farms with flies buzzing and pigs squealing and biting, and the pressure and fear of making a mistake. They were now desperate to get home and the thought of more cases depressed them. And for new arrivals it was the baptism of fire they had hoped for. Keen and raring to go, the prospect of dull routine for the next few weeks held no appeal. Like soldiers waiting for battle to begin they breathed a sigh of relief at the sounding of the first shot.

Steve and Paul were at the centre, everyone wanting to know what they'd seen and done. As the evening wore on, the quiet peace of relaxation; of sitting on a river bank with a cold beer on a summer's day, washed over Steve. The tightness of his muscles and the nagging pressure in his head wafted gently away and the smile in his eyes began to sparkle. Fear and apprehension were replaced by euphoria. He was the centre of attention with street credibility; one of the lucky few to have seen the disease in real life. He was certain of his diagnosis; a classic case, and with each pint that was placed on the table in front of him his description of his post mortem technique and the beauty of the lesions became poetry.

Julie bathed in the reflected glory. Sat by his side with her hand resting on his knee she drank in each word and acted out her part to perfection. A kiss on his cheek, a light touch on his arm; letting him know that she was there, by his side. A part of his life.

And it irritated Steve. Her closeness was possessive and he did not like to be possessed. Not now. Possession was selfish, he had learnt that much from his relationship with Rachel. They had possessed each other, engulfed and choked each other like two seedlings competing for the same nutrients. Always in each other's company, always knowing what the other was thinking and doing.

Possession was destructive to love and love was a gift to be cherished and nurtured but not caged. Love was a bird free, singing for joy with the freedom to stay or depart. Possessive love was a bird in a cage, constant and predictable. Given food and water it would survive but it would not flourish, never sing a different song. Leave the cage door open, let it once fly away and it would never be enticed back home.

Both he and Rachel had been caged birds and one day she had left the cage. And instead of helping him to leave with her she had slammed the cage shut, leaving him to survive alone and continue with his sad song while he waited in the hope of her return. But the song he sang had died too and after so many years in the cage he had forgotten how to fly.

He felt Julie's fingers tighten on his thigh and looked up. Sonia was standing a few feet away looking at him.

'Who's the hero then?' she teased and the smile lit her face.

Steve flushed warm with embarrassment and desire. He knew she was teasing him and he knew why. She was teasing Julie too; a lioness teasing another for the attention of the lion. He wanted to say something witty but his desire inhibited him. He shrugged his shoulders and raised his eyebrows instead, a gesture of nonchalant self-satisfaction and indifference. It had the effect he intended. Sonia continued in a more seductive vein.

'Would you bet your happiness on it being Swine Fever?' she said. 'How certain are you? Would you bet your happiness on it?' she was murmuring the words now, with a lust of her own.

'My happiness is my own and can neither be won or lost,' said Steve. 'A man who would bet his happiness would bet his soul.'

'A philosopher,' said Sonia. She was back to teasing now.

'I would like to help you with the slaughter if it is positive,' said Fernando.

'I'll ask Bluster tomorrow,' said Steve, glad to have someone like Fernando around. 'I'm sure he'll agree if I tell him I need you.'

Fernando laughed, a cheerful open laugh. The harem that accompanied him laughed too.

Steve and Julie left the bar at midnight. There would be a detailed report to write in the morning whilst they awaited the lab result. The one thing he was certain of was that there were a lot of pigs going to need killing.

Once in his room, Steve's thoughts returned to the stalker. Julie, irritated by Sonia's and Steve's exchange, derided his over imaginative mind. The stalker wasn't a stalker she said, he just looked like one. He'd probably left something behind and gone back to look for it or was just checking that everywhere was locked.

'Your imagination is too wild,' she said. 'Now come to bed and screw me.'

Steve arrived at the office shortly after 8.30 a.m. and went straight to the canteen for the morning's briefing. Bluster was already in full flow, the hush over the audience reflecting the sombre tone in his voice.

'We're targeting farms in the 3 Km protection zone around this new suspect IP today. And remember, if you find pigs with PDNS you must treat it as Swine Fever.' Bluster's jaw was set square and defiant, daring anyone to question what he was saying.

'If you've got a herd of five thousand pigs you're bound to have a few that are sick for one reason or other. Some of those will have high temperatures and I suspect spots as well. We surely don't have to treat that as suspect Swine Fever unless there are other compelling reasons. Do we?' someone asked.

Herbert Bluster shifted uneasily, his face purpling, his ears twitching like a mule's. He did not like people challenging his instructions, particularly people he'd never spoken to before in his life.

'Use your veterinary judgement,' he barked back, 'that's what you're paid for.'

An audible muttering of disapproval went round the room. It was a reasonable question from a fellow professional. On one hand they were given prescriptive instructions, and in the next breath told to use their veterinary judgement. Everyone felt short changed. Bluster was the master when it came to lowering morale.

'There are copies of the instructions on the table here at the front,' Bluster said. 'It's been modified in the light of yesterday's events so a lot of it is crossed through and replaced with other sentences but it should be clear enough.

'Ah Mr Turner, good of you to turn up.'

Steve wasn't sure if he was joking. He suspected not.

'Tell us everything about yesterday evening and what's happening.'

'Not everything,' Julie whispered in his ear.

Steve smiled. Remembering. He skipped through the events and finished with the thought that in his view this was almost certainly a positive case.

'Are the samples away?' asked Bluster.

'Christopher's packing them up now. I'll go and see how he's getting on.' He turned and left the room, catching the exclamations of those who were already reading the new instructions.

'This is ridiculous.'

'How can they expect us to follow this?'

'If my child sent homework in like this he'd be made to do it again.'

'What a load of shite!'

Steve giggled. Head office control freakery was alive and well.

Christopher was packing and labelling samples in the lab.

'How's it going?' Steve asked.

'Fine. I've done the samples for Classical Swine Fever. Where did you put the ones for African?'

'How do you mean?'

'I can only find one set of samples in that box in the fridge. I assumed you'd put the others somewhere else.'

A short sharp jolt. Hollow and churning in his stomach.

'No, I just took the box you gave me from the back of your car and put them in the fridge. They must be there.' He looked in the box on the table. It was empty. He went to the fridge and opened it. That was empty too. 'They must be in another box in your car. Give me your keys and I'll have a look.'

'I've looked already,' said Christopher. He was thorough and efficient. Steve knew that.

'I'll have another look anyway,' said Steve and he hurried off down the corridor bumping into Julie.

'You're in a rush,' she said in a voice that annoyed him.

'Something important,' he muttered. 'I'll speak to you in a minute.'

The tone stung her, the taste of soured milk in her mouth.

Julie looked past him to Christopher and he shrugged. 'Some of the samples are missing,' he said. It was an explanation.

Steve spent fifteen minutes rummaging in Christopher's car. He took everything out and put it all back. He felt down seats; looked under seats. Checked pockets of dirty overalls. As each minute passed the pressure in his head grew and the heat built in his body, rising up through his chest and to his neck and face which began to burn. His hands were clammy with sweat and he could feel the moisture on his forehead running like a small stream. An unpleasant taste in his mouth, metallic, harsh and pervasive.

'Shit,' he said. 'Shit, shit, shit. Fucking shit.'

His head ached now. It could have been the beer from last night or the lack of sleep but he knew it was the pressure inside as he searched his memory for a clue as to what he might have done with them. The pulse in his temples was pumping, he heard it pass through the bone of his skull to his inner ear, amplified by the repetitive nature of the beat. He felt his heart thudding in his chest, the close intimacy of his mind with his body shocked him. The thought of it failing, stopping, a real, helpless fear.

Had they left them on the farm? Possibly. Probably. Or maybe Paul. That was it. Paul must have them. They'd be in Paul's car.

He ran up the stairs to the canteen, ashamed at his sudden breathlessness. He was only 44 and he was panting like an old man. The sound of his breathing as he went through the swing doors caused a couple of young admin girls to look at him and giggle. He went into the loo and looked in the mirror.

His face was red and blotchy and covered in sweat. His hair stuck to his forehead. There was a puffy, bloated look about him. His skin, particularly around the base of his nose had the tiny tell tale purpling colour of broken blood vessels. He stared in disbelief. This was not the Steve Turner he remembered or imagined. He was turning into a bloater. He had to stop pissing it up every night and take some exercise instead. If he didn't he would turn into a fat middle aged pisshead. The oldest swinger in town. A truth he suddenly accepted. He wasn't a young student anymore. He was behaving like one but he wasn't one.

'You're too boring,' she said. Fifteen years ago he was a young man behaving like an old bore. Now he was an old bore behaving like a young man. He shrugged, One day he would get it right.

He washed his face in cold water. The astringent effect made his skin tingle, the mixture of water and salt sweat like aftershave. He washed it for a full minute and looked in the mirror again. His hair was even more plastered down but his skin had improved. The redness had given way to pinky brown. Some of the puffiness had gone too. His eyes were still clear. Brown. Very brown. Small and piercing. Like an animal's eyes. Years ago as he had lain in the arms of another girl, she'd said to him: 'How can you have such small eyes and such big eyes at the same time?'

He had never forgotten.

He dried his face with a paper towel. Rough like sandpaper. Government policy, value for money and all that. His breathing was easier now, nearly silent. His heart too.

He marched to the canteen. Paul was at a desk writing.

'We can't find one lot of samples Paul,' said Steve. 'Any chance that they're in your car?'

'No chance,' he replied. 'I emptied it this morning. There was nothing except the used boiler suits and the old needles.'

'Shit, I've lost the bloody things then. It's not the end of the world I suppose. It's not African Swine Fever, we know that. Bluster won't be pleased when I tell him though.'

'Anything I can do to help?' Paul said.

'No. But thanks anyway. I can take the flak.' He tried to laughed it off.

He went back to the lab where Christopher was still working.

'Well, I've lost them,' Steve said bluntly. 'Get the others away with the courier straight away. I'll phone the farm just to check I haven't left them there. It'll look incompetent but I can't help that.'

A quick phone call confirmed what he already knew and he took his incompetence on the chin. So what had happened to them? The uneasy scent of intrigue nagged away at him. Too many coincidences that didn't quite add up. The sound of swing doors late at night; the light on upstairs; the stalker in the car park trying all the doors; and now the samples missing. Of course there was a simple explanation for it. There had to be. What would the stalker want with the samples? To get him into trouble? It didn't make sense.

He went to see Bluster who was pouring over expense claims.

'How some people expect me to sign these I just don't know,' he said with an air of pompous self importance. 'They haven't even put down the time they left the office or the reason for going to the farms. And the cost code centre and task code are all wrong.'

Steve wanted to ask him what fucking difference any of those things would make to the value of the claim but knowing the news he was about to give Bluster, he thought better of it. And to his surprise, Herbert Bluster was remarkably relaxed about the whole thing. He agreed that it was not of huge importance in the great scheme of things, and that though unfortunate it was not likely to affect Steve's annual Job Appraisal Review.

'But I didn't lose them,' Steve finished. 'They must have been taken by someone.'

Herbert Bluster looked at him and the head began to twitch and tremble in that familiar way.

'We're all under pressure,' he said. 'Mistakes will be made. Put a report on the file saying that they've been lost and that will be the end of the matter.'

How very peculiar thought Steve as he made his way to the Accommodation portacabin. He had not expected that sort of reaction from Bluster. Petulance, castigation, a degree of 'This is not good enough Mr Turner and you will pay for it at staff reporting time.' It was something else that didn't quite add up.

He entered Accommodation and spoke to the guy in charge of building maintenance.

'How do the lights in the corridors work?' he asked. 'Who switches them off at night?'

'They're on a time switch,' he replied. 'They go off automatically at

6.00 p.m. and are then activated by movement sensors. If someone enters the corridor after that they switch on automatically. If there's no more movement they go out after five minutes. Why?'

'I'm writing a thesis on energy saving devices and thought there might be some mileage in the lights.'

'Sounds interesting,' said the guy.

Like bollocks, thought Steve. But he was excited. Detective work. Perhaps he should be in epidemiology. That's all that was really. Sure plenty of people dressed it up by talking in jargon and about mathematical models and statistics, but at the end of the day it was all down to nosing out information and applying good veterinary science and common sense to what you found. Perhaps he would try and get into epidemiology. He was fed up with examining and bleeding stinking pigs.

His spirits were lifted by his findings too. Lifted by being proved right. There had been someone in the building, someone that hadn't answered when he'd called out and the samples were missing. It didn't add up to a conspiracy but there was something odd about it all.

He kept his thoughts to himself and started writing his report. The day dragged. It was hot and steamy and most people were out in the 3 Km area around Lower Wood. The sandwiches came at noon and again at four thirty. With so few others around he had the pick of them, concentrating on the prawn mayonnaise and the BLTs. The coffee and soup machine went unused. Too hot. The cold mineral water dispenser was a Godsend.

As the afternoon wore on people reappeared clutching their boxes of blood tubes or their plastic bags of post mortem samples. The smell of pigs invaded the building, a smell that mixed with sweat and rose with the heat of the day. The building awakened with the sound of chatter and movement.

Steve wandered down to epidemiology and went into the room. There were five vets inside and a young bloke who appeared to be admin support. At one end behind a desk sat the DVA in charge, Graham Thompson. He sat, stony faced, his head supported on both his hands, eyes closed, as though meditating.

The other five vets were crammed in, files and spreadsheets open in front of them; feed lorry movements; personnel movements; pig movements, anything that might be responsible for transmitting virus from one premises to another. They pored over them in silence like Victorian clerks, looking for a link no matter how tenuous. In spite of the heat everyone was wearing a tie.

Trevor Stevens looked up at Steve, eyes blinking in his podgy face like a rabbit caught in car headlights.

'Good to see you again,' he said, 'even though you are the one causing us all the trouble today. What did you have to go and find another case for? Things not exciting enough for you?'

'What are your thoughts on how it might have spread to Lower Wood Farm?' Graham Thompson asked. A direct approach and it put Steve on the spot. He thought for a few seconds before answering, wanting to give a good impression.

'There are a couple of possibilities,' he said. 'Firstly, Lower Wood is only a mile away from IP Number 5. From what I've heard, that wasn't the cleanest of farms, dead piglets and afterbirths lying around and I think there was evidence of scavenging by foxes wasn't there?

'Foxes are pretty common at Lower Wood too with a couple of well used earths just a hundred yards from the pig sheds. It's not impossible that a fox brought some carrion back a few weeks ago. The cubs will be well grown by now but the adults would still have been bringing food to them in early August. There are a few outdoor pigs at Lower Wood, dry sows, and they could have got access to infected carrion and started the whole thing off.'

'And the second?' asked Graham listening intently. He looked straight at Steve, daring him to look away.

'That's more likely I think,' said Steve. 'The farmer used an itinerant pigman to help out about three weeks ago when one of his own men was off sick. Just for a couple of days but he was working in the dry sow house where the sick pigs were yesterday. What was his name, Donald.., Donald..'

'Walker?' said one of the vets turning round.

'That's the one,' said Steve.

'I think we have a source then,' said the man. 'Donald Walker, mucky sort of bloke, was working weekends at IPs 3 and 4. I've spoken to him a few times but he's never mentioned Lower Wood Farm.'

'You'd better get in touch with him then and find out where else he's been and never mentioned,' said Graham Thompson pointedly. 'We need to explore all possibilities and not jump to conclusions, but I suspect you're right,' he said to Steve.

Steve thought he smiled but could not be sure.

'We'll see if the lab confirms it,' went on Graham. 'If they do I suspect there will be others.'

It was then that Steve noticed for the first time Trevor's withered arm. It was the left one and it hung loose by his side like a piece of washing on a line. With each movement that Trevor made it responded with a gentle flap.

'What happened to your arm Trevor?' he asked. He was more than satisfied with the impression he'd made on Graham Thompson.

'I had a rather nasty altercation with a lorry,' he drawled, smiling like some huge lizard about to snap up a frog. The arm was smashed up completely, all the nerves torn out of the brachial plexus. The surgeons wanted to amputate it but I persuaded them that I would rather wear a jacket with two sleeves even if it didn't work very well. It's quite handy in pantomime and my kids' friends like looking at it when they first meet me,' he was laughing. 'It's difficult to get it swinging with the right rhythm when you're walking though; people think you're taking the Mickey out of them. What's happening with you? Didn't you marry Rachel Jarvis?'

'I did,' said Steve, 'and it's a long story.' He wished he hadn't asked about the arm though Trevor seemed comfortable with it. And although Steve didn't have something as obvious as a withered arm, he suspected he was the more seriously and permanently damaged of the two of them. Not suspected. Knew he was. He carried more uncomfortable baggage with him than the outsider could possibly know. Uncomfortable? It was so uncomfortable it bloody hurt. Hurt with a pain that, though dulled by the passing of much time could still be rekindled by the slightest gust of ill-chosen comment.

'Right, I'll catch you later,' said Steve knowing that he sounded abrupt.

'Thank you for the information,' said Graham Thompson.

Steve returned to the canteen. Paul was eating but came over to him immediately.

'I didn't lose the samples,' he said. 'I hope people aren't blaming me. It's not my fault.'

His overreaction puzzled Steve and he tried to calm his fears. Paul had struck him as a sound, rational sort of guy. His behaviour now was... well it was odd.

'Is something the matter Paul?' Steve asked him. It was a direct question that demanded an answer. Steve looked at him carefully, straight in the eyes, trying to read the thoughts behind the nervous gaze.

'No, nothing,' said Paul. 'I mean, yes, there is something,' his face was twisted, not with pain but with indecision. His cheeks were flushed and his pupils dilated. He couldn't hold Steve's searching look, instead he glanced from left to right like a naughty child caught doing something forbidden.

'Is it something to do with the samples?' Steve asked.

'I can't tell you here,' said Paul. 'There're too many people around. It's probably nothing. I'll speak to you tonight at the hotel. It's nothing important I'm sure. See what you think later,' his tone apologetic and self doubting.

Steve did not like to press him further.

'Okay,' he said, 'I'll see you in the bar later. But don't worry about it, no one's blaming you.' He felt the desire to pat him on the shoulder. 'In any case I think I'll piss off to the hotel now and have a long hot bath. I don't think the results will be through today now. I'll catch you later.'

He ambled to the door thinking. He was intrigued to know what had caused the change in Paul. He had no idea. When he reached the door he glanced back round to where Paul was sitting, now staring out of the window his lips moving slowly as though talking to himself; and the ear that Steve could see was red with the redness extending down his neck to below his shirt collar. Steve glanced at Paul's hands and saw that they were shaking. He thought about going to speak to him again but decided against it and at that very moment Paul turned to look at Steve. He had the face of a startled deer.

Chapter 17

Paul didn't appear in the bar. About ten o'clock Steve phoned his room but there was no answer. It couldn't have been that important he thought.

Julie forgave Steve's abruptness of earlier in the day. She had spent the afternoon inspecting and bleeding pigs on a farm next to Lower Wood and saw nothing suspicious. She was relieved. Outwardly confident she had a deep rooted insecurity both professionally and personally, and she felt some disappointment, shame perhaps; no shame was too strong a word; regret; regret that she had not achieved more.

Her life was a series of short, unrelated events. There had been and still was, no direction to it. She'd had jobs and lovers in almost equal amount. Steve she thought, was an opportunity. Perhaps her best opportunity yet for lasting, long term happiness. He was kind and gentle, intelligent but not bookish. He looked young for his age and he was usually cheerful. The problem was his privacy. He kept her at arm's length, not volunteering information about his life. He told her he'd been married but he told her nothing more. She was certain that there was a story to tell and she knew she must be patient. There was a barrier and she had driven away men before by clinging too tightly to them. Restraint, she reminded herself. Be gentle and patient.

She disliked Sonia intensely. Sonia was her but with self belief. Julie's skin prickled with envy and her eyes watered the minute she saw Sonia flashing that radiant white-toothed smile. Her stomach sank to her boots, the corners of her mouth turned down and frown lines sprung up across her forehead and around her eyes. An inner ugliness settled on her face like a sickness. She did not like it but she could not prevent it. The self belief and self worth were missing.

She knew that Steve found Sonia attractive. He could not hide it and did not try to hide it. Sonia was available and the sort of woman who would steal a man for mischief, for the laugh it gave her. Julie had met women like her before and she wished that she had never turned up at Broadwich. She wished she had stayed in bloody Australia or Vietnam or wherever it was she'd led Steve into thinking he could go with her. She was the sort of woman who could ruin all Julie's plans.

'Any news on the results?' Fernando asked Steve.

'Not yet, but I spoke to Bluster about you helping me at the slaughter and he gave it his blessing. I sorted it out with Raymond in Allocations so we'll be ready to go first thing tomorrow if the results are in. If they're positive of course. I think they will be. Did you see Paul tonight?' he asked casually.

'Yes he was there doing some work in the lab when I came away.'

'Stop worrying about him,' said Julie irritated. 'You're not his mother you know.'

'Just taking an active interest in the staff,' Steve laughed. 'Investors in People and all that. Just trying to improve my people skills and make sure that the Ministry is looking after its employees.'

The Spanish contingent smiled in a very Spanish way. The elegant one, tall and her long black hair shiny wet from her shower. The Tomboy, short and imp like. 'Puck' should be her name thought Steve, her dark hair streaked boldly with grey, matted and felted like sheep's wool after heavy rain. Short legged, baggy trousered, hands in pockets; what you saw was what you got.

'Are you to sing tonight?' she smiled cheekily, but kindly too. Good humour; perceptive; teasing; but not cruel. Steve felt an empathy with her.

'Only if you insist,' he laughed.

Julie laughed too. Neither were a threat. She knew already they were not Steve's taste in women. As friends yes. As lovers, no. Sonia was the one to watch. She was the vixen. With that thought and on cue, Sonia entered the bar. Her hair was wet from a shower and she smelt of expensive perfume.

'Interesting day?' Sonia said to Steve, singling him out for attention. He felt Julie's hand rest on his thigh and grip it gently, rolling the flesh between her finger and thumb.

'It could have been better. Could have been worse too,' he said. 'A lot worse really. I lost some samples and Bluster didn't go ape shit. I thought he would.'

'How did you lose them?' Sonia asked sympathetically.

'Oh, I thought I put them in the fridge last night with the others but this morning they weren't there. I can't have done I suppose. It's a mystery though,' he added thoughtfully as he glanced over to the bar to see that the stalker was listening to everything he said. 'I thought somebody could have taken them. Thrown them out by mistake,' he raised his voice to ensure that the stalker heard all that he said.

'Why would someone take them?' asked Fernando. 'Except by mistake?' His eyes widened as he asked the question.

'No reason I can think of,' said Steve. 'I probably put them down somewhere and they got thrown away.' He knew that was impossible. They were all in the same box.

'What time do you usually finish Conrad?' he asked suddenly. 'You seem to stay quite late.'

Conrad was taken unawares at being spoken to and the lopsided grin slipped from his face to highlight his small shrunken eyes; unhealthy eyes that were dull and slightly opaque. His lips were the sort that always had dried flakes of skin sticking to them. The sort that you had the urge to plaster in lip salve to moisten and shine them up. They were pale lips. Pale purple instead of pink. Not the sort of lips that a woman would want to kiss Steve thought.

'Late usually,' said Conrad. 'Between eight and nine, I suppose. I can get more done when there're less people around to interrupt me.' He smiled, the dry lips pulled back to reveal crooked brown stained teeth. A smoker's teeth.

I bet you can thought Steve, not wanting to alert him that he'd seen him the previous night trying all the doors. Yes, I bet you can Mr Stalker. But he was disappointed that Conrad remained so composed, hoping he might have given the game away.

Still Steve was suspicious. The guy was a loner. He sat and listened to other people's conversations without taking part and worked late so that others couldn't see what he was up to. He looked like someone up to no good, greasy straight brown hair, pale washed out complexion, opaque eyes, flaky lips, and he didn't look after his teeth. Yes Steve was certain he was up to no good and equally certain the missing samples were his doing. But what was the motivation?

He said no more and put his arm round Julie's waist giving it a squeeze. He saw the tiniest wince cross the stalker's face and then he knew. Conrad was jealous of him. He was driven by envy and he hoped that by taking the samples he would discredit Steve. It all fell into place, straightforward and uncomplicated. Yes, epidemiology was the place for him, he had an analytical mind and the ability to fit all the pieces together.

He looked across to Conrad again but the lop sided grin had returned. Steve wished that Sammy and Willie were there. He could confide in them more than in anyone else. He would be on his guard now. If Conrad had done this once then he could do it again, probably would do it again. He would have to catch him; set a trap for him. Nothing like this had happened before. The idea excited him.

Then he was back in Lima and the ideas of how he could tame this woman that was his wife flowed through his blood, a boiling cauldron of excitement and self belief. Tame her and keep her for himself and fight off the dogs that would come calling and cock their legs on his gate post. Then as now the ideas floated out of reach, a hoard of butterflies on a summer wind, tantalising and bewitching, taunting and always on the move. The ideas he let go and instead put his faith in the rings she wore on the third finger of her left hand. A plain white gold band nestled against a white gold ring with a half carat solitaire diamond mounted in platinum.

'You can't buy a better quality diamond Sir,' the jeweller said, oily like an eel, 'only quantity.'

It cost him two month's salary and it was there for all to see like a collar and name tag, showing that she belonged to someone that cared for her and loved her. Showing that she belonged to him.

Lima was the start of the loss of the dreams in his life. Their wallet was stolen and their five hundred dollars went with it. It was a strange relief, fate intervened and decided their destiny for them. They could not set off for Cuzco or Chile or Bolivia or Brazil. They must go home to make a home of their own at last. They gave their old blue Pontiac to the Automobile Club of Peru and bought airline tickets with American Express and they arrived in England without the money for the taxi from the station to Steve's parents' house. Dreams and ideas of another time and the rings that she wore on the fingers of her left hand were Steve's security that she was and would always be his.

The next day he awoke early. It would be a day of killing pigs and loading the carcasses into lorries and he felt neither sadness nor distaste at what he was about to witness. Swine Fever was not pleasant for pigs and the sooner it was eradicated the better; this was a sacrifice to the greater good.

He left the hotel with Julie just before eight. It was a five minute journey to the office and it was another day that promised great heat and humidity too. The smell of late summer filled the air; the thick heavy scent of flowers in the roadside gardens dusted with evaporating dew. The roads were filled with people on their way to work and none of them had any idea of what he was about to do that day.

'What's happened here?' said Steve as they pulled into the Animal Health Office car park.

There was a crowd of people standing in the car park. They talked in groups, dressed in the bright colours of summer with bare arms and legs. Men and women talking, looks exchanged revealing the secrets they shared of the previous night. Beyond the main mass of people he could see an ambulance, doors flung wide, blue lamp rotating slowly. Three police cars, half a dozen uniformed policeman and others in suits and ties. The doors down by the lab were cordoned off with coloured tape.

'Someone hit by a car maybe?' said Julie.

A dryness caught at Steve's throat, a dry cold pulse touched his abdomen. 'There surely wouldn't be all that lot here just for that,' he said. 'And anyway it looks like something's going on in the lab, not outside,' he added as two men in dark suits went through the lab door which was opened for them by a uniformed Constable.

'What's going on?' Steve called through the car window to a couple of young girls standing by the main entrance.

'I don't know. We've just arrived and were told to stay out here.'

Steve parked and made his way towards the lab. Fernando and his Spanish girls were there. Christopher too, and over by the wall MacSporran. Everyone was speaking in hushed voices and one or two of the girls were crying. Not hysterically but with sombre restraint. This is weird he thought. This is very weird.

'Steve,' Fernando called his name.

He turned and saw the discomfort on Fernando's face and strode over to him.

'What's happened Fernando? Do you know?' He felt his neck flushing red and his pupils dilating with apprehension. 'Why the police and ambulance? Who's hurt?'

'I don't know the full story,' said Fernando. 'All I know is what MacSporran has told me. It seems that they found a person dead in the lab this morning.'

Chapter 18

'What?' said Steve, his face twisted and wrinkled, his breathing fast and shallow and shivery despite the sun's warmth. 'Who? Someone old? A heart attack?'

'I don't know,' said Fernando. 'Someone was in early to organise the stores and found them lying on the floor. That is all I know. It is terrible.' His eyes rolled, the whites widened.

Julie squeezed Steve's arm as a hush fell over the people next to the lab door and spread back through the crowd, a ripple on a pond. Steve moved to get a better view, a chill numbness caught him unawares, childhood nightmares relived. His hands tingled, burning hot and he stared at what was happening.

Two paramedics in green overalls were carrying a stretcher towards the open door of the ambulance. A dull blue blanket lay draped over the stretcher, rising with a lump down its entire length where the body beneath lay still and lifeless. Steve had never seen a dead person, not even one hidden by a blanket. Human death unsettled him. The sound of girls sobbing and then the hot salty tingle of tears on his conjunctiva and the moistness reaching his nostrils. He took out his hanky and wiped the moistness away. Julie squeezed his arm again and Fernando put a hand on his shoulder. Emotion danced on the faces of those around him.

The doors of the ambulance were closed firmly, a stark and final act. A full stop on that person's life. It was over and done and depending on their achievements and personal relationships they would be talked about much or little in the years ahead. The strangest thing was that on this hot, sunny, late summer morning he was more or less cheerfully preparing to supervise the slaughter of five thousand pigs. Yet this sudden death of an unknown human being had kindled a grief that was hard to explain.

He put his arm round Julie and held her close to him and in that moment of vulnerability it was in her power to entrap him; to imprint on him a need for her forever. She knew and she squeezed his back with both her hands and drew back a little to look up at him. His eyes focused on hers and in the dewy glistening film that covered them she saw a compassion and depth of understanding she had never known was there. She looked through his eyes straight into his mind, a porthole into a world that was confused and had suffered much but which had been reorganised and was stronger for the experience. She felt her own eyes moisten and knew that now was the time to spring the trap. Once sprung the beast was caught and it would never be so wild or sensuous or as exciting again. But it would be hers to tame and enjoy for the rest of their lives together.

Keeping his gaze she opened her mouth slowly and tenderly. She held her lips parted for a second, savouring the moment, maintaining the suspense until she could bear the intensity of the pleasure no longer. The words 'I love you' sprang into her mind, bouncing in all directions before settling like butterflies on her vocal chords.

'I..'

'Are you alright Steve?' Sonia purred and Julie saw everything that was in his eyes flow over her shoulder and into Sonia behind her. The thing was broken, cast down and smashed irrevocably. The moment had passed without consummation, she bled into her soul, the blood drained from her skin and extremities and settled like a stagnant pool in her abdomen, heavy and lifeless. The moment had gone, she had waited too long, the beast had moved away to the cover of the reeds and would never appear as defenceless again. She wept, not for Steve and not for the body in the ambulance that passed slowly through the crowd of onlookers and out on to the main road. She wept for herself.

'Any idea who's died?' asked Sonia. 'Nobody seems to know.'

Julie felt Steve let her go and saw his face brighten at Sonia's voice. She knew that everything was lost and she wanted to cry and scream and shout like an injured child. She knew that this was a defining moment in her life. Like standing at the top of Niagara Falls and deciding whether to jump. Her timing had been almost, almost perfect. Damn you Sonia she thought. Damn you and rot in hell.

She shook with the violence of her thoughts and was shocked that she bore such malice and desire for revenge. She wept silently and everyone who saw her thought it was for the one that had died. She wept to excise and dampen the pain; the dull aching pain that cradled her body from her lower abdomen to the root of her breasts. Where there had been a fire laden passion was now a smouldering rain soaked pile of ash. Her spirit sagged and the lines on her face seemed etched in stone.

Steve spotted Bluster standing by the doorway. He strode over to him; he wanted an answer and Bluster could give it to him. Herbert saw him coming and his face twitched involuntarily.

'What's happened Herbert? Who is it?' said Steve.

A hot rancid taste plucked at his throat with a sickening memory. He wanted to turn and walk away. Return to his hotel and pack his bags and drive north, back through fifteen years to where Rachel waited for him, eyes bright and shining, lips parted in a smile. He could see her in front of him, hear her and smell her.

'Hello Sunshine,' she said and Steve trembled at her voice and the touch of her hand as she placed it on his hips. The smoothness of her skin, the yellow curls falling to her shoulders he pushed away with his face as he kissed her gently on the neck. The smell of her skin and hair, a subtle enticing perfume of the fields and storm laden skies. He rested his hands on her shoulders and brushed her lips with his own, and his hands slipped down to her waist and he pulled her body into his with firmness that could not be resisted yet was gentle and loving.

He wished he could drive back to Rachel's arms and talk with her about their dreams. Dreams of a farm that they built from nothing, where fat pedigree sheep and cattle grazed. Built from the acid peat soils and rained drenched Pennine air where curlews and snipe called and they looked from their bedroom window down a long flat valley with a winding stream and the pond that they had dug. All this he wished and more.

'Paul Smythe,' said Herbert sombrely. 'He was found about six thirty this morning lying on the floor of the lab. They tried to revive him but it seems he'd been dead for hours.'

'Paul?' said Steve, his voice splintering, crackly. 'Paul? But he's just a young bloke. He was at Lower Wood Farm with me the day before yesterday. He was a big fit bloke. I saw him yesterday evening. There wasn't anything wrong with him. Did he slip and bang his head or something?'

'It's more sinister than that,' said Herbert. His face aged, the complexion changed from a ruddy bluster to a sombre slate, almost blue. 'They found an empty bottle of ketamine and a syringe and needle on the desk. It looks like he was a ketamine user and overdosed himself; by accident or on purpose we don't know. The police will find out I suppose but as far as I know there was no suicide note.'

'Paul Smythe,' Steve repeated to himself. It was impossible that the guy had been alive last night and now he was dead. Stone dead. People became old or ill and then died, didn't they? Fit healthy people, especially those he knew didn't just die unless they had a car crash. It was all too weird.

'The results were positive for Swine Fever anyway,' said Herbert. 'We got a fax this morning. So we've got to get on and kill the farm out. Do you feel up to it?' he said.

'He was worried about something yesterday,' said Steve. 'When I spoke to him yesterday evening he said he had something to tell me and that he'd see me in the bar later. Of course he didn't come to the bar later but I just thought he was tired and had gone to bed. If I thought anything at all about it,' he added. 'But that's why he didn't come. Whilst we were sitting in the bar pissing it up he was lying dead or dying alone by himself in the lab. I can't believe he didn't say something to me yesterday: tell me how he was feeling. I can't believe he's killed himself. He was such a bright, cheerful sort of bloke. Full of himself, easy going. It has to have been an accident Herbert.'

'Let's hope so,' said Herbert. 'For his parents' sake.'

Steve knew he was crying but he didn't care. Crying was strength not weakness. It had saved his own life in the past.

Touchy feely was not Herbert's style. Stiff upper lip and square set jaw take-it-on-the-chin type. He shuffled nervously from one foot to the other, playing with his hands. He searched around for a friend of Steve's to come and take charge. He wished that Sammy was still there. He saw Fernando and Sonia and Julie and he motioned to them that help was needed.

Julie put an arm round Steve but he did not respond. He was trying to cope, recognising the symptoms of denial, of an illusion. Incomprehension swirled in his head like flies buzzing around putrid meat; sand dunes shifting in the wind; shingle on the turning tide.

The symptoms were old friends of his remembered from fifteen years back. A thousand times, ten thousand times it had gone through his head. Several times a day everyday, trying to understand and accept that she was gone. And denying all the time that it had happened. Denial; not accepting; trapped; unable to move on. Self pity eating away his life, trapped inside in his head where he was fifteen years ago. And like Julie he wept. Wept for Paul and for himself.

'Take the day off Steve,' said Herbert suddenly, surprising himself with his own compassion. 'Fernando, can you take charge of the slaughter at Lower Wood? Speak to MacSporran and get someone else allocated to help.'

'Yes of course,' said Fernando. 'I am happy to do that. I will see you later Steve,' and he patted him on the shoulder.

'Will you take Steve back to the hotel please Julie,' said Herbert. 'Stay there with him if you like. I'm going to talk to the Chief Inspector in charge. Then I'd better phone Sage Street. I don't envy them the job of notifying his next of kin.'

Chief Inspector Tom Draper was in the lab when Herbert Bluster found him.

'Ah. Mr Bluster,' he said. 'Just the man I was looking for.'

'Well? What do you think's happened?' asked Herbert nervously. 'Was it an accident or was it suicide?'

'I shouldn't like to speculate just yet,' said Tom Draper. 'The body is away for post mortem examination now. We might know something more later today.

'How long had you known Paul Smythe? And what do you know of him?'

'Not much at all,' said Herbert. 'I think he's been with us ten days or so but there're so many people coming and going it's hard to keep track. There're a lot of staff I still don't know, both temporary and permanent. I probably only spoke to him a couple of times. I can't say I knew him.'

'Did he have any special friends or acquaintances here? A girlfriend? A boyfriend for that matter?' he added absentmindedly.

'I don't know,' said Herbert. 'One of the Veterinary Officers, Steve Turner, seems to have got to know him a bit. He was very cut up this morning when he heard he was dead. I sent him back to his hotel, The Swallow. He was in no fit state to carry on working today. Apart from that…' he considered, 'I honestly don't know.'

'Can you let me have a list of everyone who works here please?' Tom Draper said. 'From those at the top right down to the cleaners. I might not need it but if I do it would be as well to have it to hand.'

'I'll get personnel to sort that out for you,' said Herbert. 'Can I ask why you want it? I don't think many people will know much about him.'

'No reason really,' said Draper. 'A hunch maybe. Things aren't always what they seem to be on the face of it. Let's just say I've got an inquisitive mind.' He smiled.

Herbert Bluster tried to smile back but he had to fight to stop his face twitching and he simply stared. Draper, a keen observer of human emotions thought he saw a look of apprehension in the big plain face.

Chapter 19

Everyone was talking about ketamine. The vets knew it as a useful anaesthetic agent for cats, particularly cats that were difficult to handle. And many of them were aware of its use as a 'designer' drug and the need for veterinary practices to keep it under lock and key. One or two boasted of having tried it out.

Steve spent the day in his room. He phoned Sammy and she promised to return the next week. It lifted his spirits. His relationship with Julie was lurching in ugly inevitability to its end point.

Sarah Fowler arrived at The Swallow at 8.00 p.m. She had spent the day at Lower Wood Farm with Fernando and the two of them had seen the job of slaughter through to the end. It went well and when the last lorry load of carcasses left the farm Fernando suggested that Sarah join them all for supper. She hurried home to feed her mare and her cat and to take a long hot shower. A glow of excitement was inside her; a memory from her teenage years and she giggled to herself. Fernando interested her. He was a gentleman but not smarmy. He treated her with politeness for her femininity but without deference; as an equal with different needs.

The shower tempered the smell of the pigs and removed the dust from her eyes and ears. She dried herself in front of the mirror. She was not vain but she was pleased to note that her body was in good shape. There were no bulges or pads of sagging wrinkled fat; no orange peel effect on her thighs or buttocks as a result of the dreaded and elusive cellulite beloved of glossy women's magazines.

How old was Fernando she wondered. She did not know and she did not care to find out. Was he too young for her? Was she imagining his interest? He was just a guy who liked to be friendly. A continental with a Latin temperament. She often holidayed in Spain and was inundated with offers from the locals. Good natured and charming offers in the main but in jest rather than seriousness. Fernando though was different to many of his countrymen. He was sensitive and humorous. His humour was intelligent, penetrating, with an understanding of life beyond his years. She was fascinated, intrigued, tempted. She nodded at herself in the mirror and laughed. The thought delighted her.

The evening was cooler than of late. She dressed casually, jeans and a jumper, the tiniest dab of Poem by Lancôme. No reason to scare him or to expose herself if she'd misread the situation. She knew there was nothing more off putting than a slightly desperate older woman. She brushed her hair. She had good hair and it shone. Simple and plain but shiny. A mix of colours so that it glinted brown and chestnut and tawny. A tingle of anticipation skipped along her spine, warm and fluid. A confidence gripped her. There was nothing to lose. 'Just be yourself,' she said aloud.

She had never met Paul but she was sad at his death in circumstances that appeared to be those of personal tragedy. You read about similar instances in the paper every day, it was mere coincidence that this time it was on her 'doorstep'. Suicide was the fastest growing cause of death amongst young males. She was certain it was suicide. She knew enough about ketamine to know that the recreational and lethal doses of the drug were separated by a factor of ten or more. Only someone drunk or stupid could kill themselves accidentally with it.

No, it was suicide, she was certain. Apparently a rich bloke; born with a 'silver spoon' in his mouth. Everything handed to him on a plate. It would be the familiar problem. Poor little rich boy; too much too soon. Nothing to strive for. Ambitions all met by thirty. No material challenges left and probably a sense of isolation or loneliness. Personal problems too probably. Conflict with his family perhaps. No wife or girlfriend to share the burden with. It was clear in her mind and it was nothing to do with her.

By the time she reached The Swallow her confidence had seeped away. Her stomach had a dull, tight knot, her palms moist, and she shivered in spite of the woollen jumper. At the entrance to the hotel she stopped and wondered why she was really there. You're forty one she told herself. Behaving like a teenager. Uncertain whether to go in or run away home. Running home would be easiest she thought. Anticipation was the best part and that had been and gone.

'You've nothing to lose,' a reassuring voice from her past. 'In you go and act normally; you're just here for your supper, nothing else.'

She wavered on the doorstep, took a deep breath; pulled her lips into a smile and went in.

The bar was busy but not boisterous. She glanced around, recognising the faces from work that were somehow different in their casual clothes and the softer lighting. She saw Fernando. Beautiful, sexy, Fernando. He sat at a table talking to Steve Turner, and there were four women hanging on his words.

Sarah decided to leave. She should not have come she knew that now. She had built up in her mind something that was not there. She glanced away, knowing that many people must already have seen her. She looked across at Fernando. He was smiling, wide eyed, teeth showing in a happy grin. He was smiling at her. She felt a warm flush of pink embarrassment and a floating, faint feeling in her head.

'Sarah,' called Fernando, unable to hide his delight, 'you have made it. Come and join us, we were waiting for you before we ordered.' He stood up and came towards her and gave her a kiss on each cheek. Flustered and elated she said nothing.

'That is a very nice perfume,' said Fernando. 'What is it?'

'Poem,' she murmured and could say no more.

'Come and sit with us. Do you know everybody? Steve, Julie, Luciana, Adriana and Sonia. Are you hungry? Here is a menu. The sheep's cheese and wild rocket salad is very special.'

Luciana and Adriana stood and kissed her too. Sonia and Julie resisted the temptation and Steve managed a smile and a wave of the hand. His eyes were rimmed red, his eyelids swollen. There was no energy or electricity in his face she thought. Not like she remembered. He looked older.

'Fernando tells me it went well today,' he said. 'I'm sorry you got landed with it. I just couldn't face it. It's not a great job at the best of times but today, I just couldn't have faced it,' he repeated and looked at her apologetically.

'I didn't have anything else to do,' she replied. 'It was a relief to get out of the office and away from all those police. They've been interviewing all the DVAs today and have a whole list of others they want to talk to. I guess they want to find out what made him do it. It's very sad,' she added at the end, mainly because she thought she should.

'What will you eat?' said Fernando. 'And can I get you a drink?'

'Yes please. A glass of dry white wine and I'll try the salad you recommended.'

'I hope you like it,' he said.

Steve fidgeted in his seat and his eyes flicked uneasily around the room. He had tried to relax all day but his nerves were like serpents, wriggling and writhing and spinning him round.

'Sit still,' Julie said, too loudly and she regretted it immediately. She placed her hand on his knee under the table but he pushed it away. It was over.

'How are you feeling Steve?' asked Sonia gently.

Julie reeled with this head on attack.

'You worked with Paul didn't you?' she continued.

'Yes,' said Steve. 'And I feel like shit actually. I can't believe he's dead. Like all those pigs that were killed today. Just finished; gone. What really bothers me is that he was worried about something and he wanted to tell me about it, and I just wish I'd sat down with him yesterday evening and listened. Because whatever it was it must have been awful for him to make him take an overdose.' He couldn't bring himself to say the words 'to kill himself'.

'Don't blame yourself,' said Sonia. 'None of us can know what was in his mind. It might have been a long standing problem. He'd only been here two weeks so who knows what his history was. He could have had a mental illness; schizophrenia even.'

'I hadn't thought of that,' said Steve. 'Thanks.'

Sonia smiled at him and he smiled back. Julie bit her lip and held back the tears. Her own world and the hopes and dreams she had were as dead as Paul's.

They ate in silence save for Fernando and Sarah who spoke in whispers and expressions. Steve watched their body language and took pleasure at the sparks that crossed the gap between them. Thrown together by fate. And twists of fate fascinated him. Good things come out of bad too, he thought, seeing the past clearly.

They saw the farm for the first time one afternoon as they drove into the hills looking for a place to walk their dogs. They followed a tiny black top road that the map showed led to a narrow track out across the Pennine moors. It was February and the grey sky dumped its rain and the gusting wind carried it to the ground and blew it against the windscreen and rocked the car on its wheels. Small banks of snow lay against stone walls and in ditches and hollows where the sun didn't reach and Swaledale sheep, skinny and weakened by the winter storms and poor grazing stared at them as they passed. Everywhere was grey emptiness stretching to the horizon. They came to a wooden gate across the public road at the top of a hill and they passed through it and drove to where the road dropped down into a little valley. On the far side stood a stone built slate roofed farmhouse with windows that reflected the moors and a wooden front door painted dirty green.

The road went up past the side of the house to another gate that opened to a stone track that headed further out to the moors beyond, a great open sea of waving yellow grass dotted with patches of snow. They drove slowly up to the house, a thin wisp of pale grey smoke, the smell of burning wood hanging in the air. Outside on some rough stone steps an old man was chopping wood, cigarette dangling unlit from purple lips, grey Mackintosh tied with baler string round the waist. He raised his head for a moment to acknowledge them as they passed.

'I couldn't live here, could you?' Steve giggled as they passed.

'Of course not,' smiled Rachel, and she ruffled his hair and kissed him on the face.

Three months later they saw an advertisement in the local paper for a small hill farm for sale. '100 acres of hill land with some improved pasture. Traditional, stone built farmhouse and large modern sheep house. Guide Price £42,000.'

When the details arrived Steve laughed out loud.

'It's that farm we passed in the winter,' he said. 'Not even worth looking at.'

'No harm in looking,' said Rachel.

They arrived at the gate at the top of the hill on a bright blue day of Caribbean skies at the end of May. Clouds of white goose down floated and sailed above them and on the land below the white bent grass was turning a powerful, intoxicating green. They climbed out of their car and leant against the gate, the air fresh and powerful in their lungs. Steve knew he was flying with the angels as calling curlews skimmed across the sky like great yachts. The gurgling of the peaty watered stream hidden by the rushes in the valley below, the meadow pipits flicking their tails as they perched on clumps of grass, the buzzard soaring across the slope to their right and behind them the unmistakable call of a red grouse on the heather moorland.

He was Heathcliffe and Rachel was Cathy and in that moment they were captured and held captive by the raw beauty stretching out in their mind. The rugged simplicity of the terrain; the spiritual proximity to the Creator.

'What do you think?' asked Rachel

'We have to live here,' said Steve and he held her close and wished he could lay her down on the green spring grass amongst the rushes and make love to her with the whistling of the curlews above them.

They drove down the hill to the farmhouse. Rabbits scattered in front of them and pied wagtails fluttered onto the stone walls at either side of the road. A stream ran down one side, a dry ditch on the other.

'We could plant trees all along here,' said Steve. 'Like a driveway up to the house.'

The old Shepherd welcomed them suspiciously. He had lived there for many years and did not want to be turned out by his employers. He told them of all the difficulties of living there; no mains electricity; water from a spring; no central heating; the nearest shop seven miles; snowed in for weeks in the winter.

Inside the house was poorly furnished. Bare floorboards in all rooms save the living room kitchen which was covered in mud-caked lino. On the north side a small back kitchen, Steve had to stoop in it to avoid hitting the ceiling. A sink at one end atop an old Formica kitchen unit that contained hidden delights. At the other end a huge walk-in larder with old scrubbed oak shelves covered in mouse droppings.

'Imagine this filled with jams and pickles and home grown veg. And hams and salt beef from our own animals. Rabbits and hares hanging from those hooks in the ceiling.' Rachel's eyes gleamed.

In the centre of the house opposite the front door, a straight wooden staircase with handrail climbed steeply to the landing at the back of the house. At the top to the right was the largest bedroom, empty now and with large patches of damp where the ceiling met the outside wall. A sash window to front and back lit it adequately and the two of them crossed the room to look out to the front. Their hearts quickened with the view, expansive and timeless. To the left the road arched up the hill to where they could see the gate at the top. To the right of the hill was the stream and the surrounding marsh and rushes, like a flood plain, disappearing into the middle distance at the boundary fence, four, perhaps five hundred yards away.

Further to the right still, a great long incline sloping up and away from the stream. Where in February it had been white it was now green;

a deep vibrant green with the occasional off-white sheep dotted around on it like sequins on a dress. The stone wall running up the hill was the far boundary. It was falling down in places but there was a wire fence the other side to keep the sheep from straying. Beyond the wall the view extended down a long flat valley for three or four miles. There was no other dwelling or building in sight.

To the left of the staircase was a short hallway and a landing window that looked out onto the sheep shed, the handling pens and dipper, and the hay barn. The pens were overgrown with grass and weeds, the dipper filled with an ominous looking, black fluid. The sheep shed with Yorkshire boarding and metal sheet roof was new and looked well built.

The first door on the left of the landing was to a small L-shaped bedroom. Big enough for twin beds. It had the same view from a sash window set right above the front door. The second door on the left was a double bedroom, above the living room with the open fire and range, the heat wafting up through the floor kept it warm. It smelt of coal tar and smoke and here the shepherd had his bed. The view from the window the same again and here there was less damp on the walls, the result of a better roof or the warm chimney breast. At the end of the landing was a small bathroom with a white enamelled bath, sink and toilet bowl, and an airing cupboard in one corner.

'There's a back boiler in the range downstairs,' the shepherd said. 'You'll never be short of hot water.' He was warming to them. 'And there's a phone now,' he added.

They went down the stairs, to the left was a door to a large lounge, used as a storeroom for old bits and pieces of furniture, a host of tools and farm chemicals and medicines. It smelt of damp, a fusty, musty smell of mould. You could feel the mould spores catch in your nose, and it set Steve off in a fit of sneezing. The walls were moist with droplets of water and in places small rivulets ran down leaving streaks. The air inside the room was cold; paint cracked and peeling from the window frames. It had not been used for many years. A room with potential.

On the other side of the stairs and between them and the living room was a large understairs walk-in cupboard. Perfect for coats and wellies.

They went outside into the little walled front garden. A mass of junk wood was thrown against the wall at one end; thick rushes growing up and covering the cobbles by the house and the soil in front of the wall. Attached to the house was an old traditional stone byre with a stable door. Swallows flew in and out of the upper half. They would have their own swallows. The byre was in poor condition, dirty and full of dog faeces. The shepherd's dogs were chained there. There were three old stalls for tethering cows or horses along the wall that adjoined the house. And opposite the front door was a back door that led into the new sheep shed. Stuck out in the middle of the northern Pennines it was 60 feet wide by 90 feet long; big enough to house 400 sheep. Light and airy and well drained with a rubble floor it was an asset that many farms could only dream of.

'What a building,' said Steve. 'We could keep anything in here. Sheep, cattle, pigs, poultry. There's more than enough room for anything we wanted.'

'Horses too,' said Rachel.

'As soon as we could afford them,' said Steve, and bit his lip.

Beyond the sheep shed was a hay barn of corrugated iron. Not pretty but in good order. The infrastructure was sound. The house was the worst thing, but there were only the two of them and they were young and fit and had each other to keep them warm.

They walked down the tarmac road and out onto the flat rushy valley bottom with the gurgling stream. Lucy their lurcher put up a rabbit and snapped it up after twenty yards. Even the shepherd was impressed. He showed them the spring where the water for the house rose up out of the hill and the damp concrete sided pit where the hydraulic ram was chugging merrily away, driven by the force of the water running through it.

'You have to have the ram set just right,' said the shepherd. 'Too fast and the header tank that drives it runs out and the ram stops. Too slow and it won't pump any water.'

Steve dismissed it as not a problem. He did not want to hear of problems. He was hooked. Nothing would sway him now.

He and Rachel left the shepherd and walked up the long sloping hill to the west. The grass was long and rank, white bent and purple flying bent. Sour grasses that spoke of low fertility, impoverished, acid soils. Water logged soils. A short growing season from May to September with long drawn out winters giving hardship to the stock and the people too.

'We could improve it with lime and reseeding,' said Rachel. 'And if we had top quality pedigree stock we could house them all winter and buy in the food we needed.'

They were both committed. The opportunity had arrived sooner than either of them had anticipated. Steve was 25 and Rachel 27. They had expected to be in their mid-thirties before they could afford a farm. And *now the opportunity was there, dangling like a rope. They had only to grasp it.*

'Can we afford it?' Rachel asked. 'Forty two thousand pounds. It's a lot of money. We might have to offer more than that. We only paid thirty thousand for our house.

'I'm sure we could,' said Steve. 'It would be hard for a few years but just think of owning this and being able to live here. We've got to go for it. Haven't we?'

She looked at him with excitement and love overflowed from her eyes.

'Oh yes Sunshine,' she said. 'With you I could do anything.'

They held each other tight and looked around at the views to right and left, north and south. The high of adventure settled on them and burrowed deep under their skin like a cancer, throwing caution and reason to the wind. They had been through revolutionary Central America together. This would be a breeze in comparison.

The clear bright air surrounding them infiltrated their hearts and minds like a mind altering drug. They came nearer to flying that day than ever before. Curlews called and larks sang and the distant sound of red grouse tugged at their souls. A pair of lapwings flew overhead, diving and rolling in broad winged courtship. A few hundred yards away they saw the buzzard again and they heard the rough harsh croak of a pair of ravens in the crags up beyond the house.

Snipe rose in front of the hunting dogs and zig-zagged their way to safety in rapid silent flight. Nature was there with them, all around them to witness their joy. It would be theirs to have and to hold, like each to the other. The emotion and beauty of that moment brought tears to both their eyes. Tears of joy and love, excitement and expectation. Tears that would turn to pain and bitterness and flow freely in the times that lay not too distantly ahead.

Chapter 20

When Steve awoke the next day he had a pounding head brought on by eight pints of lager. Lager to drown his sorrows. Lager to lift his spirits. It had done neither. He groaned to himself and reached out with his hand. Then he realised he was alone. The first time he had been alone for several weeks. Julie was not there.

He hated it at first. Sleeping alone again. An empty tightness gripped his stomach at the first conscious thought of his waking moment. At the start he could not sleep soundly. He woke four or five times in the night and always and always the painful ache was there. Sometimes so painful that he staggered to the toilet and was sick. The relief was temporary. Always the pain returned. He remembered lying alone in bed in the mornings not knowing what to do to bring about a cure. Not knowing if a cure existed. But knowing he did not want to feel this way.

He remembered wishing he could sleep forever. So that consciousness did not intrude on him. It was the conscious thoughts that hurt. Dreams he could dismiss for what they were. But conscious thoughts were real; swirling hateful demons that tormented his mind and painted it with black and purple in dense clouds of fog that threatened to choke the breath from his lungs and sent him into bouts of rapid shallow breathing from which he could not escape.

It was loneliness unimagined. It was not the loneliness of a parting too long ago made or the loneliness born of a need for support and encouragement. It was the loneliness that Jesus must have felt on the cross. A loneliness born of despair and betrayal. A loneliness deep within the mind, touching the soul. A loneliness within the chemicals and energies that make up a man's worth and hold on life. A loneliness so powerful and complete that at times and for some it is too much to bear.

He wondered then if that was how Paul had felt. If he had but known he may have helped him. Through his own pain and experience he had come to understand the pain of others. He could let them know that their suffering was not unique. That there was another side to the abyss that they were gazing into. A side where the sun shone again but with a different light. Yes he had looked into the abyss. Entered it with its thorns and poisoned snakes and wild beasts. But he picked his way through it and pulled himself up the other side. A changeling. For better or worse was not his judgement to make. More worldly wise; more cynical; and more compassionate too. Until then he had never known suffering in his life. Nothing bad had ever crossed his path and he had a conceited view of himself and his life. He believed he was immune to suffering. Suffering did not affect the chosen ones. People brought suffering on themselves: for the most part it was deserved.

He despised himself now for what he had been. Despised himself for the way he used to feel. His own suffering came out of the blue and hit him square on the jaw; smack between the eyes; like a lorry on the wrong side of the road from around a blind bend. His own suffering opened his eyes to a world of injustice and suffering, pain and personal trauma that he never knew existed. It took him by the emotional lapels and dragged him into adulthood and for that at least he was grateful. In his darkest hour, his hour of greatest need, Christ had forgiven. Steve was not yet ready to forgive.

And now there was the problem of Julie. He winced with discomfort. Partly from the headache and partly from his memories of how the evening had ended. He had rowed with Julie and told her it was over; finished. He did not regret the end of the relationship. That was the nature and pattern of his life now. He promised nothing to women and expected no promises in return. He did not lie to them or encourage false hopes. If they harboured them then that was their problem and his signal to call it a day.

But he regretted the manner in which it was done. He was unkind. And his reference to Sonia's attractions was spiteful. He blamed the drink and the state of his mind after Paul's death. They had come to his room and Julie accused him of flirting with Sonia. Her possessiveness annoyed him, made him burning hot. He was not to be possessed, never again.

'Don't think I didn't see you drooling over Sonia,' Julie said. 'She's a nasty painted bitch.'

He ignored her at first but she persisted.

'She's only doing it for mischief you know. Don't think she really fancies you.'

He became annoyed. 'I'll choose my own friends and company. If you don't like it you can leave now. In fact, just leave, I'm not in the mood for your petulance. That's it. It's over. Just fuck off.'

He flinched now at the harshness of his words though not at the sentiment. He did not like it to end like that. But Julie had got on his nerves those last few days and Sonia was a beautiful woman whom he was free to pursue if he wished. He was pleased to be on his own again. He was confident it would be temporary.

Sarah Fowler woke with sunlight blazing from her eyes and lighting the room. That 'teenage thing' feeling stripped the years from her and she glided round her cottage, singing and giggling, twirling and skipping as she fed the cat and went out into the garden to smell the early morning air and hear the call of the swifts as they rushed by. They would soon be gone, the autumn just around the corner. She thought back to the previous evening. Unbelievable, her excitement tugged at her, her skin prickled and moisture came into her eyes, shining and gleaming in the morning sun. She skipped around the garden like a young girl, the honeysuckle was still in bloom though its perfume more subtle, less overpowering. Early morning bees buzzed in the warming sunlight, butterflies too; soon they would be dead or seeking out places to hibernate.

She had left The Swallow about midnight and Fernando had insisted on walking her to her car. When he said goodnight to her he kissed her on both cheeks and held her with both his hands on her waist. He lingered longer than was purely necessary for social etiquette.

'I have enjoyed tonight in spite of the earlier sadness of the day,' he said. 'Thank you for coming.' He hesitated a moment, and she, anxious to put him at ease had placed her hand on his arm.

'I've enjoyed it too,' she said.

'Would you like to go for something to eat tomorrow night with me?' he asked. A note of nervousness in his voice. The answer was important and not taken for granted.

Sarah looked at him with cautious curiosity and saw no hint of deception or cunning in his face.

'That would be lovely,' she said and smiled softly.

Fernando smiled too, bent forward and gave her the merest of kisses on her lips. He simply brushed hers with his, momentarily, electrifyingly.

'Please drive home carefully,' he said, and opened the car door for her.

When she drove off he was waving. She watched him in her rear view mirror until the dark and the dazzle of lights took him from view. Her heart beat faster and her breathing was in short, sharp, gasps. At the T-junction on the edge of town she almost had an accident and she made an apologetic gesture to the other car driver. She was euphoric, high, a drug induced high she remembered well. She had taken ketamine herself a few times many years ago at the dirty end of an important relationship. It helped her through a bad experience for a few weeks and she had not become dependant, stopping before it took its hold.

The way she felt now was like that. She sang to herself, 'Help me

121

make it through the night.' Such a sad song yet so beautiful and so uplifting. Beauty and sadness. Not much lay between them.

Steve arrived at the Animal Health Office later than usual, and the thought of bleeding more pigs sank his spirits. He'd enjoyed the experience to a point but now he'd had enough. He wanted to move on. He wanted to get into epidemiology. The chance to use his brain a little. He went to see Herbert Bluster.

Herbert was in his room, shaking his head over more expense claims. He glanced up at Steve.

'The police want to interview you,' he said. 'Did you know Paul very well?'

'I worked with him at Lower Wood Farm,' said Steve. 'I don't think anybody knew him very well. I suppose I knew him as well as anyone.'

'Graham Thompson wants to see you too. You must have impressed him. He's asked if you could join the epidemiology team. Are you interested?'

'Yes. Very much,' said Steve. He felt better. From depressed to excited in one easy step. Chemical transmitters in the brain were wonderful. Instantaneous. What a pity they were so transient. 'I can do a good job there,' he said out loud.

'Well go and see Graham then,' said Herbert. Steve thought he had the makings of a smile on his face. 'And here's the number of Chief Inspector Draper. Give him a ring will you?'

Steve scuttled along the corridor to epidemiology. This was something to get stuck into. Sure the epidemic might be near an end but there would be plenty of loose ends to tie up and it could only be better than crawling around in filthy stinking pig pens all day. He knocked on the door and went in.

Trevor was there; a guy called Neil Franks; a few others he didn't know, and Graham Thompson.

'Ah Steve, I've been looking for you,' said Graham. 'Dreadful business about Paul Smythe. I'm very sorry about that. Was he a close friend?'

'Err,.. not really,' said Steve. 'I met him for the first time a couple of days ago.'

'I'm sorry,' said Graham. 'Somehow I had the impression he was an old friend. I don't know where that idea came from. Anyway, how do you feel about coming to join us? Jim here's going home for a few weeks and we need someone to replace him. You'll get the chance to do some proper veterinary work.'

'Sounds good,' said Steve.

'There's a desk and chair over there,' he motioned with his hand.

'Oh no, not Steve Turner in 'ere as well,' said Trevor. 'I had enough of you at college. And is it you driving that poncey bloody Austin Healey around? Not a very practical veterinary car is it? You seem a bit old to have one of those. Mid life crisis? I expect it helps with the ladies does it?'

Everyone laughed... except Graham.

'I need to speak to the police before I do anything,' said Steve. 'They want to interview me about Paul. I suppose I was one of the last to work with him.'

He went down into the car park to use his mobile. He had an uncomfortable feeling about it. There were a lot of things that didn't make sense and he wasn't sure why the police wanted to talk to him. Why they really wanted to talk to him.

Chief Inspector Draper was very appreciative and seemed a little surprised when Steve phoned him.

'Could you spare the time to come down to the station?' Draper asked, and without giving it much thought Steve said yes, he would come straight away. And now walking into Broadwich police station he had a feeling of discomfort somewhere in his guts and the rotten fish stink of guilt. Guilt at some unknown crime. His face flushed red and hot when the Constable on the Enquiries Desk said the Chief Inspector was expecting him. He hoped he wouldn't be there long. He wasn't sure what help he could give.

Draper appeared with another policeman that he introduced to Steve but he was suddenly too nervous for the name to sink in. He had never experienced this before; his heart was beating like at college before the start of those awful oral exams.

'Sit down Mr Turner,' repeated Draper. They had entered Interview Room 1 and a female Constable had joined them, tape recorder at the ready. They explained a lot of things to him but he wasn't really listening.

'How well did you know Paul Smythe?' Draper began. It was the third time he'd been asked the question that day. It was beginning to irritate him. He answered: truthfully and carefully.

'The afternoon before he died. Did he seem depressed to you?'

It was suicide then, thought Steve. They think he killed himself. Poor guy. What was going through his head?

'Not depressed really,' said Steve. 'He was more agitated and anxious I think. He said he had something to tell me but that he couldn't tell me there. He said he'd tell me later that evening. But of course he never did. Do you think he killed himself?' He blurted it out, lips trembling. 'I'm sorry to ask but it's been bothering me that maybe I could have stopped him if I'd realised he was feeling like that. Perhaps if I'd made the time to speak to him there and then and given him a bit of support and reassurance. What do you think?'

Draper looked at his colleagues. Not for long but it was a meaningful glance, of what, Steve was not sure.

'Any ideas about what could have been worrying him?' Draper went on.

'The only thing I can think of is the samples that went missing or were lost. I got the impression that he somehow thought it was his fault and that he was going to get blamed for it.'

'What samples are you talking about?' Draper asked.

Steve explained it all. Including how he thought he'd heard someone go up the stairs and seen the light and the stalker trying the doors outside.

'What's the significance of the samples you lost?' asked the man with Draper.

'Well nothing really. They were duplicates to look for African Swine Fever but since we know we're looking for CSF,.. sorry, Classical Swine Fever, they were really pretty irrelevant. Even our boss Herbert Bluster wasn't bothered.'

'Yes, Bluster. I've met him. What sort of a bloke is he?' said Draper.

Steve smiled. 'Bluster by name, Bluster by nature. I know I shouldn't say it but it sums him up in one short sentence.'

Draper laughed but did not disagree.

'But tell me,' said Steve, suddenly serious again, 'you didn't answer my question. Did Paul kill himself or was it just a nasty accident?'

Draper looked at his colleagues again and then back at Steve.

'I can tell you,' he said, 'without doubt, that Paul Smythe did not kill himself and neither was it an accident. Unlikely as it may seem, Paul Smythe was murdered.'

Chapter 21

There was silence. Silence in which a heat that started in the depths of his stomach spread out through his body, burning and scorching every part of it as it seeped into tissues and organs, muscles and nerves.

He wanted Sammy. He needed Sammy. Oh so badly he needed her there. To talk to. To cry with. To embrace. He lay on the bed in his hotel room. The heat spread up to his face and deep inside his head. Molten heat. White heat. His eyes were sore with it. No matter how many tears he shed they could not quench the burning sensation inside. The sensation that all his nerve endings were aflame. Burning and sizzling. Fat dripping. The smell of burnt fat. Black smoke swirled in his head. The fat dripped, the flames crackled higher.

There was a knock at the door. He ignored it. It came again and again. Urgent. Frenzied.

'Steve. Steve. Are you alright? Are you there?' It was Julie's voice.

He did not want her. Not now. Not ever. He was finished with Julie. It was best that way. She tried to get too close. That was her mistake. It wasn't her fault but she tried too hard and that finished it for her. He stayed silent. She couldn't be sure he was there.

'Steve. Please answer me. I just want to know that you're alright. I'm sorry about last night. It was my fault, I won't do it again. I'm sorry about Paul too.' She was pleading with him. It would not do.

He lay quiet and still. In the dark. The dark soothed and comforted him. Like someone with sunstroke or a fever the dark dulled his senses. Julie knocked again. He wanted to call out and tell her to go but he knew it wouldn't work.

He stood outside Rachel's door in the hall of residence where they stayed. Late at night. Drunk and crying. Sobbing and pleading. They had gone out together for just a few months, the happiest days of his life. Days when he thought of nothing other than her. Days when he rushed home from lectures to return to her room to lie by her on her bed; to touch her, to smell her; to listen to her; to speak with her; to stroke her skin and caress her hair.

And then later when it was over, then he stood outside her room. Always when he was drunk and too weak to resist. His heart breaking and bleeding and tearing at his chest. Then he stood by her door, speaking softly to it, salty tears streaking his cheeks and spilling onto the grey lino floor. Oblivious to the other students that passed along the corridor. Wondering. Late into the night he stood there until he was ashamed. Ashamed at his weakness and lack of self respect and he made his way to his own room and he lay in bed and shook with disgust and self hate.

And just once she let him in. Let him in to make love to her like old times and he thought it would be alright. Thought she was his again and his heart had grown strong and spirited and his mind sharpened and sloughed off the dull thoughts of previous weeks. But in the morning she turned away from him. She had needed him she said and she knew that he would not talk. She had needed him last night and she did not need him now.

Perhaps he should let Julie in. Perhaps he needed her now and he should let her in to comfort him. She could lay by his side and they could do together the things that they had grown used to doing. Julie would be happy and... it would be pleasure enough for him. He glanced from his bed to the door. He could just make out the handle across the dimness of the room. He had only to open the door.

Julie knocked again.

'Let me come in Steve, please.' She was pleading.

He could imagine her in the corridor. The carpet at least would absorb her tears. Many of those passing would be unknown to her. She would not have to face them at breakfast, to offer explanations.

'Paul Smythe was murdered,' Draper said. The words never far from his thoughts.

'Murdered? How? Why?' he asked.

'With etorphine. A morphine derivative. Apparently it's a constituent of Immobilon, a horse anaesthetic.'

Steve knew. He'd used it himself for castrating horses. Very safe in horses. Lethal to humans. Several vets had died through accidental self-administration. Pricking themselves when trying to inject a horse, or climbing a gate with an unguarded needle. That was all it took. Others had used it to take their life deliberately. His was a high suicide profession. High rate of alcoholism and drug abuse. And a high rate of self destruction. Easy access to the means of doing it. Everything you needed in the boot of your car. No planning required.

Immobilon. So dangerous that you were required to carry the

human reversal agent or antidote, Narcan, whenever you used it. Carry it and instruct someone what to do if you suddenly collapsed and went unconscious. A mere splash of Immobilon on the skin or on the eyes could be enough to put you to sleep.

'How do you know?' Steve had asked.

'The pathologist found it in his blood. He was suspicious. Ketamine is too safe, it wouldn't be easy to take your life with it. He found an injection site on his thigh and traces of blood on the inside of his trousers. Someone stabbed him in the leg with Immobilon and gave him intravenous ketamine when he was unconscious or perhaps already dead. To make it look like suicide or an accident. There's a killer in our midst, and we don't have a motive.'

Steve could think of no motive either. And the thought of someone killing Paul, murdering him in cold blood. He was sick in the interview room. Into the waste bin. Embarrassing but he had no choice. It made him sick. Horribly, terrifyingly sick. And then it dawned on him. That he was a suspect. That they thought he killed Paul. He worked with him. He said Paul was scared. Trying to give himself an alibi.

Draper sent him home. But asked him to let him know his whereabouts if he left Broadwich. He said he would talk to Steve again.

Please go away Julie, thought Steve. He could not let her in. It would be the greatest cruelty. To encourage her hopes for his own indulgence. He had suffered that cruelty. He had not yet inflicted it. He lay in silence and tried to sleep. The ticking of the clock in time with his heart. The sound of CNN from the room next door.

He went in and out of sleep. His dreams came and went. Julie and Rachel were there. Paul lying dead on the floor. Conrad watching from a seat in the corner, lopsided grin on his face, a syringe and bottle of Immobilon in his hand. Conrad stood, the grin became a wide smile. He filled the syringe with Immobilon and walked towards the two girls. They were talking together. Julie and Rachel were talking together about Steve. They were laughing and giggling together like old friends comparing notes.

'He's just a little boy,' said Julie.

'Like a pet Labrador,' said Rachel and howled with laughter.

And suddenly it was no longer Conrad with the syringe but Steve. He clenched it tight in his fist and jammed it hard into Julie's left buttock. That perfect, firm and smooth skinned left buttock. She turned and smiled at him as her knees buckled and she fell, oh so gracefully to the floor.

'There's a good dog,' said Rachel giggling. 'Are you angry? Let mummy give you a big pat.'

He raised his arm and stabbed the two inch long hypodermic into her chest. She smiled at him, the pale blue eyes looking deep into his.

'I've never loved you,' she laughed. Gleefully. With relief yet taunting and callous too. 'I know that now. I've never loved you,' she repeated it enjoying the look on his face and the despair in his eyes. 'Did you really think I did?' she asked. 'Did you really think I could love you?' She threw her head back and tossed her curls so that they bounced, and her blue eyes sparkled like fish scales in tropical sun on drops of turquoise water on white sand beaches and flashing coral reefs that skimmed above the rippling waves. Light reflected in deeper pools of lust and passion, now foregone and tossed aside like wrapping paper on a diamond ring. With no guilt. There was no guilt.

'You're so boring,' she said. Almost nonchalant. An afterthought. An aimless kick at the faithful dog that gambolled at her heels in the hope of a kindly pat or word.

He pulled the needle out and in desperation plunged it deep into his own chest, wanting now only to take away the pain and the hurt. Gently he felt sleep tugging at him. A heavy irresistible sleep. A sleep of longing. A sleep of relief and restfulness. And before he closed his eyes he looked at Rachel one last time, hoping desperately to see something to hold to, to cling to. He saw her eyes looking at him, bright and clear in steadfast self belief. She was laughing.

The knocking on the door stirred him. It was a different voice. More measured. Less frantic.

'Steve, are you there? We are going to eat and we would like you to come with us.' It was Fernando.

Steve opened the door. Fernando stood there in the corridor smiling sheepishly. Spontaneously they embraced.

'You've heard that Paul was murdered?' said Steve.

'Yes,' said Fernando. 'Everyone knows this now. There have been many police at the office today. Lots of questions. They have set up their own portacabin for interviews. I think they will be talking to everyone that works there. Herbert is very unhappy. He is concerned about how it will affect the disease control effort. So much disruption.'

'Concerned about his staff as always,' said Steve sarcastically. 'Give me ten minutes Fernando and I'll be down.'

'Okay. There is someone waiting to see you,' he smiled.

Steve showered and dressed. Not Julie. Please God not let Julie be waiting for him. Please no. He couldn't handle that. He took the stairs rather than the lift, terrified of meeting someone he didn't want to talk to. He walked into the bar. Uncomfortable. As though a hush descended on it when he entered.

'Steve.' The familiar voice lifted him.

'Sammy,' he shouted it loud and rushed over to her, grabbing her in his arms gently but tightly. He felt the tears well up in his eyes and he buried his face in her shoulder.

'How come you're here?' he cried. 'I didn't think you were coming till next week. Oh Sammy, it's so good to see you.'

Sammy laughed and patted him on the back. 'You big sook,' she said and the moisture in her eyes shone back at him. 'I couldn't leave you down here all by yourself with no one to look after you, could I? I spoke to the powers-that-be and they said I could come down now so, here I am, for as long as I want to stay. Did I ever meet Paul?' she asked, serious now.

'I don't think you did,' said Steve. 'Oh Sammy,' he whispered to her. 'The police think I did it. They were questioning me today and I've to tell them where I go if I leave Broadwich. I didn't do it Sammy. You know that don't you?'

'Of course I do you bloody idiot,' said Sammy. 'Don't be so bloody daft. Nobody thinks you did it. Now Fernando has asked us to go out for dinner with him and Sarah. They were going by themselves but he thought we'd like to join them so I said yes.'

Sarah smiled. If she were disappointed she did not show it. 'How about Chinese?' she said. 'There's a good place not far from here.'

'Okay,' said Steve, his arm still round Sammy's shoulders. He shivered as he saw Conrad seated at the bar. He was certain he was watching them and he was equally certain he'd killed Paul. For what reason he had no idea. The whole thing was senseless. All the strange coincidences. Were they just that, or were they all linked? He didn't know. He was a vet, not a detective.

Now though he was working in epidemiology. The skills needed for detective work were pretty much the same. Finding out the facts and then establishing a link between them all. Yes, the only difference was the subject matter. And now that he no longer needed to crawl around on his hands and knees bleeding stinking pigs and taking their temperatures, he could start to use his brain. He would do a good job in epidemiology and he would use it as an opportunity to do some snooping around and serious thinking about everything that had passed.

'Are you ready then?' said Fernando smiling gently and placing a protective arm around Sarah's waist. 'Shall we go?'

'Yes, let's,' said Steve, immediately feeling more cheerful now that he had the semblance of a plan. He felt guilty about Paul's death and had not known how to make amends. Now he did. He would carry out his own enquiries from the inside. He was in a unique position to know what was going on, to hear the gossip and read the signs. 'I'm sorry for what's happened Paul,' he said to himself, 'but I'm going to make it up to you. I'm going to find out who the bastard is that killed you… and, on top of that, why?'

Chapter 22

Steve's new role in epidemiology was to write the final report on each IP and on farms that had been slaughtered as Dangerous Contacts or DCs, to present to the European Commission. Whilst most farmers were willing to help and co-operate, some were tiring of the whole thing, and others were overtly hostile.

One afternoon, he visited a farm where 240 pigs had been slaughtered as DCs solely because they were within one kilometre of an IP. It had represented a change of policy, to clear all the pigs from the 1 Km zone to stop the lateral spread of infection by foxes or other vermin. He tried to phone but it rang out time after time. He decided just to pitch up in the hope of catching them home.

The house was up a short muddy track that he eased his Healey along, the chassis scraping on the deep ruts made by a tractor or four wheel drive. The rain was falling for the first time in several weeks, everywhere the dust replaced by a thick brown sludge. Anger was on the woman's face the moment she opened the door. When he told her who he was and why he had come the anger spread, festering and ready to burst like a boil. Tight lipped, a harsh deep grey in her cheeks and on her forehead, no hidden smile.

'You have the answers already,' she snapped at him, like a dog held back by the scruff of its neck. 'There was nothing wrong with our pigs. Ten years work destroyed. The kids aren't over it yet. I can't tell you any more.' She made to close the door in his face.

Steve sympathised. He put himself in her position. He had learnt to do that over the years. Rachel would not recognise him.

'Look, I understand your feelings,' he said gently. 'I don't want to give you extra hassle or make things more difficult than they already are but...'

A little girl appeared from the shadows. A pretty girl of four or five with conker brown, wide open eyes, like Fernando's. Straight brown hair needing combed. A teddy in her arms.

'Is this the man that killed our pigs?' she asked.

The words struck at him, catching him in the chest, barbed, unmoving.

'Did you kill Pickles and Spotty and Piglet?' she asked Steve, looking him in the face without flinching.

Did I? thought Steve. Did I kill them? I'm part of the machine, supporting it and working for it. It wouldn't work without people like me to do its bidding. How could he answer this little mite? Honestly and gently. What could he possibly say to give her comfort?

'I wasn't here when they were killed,' he said. 'It's very sad and I'm very sorry about your pigs. Sometimes things like this have to be done to try and save other pigs. It's a horrible thing to have happened.'

The little girl looked at him suspiciously.

'Are you a vet?' she asked.

'Yes I am,' said Steve.

'I wanted to be a vet,' she said, 'but I thought vets looked after animals and made them better.'

Steve felt the tears salty in his eyes and he blinked them away.

'I thought so too,' he murmured to himself. 'I never thought I'd be doing something like this. God I never thought I'd be doing something like this.'

'Go in now Chrissy,' said the little girl's mother, embarrassed by her daughter's clear and uncomplicated view of things.

'She's fine,' said Steve calmly, and he squatted down on his knees

131

so that his face was level with hers. 'Do try and be a vet Chrissy,' he said to her smiling. 'Being a vet is about looking after animals. You wouldn't have to do something like this.'

She managed to smile back at him and then ran off further into the house.

'I'm sorry,' the woman said, her face softened by the exchange between Steve and her daughter. She knew it wasn't his fault. He was just there to do a job. 'Look, I can't see you now, I have to collect the other children from school. If you can come back at six thirty this evening my husband will be home from work and he'll see you.'

'Thanks,' he said. 'I'll come back then.'

He walked back to his car through the rain. Relieved to get away. A chance to think and to reassure himself. He sloshed through muddy puddles to where he'd abandoned his Healey on a patch of gravel. He cleaned and disinfected his boots as best he could, the rain running down inside his collar, his shirt wet and sticking to his skin. He had three hours to kill and the office was an hour away. Chrissy's words were sticking in his heart, pricking his feelings as to why he was doing what he was. He had become a vet because he was fascinated by animals. By being a vet he was able to heal and help them. That was what he had set out to do. For how much longer could he carry on with this?

He revved the engine and set off down the road at speed. The tightness in his head was agitating him, a tension in his neck and back, a tautness in his muscles. He needed speed, a release from the pressure; to burn it off like gas on an oil field. He threw the car round the narrow bends, too fast he knew but it was important to him. Water on the road, dull matt black, shining in places where the puddles formed.

Drops of rain bounced off the road; off the windscreen; off the bonnet. A deep rattling sound on the hood; a stream of water down the inside of the windscreen and onto the floor, wetting his shoes. It was a small price to pay. The CD player pounded Brian Adams' 'There will never be another tonight.'

He accelerated faster. Not thinking now. Lost in the thoughts of years gone by. He was a little boy back then. A little boy in an Austin Healey Sprite without a care in the world. And now he was a middle aged man. A middle aged man in an Austin Healey 3000 with more cares on his mind than he dared to think about. 'Put on your best dress darling,' the words blared. Yes, put it on Rachel, he thought. Put it on and fuck yourself. He was angry at the strength of feeling he still had. 'Let it go,' he said out loud. Let it go to drift away like a piece of rubbish on a raging sea. Let it go for good, cut out the biting cancer that still wraps round your heart. Let it go and the pain goes too. Let it go and you are free; free to go forward unhindered by the past. 'Let it go,' he said louder, but he was still not ready.

The sharp bend to the left came up on him quicker than expected. He felt the back end slide out and he corrected it with a clockwise flick of the steering wheel, resisting the temptation to apply the brakes. A massive release of adrenaline and a sharp, cold, shiver through his body, he hit the standing water on the road ahead and the car aquaplaned sideways, front wheels pointing in the direction of travel, perpendicular to the long axis of the car. As the bend straightened out he saw through the spray a lorry, fifty metres away, bearing down on him as he straddled the white line sideways.

The car began to straighten, slowly, too slowly it seemed. His body was cold and clammy now, he braced himself for the impact, it would catch him bang square in the driver's door. The sound of the lorry's horn, the screech of airbrakes, a vision of twisted steaming metal and blue flashing lights and then the rear wheels gained traction and he whipped back onto his side of the road as the lorry slid past in a haze of spray and gravel and burning rubber.

'Yoooow,' he shrieked loud and long with relief and defiance. 'You've not killed me yet Rachel you bitch,' he screamed, 'not by a long way.'

A few miles up the road he came to an antique and craft complex. Old farm buildings long redundant from holding pigs and straw, tractors and potatoes, converted into up-market retail units and a café. The rain streamed down, heavy blobs of water on the roof as he swung into the car park. Thick gravel ruts, water in lakes and puddles, people running to their cars with umbrellas and hats, windows steamed up, coffee smell coming in his window. Cold and damp, the heaters in these old cars were crap.

He climbed out and stretched. He needed a coffee and a piece of cake too. He needed cheering up. His feet went into a puddle.

'Shit,' he said. The cold wet feeling spread out in his shoes. Wet toes and socks; they would begin to ache soon. His mother had always told him not to get his feet wet, it would lead to rheumatism and arthritis. His feet certainly ached now. So did his shoulders and knees. Rugby and football probably. And getting older.

He ordered himself a cappuccino and a buttered scone. Funny to be doing this sort of thing by himself. Rachel had always wanted to stop at places like this and he'd always refused. Waste of money; none to spare. Take a flask and sandwiches with us. He remembered the last time they'd had a coffee together.

'This must be really hurting you Steve Turner,' she said and laughed. Sneeringly. Gleefully.

He smiled to himself. Funny the things you remembered. He picked up a newspaper and settled down to read. Luxury. He hadn't looked at one in weeks. The cappuccino was warming and sweet. A bit too sweet but uplifting. The scone light and fluffy. He glanced up at the sound of the door opening. It was Sonia. She was soaked through and her breasts poked out through her wet T-shirt, nipples erect. Her hair was plastered to her head, golden and shining. Rain drops ran down her face like beads of sweat, all desire and moistness, heat and sticking flesh to flesh; salty taste of oysters; smell of pale wood smoke and musk. It was the most erotic image he'd seen in years.

'Sonia,' he called.

She turned and waved. 'Steve, can I get you a coffee?'

'Yeah, another cappuccino please,' he said, his stomach knotting tight. No shame or pity for Julie. She was his past. There was no pain for him there. No promises made. Time to move on. Time to tempt someone else. And Sonia he felt, could be tempted.

'What happened to you?' Steve asked as she set the coffee on the table in front of him. 'Have you been swimming?'

'I was out on patrols,' said Sonia. 'Walking the roads looking for backyard pigs in the Protection Zone around Stevenson's IP. And then the sky just turned black and down it came.'

'Didn't you have a car?'

'Yeah of course but it was a couple of hundred yards away so I stood under this tree which was fine for about five minutes and then all the branches just seemed to decide to point down instead of up and dumped about a million gallons of water on my head.' She giggled in delight; delicious and appetising.

Steve laughed out loud. 'You look like you're in a Miss Wet T-shirt competition.'

'Yes,' she agreed. 'Would I win do you think?'

It was a 'come-on', it could be nothing else. It was blatant and she stared him straight in the face, letting her lips part ever so slightly, so that he could see the tip of her pointed, bright pink tongue, moist and tempting.

'You'd win,' he said.

She leaned forward until her forehead was almost touching his, her breasts pointing at his throat just inches away.

'I'm frozen in this T-shirt,' she said. 'I need warming up. I need a screw. Now. Meet me in the women's loos in two minutes; they're round the back,' and she was gone, her T-shirt stuck to her straight slender back, shoulder blades protruding provocatively.

Steve's mouth was dry. He often fantasised about this sort of thing but it never happened.

'You need to decide,' he said to himself. 'Two minutes the lady said.' He laughed. 'The lady.'

He left his cappuccino to go cold and went out through the side door. Sure enough the loos were where she had said. What if she were joking and there was someone else in there. He would look a fool. But why would she joke about this? He hesitated, aware that he could be accused of loitering. I could pretend I went in the wrong one, he thought. He took a deep breath, pulse racing and pushed through the door with the picture of a girl in a dress. There were three cubicles and three wash basins. 'No urinals,' he murmured, genuinely surprised. One of the cubicles was closed.

'Sonia?' The bolt slid back and the door opened.

'I wasn't sure you'd come,' she said. 'I'm glad you have.'

He went into the cubicle and she locked the door. She kissed him on the lips. 'Now Steve,' she whispered. 'Now we'll see what you're really made of.' She was purring like a cat; a cat stretching itself in the sun, then rolling and wriggling in ecstasy on the ground. 'Now we'll see what sort of travelling companion you'd make,' she held his face tight in her hands as she breathed warm and damp into his ear.

He lifted his hands and peeled the T-shirt from her wet body. Time settled like a beautiful butterfly. Seconds became minutes, minutes an eternity; and eternity passed in the touch of skin on skin, lips on lips, the soft caress of fingertips and beads of sweat mingling with rainwater and the taste of late summer. He placed a hand on her face, felt her eyes wide and gasping, the wet hair now steaming and slightly oily; the pinkness spreading up from her chest onto her neck; the shake of her head in disbelief; felt her nails dig tight into his bare shoulders and saw the steam rising from her like in a sauna.

'I feel warmer now,' she breathed, resting her face on his neck. 'Perfect. Perfect.' She stroked his arms gently and held his hands.

'Have you ever screwed in a public toilet before?' she asked him.

'No,' he whispered, 'have you?'

'No,' she replied. 'The idea just came to me when I saw your brown eyes staring at me over your coffee cup. And how was it for you?'

'Wonderful,' he said truthfully. 'Just wonderful.'

'Can I borrow your T-shirt?' she said.

Steve smiled at her. 'Of course. Keep it as a memento.'

'You could keep my knickers,' she said, 'but I don't wear any.'

'I have your picture, he said. 'In my mind I have your picture. It will never leave me. It will never go away.'

Just like the picture I have of Rachel, he thought. The picture of her in the passenger seat of my Sprite in her cheesecloth shirt and sunglasses; the picture of her lying in my single bed, sheet pulled up around her neck, laughing when she had had all her hair cut off; the picture of her coming home one night in tears, black rings of tiredness around her eyes. A gallery of memories hung in his mind. Down every passageway, through every door, another image that was a part of his life. Another image that explained how he was today. Who he was today.

Sonia pulled on his T-shirt and hitched up her jeans.

'I'll see you this evening,' she said, and, giving him a kiss on the lips, turned and was out the door and away.

He was stunned by what had happened. He was forty four and he was in a woman's toilet having just screwed this gorgeous blonde who he had only ever spoken to before today. It was bizarre. And it was brilliant.

He left the cubicle and walked across to the main door. He opened it just as a large, round woman with a heavy dark moustache was about to come in. She looked at him with a startled expression, like he was some kind of lower primate.

'Sorry,' said Steve. 'I came in the wrong door. Silly mistake. My eyesight's not what it used to be. Shouldn't be driving really, blind as a bat. Sorry about the inconvenience.'

He dodged past her and headed for his car. He risked a glance back, she was staring shaking her head. If only she knew, he thought. That would give her something to shake her head about. He unlocked the driver's door a smile dancing on his lips.

'Oh Mr Turner,' he said as he looked at himself in the mirror. 'You've been a very naughty boy.'

Chapter 23

Another outbreak. It had been quiet for three weeks and now there was another outbreak. Fifteen miles from the nearest IP and six thousand pigs needed to be slaughtered. There was no connection with any other IP. No movement of pigs or personnel; no shared advisers or staff; no feed lorry movements or foxes or anything that could be remotely suspicious.

Ron Steady the PVO was not happy. He wanted answers from epidemiology. And if they had none he wanted to know why not? He came on the phone to Graham Thompson one afternoon and the others in the room could hear the raised voice spurting from the earpiece.

'We've checked everything and we're checking again,' said Graham. He looked sombre, hawk like.

Steve and the others busied themselves with their files; a rustling of paper; some sighs as well. Faces moved in mock concentration; just to show how hard they were working on it. How hard they were trying. Everyone in the room could feel the energy at work; but the PVO could not.

'Yes we'll go over it all again and again until we do have an answer,' said Graham. 'Rest assured we will find an answer. Yes. Okay. I'll speak to you tomorrow.'

He put the phone down. No one said anything. He leant back in his chair and rested his hands on the desk in front of him, eyes closed, trance like. Steve risked a furtive glance at him. He appeared to be meditating. The other vets looked around daring each other to speak. The Veterinary Service was still strictly hierarchical and whilst the DVAs were not saluted or addressed as 'Sir', the VOs had the distinct impression that they would like to be. As for the PVO, some considered him second only to God.

'The PVO is not pleased,' said Graham at last choosing his words deliberately and carefully. 'He wants to know how the disease has travelled to this new IP in spite of all the movement restrictions in place. Now you heard me tell him that we will find the answer and I meant it,' he paused.

'The answer's there,' he said dreamily. 'It's there in those files and spreadsheets in front of you. It's a question of picking out the relevant information from everything that's hiding it. There's no short cut other than painstaking investigation. It's there and we're missing it.' His eyes were still closed and the vets exchanged glances again.

'Ron is sending Sally Pringle down tomorrow to see if she can come up with anything. Let's see if we can have an answer for her by then.' He stood up and went out of the room. There was silence for a few moments and then Steve spoke.

'Who's Sally Pringle?' he asked.

'She's one of the PVO's babes said Trevor. 'See if she can come up with anything,' he said sarcastically. 'I might come up with something if she sits on my lap. Something considerably bigger than what she's got in mind. That would give her quite a surprise wouldn't it?'

Everyone laughed.

'If any of you want to hear it, my own theory on how it got to Mr Fisher's farm is that Colonel Merrydew from IP 7 is having an affair with Mrs Fisher. And a few weeks ago he went over to see her and found her working in the pig pens. And whilst he was giving her a damn good seeing-to amongst the weaners, a couple of dead piglets that he'd picked up on his own farm earlier that day fell out of his pocket. I don't know if that's the sort of theory that would interest the PVO or Sally Pringle for that matter?' His eyes bulged like an iguana's, his lips parted slightly in a smile as he stared around the room at the others.

'I'll give Colonel Merrydew a ring now and see if that's what happened shall I?' said Steve. 'There's nothing in the preliminary report to suggest it but maybe the vet concerned just didn't think to ask the right questions.'

'Good idea. And while you're on to him,' said Trevor, 'just ask if he's ever slipped Sid Potter's daughter a length at IP 12 because the link we have for that is pretty tenuous. It would be nice to think he could have dropped a couple of dead piglets there too. And how's that poncey car of yours going Mr Turner? Still firing on four cylinders is it?

'Like a dream,' said Steve. 'Seriously though, has anybody got any idea of how disease got to Fisher's? It's sort of stuck out in the middle of nowhere. Presumably all the different groups of pigs are being bled at slaughter so we can pinpoint where it came in and get an idea of how long it's been there?'

'Yes we've got people out there today doing bleeds,' said Neil Franks. 'The problem is getting the bloody results back. The lab send them to Sage Street who refuse to send them on to us. Too many people building Empires and ivory towers if you ask me. Running things from there isn't the best way of doing things. They're not close enough to the ground to know what's really going on.'

Neil Franks was pissed off with it. Not just pissed off, he was bloody furious. He'd worked on a host of disease eradication campaigns, none of which had been run quite like this one. The field staff were working beyond reasonable limits with Health and Safety issues largely ignored. He could not devote the time needed to real epidemiology because of the paperwork and the bureaucracy. The system was crumbling under the weight of paper and the inability to make decisions at local level because Head Office insisted on controlling every last detail. Centralisation gone mad. No one trusting anybody else to use good veterinary common sense. Tried and tested procedures were being torn up daily and the wheel re-invented by jumped up administrators in Armani suits who probably couldn't recognise a pig if they saw one.

'Thank God this isn't Foot and Mouth we're dealing with,' he said to Graham the next morning. 'In our current state of preparedness this would be a disaster.'

Graham looked at him, sombre and worn out. Tired lines from his eyes to his mouth.

'This is what The Service has come to,' he replied. 'It's all business plans, setting and meeting targets and number crunching with computers. What happens on the ground is no longer important, it's what it says in the report that counts. You can't turn it back though. That's the direction it's headed in and the direction in which it will continue. Ron Steady may or may not like it, I have no idea. But he'll get on with it because that's what his political masters and the administrators want. If he says "No" he may as well look for another job. So what would you do in his position?'

Steve overheard it all. It confirmed his own views which were considerably less charitable. After all, Ron Steady had personally overseen the closure of goodness knows how many Divisional Animal Health Offices and cut the number of vets back to the point where the right level of training and expertise couldn't be maintained. If you doffed your cap and took the salary when times were good, then you had to take the flak and responsibility in times of crisis. And deserved to burn in hell when the shit hit the fan.

Sally Pringle arrived that afternoon. She was one of the new breed of epidemiologists: all numbers, statistics, computer models and predictions, and no muck on her wellies. Important sounding words for simple old fashioned ideas. She talked of spatial and temporal distribution instead of where and when disease outbreaks occurred, and 'confounding factors' instead of 'false leads'.

Steve was intimidated at first. The language, though not alien did not trip off his tongue. But he knew it was easy to hide behind language; professionals did it all the time, part of preserving the privileges they enjoyed.

She sat in the middle of the epidemiology room perched on a chair, with the rest of them surrounding her, like a nursery teacher about to read a story to her pupils. We should all be sitting cross-legged on the floor thought Steve, with our little bottles of free milk and our grey shorts and scabby knees. Trevor sat chewing gum, his eyes bulging as he stared at Sally in her black mock jodhpurs, and exquisitely cut white silk blouse and orange scarf. Steve caught Trevor's eye and made a gesture that could only be a reference to what he'd said the day before. Trevor smiled lazily.

'This new epidemiological mathematical model we're using is called DIsease Control MANagement, or DICMAN,' she said, straight faced without the glimmer of a smile. 'We're using it to plot the temporal course of the outbreak and predict where the disease may surface again. The data we're putting in is collected by the investigating vet and of course yourselves in your more detailed enquiries. You're our link to what's happening on the ground. The information we get from you is absolutely critical.'

'Did the model predict this last IP?' asked Trevor, his eyes glistening with mischief.

Sally's face coloured a hint of pink beneath the thick layer of pale foundation.

'No it didn't,' she replied, 'and we've done some fine tuning since then to reflect that new outbreak. The model in fact predicted that the epidemic was over and that there would be no further IP's. So this one came somewhat out of the blue and took us all by surprise. Yourselves included,' she added, not venomously but with a certain pointedness that indicated she would take shit from no one.

'How did it get there?' she asked.

'Trevor has a theory you might be interested to hear,' said Steve innocently. 'It's less conventional than some but I guess we should take all possibilities seriously until proven otherwise.'

Trevor's eyes bulged to the point where they looked as if they might pop. 'I don't really think it's a serious option,' he said, trying to keep his face straight. 'I'll give it some more thought before making it general knowledge.'

'Is it possible we're missing other cases on the ground?' said Sally. 'Confusing them with PDNS? Taking and recording temperatures as per Emergency Instruction 2000/136 should prevent us missing disease shouldn't it?'

'Not necessarily,' said Steve, aware that he was going to put his foot in it but prepared to carry on anyway.

'Taking temperatures is a red herring. A friend of mine went to a farm a few days ago to inspect twenty fatteners. He told me that when he got there they were the healthiest looking pigs he'd ever seen. It was a stinking hot day though and by the time they'd been chased around and caught for blood sampling the last few had temperatures of over 107 F. Like he said, he wasn't going to serve Form A and start killing pigs to post mortem.'

'But he'd have to if he recorded their high temperatures,' said Sally. '2000/136 is very specific on that.'

'Exactly,' said Steve. 'So he did what any sane person would have done. He recorded them as normal. That's the problem with the prescriptive nature of the instructions that we're getting. If we're not allowed to use veterinary judgement then why not just send a typist out with a tick list. It forces vets to lie, to hide the fact that they've made a veterinary judgement, which is of course exactly what they should be being paid to do. We need to encourage the vets to make clinical judgements instead of blindly follow instructions approved by administrators.'

Sally Pringle's face assumed the look of one who has just trodden in dog shit and Graham shifted nervously in his seat. Trevor appeared relieved that someone had at last spoken a plain truth in a brutally frank manner.

'We haven't got a good source for Potter at IP 12 either,' reminded Trevor.

'What have we got?' asked Sally.

'The pigman from IP 8, two miles down the road, drove a tractor and trailer past Potter's place two weeks before Potter's outbreak. He didn't stop and the pigs are at least a hundred metres back from the road. It's a bit of a long shot isn't it?'

'It's not a lot,' agreed Sally, and gave a disarming smile that made Steve warm to her. 'We'll keep our options open shall we?'

Sonia met Steve in the bar at The Swallow later that evening.

'Oh what a day,' she said, giving him a long sloppy kiss on the lips and draping her arms round his neck and her pelvis round his.

'Pot bellied pigs. Why the hell keep those fat ugly bastards as pets? They're more trouble than a thousand sow outdoor unit.'

'A problem today?' he laughed, kissing her closed eyelids and holding her buttocks in both hands.

'Yeah, we had to go and bleed a couple of pot belliels over at Taneworth. They belonged to this young businessman bloke; country house; big Porsche in the gravelled driveway; all the trimmings of new wealth, including the two biggest, fattest, pot bellied pigs I've ever seen. Frank and Betty; you'd have thought they were his children; or worse,' she added. 'Come to think of it there were no women about the place. The AHO I had with me, Geoff, never stopped talking and bloody hopeless really.'

'Yeah, I know him. He's a nice enough lad but he can't bleed pigs. Not that I'm much good at it either. Don't want to be if the truth be known. Can't think of a worse way of earning a living than bleeding pigs,' Steve laughed.

'Likewise,' said Sonia biting his left ear lobe as she whispered, 'I want you. I can't get enough of you. I don't want to wait till later.'

He laughed. 'What happened about the pigs?'

'Oh I put a snare on Betty's top jaw and of course she started squealing as though I was killing her and this bloke started hopping from one foot to the next saying "This is awful. This is inhuman. You can't do this to her." I thought he was going to cry. Or hit me. Perhaps both,' she mused.

'So I said to him, look it doesn't really hurt, she's just annoyed and Geoff tried to get some blood out of her neck but I suppose it was just like sticking the needle into a tub of lard. So after about five minutes of this high pitched squealing and him prodding and poking, if you know what I mean, and Mr Poncey sweating and pacing up and down and looking at his watch saying he was going to be late for a meeting, I suggested to Geoff that he tried the tail. So he got about two drops of blood out and I said that'll do and let the bloody thing go. By which time Frank had gone into the corrugated iron ark which had a tiny low door so that a person couldn't get in and there was no way he was going to budge himself out.'

She leaned forward again and put her tongue in his ear. 'If I wore any knickers I'd want you in them,' she teased.

'Anyway, this young bloke disappears and comes back with a banana. "He always comes out for a banana" he said and I thought, oh yes, I bet he does, but of course after hearing Betty, Frank is having none of it and just stands at the entrance whilst Betty potters round the pen with blood dripping from her tail like she's some sort of haemophiliac.'

'Oh God,' said Steve in genuine sympathy. He squeezed her hips in support and kissed her on the neck. 'Just be patient and you can have as much as you want,' he whispered.

'So then I said, look Mr Gerard, you're getting upset about this quite needlessly. Why don't you go off to your meeting and leave us the bananas and we'll coax Frank out and you won't have to go through the trauma of it all. And you know what? He agreed. I think he was grateful for the excuse to get away, it was all too horrible for him. So we sat around for about half an hour whilst he went and put on a suit and then we heard the Porsche start up and he roared off, not quite into the sunset, but you know what I mean.'

'So did you manage to tempt Frank out with a banana?'

'No, I just shoved the snare over his nose and dragged him out squealing and luckily Geoff hit his tail vein first time. Then I caught Betty again and we took the bung out of a tube and by pumping her tail up and down like a water pump we managed to get enough blood flow to catch the drips and fill a tube.'

'So you're quite deceitful then really,' said Steve teasingly as he patted her hips with the flat of his hand and brushed her lips with his own.

'You'd better believe it. Like all women I can lie to perfection when the need arises. Now take me upstairs and make love to me like I've been away from you for a year.'

Steve glanced over her shoulder to where Sammy was talking to Fernando and Sarah and he winked at her. She smiled but there was sadness in her eyes. At the other end of the room sat Julie, her eyes fixed purposefully on Sonia's back. She caught Steve's gaze and the hate in her eyes and face took him by surprise. Even more surprising was that she was sitting next to Conrad. I wouldn't have thought he was her type thought Steve. Still, none of my business.

He whispered in Sonia's ear, she giggled and pushed against him, then draining his glass he led her through the rapidly filling bar and up to his room. And at that moment it was over twenty years ago and he was leading Rachel back to his room for the first time. He was twenty years old with a sensation of tiny burning pinpricks inside and on the surface of his skin. Rachel was a goddess then, an Amazon in her power and beauty and he was possessed, bedevilled, with lust and want. He led her to his room and laid her down on his bed and like a little boy held her to him through the whole night until the morning sun cast its light through the curtains onto her proud and sleeping face.

Chapter 24

Those ten weeks of summer were the best of his life. Ten weeks of bright summer sun with the smell of cut grass and roses in the gardens at the Hall of Residence at the Vet College field station. Evenings playing croquet and tennis or walking in the fields where blackbirds and blue tits flitted in the hawthorns and rabbits played in the gathering dusk. Lying on dry ground in the shade of rhododendron bushes, head on Rachel's lap as she stroked his hair with tender movements of her slim smooth fingers, catching in his curls and teasing out the knots.

An age of cheesecloth shirts in blues and whites, purples and greens. Slim taut bodies, brown and silky soft with youth; short skirts and shorts of pale blue denim that hugged the curves and fissures of her body.

Long glasses of ice cold lager, golden with bubbles rising in streams of light and sun-drenched mist. Each day a day of gentle paces without cares or worries. Simple pleasures of friends and company; boating on the river at the weekends; picnics of fresh bread and salads with chilled cheap wine. Grown up pleasures in youthful disguise of innocence and inhibition; parties with home-brew brewed in baths. The thump of music, floors moving up and down with the weight of people, sweat and beer stained shirts late into the night, pressing against each other, seeking out the one desired.

And always, always, Rachel by his side. Into the night from earliest waking. Touching, stroking, always, always. Each minute that passed. Each moment of time. The smell of her hair. Her tender lips. Her smile and laughter, not forgotten. 'I love you Sunshine,' she said, time and again and the light from her eyes told him it were true. A lifetime lived in ten short weeks that brought the taste of sweetest honey to his heart and the bitter taste of betrayal to his mind.

A year of terrible pain. A year when waking was a heavy heart and he followed her as a puppy follows its Master. Laughing at her jokes. Gambolling in her shadow for some recognition of the sickly devotion that he showed.

Drunken longing. Standing at her door in the grey tiled corridor in the darkness of two o'clock in the morning and then walking to his Austin Healey Sprite and driving quietly to beneath her window, then making the engine roar and the tyres scream as the wheels spun and he was out of the car park and onto the road and with each bend the tyres screamed louder and he knew she could hear and he hoped she would fear him killed and he did not know if she would or if she cared anyway.

He could still see the grey tiles of the corridor lit by the fluorescent lights, the veneered doors with the room numbers in gold figures. He knew the sound of the doors when you hammered against them with your fist, the hollow dull ring that echoed down the corridor and the creaking of the frame when you put your shoulder against it. The grating noise when you worked the handle up and down in rage and the metallic click when the handle sprung back up; the feel of the door when it was locked. The sound of a door opening further along the corridor, the shuffle of feet as they made their way to the bathroom; the involuntary sigh of disapproval when they saw he was still there.

He could recognise the change from grey to grey of the curtains over the corridor window as the morning sun inched towards the horizon and it was time to creep back to his own bed so that no one should know how long he had stayed. He knew the feel of a cold bed in the early morning. The lonely feel of such a bed and the loneliness of a heart in such a bed.

The pain had continued for two terms until Rachel had completed her degree and left. The unhappiest terms of his nearly five years at University, when every day he knew that he would have to see her, and every day he wanted her and every day he would cry for her in his room. Tears of love and lust and injustice like he was the only one in the whole fucking world who had ever lost in love.

And other women held nothing that was comparable for him. There were others he took out and slept with. He liked them. Enjoyed them and their company. But they had no depth for him. Flirtations of the body. Diversions of the mind.

When she left, his relief swamped him like a flood. A blind man who could suddenly see in vivid colours; a lame man able to walk again. It was spring in the world and spring in his life, and light burst in on him with devastating effect. Smiles and happiness danced across his face and lit the faces of others where there had previously been darkness. He felt the thrill and power of a salmon that has shaken out the hook, a falcon that has slipped its jesses on a full stomach and has no reason to return. He need never see her again. Never hear the voice that twisted his heart or smell again the scent of her hair and skin, or observe the movement of her hips and breasts, the carriage of her arms and shoulders; the drop and bounce of her hair; the curve of her thigh; the arching of her back when she had lost control.

All would have been well had it not been for the destructive spark that glowed deep inside him, red and waiting for a breeze to fan it and rekindle the flame. Though she were no longer there and the pain was less she still had a hold on him, a distant power that unseen was real enough and held him by a thread to her own heart. A thread down which she sent the tiny pulses of lust and tender memories; the feel of her life's blood pulsating in his own heart, warming and nourishing his pangs of love and loss so that they would not die completely.

The thread sent strange messages to him that lifted his spirits and dashed them in the same instant like wicked jokes played on young children by their older siblings. He thought to cut the thread like an umbilical cord but he felt the need of the nourishment and comfort that it gave to him and he revelled in the self pity that was behind it, not yet ready to cast himself adrift and completely free.

And he had a plan. A vague but wondrous plan, a trap to set to entice

*and snare her back into his life. He too could be cunning. He could stalk
her too. In her mind when he was not there. Especially when he was not
there. Then she would have to think and imagine what he was up to.
So he sent her a birthday card:*

*To Dear Rachel,
Love Steve*

*Short and simple and he posted it and he said no more and he waited.
The hunted must become the huntress. He must become the prey. To lead
the way so that she would follow him.*

PART TWO

Armageddon

Chapter 25

Another dreary February day. Grey and more grey. A fine mist of water hanging in the air instead of falling earthwards. Grey sky and grey buildings merged with the shining black tarmac of the car park. Droplets of water covered the cars that he could see from his window, their colours dulled, the light too subdued to make them sparkle.

Steve Turner felt the same. Swine Fever had finished a month past. All clean and tidied away. Herbert Bluster had already booked his seat at the Minister's 'Thank you' drinks party at the end of the month. He'd probably booked an appointment at the Palace too for the birthday honours list, thought Steve.

He sighed. He felt worn out; needed time to recuperate. Time away from the pressures and the memory of what had gone on. Like the death of Paul and the knowledge that the police were still no nearer to finding his killer. In spite of his own snooping he'd uncovered nothing. No motive, and apart from Conrad, no suspects.

His relationships with Julie and Sonia had disorientated him. Two beautiful women who were besotted with him and he walked away from both. Neither were amused and Julie was vengeful. It was not the way he liked to end relationships, preferring to shake hands with a parting kiss on the cheeks. Most were satisfied with that and if not, well he could usually pull them round. Not Julie though.

He heard Willie whistle down the corridor.

'Coffee's ready,' he shouted.

'Okay, coming,' called Steve.

The coffee room was unusually quiet. Just Steve and Willie. Like an early morning bar session back in Broadwich. The two with the most staying power; to the bitter end.

'Have you seen this Mr Turner?' mocked Willie. 'It's from Sage Street. They want us to put down on paper all our thoughts on the Swine Fever campaign, good points and bad. And no matter how small they want to hear about it because, as they say here; "It could be vital." So are you going to do that for them?'

'I rather think not,' said Steve. 'They probably won't even read it. Just hang it on a rusty nail in the shitter.' He giggled.

Willie looked hurt. 'So you don't like the idea then. I must say that's a very cynical attitude you're taking there Mr Turner, because remember, no matter how small; it could be vital.'

Steve laughed again.

'I suppose you've done yours have you?'

'As a matter of fact,' said Willie, passing over a sheaf of papers, 'I have. See what you think.'

Steve read through the notes as he drank his coffee. Willie had some good ideas and constructive criticisms. He had put a lot of work into it. He had shone throughout the campaign. Competent and resilient. Cheerful too.

'Bluster's back in this afternoon,' said Steve. 'That's very good Willie,' he continued, passing the papers back to him. 'Some good ideas that I'm afraid will be instantly consigned to the dustbin of indifference. No one can say you haven't tried though.'

Later that afternoon Steve sat in his office with Bluster opposite him. More bluster than usual and looking tanned having spent a couple of weeks away with his wife in Madeira.

'Very nice,' he said in response to Steve's cue. 'It was a family run hotel; we were soon on first name terms with the owner. Great selection of malt whiskies, no measures just a tipping of the bottle into the glass,' he chuckled as though he were party to some luxurious conspiracy. 'We met a couple from Edinburgh, retired accountant, fascinating bloke. He'd worked for Edinburgh City Council and knew some of the big noises at the Scottish Executive. Very interesting chap.'

I bet, thought Steve, cringing at the sort of holiday he would despise. Fuck you Herbert Bluster and your pathetic name dropping and your big malt whiskies. The guy probably waters it down or pours cheap local stuff into the bottles to fool the likes of you, he thought.

'Well you made quite a name for yourself at Broadwich,' went on Bluster. 'Good team player. Good clear reports. You've been noticed which can't have done you any harm. The PVO even mentioned your name to me on a couple of occasions. You may well come under pressure to seek promotion.'

Steve laughed to himself. A mention by the PVO. Just the sort of thing that would ring bells for Herbert Bluster. A bit like being mentioned in dispatches. Promotion? For what? To pore over business plans and become an administrator? Not likely. That route wasn't for him. Swine Fever had its enjoyable side but it had also confirmed his worst suspicions that The Service was being taken over by administrators. He kept his mouth shut on that matter.

'Ah well, the cream always rises to the top,' he said with an effort.

Bluster winced as though with tooth ache and his jaw trembled. He was confused by the contradictory signals radiating from Steve. A capable VO; good at his job, but with a flippancy and disrespect for senior management that Bluster found only mildly short of anarchic.

'Epidemiology was fascinating,' said Steve, aware that he must say something positive to relieve Bluster's anguish. 'I felt I was using my brain and my veterinary training for a change. It was a challenge. Hard work and I wouldn't want to do it again for a while. I still feel, well, drained by it and in need of a damned good holiday. In fact I picked up some travel brochures at lunchtime today so I might be applying for some leave soon.'

It was three thirty when Herbert Reginald Bluster left for another meeting. Steve saw him walking across the car park in his pale beige hush puppies and blue double breasted jacket swinging his leather brief case with the initials H.R.B. embossed on the front in gold lettering. He glanced left to right, furtive; like a hunted animal on strange territory, unsure of himself.

What a man, thought Steve. He had to smile. The phone rang. It was a vet from the main regional office.

'Has Herbert left yet?' The voice was hurried, agitated.

'He drove out of the car park two minutes ago,' said Steve. 'What's new?'

'It may be nothing, probably is nothing,' he said, 'but there's a suspect Foot and Mouth case at an abattoir down south. A pig apparently. No doubt it'll be negative. Probably a *Staph* infection or something like that. I just thought Herbert should know but it'll keep till tomorrow. How are things with you anyway? Recovered from Swine Fever yet?'

'To be honest, no. You were in Sage Street weren't you? What were things like up there?'

'Like a bloody circus. A lot of people building their own little Empires and sucking up to Ron Steady. You know how it is. A lot of egos around. That bloody DVA from Western Region. What a bloody idiot. Kept removing things from the IP map without telling anyone. Had his sidekick with him, a skinny bloke in a sharp suit.

Wouldn't dirty his hands answering the phone but quite happy to dirty his nose up the PVO's arse. It opened my eyes anyway.'

'Where is the FMD suspect?' Steve asked, not overly thrilled.

'An abattoir in Northamptonshire I think. Apparently the pigs arrived last Friday, too late to kill them so they stayed in the lairage over the weekend. Yesterday morning the Official Veterinary Surgeon saw what he described as classical signs of FMD. Like I say it'll be negative. Where could it have come from? There's none in Europe at the moment.'

'Oh well, a bit of excitement to keep Sage Street on their toes,' Steve laughed. 'I'll speak to you later.'

The light outside was fading, it looked as though it might snow. The smell of Christmas long past, spring too far away to offer summer's cheer. A bad time of year for Steve.

Long days of leaving the farm in the dark and returning home in the dark, fearful of the snow coming and blocking them in or out. Longing for the safety of the weekends when they could stay all day, waking early and boiling water on the Belling gas stove in the light and roar of the Calor gas lamp hung from a hook in the ceiling, the first sip of scalding tea breathing life and fire into their hearts and minds, giving courage and strength of purpose. Then outside to feed the stock in the great wooden shed, the ewes with their lambs growing inside and the heifers they were rearing to be their suckler cows. Barley and soya mix spread in their troughs, hay and straw to follow. The peace and joy in standing to watch them eat, their jaws moving rhythmically with the healthy hunger of beasts well nourished.

Pride burst in him as he watched. To create this from nothing other than a dream and a desire. To follow the dream and see it there in front of him; to reach and touch and to find it real. Leaning on the gates shoulder to shoulder words passed between them like electricity down a wire. Excited voices, bubbling and brewing over, a boiling pot, lid rattling with the heat. So much to see and do and experience. The impatience of youth cramming ever more in, no minute or second wasted in peaceful contemplation.

In summer the light came up at three or four in the morning. No curtains at the windows, the view too keen to waste and hide away. On still days the sound of the stream carried through the open window, the scent of dew drenched grass, the buzz of dragonflies skimming the pond, the gentle smell of summer earth and summer sounds of songbirds in the thickets they had planted. Bleating lambs and baaing ewes, the tramp and swish of young heifers in the rushes on the fell, the musk of fox as he climbed the wall and disappeared beyond.

To stare from the window at six in the morning was to be beckoned outside onto the green grass with the dogs. To follow the line of the wall where rabbits ran for cover and a short eared owl hovered and taunted the terrier. And roe deer amongst the newly planted trees, russet red with spindly legs leaping and jumping at your approach.

An hour to walk the boundary, to take in all that was his and remind him of what they had achieved. This was his home forever, for eternity. His ashes would be scattered on the bank opposite the front door, beyond the pond where he could lie and watch the comings and goings of the new owners down the years and centuries. It would be his until the world ended. He would never leave.

Then inside to cook a breakfast of eggs and bacon, fried mushrooms, fried bread and mugs of steaming tea. Eaten huddled round the gas fire in winter or sitting on the stone bench in summer sun to wait the postman and his letters... and his bills.

Steve smiled to himself. He was getting soft in the head. He switched his computer off and stretched in his chair.

'I'm off home,' he called to Willie, 'I've had enough.'

'Aye well it wouldn't do to be late twice in a day,' came the reply.

When he arrived at his cottage it was dark and cold. The Rayburn was nearly out, he heaped coal on from a scuttle next to it. He felt alone and suddenly depressed. This wasn't how his life was meant to be. He should have made it by now. He should be established. A part of the community. He and Rachel together.

He went to the fridge. There was nothing there worth eating, he'd forgotten to shop again. It happened a lot since he returned from Broadwich; used to eating out all the time. He didn't feel hungry anyway. He picked up the letters from the hall mat. A letter from his mum: he should phone her more often. He knew she worried about him, even now at his age.

There was another letter too. The address was spelt wrong. That was the trouble with computers, he thought. Once something was entered it stayed there until somebody who had power of data input corrected it. Which they hardly ever did. He ran his finger under the edge of one corner and slid it along the top.

'Ow!' he shouted. Blood flowed onto the floor from a neat fine cut in the fleshy part at the end of his finger. He grabbed a piece of kitchen towel and wrapped it tight round. The stinging sensation made him feel faint. He was not good with self-injury. He peeled the kitchen towel back and looked at his finger. Blood filled the wound but he could make out the extent of it, about a centimetre long. Deep enough for some stitches but he'd had a finger stitched once before and he was not prepared to repeat that. The doctor was inexperienced and trembling as he administered the local anaesthetic. The pain of the hypodermic and the irritant local in the sensitive tip of his finger was a still fresh memory.

He held the kitchen towel tight on his finger and hunted in a draw for a roll of sticking plaster. Then, squeezing the cut surfaces together he wrapped the plaster round the finger several times; tight, but not so tight. A faint red tinge showed through the plaster but it seemed to have stopped.

He gingerly took hold of the envelope and with forceps and scissors cut it open. The words 'Wilkinson Sword' flashed at him, black lettering against shiny steel. The thinnest of razor blades was stuck to the inside of the envelope, a fleck of dried blood on one end of it. It had been concealed, carefully and lovingly, for one purpose alone. Using the forceps he removed the letter and unfolded it. It was short and to the point.

I've seen how you treat women. I've been watching you. I don't like it. Poor Paul. Such a nice lad. Such a nasty accident.

His legs wobbled and he squatted down to fend off the fainting. His mouth was dry, his lips stuck together, the dryness caught at his throat. A sharp coldness, frost or ice massaged his neck and shoulders and disappeared into his guts. His empty stomach filled with nausea. He ran to the kitchen sink and was sick. Yellow, hot tasting bile. Sour and slimy. Sweat on his forehead and on his cheeks, the cold inside him matched by a heat and claustrophobia on the surface of his skin.

He was scared to be alone. The cosy comfortable cottage now shadowy and sinister; the creaks of the doors and floorboards caused his heart to thump and pound. The limbs of trees moving outside the window brushed against the panes of glass like death, gentle but without compassion. Vulnerability smothered him. Alone with no neighbours; alone with his thoughts and fears; like at the farm. He shuddered. The cold grip tightened on him; squeezing his chest; compressing his heart and lungs; gently, gently, ever tighter, a python constricting a monkey; he felt the force and power of breathless fear. A rushing in his ears, the hot metallic taste of blood in his throat. The trees rustled again on the window pane and he ran for the door, running, running up the side of the cottage until he reached his Healey. He clutched the letter in his hand, fumbling for the keys in the dark. Every sound was a demon, a monster, nothing was straightforward now. Everything had changed.

He arrived at Willie's house, not knowing the route he'd taken, his breathing was becoming normal; slow and steady, but he felt like shit. Nothing like this had ever happened to him. No benchmark against which to measure it. He trembled as he knocked on Willie's door.

Morag opened it and her face sparkled when she saw him.

'Steve. Come in. Willie's not home yet.' Then, 'What's wrong?' when she saw the hunted look in his eyes; the trembling of his lips.

He threw his arms round her and held her tight. She patted him on the back.

'I've just had this letter,' he said handing it to her, 'with a razor blade hidden in the envelope.' He held up his taped finger.

She read the letter. 'That's horrible,' she said. 'Was Paul the guy that was murdered?'

Steve nodded.

'Have you told the police yet?'

'No, I was so terrified I just ran out of the house and came here.' He smiled sheepishly, embarrassed at his reaction.

Willie and Morag's kids trooped through to see him. He wiped his eyes with his sleeve and tried to smile at them. The youngest, Katie, came over and held his hand.

'Don't cry,' she said. 'When I'm sad I think of something nice to eat and that cheers me up.'

Steve laughed and ruffled her hair.

'That's Willie arriving now,' said Morag. 'Stay for dinner and phone the police.'

Chapter 26

It was nine thirty by the time the police finally left. They had taken the letter with them and had gone to the cottage to retrieve the envelope and look around. The Inspector was of the opinion that it was a hoax but couldn't rule out that it was sent by the person that killed Paul.

'Murderer's do sometimes draw attention to themselves,' he said. 'It's a sort of taunting cockiness that they seem to enjoy. And sometimes people who aren't involved try to get in on the act. It's a game to that type. We'll get in touch with Broadwich and see what stage they're at with the investigation and get this evidence to them.'

'Thank God that's over,' said Steve. Morag gave him a hug.

'Do you want to stay here tonight? I can move Rory out of his bedroom and you can sleep there.'

'Thanks, but no. I'll go home. I feel better now. It's not as though anybody has been inside the house. It's only a letter they've sent.'

'I'm going to put the ten o'clock news on,' said Willie. 'Let's see what else is happening in the world.'

'The first case of Foot and Mouth Disease to be diagnosed on mainland Britain since 1967 was confirmed today at an abattoir in Northampton,' said the newscaster. 'The government's Principal Veterinary Officer told our reporter that it wasn't known where the disease had come from but that Ministry of Rural Affairs vets were visiting several pig farms that were known to have sent pigs to the abattoir during the last week. Our agricultural correspondent Cameron Mason, has sent us this report.

'Oh shit,' said Steve. 'Just what we didn't need. I bet Bluster is in his element.'

'... restrictions have been placed on an area of approximately 10 kilometres radius around the abattoir and Ministry vets will be visiting farms in this area at the earliest opportunity. It's hoped that the outbreak will be brought quickly under control and in the meantime farmers are advised to be vigilant and report any suspicious signs of disease to their Divisional Animal Health Office. This is Cameron Mason....'

'Looks like we'll be heading back down south then,' said Willie, giving Morag's hand a squeeze. 'Just when you thought you were going to have to put up with me again for good. What do you say lass?'

Morag simply smiled back at him and Steve sat and looked at them. What luck to have a wife like Morag. A tinge of envy, his cynicism weakened.

'No doubt Bluster will be on the phone first thing tomorrow,' said Steve. 'Dusting off the contingency plans and the official name badges. His wife's probably already pressing his best suit in case the TV cameras are around. Thanks for dinner Morag... and for the company.' He kissed her on the cheek. 'See you at the office tomorrow Willie.'

'Aye you're right,' said Willie laughing.

Steve let himself into the cottage. It had taken time to learn to be alone again. And always waking in the morning had been the worse. For months and years as his body stirred he reached out and searched for Rachel's warm soft presence. Her shoulder, her thigh, the gentle wisp of pubic hair, her breasts, her face, the curve of her buttocks, the concavity of her arched back. His hand would move and then search blindly, frantic, frenzied, always finding a cold smooth mattress, no comfort there. Then the aching inside would come. The twisting tearing knife, always to hand, cutting and gouging his insides until he was forced to get out of bed and take a hot shower to warm his soul.

It had taken time, so much time that he thought it would never pass. Never thought he would wake again in peace or murmur the name of one that was loved as she. The scar, tight and twisted, pulling him out of symmetry, out of balance like a mistimed engine. Sometimes at night he would cry her name out loud, waking himself in excitement and expectation that she were there, looking at him through her moist blue eyes just inches from his. He would search for them in the dark, straining his eyes as his pupils enlarged but always it was the same, an unruffled pillow by the side of his; a flat sea of undisturbed quilt. Then he would lay in the dark and go over it in his mind, carefully and painstakingly dissecting out the tiniest detail, teasing it free from the confused whole, to unravel the route of every beginning and trace it to its end. By that process his understanding grew but in time it was altered by perception, changing softly and gently with each retelling like a legend passed down through generations and over centuries. Perceptions became truths, and truths faded into recesses of the conscious mind that were seldom visited and searched. History rewritten. One person's truth, another's misrepresentation.

He was not ready for bed. The events of the evening had strengthened his spirit. He went to the cupboard and took out a box folder. He sat down next to the Rayburn, the warmth was comforting and gave him courage. The lamp on the wall cast an intimate pink-laced light. He opened the folder and saw that his hands were steady, untrembling.

A heap of letters in pale mauve envelopes, cards with hearts and furry animals. He caught his breath, like a child opening a packet of brightly coloured, cheap imitation jewellery. Nothing more than that he told himself. No gold or diamonds, just base metal and plastic thoughts. He took out a letter written in blue ink, a slight smell of perfume still; nostalgia forced a smile, of fond memories and bitter sadness.

Dear Steve,
I cannot start to tell you how much I love you. When I saw you again on Saturday I just knew and I can't believe I ever let you go in the first place. You're so big and kind and I just know I want to spend the rest of my life with you. I know this thing is going to grow and grow.
If you can't feel like that about me I want you to tell me now. It would hurt me badly but I couldn't bear to be given some hope and then be let down. Please don't string me along Sunshine.
I love you forever,
Rachel, XXXXXXXXXXXXXXXXXXXXXXXXXXXXXXXXXXXXXXXXXX

He grinned to himself and read it again. Straight to the point. When she wanted something she went for it. No hanging back. He found another, dated two weeks later.

Dear Steve,
I can't wait to see you at the weekend, I have been thinking about you all day every day, I can't concentrate on my work. When I read your letter I just couldn't believe you felt the same way about me. I can't believe how lucky I am having someone like you. You make me feel warm and safe inside, like I could

tackle anything if you were there to help me.

I keep thinking this is all some weird dream, like it's not happening to me. Please tell me it isn't. I am very jealous of you know who but I know I've no right to tell you to ditch her. I will just have to let you decide what to do because I can't risk losing you.
Loving you more and more for always,
Rachel, XXXXXXXXXXXXXXXXXXXXXXXXXXXXXXXXXXXX

Steve laughed out loud. He remembered it vividly.

He was going out with Tanya and Rachel came back to college to see The Final Year Variety Show. He saw her from the stage, down near the front, laughing and smiling at him.

Later at the party Rachel pursued him on the dance floor. He feigned indifference, to protect himself. He would not encourage her and let her tread on him again. Press him down into the mud with her heel from where he had only just emerged. And he liked Tanya. Lean and lithe and muscular; a cat. Articulate and witty. He would not push her away; discard her like unwanted baggage.

But Rachel persisted. She was there at every dance, holding him tight against her, head on his neck and shoulders whilst he touched her hardly at all, his hands resting only lightly on her waist. Tanya left early and Rachel seized her chance, using it with consummate skill. As the night closed in she danced a final dance with him, closer than ever before, pushed tight against his body, her mouth pressed up against his ear.

And then the cruellest blow.

'I love you,' she whispered.

It was a whip cracking, a flash of white lightning lighting up a sky of sombre grey; a heart stopping, gut wrenching, life changing statement. The hot sharp burst of arousal jarred his body at the words, appearing from nowhere, never expected, never imagined; flying from infinity to make their devastating impact on his world. Three words whispered in his ear late one November Saturday night. Whispered with passion, in earnest, amongst tears and caressing hands that clasped him to a body that melted and metamorphosed to the shape and feel of a woman helplessly in love.

And then he moved his hands from her waist and lifted them to her shoulders and covered the bare skin and bones with the flat of his hands and pulled her gently towards him, yet with force and he felt her shake with her sobbing and he knew that his feelings for her were the same as ever only he could not let her know that she had won so easily this game she played so he said nothing in return.

And later when he lay in bed in wonder and amazement at what had happened there came a knock to his door and it was her. Tear stained cheeks and soft smile of guilt that she had left her boyfriend to wonder where she was and walk the corridors of the Hall of Residence to look for traces that she had passed that way.

'Can I come in Steve?' she asked and he returned to his bed without a word and she locked the door and slipped in bed by his side as if she had never been away, working her magic and charms with honey and the smell of salt spray burnt by midday sun; coconuts and ripe mangoes; a dash of tequila and lime; fresh oysters sprinkled with the hot delicious scent of cayenne pepper.

The smell and the taste of her were paradise remembered from his childhood. Of warmth and comfort. Loveliness and love. Of Christmas and birthdays, Easter and summer holidays; scooped up in his mother's or father's arms on coaches and trains; with his brothers and sisters playing on the beach and swimming in the sea; fishing for crabs and small fishes in the rock pools.

And paradise from his adolescence; moist sloppy kisses and satin smooth skin. Of folds and creases and the smell of musk and petuli oil; darkened rooms and the warm scent of bras.

A third paradise still from that summer term nearly eighteen months previously. Of manhood and fulfilment. Of finding that which he had sought. Beauty and friendship. A love hot with passion, molten metal, white with intensity, flowing and solidifying. Soft and tender too. As a butterfly landing on a flower to sip the sweet nectar, drunk with the loveliness of the taste and texture, the bright colours and the delicate aroma. The best paradise of all.

He picked up another letter.

Dear Steve,
Every day I need you more and more. You are the best thing that has ever happened to me. When I'm with you I'm so strong and confident. Without you I'm small and insignificant. I just wish I could be with you all the time. I could do anything then.

Sometimes at night I sit in bed and think of you. Imagine

you're here with me and I can't stop smiling. Is that stupid or do you know what I mean?'

He searched through the box, opening the Valentine cards and reading them silently to himself. Here was one from him to her, a big soppy puppy on the front with a licky tongue and heart around its neck.

'To my Darling Rachel,' it said. **'Loving you always and forever.'** Hardly original but heartfelt at least.

He opened the door to the Rayburn and laid the card on top of the glowing coals. Hot flames appeared, magically conjured up by the chemistry of combustion. The puppy shrivelled and twisted, the heart split in two, an acrid smelling smoke reached his nostrils.

'I should have done this years ago,' he said to himself as one by one he floated each card, each letter and envelope into the orange flames, watching as the flames turned them to a thin, crisp sculpture, and then to dust. Ashes to ashes, dust to dust, it was a funeral of sorts, the burning of a life lived long ago and long since passed. And with each letter that burned he felt a pulse of energy. A pulse that gave him hope and joy and chased away the background bitterness that like a clinging fog had smothered him too long. He felt younger, a heavy, forcing weight lifted clear. He was almost at the bottom of the box when he found the photograph. A photograph of Rachel and him, arms around each other's shoulders, laughing. Was I ever that young? he thought to himself. Was Rachel ever that young? He hesitated. Perhaps he should keep it for old time's sake. Not to look at; a memento; a reminder of his former life. He held it gently in his fingers, twisting it in the dim light, watching the flames reflected from the surface. Warm sweat stained nights in cotton sheets; thick blue tinged snow in drifts that kept them in their wind whipped home. Standing on the doorstep with water dripping from his hair, his face cracked with pain and confusion. Rachel laughing at him through eyes of malicious pity. He remembered the hard blue grey steel of the shotgun; smooth and cold to the touch; humane in its power. He felt his cheeks wet with tears, salty and tingling.

He took the picture and committed it face up to the flames. His own image quickly burned but Rachel's smiling face, lit by the orange tongue of flame surrounding it shone back at him like an angel with a golden halo. It held his gaze, mesmerised by the image of this beautiful girl burning in the flames. And then the paper crinkled, the face contorted to a cackling witch with hollow eyes that screamed and shouted as her skin melted to leave a heart of blackened stone.

And suddenly; suddenly he felt like a wild bird released from its cage after a lifetime's captivity. He could fly and soar and spin in the wind. He was a salmon rushing upstream against the pounding rapids; leaping the rocks and waterfalls with ease and with grace. He was a cheetah escaped from its Indian Prince, running down the antelope when and where he pleased.

After fifteen years and a million bitter tears, he finally thought he was free.

Chapter 27

'More bloody pigs,' laughed Willie as he and Steve put their boots on at the farm gate.

It was the last Saturday in February and the forecast was for snow. The whole UK livestock industry was paralysed by a ban on livestock movements that had come into force the previous day, three days after Foot and Mouth was confirmed at the abattoir in Northampton. A brave decision by the PVO amidst criticism from many quarters that he had overreacted.

Tracings had pinpointed the source of disease as pigs from Warren Farm, not far from Morton Animal Health Office in the north of England. The farm had sent pigs to the abattoir on the previous Thursday and they had been killed on the Friday. Pigs arriving from the south of England on the Friday had been kept in the abattoir lairage over the weekend and on the following Monday had shown classical signs of Foot and Mouth. EVRI, the Exotic Viruses Research Institute, a world reference laboratory for FMD had typed it as the highly virulent Pan Asia strain that had devastated livestock in a number of countries in the world in the last few years. Taiwan, Japan, South Africa, all had been badly affected with millions of livestock slaughtered costing billions of pounds.

FMD control could follow one of two main strategies. The first was 'Stamping out', the slaughter of infected and exposed animals, depriving the virus of its lifeblood. The alternative was vaccination, seen by many as causing more problems than it solved. Vaccinated animals might carry the virus, and blood tests to distinguish between them and animals that had had natural infection weren't yet internationally recognised. The problem, went the argument, was that you couldn't then tell where the virus was.

During the 1980s most of continental Europe had relied on regular vaccination to keep the disease at bay. Then in the early nineties Britain had persuaded the European Union to change to a Stamping out policy and vaccination was banned. The whole ruminant population of Europe was now a tinder box awaiting the spark of FMD.

On the day after confirmation of the disease at Warren Farm, the e-mailed requests to Divisional Animal Health Offices to provide names of persons willing to travel to Morton caught the attention and imagination of Herbert Bluster. Willie, Steve and Sammy were all anxious to go. Foot and Mouth was the big one, la crème de la crème. The one that spread like wildfire and caused fear and panic throughout the livestock industries of the developed world. Huge herds and flocks of cattle, pigs and sheep, all with complete vulnerability to attack from the virus. It was the disease equivalent of dry brushwood waiting for the virological spark. And now that the spark had lit the fire, there was no telling where the flames would spread.

But Willie was upbeat that Saturday morning as he took out the needles and blood tubes. They had sorted Swine Fever; they would sort this too. He looked around the entrance to Warren Farm, there was filth everywhere. A fifteen foot mountain of rotting compost sat in the yard. Wisps of smoke rose from three or four places on its slopes, like fumaroles on the side of an awakening volcano. Half a dozen moth-eaten rats scratched at the surface for food.

An old portacabin raised on blocks of wood stood to one side, the paint long since disintegrated, the wood damp and soft, rotting where it sat. A set of metal steps, black and grease covered, rose to the door that was a mass of muddy dog footprints and scratch marks. The whining and yapping of dogs from inside was clearly audible.

Heaps of twisted metal, barbed wire, car tyres and plastic dustbins were strewn around. Paper sacks and polythene wrappers fluttered in the wind, hooked like decorations on a Christmas tree. Crows perched on the roofs, like the black vultures in Mexico thought Steve. The stench of pigs and rotting garbage, grease, foul water, was all around.

'The man likes to keep a tidy place I see,' said Willie.

'That's obviously the way he likes to work,' grinned Steve. But inside he was scared. This was not Swine Fever. Swine Fever would be seen as a picnic compared to this unless they were very lucky. Swine Fever only affected pigs and was mainly spread through the movement of animals. Fomites like infected clothing, machinery and equipment were more easily controlled. Not so with Foot and Mouth. It was widely reported to be the most infectious disease agent known to man. It could spread on the wind, in milk, on the wool of sheep, under people's fingernails, even trapped in a person's throat. And pigs were the worst virus excretors. It was a fact that an infected pig would breathe out up to three thousand times the quantity of virus exhaled by an infected cow. If the disease had been on the farm for a while it did not bode well.

Neil Franks, the guy from epidemiology in Broadwich came around the corner of the portacabin, dressed from head to foot in green plastic waterproofs. There were two other men with him dressed the same, and a rough looking bloke in overalls stained with what looked like vomit, but was probably pig swill. He was fat and gruff; weather beaten broken veined purple face with grey stubble that held further traces of swill.

'I don't know how it's got here,' he said. 'Must have been in the air. The pigs were healthy until a couple of days ago. Big healthy things with fine appetites. They only get the best you know. Chinese restaurants and school meals. If it's good enough for the bairns, it's good enough for the pigs I say.'

No one answered. Neil came over to Steve and shook his hand.

'Good journey down today?' he asked. 'Early start I suppose?'

'You could say that,' said Steve. 'Not much traffic so that was something.'

'This is John Stevens and Anders Thorsen from EVRI. They've come to age the lesions on the pigs as we slaughter them. We want to try and get an idea of how long it's been here. First impression,' he added grimly, 'is that it's been a while.'

'What do you want us to do?' asked Willie.

'Bleed pigs,' said Neil cheerfully. 'You should be good at that after your starring role on Sky TV down in Broadwich. Right up your street isn't it?'

'I...'

'am a shit hot pig bleeder,' cut in Steve. 'Yes we know you are Willie. Are there any others coming to help?'

'Yeah, another couple of teams. We might as well get cracking though, the slaughterers are here already.'

'When will I get paid for the pigs?' asked the farmer. 'It's going to be difficult enough managing without any income coming in. It's not my fault this has happened. Good healthy pigs they were; still are most of them. It's a lot of fuss over nothing. They've just got a touch of cold. They'll be over it in a few days. Fucking Ministry. What do they know about pigs?'

Nobody answered. The Morton staff had warned that he was an awkward bloke. Difficult to deal with. Better to say nothing and just get on with the job in hand.

Neil led the way into one of the sheds and they looked over the gate into a pen. A heap of pigs lay huddled in one corner amidst a sea of liquid dung. The air, rank with ammonia, burnt Steve's nose and throat like smelling salts; stung his eyes. Dim light, the unhealthy stench of putrefaction settled on his hair and uncovered skin, the half eaten carcass of a pig in grotesque pose stared at them through pus streaked eyes.

Neil banged on the door. Hardly a pig moved save for the laboured rise and fall of their chests, the twitching of a leg to ease the discomfort, the occasional straining of an abdomen to void a squirt of liquid dung. By now they should all have been up at the gate, grunting and snuffling, inquisitive like cats; anticipating food and curious at the noise. One managed to raise its head off the floor and then let it flop down again into the filth.

'Look in the trough,' whispered Neil to Steve.

Down one side of the pen was a concrete gutter that served for feeding the swill. In pride of place lay a couple of half eaten newborn piglets, well putrefied, purple and green with decay. They lay amidst a mix of what at first sight appeared to be the contents of a kitchen dustbin. Food scraps mixed with paper serviettes, empty soft drink cans with teeth marks, salamis still in their wrappers, cabbage leaves and potato peelings; a metal knife or fork here and there; plastic cutlery splashed around like currants in a bun; over there a cheap glass salt cellar.

'Not one for cooking his swill then,' said Steve flippantly.

Neil nodded gravely, eyebrows raised above eyes opened wide.

'And where are the piglets from?' Steve went on. 'I thought this was just a fattening place.'

'It is,' said Neil, 'but he buys boars and sows from all over the place too. Keeps them here and fattens them until the price is right and then ships them to the abattoir. And of course in the meantime some of the sows end up in-pig and they just pig down amongst all the others. Most of the piglets get trampled on or eaten. It seems he throws the trampled ones in with the swill for a bit of extra protein. These poor buggers here look too bloody sick to eat though.'

They made their way along the passageway, their eyes becoming accustomed to the darkness and revealing the hitherto unnoticed details of rats sitting in the shadows on the walls, gnawing at the carcass of a dead pig, knives and forks strewn about like confetti, old needles and syringes next to half used bottles of antibiotics. In each pen the pigs were the same, some a little worse, some a little better. In those pens where they were standing they shifted from one leg to another to ease the pain in their feet. Most had crusty, necrotic brown scabs on their snouts and many had yellow, pus filled eyes. And what struck Steve above all else was the silence. Sheds of fattening pigs just shouldn't be that quiet. They were busy, noisy places, full of grunts and snorts and squeals. Dynamic lively places with activity and pink fatness. You would have to be a fool not to know that something was wrong with these pigs. A fool or a liar, thought Steve.

'There're ten pens of about twenty pigs in this shed,' said Neil. 'Two hundred in total. Steve, I want you and Willie to stay here with Anders and supervise the slaughter of this shedful. That's the slaughterman in the doorway over there. Anders is going to age all the lesions and I want you to learn how to do it Steve. This is good veterinary work,' he emphasised the word veterinary. 'Willie, I want you to blood sample as many of the pigs as possible. Red topped tubes, we're checking for antibodies here. We want to know how many have sero-converted, how many have been infected. Label the tubes by pen number so that we get an idea of how it's been spread around the house.

'I'll go and work with John in the next house, and as the other teams arrive they can help out with blood sampling.'

The slaughterers, Frank and Bert were local men who killed pigs with efficiency. Captive bolt for the fatteners and a shotgun for the sows and boars. Frank worked with Anders' group and Steve shadowed Anders.

'This pig has early lesions on the snout and coronary band,' said Anders pointing to the small raised vesicles or blisters. 'Very easily missed if you do not know what it is you are looking for. And then this one here, this is a day later. You can see that the vesicle has ruptured to leave this raw, bright pink ulcerated area beneath it. The fluid in the vesicle is full of virus particles, very infectious.'

He moved on to another dead pig.

'Now, here we can see a three day old lesion. You can see that fibrin is beginning to fill in the ulcerated area and it has turned yellow. It is getting more difficult now to isolate virus from this type of lesion. And this one, look at the snout of this one. Here we have secondary bacterial infection with pus being formed and swelling of the adjoining tissues. This is a typical five day old lesion.'

'What about this?' asked Steve pulling at the foot of another dead pig, the hoof sloughing off in his hand to leave a red raw stump.

'This,' said Anders is probably twelve days old. 'An animal such as this will take many weeks to recover and it would most likely be always crippled.'

They made their way from pen to pen, Frank working calmly and efficiently, Willie collecting the blood, and an Animal Health Officer from Morton recording Anders' findings. The worst affected pigs remained crouched in corners and needed to be pulled out. Some were unable to stand with the pain in their feet, hooves peeling off and swollen infected joints.

'This is fucking disgusting,' said Steve. 'The guy must have known these pigs were sick even if he didn't know why.'

'It is very bad,' agreed Anders. 'The oldest lesions are I think so far 12 days. It is difficult to age them after that because of the secondary infection. But I think 60 to 70 % of the pigs in this shed are infected for sure. The quantities of virus being produced and excreted into the air outside will be very great. I suspect that we will find cases in cattle downwind from here unless we are very lucky.'

Steve nodded. This was what everyone feared. Wind borne spread, particularly from pigs, was well documented. Under the right conditions virus could travel in plumes, like smoke from a bonfire, rising up and along, drifting slowly down, perhaps rising again but maintaining the concentration of infective material. Calm days with the lightest of breezes were the best, you had only to watch the way smoke rising from a chimney on a still November day could creep and spread along a valley bottom, to understand the principle of FMD virus spread in the air. It could travel for tens of miles, like in 1982 when it had crossed from France to the Isle of Wight. That time everyone had known it was coming and Ministry Officials were waiting on the ground for it to descend. The infected herd was quickly killed out and buried, a single outbreak stopped in its tracks by forewarning and prompt, decisive action.

This time was different. This time several hundred pigs had lain sick and dying for perhaps weeks, pumping out the virus with every rise and fall of the chest, filling the shed with infection which seeped out in the air through ventilation shafts and the holes in the roof. Already the virus was out there in the surrounding countryside, a hidden messenger of death without respect or remorse.

The cold ache of disgust settled in Steve's stomach. If the public could see how some of the food on their plates was produced they would never eat meat again, he thought. He stared around him. Rats trod their well worn paths and chewed at the jagged holes in the walls. Pigs lay in comfortless squalor in dimly lit pens full of shit and puddles of stinking putrid water. Grey bubbles of scum floated on the surface and many of the pigs lay half submerged, through indifference or lack of choice. Food troughs full of rubbish so that those still with strength sorted their food like tramps rummaging for a morsel in a bin. Others reduced to cannibalism of the newborn as they emerged from the warmth and shelter of the womb.

Sleeping on cold, wet and filth stained concrete. Huddling together for warmth and what comfort they could glean from each other's touch. And on top of that this plague had descended on them. A plague of high fever and burning, searing pain in their feet that was eased only slightly by lying still and flat on their sides. No warm bed of straw to ease their aching shoulders and bruised joints. No kind words from a concerned owner or the careful, expert ministrations of a caring vet. Ignored in health and in their suffering too, another dustbin of rubbish tipped into their trough in the hope that food would tempt them back to their feet so that they would eat and continue to grow and fatten.

No eat, no weight gain, the farmer concerned only by the loss of income, loss of profit. His pigs were a factory for converting the contents of dustbins into dirt stained paper money. They were low quality pigs; other people's cast-offs, other people's rubbish. Rubbish fed on rubbish and then served up on people's plates as prime British pork. If the consumer could but see where that rasher of bacon or pork chop on their plate had lived its life; where it had lain; the rats that had shared its dinner table; shared its food and water; scampered around its living room and nibbled at the half eaten piglets that lay in the trough with it.

So this was the great, high standard British farming industry. Anger inside him, red and deepest purple. Each pig that lay in the shit was a victim. A victim and a symptom of the disease. Slaughter was a welcome escape from their misery. A welcome, dignified release from the squalid, uncared for life that was theirs. The click and pop of the captive bolt; a number written in the pages of a dirt stained notebook.

Neil came and joined them. 'This is bloody grim,' he said to Steve. 'This guy wants locking up for feeding raw swill and keeping pigs like this. Trading Standards are coming out today to take evidence for a prosecution. Apparently the Morton Animal Health Office knew this guy sailed close to the wind but whenever they visited everything checked out okay. You know what it's like. Trying to catch someone like this red handed and get the right evidence to close them down is a fool's errand. "Disrupting their trade; heavy handed officialdom; Ministry jobsworths." We've heard it all before; everything's stacked against us.'

'There but for the Grace of God .....' said Steve.

'Exactly right lad.'

'Who's in charge of the eradication campaign here?' Steve asked.

'They've brought a DVA up from down south, Colin Hunt. They've installed him at Cardington over in the west. It's bloody miles from here but as you know Morton's just a sub-office of Cardington. They're trying to organise railway sleepers and coal, diggers and everything else we need to get this lot burnt. There's going to be a pyre built in the field out the back, far enough away not to set this lot ablaze.' He raised his eyes upwards to scan round the building. 'Mind you it wouldn't be a bad thing if it did.'

A girl Steve didn't know came in breathless. 'There's a TV van turned up at the gate. Huge great thing with a satellite dish on the roof and about ten different people. They want to come in and film.

171

What do I tell them? It's a public road running almost through the yard out there.'

'Get Colin Hunt on the phone and tell him we need the police here to close the road and stop anyone going up and down it,' said Steve. 'We can't have dozens of people wandering in and out; we'll have disease spread all over the fucking county. And tell the camera crews to sod off.' He laughed. 'I didn't mean to shout at you. I'm Steve Turner, I won't shake your hand, mine's covered in blood and shit.'

The girl smiled. 'No offence taken,' she said.

'Any news of other outbreaks?' Steve said to Neil.

'I've heard there's been four report cases in this area today. One only a couple of miles east of here. Housed cattle showing foaming at the mouth. If that's positive you'd better watch out. Others will follow, I guarantee it.'

'Are they setting up a disease control centre at Morton?'

'Apparently not. They're going to run it all from Cardington. Seems crazy but that's the way Hunt wants it so it's none of our business. It'll end up like Swine Fever though. People miles away trying to make decisions when they've no idea what's happening on the ground.'

The farmer approached them.

'What a fucking mess. Good pigs slaughtered and left to lie in the shit,' he said. 'I hope you lot are going to clear this mess up before you go. And mind you don't damage my buildings, I refurbished them all not long ago.' He glanced around the pens, a gleam of satisfaction in his eyes, black grease trapped in an iron grey stubble, the purple broken veins racing across his nose.

'What a fucking carry on just because the pigs have got a bit of a cold. Blown in on the wind, no doubt about it. What a bloody shame.'

Steve and Neil said nothing.

'Are you going to spend all day talking,' shouted Willie, 'or are we going to crack on and finish these pigs?'

'You heard the boss,' said Neil. 'Get to it.'

Outside, sleet showers drifted in from the west, dampening spirits. Dilapidation and neglect is never pretty. In grey light, furred with droplets of water it takes on a greasy sickening appearance that clings to your hands and clothes, penetrates your nasal passages, the taste of neglect filling your mouth.

Someone set to work organising the contractors to dig a shallow trench in which to build a pyre. The ground was water logged, burial out of the question. Consigning everything to the flames of hell the only option. Straw bales laid end to end in the trench in three rows a foot apart. Railway sleepers laid across the rows and several tons of kindling, broken pallets, stacked on top of them. Next would go the coal, tens of tons spread along the length of the pyre, a black dirty heap like a scar across the grass. Only then could the 560 pigs be loaded before the whole lot was drenched with diesel and the flames started to do their work

As the day stretched out the wind increased its speed; gusting and whining, corrugated iron flapping and jangling its sad sound of neglect. Sleet turned to biting snow, and the bucket of the JCB tore the turf from the sodden field turning it brown and mottled with clay and heavy loam.

All day long a tiny 'Bobcat' tractor worked the passageways inside the sheds, pulling dead pigs out of the buildings and stacking them in the yard where they could be lifted into a green, tip-up trailer ready for transporting to the field. And a hundred yards away the television vans were parked with their long range lenses and satellite dishes to beam the images right around the world as 'breaking news'. Steve stepping outside for a moment to cleanse the air in his lungs saw the apocalypse unfold around him. This was how it would be in the end, he thought.

'Call them and they shall come,' he said to himself as a massive Low-loader crawled up the road with a caterpillar tracked digger on board, closely followed by a twenty ton bulk coal wagon. They tore up the roadside verges, and the mud turned to porridge in the wet and the lorries broke down fences as they tried to turn and dump their loads. Thick brown mud clung to the tyres and in the wheel arches, and squads of people drafted in from the Agriculture department worked with pressure hoses and knapsack sprayers in the chilling wind and wet as they tried to clean and disinfect. Lorries arrived with weeks and months of grease and mud clinging to them like a protective skin, a thick layer of chocolate icing baked hard. All needed to be removed before disinfection could take place. Minute after minute, hour after hour, time marched on, and darkness crept up from the east. Someone had had the foresight to order, big, powerful arc lights that now lit up the farm like a football stadium or concentration camp. Generators hummed, the electrics in the shed unusable and deadly with worn wires and blackened sockets. No one from Health and Safety had yet been near the place and common sense dictated caution. By 7.30 p.m. all the pigs were dead, the pyre half built, and everyone was shagged.

'What about my compensation cheque then? When will that arrive?' said the farmer again, as everyone washed down their overalls to clear away the blood and shit. Their faces and hair were splattered too and in the dark and cold and with the snow flying in their eyes and their hands blue and unresponsive they could not wash them. Everyone ignored his question. It did not merit the respect of an answer.

'I'm leaving someone here overnight to prevent access to the site,' said Neil. 'He's come with sandwiches and a flask and plenty of warm clothes. Tomorrow, another couple are going to supervise the finishing of the pyre and getting it lit. Steve, that suspect case on the farm just east of here has been confirmed. A lot of cattle affected, maybe sheep too. I want you to come there with me tomorrow for eight thirty. Now, let's get to the hotel and clean ourselves up. It's been a long day.'

Chapter 28

Steve awoke early. He had slept well at first but around five in the morning he knew that he was permanently awake. He switched on the bedside lamp and filled the kettle from the bathroom tap. A nice cup of tea was needed.

The room was large and rectangular. Flat walls painted in flat pale colours, a huge mirror with chrome studs reflected the chipboard furniture that filled the room. It was ultra modern, designed for practicality, mass produced so that all the rooms in the chain would be the same, whether it were Morton, London, or Edinburgh. A formula that made money by giving business clients a clean, satisfactory stay for the night with decent food and not a lot else. A world of anonymous people in anonymous hotels.

The first sip of tea was always the best. Like a smoker's first drag on the first cigarette, it kicked in and sharpened his mind. He turned the telly on, Sky News at six. The images of the pig farm stared back at him; a coal lorry arriving and dumping its load in the yard; a JCB working in the field behind the sheds; there was Neil walking from one building to another amidst the falling snow. It was real; not a dream after all.

Then an interview with Ron Steady who looked calm and composed. Yes it was a cause for concern but so far the outbreak had been limited to six cases, four down in Northampton and two up in the north. He was confident that his staff had the situation under control and that movement restrictions would limit the spread of disease. Of course it was distressing for those farmers involved but it was essential to stamp out the disease rapidly so that our lamb export trade to Europe could resume at the earliest opportunity. There was certainly no need to panic.

And then the Minister for Rural Affairs and he too was confident. The PVO would have all the assistance and resources required to get the job done. He understood farmers' concerns about their inability to move livestock but it was essential to prevent the further spread of disease so that it could be quickly eradicated.

Steve sipped his tea. He didn't know if Ron was right or not. There was bound to be significant lateral spread from the pig farm, thought Steve. Already it had reached the cattle he was going to later that morning. There would be others too. If they could get weather reports for the last three weeks they might get an idea which farms were at most risk.

In the bar last night Anders and John Stevens had reckoned that clinical disease had been present on the farm for up to three weeks. Fortunately all the pigs that left during that period had gone directly to slaughter so it was wind borne spread and spread by the farmer travelling around that was the concern. Everyone was hopeful that a lid could be kept on the thing.

Where had it come from? The untreated swill was self-incriminating. There were rumours of illegal meat from Chinese takeaways, even collecting ship's waste from the docks. But rumours were all they were. The atmosphere in the bar had been subdued. Anyone expecting to carry on from where Swine Fever left off was disappointed. Most recognised that this was a different disease with a potentially quite different scenario.

And yesterday evening Steve had been delighted to find that Fernando had arrived from Gloucester during the day. Neil had suggested that he could come to the farm with them today to supervise the slaughter, leaving Neil and Steve to help Anders and John age the lesions. Fernando was excited. Young and full of enthusiasm, raring to go.

Steve poured himself another cup of tea. They were interviewing the leader of the Farmers Club now. He stressed the importance of cracking down on the disease, getting rid of it, and above all finding out where it had come from. His members must not be allowed to suffer further. Farming had been through a difficult period with BSE and Swine Fever. Many farmers felt they were just starting to emerge from a crisis period and now this had thrown them right back on their heels. Movement restrictions, though important, had to be relaxed at the earliest opportunity. For many people lambing was underway or imminent, and ewes were in desperate need of being moved to the home farm and to the lambing sheds. Compensation levels must be adequate. No expense should be spared to regain the UK's disease free status.

Steve took another shower, he knew he still smelt of pigs. His clothes from yesterday were filthy and stinking in spite of the waterproofs, covered in virus. How long it lasted on clothing he didn't know. It would be temperature and humidity dependent that was certain, but whether it was hours, days or weeks, he had no idea. He'd tried to organise his room into a clean and dirty area. All clothes worn on farm were going into a plastic bin bag in an alcove just inside the door. Everything else was in a wardrobe and chest of drawers. It wasn't perfect but it was the best he could think of. Hopefully they could just use the hotel laundry service and get it put on the Ministry's bill.

It was a quarter to seven when he emerged from the shower. Live pictures of a lit up Warren Farm were on the telly and the reporter was suggesting that the fire would be set some time later that day. They would of course keep viewers updated with developments as they unfolded.

Steve met Neil, Fernando, Willie and a crowd of others in the dining room at seven thirty. There was a gentle buzz of anticipation, excitement even as they crowded round the breakfast table. No one except those at Warren Farm the previous day had seen FMD. Faces were a mix of daring do and apprehension. Animal Health Officer Joe Stubbs, veteran of Swine Fever, Sheep Scab and Swine Vesicular

Disease, had been a young man during the '67 outbreak and just missed out on it. He'd been with the Ministry for 33 years and worked with good, bad and indifferent vets.

'This is what the Veterinary Service is all about,' he said. 'This is our raison d'être. Forget the bullshit. This is where the real work starts.' He rubbed his hands. With glee. With expectation. With a calm self-belief.

It contrasted with the uncertainty in Steve's mind. Not knowing where they were heading in the next few weeks, a chill inside like watching a horror film, expecting to be scared but still being surprised when it happened. Something in his mind niggled. A preoccupation. A sense of foreboding. Like when Paul was murdered. Like when the letter arrived the other day. There was an underlying current of evil; doors closing shut, bolts pushed home; curtains being drawn; a man putting on gloves and taking out a piece of stout rope with a slip knot in one end; no route of escape. A cold wind blew inside him from an unknown source; the coldness down his spine as he drank his coffee black. The cold outside was nothing to this; this was a chilling cold that numbed his spirit, caressing him gently with an icy breath, engulfing him with a black, tearful menace. He shivered. Hugely and involuntarily.

'Cold already lad?' said Neil. 'Wait till you're out there in the wind and the snow.' He nodded at the dingy grey sky beyond the smoked glass of the restaurant windows.

'You're a cheerful bugger,' said Steve. The coldness had gone the instant Neil spoke. 'What's the plan today then?'

'We're meeting Frank and Bert at the farm at eight thirty. They can start shooting the cattle and Anders and John can age the lesions with you and me looking over their shoulders. I've got a copy of the vet's preliminary report. 16 sheep left the farm ten or twelve days ago for the local market. Those were the only movements in the last six weeks. Hopefully that was before FMD got onto the farm and hopefully they went for slaughter. Tracings section at Cardington are already trying to track their whereabouts so that we can get them examined and blood tested if they're still alive. Right, let's get going shall we?'

It was ten minutes to Round Hill Farm. Owned by Phil Nelson and farmed in partnership with his young nephew Bobby, it was a mixed beef and sheep farm of 280 acres. All the 220 cattle were housed, the four hundred sheep at pasture.

Phil Nelson was waiting at the gate, leaning on his stick, sombre but resigned to the day's work ahead. Most of the cattle were commercial crossbred sucklers but there were 53 pedigree Angus too. Amongst them were three stock bulls and another six bulls about a year old. Phil had bred Angus for 25 years; they did well at the shows and sold for big money. Steve watched Phil Nelson's face as he pulled his boots on. It showed little emotion but the lips moved occasionally as though he were talking to himself.

'Perhaps we could go and see the handling facilities and then Frank and Bert can organise how they want to slaughter the cattle,' Neil said. 'We'll do the cattle first and if in the meantime you could bring the sheep in from the fields in their various lots, Willie here can make a start on blood sampling them.'

'Tell me about the 16 sheep that went to market,' Steve said.

Bobby Nelson answered him.

'It was 16 cast ewes, nine mules and seven Suffolks. They went a week ago last Tuesday.'

'Which fields had they been in before they went?' Steve asked.

'The Suffolks were in the little field behind the cattle sheds. The mules were three fields away, in the direction of that bastard with the pigs,' he pointed over the top of the cattle sheds towards Warren Farm.

'Any lameness or sickness in the sheep?' Steve asked gently. He saw the wide eyed hollow look in the man's face, the darkness around his eyes and the trembling lips.

'Virtually all the Suffolks had an attack of foot rot a few days before we sent them. We put them through a formalin footbath and they were better within a couple of days.'

Steve glanced at Neil who raised his eyebrows. Just let's pray it was foot rot, thought Steve. Otherwise we could all be in the shit.

'Let's have a look at the affected cattle can we?' said Neil, and Bobby Nelson led them across the yard towards the cattle shed. Steve saw Phil Nelson wiping moisture from his eyes with the back of his hand before turning towards the house.

'Phil's going to stay in the house until it's all over,' said Bobby.

'You can too if you want,' said Steve, neither bullying or condescending. 'Whatever you feel comfortable with.'

'I want to see that it's done right,' said Bobby, 'but thanks anyway.' He turned away, voice trembling.

They walked down a central passageway in a well built and well ventilated open span cattle shed. The first pen held young Charolais cross fattening cattle, knee deep in golden orange straw. From deep grey to almost white in colour, heavily muscled bodies weighing between 450 and 500 kilos. This was the other side of the farming coin to Warren Farm's pigs; beautiful, high quality animals kept in near perfect conditions by a dedicated stockman. They stared warily at the parade of green plastic clad Ministry men leaning against the metal feed barrier. A few tossed their heads gently, more in play than in threat. Others stood passively chewing their cud. A casual observer would have pronounced them a fit, healthy bunch of cattle, no lameness, no drooling.

'Look at the froth around the muzzle of that one,' said Neil pointing, 'and the one behind it.'

A white sticky froth lined the top and bottom lips of both the bullocks. One of them stuck out its tongue to lick the froth away and a red ulcer the size of a fifty pence piece glistened.

'They're not lame,' said Steve. 'I expected to see them hobbling, like the pigs yesterday.'

'It varies very much,' said Anders. 'Fit, young, healthy cattle like these, well fed and with a good immune system, will often show little sign of disease. But breeding cattle, well, you can get abortions; sudden death in the young calves; and the cows can sometimes be very sick, drooling and lame with high fevers. It can be the same picture in sheep, the lambing ewes, under more stress, are the worst affected.'

They moved along to the next pen, this time cows and calves. As if to illustrate Anders' point a deep grey coloured cow stood in a corner alone, ears drooping and saliva pouring from her mouth. Bobby Nelson went into the pen and made her move, she was sore on all four legs.

'This is the one we noticed first,' he said, 'early yesterday morning. Since then we've been looking more closely and it's obvious once you know what to look for. We reckon that about 30% are affected. It must have been here a while without us noticing mustn't it?'

'We'll know more once we've examined all the mouths and aged the lesions,' said Neil. 'It's not something you'd have been expecting to see,' he added kindly. 'Lets take a look at your handling pens and crush?'

They continued on through the shed, and in every pen there were animals with white foam round their lips. He's right, thought Steve. This has been here a while.

The handling pens were outside, sleet falling in a biting north easterly wind from the North Sea. The north east in February, he thought. It brought back memories of driving snow and early morning dashes to work.

Mad dashes of panic across open moorland where the snow lay in drifts and walls across the narrow paved road, visibility of just a few yards when the squalls blew in. Grey skies almost black and purple with malice, like a bruise on the mind or soul. Fear of being stuck, the frantic shovelling of snow from beneath the wheels and sills, frenetic in speed, manic in intensity, strength dragged up through worry and fear; always fighting the clock to arrive at work on time. Shouting and screaming, shoulder pushed against the sheet metal with spinning wheels and cries and straining biceps as he tried to lift the car free; roaring like a gladiator as though his life hung in the balance.

'Not so much accelerator,' he screamed at Rachel. 'Gently, you'll dig in deeper. Gently, gently, STOP.' Shouted out loud, absorbed by the falling and fallen snow. Sheep huddled together in snow covered fleeces, hunger on hunger until the spring, for those that survived. Others reduced to papier mache that dissolved and washed away into the peaty soils to leave a pile of yellow sodden bones for the foxes and sheep dogs to chew on.

'It will be awful slow doing them through the crush,' said Frank. 'Each one'll have to be dragged out before we could put the next one in. How about if we shut ten or a dozen of them into one of these square pens and then drop them all before we pith them? Then the whole lot can be dragged out together and we can fill the pen again.'

'Could you reach them all leaning over the pen sides?' said Steve. 'We don't want a heap of half stunned animals on the floor with a couple of awkward ones leaping about on top of them. Until they're pithed some of them could wake up again don't forget.'

'They'll not wake up again once I've hit them with the Cow Puncher,' said Bert patting the gun metal of the cylindrical captive bolt he held. 'Not using purple cartridges anyway.' He smiled, not unkindly or savagely but with a hint of cocksure confidence.

'We'll try it your way,' said Neil. 'Where can we store the carcasses until we get the fire built?'

'I can drag them into the central passageway of the shed,' said Bobby. 'I can stack them two or three high with the Teleporter if we need to.'

'Okay,' said Neil. 'Off we go then.'

Bobby opened up one of the side gates and let thirteen, fifteen month old bullocks out onto the concrete yard. They jumped and skipped, made mock charges, slipped and skidded on the wet concrete. Excited by the change of routine and surroundings but with no fear. They were herded with ease into the galvanised tubing pen and the gate was swung round and bolted shut.

Then Frank and Bert went to work. Standing on rungs half way up the pen sides they leant over with their captive bolts poised. Frank's Cash Special was the traditional gun shape with trigger mechanism. The muzzle needed to be placed against the bullocks skull, more or less in the centre, a little higher than the point of intersection of lines drawn from each eye to the opposite ear. When the trigger was pulled, a cylindrical bolt shot out, hitting the skull a concussive blow and boring a hole through into the brain from where the bolt would be instantly withdrawn back into the pistol. The Cow Puncher worked on the same principle but was simply a metal cylinder in which the bolt was housed. Banging one end of the cylinder against the bullock's skull caused instantaneous firing of the bolt. In both cases it was the concussion produced by the bolt hitting the skull that stunned the animal, not the hole that was made into the brain. Most cattle shot with a captive bolt stop breathing and quickly die as a result, but some begin to breathe again after a minute or two and even get to their feet and recover.

To stop that happening, they must be pithed by inserting a flexible metal or synthetic polymer rod through the hole in the skull. This rod is then pushed backwards through the brain and out the hole at the back of the skull, straight down the spinal cord, destroying the central nervous tissue and killing the animal.

Steve had seen plenty of cattle shot in abattoirs. One at a time in a stunning crate, then rolled out and pithed, hung up and bled before being skinned and dressed to produce meat. There was a hint of brutality about it but it was clinical with the clear objective of turning a live animal into healthy, wholesome food. But that experience could not prepare him for the shocking violence of the mass slaughter of cattle on-farm. They were such huge beasts. So tall and strong and solid. So alive. When they fell they fell with a clatter and a thud that made the ground shake. The first two went down together, one each from the bolts of Frank and Bert. The sound of a half ton animal hitting concrete, thud, thud, like a distant explosion. Hind legs drawn tightly up towards the belly, eyes staring fixed straight ahead, no breathing; a perfect stun. The bolts reloaded. Click, click--- thud clatter, thud clatter. Click, thud clatter; click, thud clatter clang. A bullock bellowed, tongue protruding, eyes bulging.

'Keep your head still you cunt.' Click, thud clatter.

Within a few minutes the pen was full of steaming bodies, lying on top of each other, tongues lolling, blood oozing from the holes in their skulls, the occasional lazy reflex kick of a hind leg, dangerous if it hit you, full of power with sharp hooves like knives.

'You must pith them now,' said Fernando. 'As quickly as possible please.'

The gates were thrown open and an off white polymer pithing rod was threaded through the hole in the skull of the nearest beast. It was pushed home with brutal force, two feet, three feet, four feet, through the brain and down the spinal cord with a rapid backwards and forwards movement like sweeping a chimney. The stimulation of the nervous tissue made the animal throw its head around, smacking off the concrete with a sickening crack; kicking out with its hind legs, banging the metal tubing of the pens with a ringing clang.

'Don't get yourselves killed,' said Steve as Bert clambered over the top of the bodies to release another bullock's head and push the pithing rod home.

'There is a bullock here breathing again and starting to move its eyes,' said Fernando. 'Please shoot it again Frank.'

Frank was there immediately, click, the animal jumped a fraction and the breathing stopped again. Rough and ready they might be but they were anxious to please. Perhaps they had the foresight to see into the future. To see the treasure trove of government money that was even now being slowly opened up for them. X marked the spot. Just between the eyes and ears in the centre of the head. Every X with a little piece of gold hidden carefully behind it.

The pithing rods were now being used with speed; in, out; in, out; backwards and forwards like the connecting rods on the wheels of a steam engine, pulled out with a flourish and a snap, a whip cracking so that blood and brain tissue spattered across the yard. More brain dribbled out of the holes in their heads, creamy white, the consistency of Greek yoghurt. Everyone stood and watched with the pretended air of detachment until all thirteen bullocks had kicked and thrashed and Frank and Bert had completed their work.

Then Bobby Nelson went to get his tractor and Anders and John began their examination with Steve, Neil, and Fernando watching carefully over their shoulders. The first bullock's mouth was clean. The second's was not.

'Look now at this,' said Anders excitedly. There was a minimum of white froth around the lips and when he opened the mouth and pulled out the tongue, a large raised vesicle, two inches long by an inch wide stared at them. He poked it gently leaving a depression which slowly disappeared. Then, to demonstrate, he rubbed his thumb firmly along the tongue and the surface of the vesicle peeled away with an escape of clear fluid to reveal a raw pink ulcer.

'This is a typical one day old lesion,' he said. 'Almost ready to rupture and it broke easily when I rubbed my thumb against it. The fluid that escaped is highly infectious and if we take a piece of the ruptured epithelium into transport media we will find lots of virus attached to that in the laboratory. You can see here too,' he pointed to the upper jaw, 'that on the dental pad we have newly ruptured vesicles. These rupture sooner than those on the tongue because the bottom teeth are biting against the dental pad and cause the vesicle to burst. This animal is highly infectious.

'Now look between the hoofs. Again we can see unruptured vesicles and I can very easily pull the epithelium away to reveal that it is fluid filled. The same on the back of the heel here. This is a very typical case,' he beamed round with satisfaction.

They moved on to another bullock as Bobby Nelson hitched a chain round the neck of the first beast and dragged it away across the yard, the sound of hooves scraping against concrete. There was something comical about this huge animal being dragged along the floor and through the shit, its neck stretched tight, tongue flopping and eyes staring straight ahead, green rumen contents running down its nose, a lump of congealed blood mixed with brain on its forehead. On into the passageway in front of its cohorts who looked on with indifference.

By the time they had been through the whole batch the oldest lesion they had found was five days. With an incubation period of from two to twelve days, the virus could have been around for up to 17 days and a minimum of seven. Things did not look good, thought Steve.

As soon as the last carcass was dragged away another fourteen bullocks were let out and herded into the killing pen. AHO Joe Stubbs was enjoying himself, moving about like a man with a mission. 'Shooshing' cattle one minute, talking into his mobile excitedly the next.

'This beats pissing about collecting samples at feed mills,' he said to Steve. 'And you know what, there're some people moaning about having to come away on detached duty so soon after Swine Fever. Bloody whingers. This is what they're paid for; what we're all paid for. I'm only too pleased to be getting stuck in. This will do The Service a power of bloody good you know. We can show people what we're here for instead of all this pissing about stuff. Do a good job and this'll make the GVS,' he smiled and 'shooshed' at a wayward bullock that had trotted his way.

Steve nodded. Uncertainly. This wasn't why he'd joined the Ministry. He'd joined for an easier life than being in practice, not because he had a burning desire to defend the country against exotic disease. It struck him suddenly that he was a fraud.

Within minutes the next fourteen beasts were reduced to a heap of steaming, hide covered, waste meat. Heads and legs lay intertwined, the slaughterers clambering in amongst the sporadically kicking corpses to set to work with their pithing rods, back and forth; pulling on legs and tails to move a carcass to gain access to the head of another. Soon there was shit and blood everywhere, and the sleet turned to snow, blowing in cold, stinging cheeks and foreheads, hands turning blue and purple, fingers numb, stiff and powerless.

Another penful dragged away and stacked under cover in the passageway. Another gang of eager young bullocks herded into the killing pen and the clicks and thuds could start over again.

'Click,' the bullock moved its head at the moment Frank squeezed the trigger. It did not fall with a thud. It stood and looked ahead, a small trickle of blood oozing from a hole too low down its face.

'Fuck it,' said Frank, his cold fingers working as quickly as they could to reload. 'Stand still now you bastard,' he said, not with malice, more by way of explanation or wishing out loud. The bullock tossed its head as though bothered by a fly, a trickle of shining red blood dripped out of its left nostril and onto the floor. Frank inched along the side of the pen towards it but it moved away, alert now to something amiss. It stumbled on the bodies of some of those already fallen, dropping to its knees, not with weakness but with resigned acceptance.

Steve watched, helpless, lips pursed, hands held open and apart as though trying to steady it with telepathy. It was all he could do, concentrate his thoughts on the beast, wish it to remain still.

Bert dispatched the other two in the pen that were still on their feet and Frank climbed into the pen, leaning out and holding on to the bars with one hand, trying to reach the head of the bullock that rested its front half on the carcasses beneath, its rear end raised in the air. It tossed its head again, struggled forward and collapsed onto its chest, its legs trapped between the bodies of already fallen animals.

'Give me the Cow Puncher,' Frank called to Bert. It was a better shape to use than the Cash and a hit on the head would set it off at the point of impact. The beast continued moving its head, eyes rolling now with apprehension.

'Steady, steady, steady,' Frank murmured. 'Steeeaaady, steady…' The beast lurched forward again, all its weight momentarily on its neck, forehead exposed. A thrust of the arm,… click … and it was still.

'Open the gates immediately, we must get them pithed,' yelled Fernando. 'There are two breathing, shoot them again, quickly,' his voice was urgent as one of them struggled to regain its feet, trapped by the weight of others on top of it.

In seconds they were both stunned again and the pithing could start. And so it went on. Animal after animal, pen after pen, click after click, thud after thud. Two hours into the job a white transit van with a satellite dish on the roof pulled off the road a hundred yards away across the field from where they were working. It had a clear view of the yard though not the killing pens, through a small gap between the corners of the stone buildings, and soon a long lens camera could be seen pointing at them.

'Look at those bastards,' said Joe his face twisted like a snarling dog's, an excitable note in his voice. 'Scavengers and vultures the lot of them. Come on, let's block this gap off with a sheet of that old corrugated iron over there.'

He moved quickly for a man of his size, talking all the while.

'Come on, we'll stop their bloody game,' he ordered a couple of onlookers. Let's get this up over here and wedge it with that tractor.'

The sheet of rusty metal caught in the wind as he stood it on its end, bending and twisting, he wrestled to control it and the wind joined in the game, blowing in fierce gusts and then relaxing.

Steve watched them struggling with passive contempt, marvelling at the futility. Did they really think they could remove this thing from the world's gaze with a single sheet of scrap corrugated iron? It was already too big for that. And knowing now about the sheep movements there was no telling what was round the corner. They were sitting near the summit of a smoking volcano; taking notes and scientific measurements and trying to predict when and where it would erupt. It was an imprecise science, just as those working on the Galeras volcano in Colombia had discovered in 1993.

Yes, he thought. This is our Galeras, ready and waiting to erupt, to spread its death and destruction into the air and leave us helpless in its wake. He looked around with a degree of understanding and with a sense of sympathetic camaraderie. He knew how the government and those above him worked. Already as he and the likes of him were at work on the ground, the Teflon men in charge would be putting plans into operation to cover their own backs and ensure that the shit did not stick to them. Those on the front line would take the blame if things did not go well, those up top the credit if all went splendidly. He sighed. Even if we survive the eruption, he thought, many of us will be caught in the pyroclastic flow.

The afternoon came and dragged on and now only the three stock bulls remained. Big Angus bulls, weighing over a ton each, muscles rippling down their body like weight lifters or body builders; huge granite heads held low pointing at the ground; tiny bulging eyes that looked from beneath a bony brow with a transfixing glare. They walked with deliberation, massive shoulders straining with power and strength, necks arched, a great curve of muscle and ligament that supported the heavy bone laden head. Steam came in bursts from their flared nostrils, the sound of a whale exhaling through its blow hole. The hind quarters, a mountain of flesh and curves; an Adonis.

Everyone knew they must be treated with respect. Firm but sympathetic handling was needed, keep them quiet so that the adrenaline was not released. They were guided into the pen.

'These are big cunts,' said Frank. He took the Cash and loaded it with a purple tipped cartridge. 'This should do the trick though,' he said. His hand and gun were tiny against the forehead of the nearest bull. He pushed the Cash firmly against the skull and pulled the trigger. 'Click,' nothing happened. The bull didn't move. He reloaded and pushed the muzzle of the pistol harder against the skull. Again a click and this time a mild shake of the head and an eruption of damp steam.

He took the Cow Puncher from Bert and loaded that with another purple cartridge. He banged it on the bull's head; a click and the bull sank to its knees but not onto its side, its head raised aloft off the ground. Frank shot it again, slightly to one side of the original hole and this time it lay over on its side, its breathing shallow and rapid.

'Shoot it again,' said Steve reflexly, wanting to do something but not knowing what. Another shot and this time thank God the eyes stared and the breathing stopped. The other two bulls stood impassive, gentle gusts of steam from their nostrils, low rumbled moans with each breath.

'Can you pith it through the bars?' said Steve.

'I'll try,' said Bert on his knees, jamming the pithing rod home for all he was worth. The great bull moaned as the rod disappeared into its skull and the great neck strained and lifted its head high before crashing it down again on the galvanised bars. Further in went the rod, the bull's front legs paddled and clattered, its head thrown high in the air, the pithing rod protruding a couple of feet from the hole in its skull. It lay still again and Bert pushed the rod right the way home. Another giant spasm of the whole body, a final lifting of the head and a hollow, dull crash as it was thrown back down onto the concrete.

'These fuckers are almost too big for a captive bolt,' said Frank.

'Yes, the skull is very thick,' said Fernando.

Steve felt a sickness inside him. It was like seeing some great prehistoric beast slaughtered by Stone Age man. The corralling; the gradual weakening with blows to the head from a mechanical club, and the final almost ritualistic destruction of the brain and spinal cord in front of a crowd of onlookers. Like the removal of still beating human hearts by the Aztecs; the public 'drawing' of the innards of condemned yet conscious men in London centuries ago; this was how it must have felt to be there. It was chilling that already it had come to this. Steve glanced across at Bobby Nelson. There were no tears, but a look of wide eyed shock.

Steve wanted to shout out, 'This must stop,' but he knew that if they were to stamp it out, that slaughter was the only way. No half measures; all or nothing.

'Do you want me to use a live bullet on the others?' asked Frank.

They considered it for a few moments and then Steve spoke.

'I don't think so,' he said. 'Human safety takes preference over animal welfare. The last thing we want is somebody getting hurt. Use the Cow Puncher and shoot them again immediately if they don't go down.'

'Aye, I think so too,' said Neil. 'On you go Frank.'

The remaining two bulls went down with the first click and Frank shot them again on the floor before pithing them. The cattle were finished.

Relief. It came over him like the sun rising after night terrors in the darkness. Like the phone call to say that a delayed loved one has arrived safely; that the tumour was benign, the blood test negative. Legs turned to liquid, his brain dull witted, sleep beckoning him, the safety of a warm bed. The carcasses of the bulls lay steaming in the falling sleet. Saliva and blood, shit and brain tissue mingled on the floor of the yard. He glanced across to the shed, now empty of life. A crude mountain of bodies piled high, legs and heads sticking out of the mass at strange angles, and a silence, a spontaneous spiritual silence of awe and reflection as though no one believed what had happened. This is what it must be like after battle, thought Steve. Only the cattle carcasses would be those of human beings, torn and ripped apart. Friends and comrades. How could people cope with that?

'The oldest lesions we have here are 10 to 12 days,' said Anders. 'The infection has been here longer than we had hoped.'

'Let's go and see how they're getting on with bleeding the sheep,' said Neil. 'We can't do any more here.'

Willie McDonald was in his element.

'How are you doing Willie lad?' said Neil.

'Oh aye, we're getting on just fine here. We've done the first three hundred that came from those two fields over towards Warren Farm, and the Suffolks that were around the sheds here. There's only another 70 or 80 so we're nearly through them.'

'Good lad,' said Neil.

He followed Steve into the low roofed lambing shed now packed with crossbred mule ewes. They were big and heavy with lambs, the start of lambing just ten days away. Neil and Steve moved slowly amongst them, most looked bright and in the peak of health. They caught a lame one and turned it onto its backside. Both front feet had a necrotic patch of skin between the two hooves, with yellow, foul smelling pus glistening on the surface. They looked carefully for blisters along the coronary band, where the hoof joined the skin, but there was nothing. They opened the mouth and inspected the dental pad on the upper jaw and shone a torch to look at the surface of the tongue. All was normal.

'It looks like classic foot rot,' said Steve, and Neil grunted agreement.

'One of the problems is that we hardly ever look in sheep's mouths other than to glance at the front teeth to check their age,' said Neil. 'This will be a rapid learning exercise,' he grinned. 'Let's grab a few more of the lame ones and we'll go through the whole lot as they're slaughtered. Sage Street don't understand the problems.'

Frank joined them, Cow Puncher at the ready.

'How do you want this done Neil?' he said.

'What do you suggest?'

'Well, we could shove 50 or so in that long pen at the side. Bring gates in to keep them jammed up tight one end and then me and Bert can move in amongst them and pop them one at a time. Then another lot, and another lot and if we run out of room we can push the dead 'uns up with the Teleporter. This won't take long.'

'Shall we try that Fernando?' said Neil. 'If you can make sure all the sheep are dead. Any that are breathing need shooting again.

'Yes, that sounds fine,' said Fernando. 'Frontal stunning of sheep with a captive bolt is usually a stun kill. We can pith something if we feel it is necessary.'

'Right, Steve and I can check for lesions. Anders and John are already getting cleaned up. Someone is coming to collect them and take them to the airport.'

In dim light and falling temperatures a mass of sheep were herded into the pen and chased up to one end. The emptiness of depression drifted in on the wind and settled silently on Steve, ice cold and dry, searing his thoughts. He was ready to retreat to the hotel, to the comfort and safety of a hot shower and a hot bath; to lie on the bed and watch the news or read the paper with a refreshing beer in his hand and to close his eyes and think and understand what was happening. Instead another few hours work stretched out in front of him, in the cold and dirt and damp of a February evening.

Frank and Bert climbed into the pen and waded in amongst the crowd of off-white fleeces, tightly packed and unable to escape. Click, click; there was no thud or clatter to follow this time, just a gentle sinking to the straw covered ground, sometimes held up by the supporting crowd so that the only indication of death was the blood stained brain tissue oozing from the hole between the ears and trickling down the long Roman nose, the glassy, desert-yellow eyes no different in life or death.

Click, click, reload, click,... click, reload, click, click; rapid and unpausing like at the fair. The sheep took their death in the silence that was the nature of their species. Passivity and acceptance; not wanting to cause a scene. Frank and Bert clambered over the fallen bodies, some that now kicked reflexly and violently, threw their heads around sending blood and brain flying in the air in tiny droplets.

Fernando worked as best he could in the dim light, checking their eyes for reflexes and their torsos for signs of breathing. Whenever he found the rhythmical rise and fall of the rib cage he called the men back to shoot again or even a third time. And within a few minutes there was a heap of 40 or so dead or dying sheep, some buried under the bodies of others, impossible to inspect.

'We will need to pull some of them back so that I can check that they are all killed,' said Fernando.

'Aye, for us to check for lesions too,' said Neil. 'Can you two guys shift them please,' he said to a couple of helpers. 'Spread them out one layer deep so that we can see them all.'

'If we tie gates together behind them we can make up another pen and get slaughtering again while you're doing that,' said Joe. 'We need to keep it all moving so we're not hanging about. Good job the TV cameras can't get in here too,' he smiled, licking his lips as though about to start a feast.

Fuck the TV cameras, thought Steve. If it were up to me I'd let them in so everyone could see what was happening. It might be unpleasant but it was real. He noticed a sheep breathing now that those on top of it had been pulled away and he called Bert back to shoot it again. Then he and Neil examined every foot and every mouth. They found nothing, and by the time they'd finished, there was another pen-full to work on.

It went on for two hours. From time to time the Teleporter was called in to lift the bodies and push them further back along the passage in a heap to make room for the next batch. Steve felt pale weakness arrive. Aching calves and biceps, chilled feet; a sombre tiredness. He had had enough. He wanted the day to end yet Neil seemed possessed of an inexhaustible energy, striding around in his long waterproof coat, like Wellington at Waterloo, rallying the troops. Directing operations here; hands on activity there, and a crystal clear knowledge of which sheep were from which field and how long they had been there. Eventually, around 6.30 p.m. it was over.

Steve wandered around the buildings alone. There was a silent sadness, like the end of a love affair. Eerie like bats leaving their roost at dusk. Christmas without presents; a double bed without a wife. He felt the sadness, bitter on his tongue, salt in his eyes; and there was something else too. A macho scent wafted in on the cold February air; the scent of bravado; a sense that he was wrapped up in something tough and ruthless, and necessary. Self satisfaction whispered his name, the hot air of inflated self importance breathed its life into him. He Steve Turner was at the heart of it; at the start of it.

Willie joined him. 'Fernando and I are back here tomorrow to get the fire built. It'll be some barbecue.'

'I'll bring the beer and rolls,' said Steve.

They made their way to the farm entrance and joined the melee of people washing down and disinfecting their waterproofs. Frank and Bert were smoking, blood stained and brain spattered faces and hands. They laughed and joked; it had been a good day's work.

Bobby Nelson's face smiled with relief that it was finished. He accepted a cigarette from Bert and took a long, eyes closed drag, savouring the warmth and taste of the smoke. It was all out of his hands, there was no waiting left for him to do. That experience was one that would be felt by the thousands that were to follow.

Chapter 29

In the hotel that night the number of Ministry vets had more than doubled. Temporary Veterinary Inspectors (TVIs) had been arriving throughout the day in response to appeals from the Ministry and the British Veterinary Club. No one knew how the outbreak was going to develop, whether it would be stamped out in a matter of days or whether it had already spread further afield. Personnel needs were unknown. It was better to be prepared.

There had been a shock for Steve too. He had bumped into Sonia in the corridor and they had greeted each other with a kiss on the cheek and a hug. Sonia's face had lit up and she had placed her hand on his forearm as they talked. She had been staying with her mother since Swine Fever ended, only forty miles from Morton. When she heard about FMD she contacted Sage Street and they signed her up straight away.

'It's good to see you Steve.' She purred, cat like, bright pink tongue protruding slightly between her teeth. 'Are you staying here?'

'Yes,' he replied and she squeezed his arm with memories.

Later at dinner a crowd went to the hotel carvery and Jeremy Roberts, a vet from a local practice held the stage. Fast moving eyes, flicking backwards and forwards like a stoat watching for prey, his head twitching from side to side, watching and talking, talking and watching.

'You're an epidemiologist Steve,' he said, 'you know what we should do. Here have some of this wine, the practice will pay.' His eyes darted round moving from person to person. 'How do you think it's going Steve? Lot of cases do you think? Maybe take out the whole three kilometres around the pig farm; stinking place wasn't it? The bloke should be locked up; here let me top you up. Big decisions ahead I suppose. What do you think?'

'It's difficult to...' He was cut off in mid sentence.

'I saw Ron Steady on the telly again tonight. Sounded impressive, almost statesman like. Steady bloke at the helm is he? Another bottle of this red wine please,' he plucked at the sleeve of a passing waiter. 'Drink up Steve.' He emptied the bottle into Steve's glass. 'Can't wait to get started myself, I don't like this sitting around. Can you send me out on a visit tomorrow? Something decent. Can't wait to see the disease. Is it easy to spot? Got to be really hasn't it?'

Steve's head rolled and the pressure pushed outwards squeezing his eyes together, the rushing of blood in his ears burning the back of his throat, his intellect draining down to his stomach and mixing with the hot acid and the red house wine. He did not need this; not after today, he thought. He looked at the guy and smiled. He couldn't help liking him. Behind the brashness and hyperactivity there was an openness that you could not help but warm to. If you dressed him in shorts you felt that you should comb his hair for him and ask him if he had a hanky in his pocket.

Sonia was seated at the other end of the table. From the corner of his eye Steve saw her looking at him. She was as he remembered her. Honed and smooth, skin like a polished pebble, long straight fingers that caressed with the touch of goose down; a pink tongue that could work magic and tasted of molten honey; blonde hair that fell long and loose and brushed against his thighs as she arched her back, and the scent of the sea and tropical fruits. Perhaps he had been too hasty, he thought. Perhaps there was a case for a second try.

Monday morning and the office in Morton sang with the song of a football crowd frustrated at their team's performance. The job allocations were being organised from Cardington; phoned or faxed through and the system was at meltdown. The Veterinary Officer brought in and put in charge was called Beryl, and she spoke with a slow monotone that gave the impression of being permanently stoned. People were running up and down, shouting and clamouring, demanding information about what was required of them. She looked each one of them straight in the eye, calmly, unflustered and reliably, and told them she did not know. Her second in command was Tommy. A ruddy faced farmer's son from the south Pennines he smiled regardless of the news he was receiving or imparting. Steve knew him from a meat hygiene course of several years back. He had great respect for him.

Fifteen or twenty vets milled around with no one to organise them. Steve heard his dinner companion from the previous night talking in a loud voice.

'I just hope I can get out there today and get stuck in,' Steve heard him say as he pushed through a set of double doors to where he knew Neil had set up an office.

'Well, what do you want me to do today?' asked Steve.

'Bad news I'm afraid lad,' said Neil. 'Colin Hunt doesn't want you

193

on epidemiology, he wants one of his own cronies. You're to go out to Warren Farm and take over from the AHO that's there and tend the fire that was lit yesterday. Load of fucking crap. It's pointless having a veterinary surgeon out there poking the embers of some funeral pyre when there's important veterinary work to be done. But he's the boss. So that's that.'

'Oh shit,' said Steve. The thought of returning to the pig farm was a kick in the teeth. He wasn't going to learn anything doing that. 'Can't they find an agricultural officer to do that? It's only a matter of stirring up the ashes isn't it?'

Neil laughed. 'Yeah, something like that. I'm going to speak to Graham Thompson at Sage Street today and tell him I need you. I'll do what I can.'

'Thanks,' said Steve. At least he was getting out of the office. He met Beryl in the video conference room talking to Colin Hunt. The link was slow and ponderous, the picture on the screen jumping so that Hunt flicked from place to place as if by magic. The camera lens zoomed in and out with a mind of its own, one minute he was like a speck in the corner of the room, the next you could see up his nostrils, his face distorted, eyes bulging with the bending rays of light.

Welcome to the new millennium, thought Steve. Modern technology at its best. The sound crackled, the voice as ponderous as the movements; Hunt reminding Beryl that Morton was an outstation of Cardington and not a disease control centre in its own right. Everything was to go through him, Colin Hunt. He was the man in charge.

Steve gave Beryl a cheery wave and left. He was best out of it. Let the brown nosers loose and see how they got on. He laughed to himself, and headed for Warren Farm.

The sky was grey like the ocean, rain dancing on the road ahead, a Monday to end all Mondays. He parked fifty yards from the farm, smoke billowing from the pyre that glowed red and orange on the hillside opposite. He put on his overalls, the rain cold and penetrating in his hair and down his neck and up his sleeves. The day stretched out ahead, a dream, a nightmare; something to endure, to tolerate, to close his mind to. He walked up the road and met the AHO, grey skinned, cinders clinging to his stubbled cheeks and chin, his eyebrows and hair singed a tobacco brown, the individual hairs contorted in misshaped spirals, his eyes pink and raw, congested blood vessels bulging.

'Thank God you're here,' he said. 'I'm shagged. I've been up all night watching this fire. I've been told to go and get some breakfast and then have a sleep.' His voice wavered with the taste of sleep, he spat cinders, black ash stuck to his front teeth.

'How's the fire going?' Steve said.

'Alright. There's a guy here with a JCB who you can get to stir it up every now and then and there's a bit more coal in the yard. There's a heap of machinery to come off today too. I've told the contractors it's off hire now but whether Cardington have told them…. who knows?' He shrugged, as though he didn't much care either. 'The problem is cleansing and disinfecting all the stuff. We're trying to power hose it clean on the road, the yard is such a fucking mess.'

'Right, you get off and get some sleep, I think someone's coming from Cardington to get the preliminary cleansing and disinfection underway.'

'There're four pressure hoses meant to be turning up today too… look out,' he yelled, and Steve jumped clear as a newly cleansed and disinfected JCB roared down the road past them.

'He's off to Round Hill now to help with the fire over there. Right,' he yawned, mouth wide and pink, 'I'll leave you to it. If you need anything give Cardington a ring.'

'Cheers,' Steve said, and continued up the road to where three men in green waterproofs were standing. One had a power hose, another a knapsack sprayer, and the third clutched a clip board inside a clear polythene bag. The road was on a steep incline and a deep bed of straw was spread on its surface for a length of about ten yards. On the top side of the straw was a lagoon of filthy water, reinforced by the rainwater streaming down the polished tarmac, and which now threatened to burst through the straw in a scene reminiscent of the dam busters, washing disinfectant and FMD virus into the little burn below which gaily bubbled its way under a fence and into the neighbouring farmer's fields. On the lower side of the straw a torrent of water emerged as though from an underground spring. The taste of acid caught in his throat with the realisation that he was now responsible for the whole fucking mess before him.

A new BMW glided down the road towards them.

'Who the hell is that?' Steve asked.

'It's one of the residents from up the top of the lane,' said a man in green. 'There're half a dozen posh houses up there. We've been stopping them all and spraying their wheels. They're a bit fed up but so far they've been pretty co-operative.'

Steve shuffled over to where the car had stopped just on the topside of the lagoon. The driver's window glided silently open. Blonde with green eyes, quality label clothes, a scent of perfume wafted towards him. The flash of white teeth, designer freckles on her nose, the sparkle of diamonds on her fingers, yellow gold splashing from her ears and onto her wrists. The look on her face said she found the whole thing distasteful. Steve felt the rain running down his face and dripping off his nose. He had the starring role in a bad farce, he thought.

'Sorry to inconvenience you,' he said. 'Would you mind driving slowly over the disinfectant mat,' he stifled a hysterical giggle at the sight of the filthy mound of straw that lay ahead, 'and then stop just past it so that we can spray your tyres.'

'Of course,' she murmured, maintaining the charade. 'It's a terrible business isn't it?'

Steve looked at her and cringed. He wanted to tell her that he didn't want to be here doing this. Wanted to tell her that the deep blue Austin Healey 3000 parked just down the road was his and that in a different life he hadn't looked like the wanker of a Ministry man that he knew he looked now. He wanted to tell her that he had once had a wife like her and that he had girlfriends like her too and that he took skiing holidays in Chile. Standing in the pouring rain next to a decrepit, stinking fucking pig farm and poking at a fire with five hundred giant pork sausages sizzling away on it was not his idea of a fun way to make a living. It was just that somehow he had ended up there, unplanned, just drifted into it.

The shiny BMW eased its way over the straw filled swamp and waited patiently for its wheels to be sprayed. Steve could see the woman's face through the raindrop covered back window reflected in her rear view mirror. She was giggling. He flushed hot and red with anger and frustration. He couldn't believe that after five years at University and twenty odd years' experience that he was reduced to this. He suffered in silence though he wanted to shout and scream. Instead he turned his back and walked up the field to where the flames from the pigs were rising into the winter grey sky.

It was medieval. The half charred corpses of pigs stared out of the flames at him. Skin cracked and shrunken with the heat, pulled back over bared teeth like savage dogs only there was no sound save the sizzling and spitting of the hot roasted fat. Pigs of all sizes from just a few weeks old to boars with giant tusks made all the larger by the contraction of their gums.

He made his way along the line, grateful for the heat. The rain had turned to sleet, driving in under his collar, but his face, pointed at the fire flushed warm and rosy red. The smell was a young farmers' pig roast, all those years ago with Rachel by his side, beer and wine and happy laughing in the warmth of summer sun and the dawn of his life.

He was joined by another man in green overalls. A man about his own age who introduced himself as an Animal Health Officer from Cardington.

'I never thought we'd be seeing this,' said Steve. 'I hardly believe it now. Like it's not real, not really happening. Even though I'm staring it in the face, smelling the meat, hearing the hissing, tasting the smoke. And it's going to get worse.'

The guy nodded as though he understood. They made their way along the pyre, thick brown mud churned by the heavy JCBs, like melted chocolate ready to cover a cake. The fire burned better in some places than others and Steve had no idea what to do or what to expect; whether more coal would be needed, or whether he should poke the thick congealing crusts of fat and coal. He was a vet, not a stoker.

He glanced across the valley to where the TV vans were parked several hundred yards away, satellite dishes pointing to the sky, cameras pointed at him. He would be seen all around the world, his Andy Warhol fifteen minutes of fame, hopefully unrecognisable in his Ministry clothes. He pulled his hood down over his forehead to shadow his face, and kept from looking directly at the camera. He didn't want to be recognised. Didn't want friends and acquaintances to know that this was how he now earned his living.

He stared into the flames, looking for something positive, searching the ashes for a sign of hope, but all he saw was destruction. In the hotter parts of the fire the flesh had already burned away to expose the soft wet guts, green and purple and black. They bubbled like a saucepan of stew on the stove, steam rising amidst the orange and red flames with a hint of blue. Stewed guts and barbecued pork with crackling thought Steve. Plenty for all; bring your own beer and wine. Rolls and salad provided.

He walked back down to where the men were trying to clean a huge digger with caterpillar tracks in the middle of the tiny tarmac road. Several hundredweight of mud was ground into the metal tracks, all needing to be washed off with the power hose before they could be disinfected. And hundreds of kilos of mud and hundreds of gallons of water flowed down the road into the straw dammed lagoon and then onward to the stream below. Hysteria burst in him like a firework. This was not how it was meant to be, disease security was non-existent.

'We can't wash off any more vehicles on the road,' he said. There's a fairly hard standing up beyond the farmyard. If we get the worst of the mud off there and then the final disinfection here, that'll reduce the contamination going into the stream.'

An old battered van pulled up and the pig farmer got out with a couple of cronies. Rough and unkempt looking men, clothes streaked with a mix of swill and manure.

'I've come to feed my dogs and check on my gear,' he said.

'You can't just come on and off here when you like,' said Steve. 'This premises is restricted until we've done the preliminary cleansing and disinfection.'

'I need to come and feed my dogs and check my gear,' he repeated. Contemptuously and defiantly as though to say 'you try and stop me.'

'We can licence the dogs off,' said Steve. He despised this man.

'Phone your boss at Cardington,' smirked the farmer. 'I've got an arrangement with them to come and check my gear. You'll see.'

Steve dialled the Cardington number from his mobile. It rang out. No one to answer the phone or not wanting to answer it for fear of what the news might be.

'I'm not having this bastard just turning up in his filthy clothes whenever he wants and spreading disease all over the fucking place,' he said to the AHO. I'm going to phone the police and get them to come up and get rid of him.'

Fifteen minutes later a patrol car arrived and Steve went down the road to meet the two police officers inside. He explained what was happening.

'What would you like us to do with him?' asked one of them.

'I don't want him coming here except by special arrangement and under licence,' Steve said. 'And he shouldn't bring all his cronies with him, there's no need for that. Let me try Cardington Animal Health Office again just to make sure that nothing's already been agreed.'

The phone was answered after three rings and Steve asked to speak to whoever was in charge of IPs.

'I'll put you through,' said the receptionist.

A man came on the line and Steve explained what was happening.

'Sounds like a communication problem,' said the man confidently and with a thinly disguised Ministry-speak superiority that suggested he thought Steve was incompetent. 'You've probably antagonised the guy with your approach. Back off a bit and show a little give and take. Come to an arrangement with him that's amicable.'

What are you fucking talking about, Steve wanted to say but he bit his lip and kept his voice calm and steady.

'But he shouldn't be allowed here should he? The place is crawling with virus and there are no animals to look after other than a couple of mangy terriers which we can licence off anyway. He's got no protective clothing and I can't believe he takes disinfection very seriously if his clothes are anything to go by.' His voice was rising with frustration and excitement.

'I know what you're saying,' said the voice, 'but I think we need to show a willingness to work with this guy.'

'So I should just let him get on with it should I? Is that what you're saying?'

'Talk to him. Come to an arrangement that suits. Show him that we're prepared to help him.'

What a load of bollocks thought Steve.

'Okay,' he said, 'I get the message. Cheers for now and thanks for your help.' He hung up; just as he had hung up on Rachel.

'Wanker. Fucking wanker,' he said under his breath. 'Arsehole. Complete stupid arsehole. Where's the enforcement in that. Where's the disease security? Wanker, tosspot, arsehole.' He was burning with rage; ears tingling red and a dryness in his throat. Still, it was Cardington's show, he thought. Let them fucking get on with it.

'Seems like I'm to let him do what he wants to,' said Steve to the police. 'I'm sorry I've wasted your time.'

'No problem,' said one of them. 'If you do need us again, just give us a call.' He smiled cheerfully. 'Cold bloody job isn't it?' he grinned.

'Bloody freezing,' said Steve. 'I might have to go back up to the bonfire to warm up again,' he laughed.

And so the day passed. Purple and red hands, cold burning cheeks and noses warmed by the fire. Steve found a couple of long metal pipes and he and the Animal Health Officer passed their day by giving the fire a prod here and there, leaning on their pokers like a pair of old stokers at a foundry with fire reflected in their eyes and cinders in their hair. They broke the crust on the coal where it had fused solid, letting the oxygen mix and mingle with the heat and the flames roared up crackling and fresh. Sleet turned to snow, blackened bones turned white and crumbled into dust, and the world was at an end, consumed by fire and madness.

Chapter 30

Julie arrived at the Cardington Animal Health Office full of the excitement of new beginnings. The months between breaking up with Steve and the day she heard on the news that FMD had broken out were a flat treeless landscape of sand, stretching away from her in front, behind, and to the sides. In those four weeks she had been with him she had known that he was the man for her; the one she had been waiting for. And then he had dumped her for that bitch, Sonia.

Heartbreak was not a word she had previously understood. A word for teenagers to describe their shallow feelings of infatuation, overplaying the pain and the loss. That was her understanding, her interpretation, her reality. And then her own heart had broken. A physical ache in the chest like a deep bruise. Persistent. Constant. There on first waking and when going to bed. Pain on pain in her heart; the centre of her stomach; the hot needle sharp pain in her head of denial and expectation that at any minute the phone would ring and it would be him telling her how much he loved her and wanted her back; that he had made a mistake. And the warm glow of how she would feign disinterest. Force him to woo her back, not crawling on hands and knees, but head suitably bowed at least. That was her dream and her belief. That was her fantasy.

As weeks turned to months the fantasy poisoned her. Grew into taking revenge. At first the focus of her hate was Sonia but she came to see that Sonia was a victim too. Steve was the perpetrator of her pain and grief. He had misled her; discarded her like a worthless Christmas present. She had loved him so. Her love had been pure and clear; birds singing on a sultry evening, the sound of leather against willow, a gentle round of applause; wood smoke in the bar towards Christmas; children singing carols and building snowmen; the smell of puppies curled under your chin.

And now the love was twisted to hate with a lust for revenge and the desire to make him suffer. To suffer as she had suffered. The doctor had prescribed Prozac to help her over it. The tablets had helped the symptoms but not the causal seed or the desire to nurture that seed at every spare opportunity. During the day whilst driving and shopping; at times sitting, staring out of the window with no thought other than that which consumed and poisoned her.

At night too. Long restless nights of fitful wakefulness and disturbed sleep when she dreamed he was there by her side, touching her, oh so gently and carefully. Lovingly. Like it had been for those few short weeks when her world was a fever with quenching cool water that steamed on the smooth skin of her breasts and desires. She was a woman whole. Fulfilled and fulfilling, now frayed at the heart of her, the edges cracked and peeling; like fruit rotting in a forgotten bowl.

And then, just a few days after the pigs at Warren Farm had been slaughtered the first case of FMD on the west side of the country had been discovered in a dairy herd of 250 milking cows not far from Cardington. The man who milked the cows at weekends worked at a market where some of the sheep that left Round Hill Farm had eventually arrived. It was the beginning of the flood that everyone had feared but had not dared to predict.

There were three satellite premises involved with the outbreak making a total of 2000 cattle and 6000 sheep spread around four farms. There were four pyres to build, and the infrastructure at the Cardington office, along with its logistical and administrative skills, creaked and groaned under the strain. All staff were working twelve and fourteen hour days. The Minister for Rural Affairs and the PVO were making ever more regular appearances on the news media to say that everything was under control. That all was well.

Back at Morton, Steve Turner knew that all was not well. After the wasted day spent tending the fire, Neil had managed to get him assigned permanently to epidemiology. There was just him and Neil and for the whole of the next week Steve trailed from one new outbreak to another in the immediate vicinity of Warren Farm and to others many miles further afield. He saw sights he could not have imagined; had conversations he would never forget.

Late one evening he visited Blackheath Farm where both the lambing ewes and the dairy cows had gone down with the virus. Lambs were dying from heart failure just minutes after struggling into the world, the heart muscle damaged by the virus. The ewes were sick and lame. Dusk was falling when Steve arrived at the farm. He recognised Jeremy Roberts who rushed to greet him.

'Hi Steve,' he gushed. 'Mr Johnston, meet Steve Turner, he's an epidemiologist. He's going to tell you how and when the virus got here. Got to be on the wind from Warren Farm's pigs hasn't it Steve?' and continued without waiting for an answer.

'The ewes in the shed out the back there,' he pointed, 'riddled with it. Mouth lesions; foot lesions; lambs dying; the lot. Five day old lesions in the mouth I'd say. What do you think? Dairy cows affected too now. Rupturing vesicles on the tongue and dental pad. Got it from the sheep almost certainly. Cubicle shed backs on to the lambing shed.

'A couple of sons, very upset. Got animals on farms away from here. Have to take the lot won't we? Course we will. Sooner the better. Stressful time for them. I've been trying to smooth it over. Follow me I'll show you the sheep.'

Steve followed blindly, shell shocked by the monologue. In the few days he'd known him he'd come to like the bloke. A man to lift your spirits when you were feeling like shit and ready to throw in the towel. But just occasionally you needed a break.

They looked at some big Suffolk cross ewes. Ragged lesions on the dental pad, some pale grey, smooth, almost healed. Probably five or six days old thought Steve. A few moribund lambs lay with heads resting on the straw, necks outstretched, chests heaving rapidly with effort, weak and fading.

'I'll put these ones down now with Euthatal,' said Jeremy. 'Can't leave the poor little chaps. Valuer's been. Just waiting for Geordie Spencer the slaughterer to arrive and we'll get stuck into the dairy cows. Ah, here he is now. Geordie, Geordie, through this way, we've got a crush set up already,' he stalked off with his overlong green coat flapping around his thighs like a skirt, leaving Steve with the farmer and one of the sons.

'It's a miserable thing,' Steve said softly, trying to empathise. 'I'm really sorry for what's happened but I need to ask you a whole load of questions,' he was in automatic mode now. 'You'll have been asked some of them before but we need to check these things as carefully as possible. We're trying to find out how the virus is spreading and where it might already have spread to. It's not easy for you I know. It's dreadful...' he tailed off.

He was babbling, offering platitudes. Because platitudes were all he had. That and a big fat compensation cheque. The Ministry gave no training in this sort of thing, dealing with people under severe emotional stress. God, there was little enough training on notifiable disease outbreaks let alone on how to counsel the victims of them.

Funnily, loosing Rachel had helped him there. Helped him to understand how it felt. To know the grating, lingering sadness. The hollow touch of sympathetic words and phrases.

'Life must go on,' they said.

But why? he'd thought. Too much effort. Too much emotional strain. Others didn't know, couldn't know unless they'd felt it. Felt it and lived it. Seen it. Smelt it. Like the smell of fear or death. Smelt the distress and the hopeless feeling of loss. Caught in a strong tide taking you struggling, further from the refuge of the shore, then struggling less; resigned to your fate. Resigned to die if that was what it took to take away the pain.

He looked at the farmer and his son. He saw sadness in their eyes shining back at him. Sadness and the resigned taint of complicity.

And then suddenly there was a huge crack like a firework splitting the dark winter sky not with light but with sound. What was that? Steve thought, and then there was a silence, broken by the bleating of a ewe as it nuzzled its sickly lamb.

Crack! Again the noise. Steve walked purposefully towards the sound, through the milking parlour and towards the sliding metal door that led out into the cubicle shed. He pulled the door to one side, it slid easily on its runners. Black and white cows milled around in the passage and Jeremy Roberts, the look of an excited school boy about his face, emerged from the dimly lit recess of the passageway, his hair flying as though electrified, Biggles moustache twitching.

'Keep back Steve,' he urged with relish. 'Geordie's using live ammunition.' He emphasised the live, spoke it like he was talking about an exotic and seductive woman. 'Best to keep behind the door. Geordie knows what he's doing.'

Steve shook his head. Too much to go wrong, and when it did it would all be too late. 'Shouldn't have allowed it.' 'Not Ministry policy.' 'The vet should have taken charge when he knew what was happening.'

He heard and saw it all and he would not be a party to it.

'He's to stop using it right now,' Steve said firmly. 'There's no need for free bullets, a captive bolt will do just as well. We don't want anyone getting hurt. That's the most important thing.'

'It's okay Steve,' Jeremy said. 'Geordie's a good guy. He knows what he's doing. He's putting each cow into the crush, catching its head and then shooting it and dragging out the carcass. It's a good system and it'll work. I know Geordie well. You can trust him.'

'I don't doubt it,' said Steve, preparing to dig his heels in, 'but you could get a ricochet whizzing round these concrete walls or hitting the metal crush and shooting off anywhere. It's not Ministry policy to use free bullets without a full safety audit. He'll have to stop.' He was adamant.

They waited for the next explosive crack and then shouted through.

'Don't shoot any more,' Steve called, 'we're coming over.'

'Stop shooting Geordie,' Jeremy spoke quickly, exhilaration in his voice. He was enjoying the experience. 'Steve and I are coming through.'

Wyatt Earp with me as his side kick thought Steve. He laughed to himself. Black humour at its best. He adored it. He had even seen the funny side of loosing Rachel.

They pushed their way through the melee of cows. There was shit everywhere, udders overflowing with milk sprayed white fountains onto the dark green slurry coating the floor, the milking cancelled on the news that slaughter was imminent. Several cows had the characteristic white foam around their muzzles, one or two were hobbling. They were restless with the change of routine; with the strange men and the clatter and clang of the gates and crush and the explosive crash of the pistol. Steam rose from their mouths and the condensation settled on their backs. It was a cold night outside but in the passageway it was clammy and steamy with the smell of cows and their dung; the sweet smell of fresh urine rising in the air. A dung smeared tail flicked across Steve's face, the taste not unpleasant, of ripe cheese and game. He cuffed his face with his hand, merely streaking it across his cheek. People didn't get Foot and Mouth. Plenty of other things though, *Salmonella; E. coli*; leptospirosis; *Cryptosporidia*. Still he'd worked with cows for years now so he must have been exposed. Eating sandwiches with dung caked hands; dung and urine splashes in his mouth and eyes. He'd had them all and so far so good.

Geordie's face had the hang cheeked look of a spaniel as he peered through the gloom, his head slightly bowed. The look of a man caught with his trousers down in a friend's house: I know I shouldn't be doing this but it seemed like a good idea at the time.

'You're not to use live bullets,' said Steve straight to the point. Not nastily or arrogantly, but simply as a statement of cool fact that he was not to be moved from. 'A captive bolt and pithing rod. We want no one hurt.'

Geordie nodded. 'I was a bit concerned myself,' he said. 'In the dark like this.'

He put his pistol away and took out a Cow Puncher. The next cow, her udder tight and swinging almost to her hocks was pushed into the crush. The gentle familiar click and a metallic clanging as her head bounced off the metal gate and side bars. Geordie flung open the crush door to release the unconscious beast and inserted the pithing rod with skill and dexterity. The clunking of hooves against metal and Steve shivered inside. The farmer and the two sons showed no emotion.

'Let's go inside shall we?' said Steve gently, 'and do the paperwork. I'll see you later Jeremy,' and he smiled.

'OK Steve. Thanks very much for coming down here and giving us a hand. Take it easy with these guys,' he said in a stage whisper, 'the older son's close to breaking with it all. Try and get Sage Street to agree to kill all the other properties as DCs. Get it all over and done with in one go: take the pressure off the farmer not knowing what's going to happen. Makes sense doesn't it? I can come back tomorrow and do the sheep. We'll finish the cows tonight, can't leave them unmilked and can't ask the farmer to milk them. That'd be too cruel. It'd kill him I should think. See you Steve.' He was off in a flurry of green crackling plastic like a swashbuckling highwayman or musketeer.

Steve went through the standard questionnaire with them in the kitchen. It was an old form created years ago, outdated, archaic. Treated with disdain, contempt and piteous neglect by successive governments, the Veterinary Service had been expected to cope and bumble along making do. Lack of training, the stifling of initiative; the brow beating of professional judgement by administrators; the conversion of all professional knowledge and advice into numbers and letters that could be punched into a computer. And what was worse thought Steve is that we've all gone along with it. Doffed our caps to those that pay us and scurried off to comply with our orders, like lemmings on their cyclical race to reach the cliff edge first.

And the shameful thing thought Steve, is that our leaders have not only condoned the running down of The Service, they have been instrumental in it; encouraged it. Whilst most people built up Empires out of nothing, our leaders have busied themselves with dismantling their own for a pat on the head from the Whitehall Mandarins, and a promise of promotion for the PVO.

Why, Ron Steady had even boasted that he was planning to cut The Service further, saving money and receiving another thumbs up from his political masters. And as usual, Steve thought, we will all just lie down and take it; then roll over and take it again right up the backside; shafted good and proper by the old Etonian and Oxbridge brigade who wouldn't know a cow from a bull and wouldn't care anyway, just so long as they could screw it.

He winced as he came to question 20 on the form. Here they were, in the middle of slaughtering a man's life's work in the cold and wet of a Pennine winter. Slaughtering his life's work as simply as breaking up cardboard boxes to throw on a fire to watch them go up in smoke. He looked at the older son. His face was white, eyes that did not see, a mouth working and twisting, his skin the colour of a cut coconut, stubbled with short, stiff, black and grey hairs.

'If they could just leave the calves,' the son said, flat and grey, not expecting any answer. 'Just leave the calves so that there was something left to start again with. There's four generations out there in those sheds. I can trace some of them back forty or fifty years to when my grandfather farmed here. It doesn't seem right to just kill everything so that you can't get it back. If they could just leave the calves we could be back to where we are now in a few years.'

It was a hopeless plea. From deep within. From his soul. Not a plea to Steve but to something or someone greater. Like others before him had done through the centuries.

Tears spilled into Steve's eyes and a faintness made him hold the edge of the table for fear of falling. Knees trembling, a prickling sensation in the skin of his back that moved up his neck and caused the hairs to rise and brush against his shirt collar.

Like he had pleaded with God to bring Rachel back to him. He stood out there under a storm laden Pennine sky and shouted at the top of his voice, 'God. Help me. Please God. Help me.' Over and over again he had screamed. He had expected a parting of the clouds. He had expected a ray of light to come shining through. He had expected to look upon God's smiling face, to see his lips move as he mouthed the words that Steve so badly wanted to hear.

'She will always be with you my son. She will be yours forever.'

Shouting and shouting. The tears had poured down his cheeks and the snot ran from his nose and despair and self pity left him diminished and debased. He had shouted until his voice was hoarse, pleading with God; threatening him; begging him; blaspheming him. Anything to get a reaction. A thunderbolt would have done. After a time his voice had grown pale, his throat hurt with the effort and the clouds had stayed stubbornly grey and the cold wind had blown from the hills with an icy feel and he had knelt down like a man before the executioner's axe.

'You're so boring,' she said and the words pierced him; a fine point of tempered steel, barbed so that it would stay forever in his flesh, working deeper still with time, clawing at his peace of mind.

The pond they had dug beckoned, five feet deep, grey brown and cold with steep clay sides. He had walked across to it and climbed down into it, the cold water filling his wellingtons and lapping at his knees. He waded towards the middle, a thick, heavy wool jumper under his green oilskin jacket with the deep pockets. The water reached his waist, his clothes were heavy; he did not know what he was doing or what he should do or what would be the outcome. He bent his knees and pushed off for the middle, gasping as the cold caressed his chest and throat, heard the rush of water in the pockets, felt the drag as he swam, kicking with slow, laboured legs with the heavy weight on his feet.

He stopped in the centre, rested on the bottom, the water to his chin, thick mud clinging to his boots so that he could hardly lift his feet. He turned his eyes upwards, in hope rather than expectation. Not a flicker. No sign that he had been heard. Nothing on which to pin his hopes and dreams of a return to normality. He looked at the surface of the water and the swirling of the mud mixing like oil, gentle and cold around his neck as he bent his knees oh so slowly. Felt the salty tingling on his cheeks, the gelatinous mucous on his top lip floating on the surface now. Perhaps he should just get out, walk back up to the house and have a hot shower. Rachel would say it was just like him. Too boring to take the risk, to take it all the way. Typical of him to bottle out.

He took a deep breath and closed his eyes and let his knees sink; felt the icy water on his face, lifting his hair from where it was plastered to his ears and forehead; felt the cold pass over the top of his head, fought back from gasping with the shock of it and pushed with wellie clad feet as he duck dived beneath the surface. He felt again the weight and the drag of his clothes pulling him up or down he could not tell. Down, down went his head, arms outstretched, fingers groping for the muddy bottom, his eyes tight shut against the cold, the taste of peat in his mouth. And then he felt the soft clay at his finger tips, he grabbed at it, digging his fingers in deep to grab a handful as proof of what he'd done.

Disorientated now with cold and emotion he turned his head for the surface, panicking and kicking with legs that had grown too heavy, too slow to respond; trying to get his feet down onto the muddy bottom, to stand and thrust his head above the surface in defiant triumph.

'You bastard,' he screamed at the sky. Not at God. Not at anyone. Screamed for the sake of screaming, knowing that no one could hear him; wishing that Rachel could spot his bobbing head and come racing down the field to his rescue, tears in her eyes, telling him she loved him and to never abandon her.

He floated on his back looking up at the sky, his clothes now water logged, the cold eating into his flesh and deeper still into his bones. He washed away the tears and the snot, the water acid and peat tasting, brown and staining with strands of peat floating in it that clung to his hands like tiny brown worms. Slowly he floated to the side, knowing now that he would not drown. He climbed onto the bank with difficulty, his movements slow and ponderous, water pouring from his body, the cold breeze chilling him.

He did not empty his boots, began to walk slowly and methodically

towards the road and then up to the house. Water followed him, squelching;
shivering violently, the skin of his hands a rich purple. Was she watching
from the window? In all the best films she would look out and catch the
moment; see the shocking sight; rush from the door and down the road
calling his name in fright; clutch him to her and warm his face with her
kisses. With every step it seemed it must happen and he slowed his walk
to give her more time. The script, the script, no one but he ever read the
script. Least of all her. He reached the stone steps, the door still tightly
closed, and he stomped around coughing and spluttering. She had to
see him or there was no point. Frustration as he stood and shivered, the
afternoon was dim and hostile. He knocked on the door. Pathetically and
predictably. She opened it, her face tired and lined as though she had been
sleeping. Steve stared up at her, his face pitiful in its desire for pity; water
dripping from his head and coat, still slurping from his boots.

'You stupid idiot,' she said. 'Go and have a hot bath.' The voice
contemptuous.

He wanted to kill himself. And her too.

He emptied his boots and stripped off to his pants on the doorstep.
Noticed the purple blotching spread out across his body, the shrivelled
impotent cold of his penis.

Yes he knew how Mr Johnston felt at that very moment. He, Steve
Turner, had been there himself.

He passed over question 20 with a squiggle of his pen and a
contempt of his own. When he was in the middle of killing a man's
life's work, ripping out his heart and soul before his very eyes, he was
not prepared to ask in all seriousness if he'd seen many hedgehogs
around recently.

Chapter 31

As they moved into the second week the number of new cases rose
daily and Cardington's nightmare began. Neil was called over by
Colin Hunt to set up a field epidemiology unit leaving Steve alone
at Morton. The memory of Broadwich was a picnic in comparison,
a mere rehearsal for the real thing. How many times back then had
they said to each other? 'We'd never cope with Foot and Mouth.'
Now they were finding out.

The reports Steve wrote on each farm started as in-depth documents but as the number of cases rose they degenerated into pointless pieces of paper containing nothing more than a few basic facts hidden amongst the guesses. Contact with Sage Street was minimal and nobody there seemed to understand the chaos that was unfolding. In the bar late into the night, Steve listened to the moans of experienced large animal practitioners, confident of their diagnosis but unlistened to by Sage Street who refused to confirm on clinical grounds, demanding instead restrictions and sampling.

'We need to be sure before we can authorise slaughter,' was the stock phrase, as though implementing a policy decision made higher up the tree. It was the same with Dangerous Contact premises (DCs); delay, procrastination, a report was needed on which to base a decision. If only each vet had been allowed to make their own assessment locally. If only trust were placed in their veterinary expertise, knowledge and professionalism to assess and make a critical judgement as to which animals were DCs and should be culled.

A treadmill of enquiries and information arrived in front of Steve as each vet returned to the office with his or her tale of woe. And Neil all the time wanting him out on farms to get information and reports written for Sage Street; and Beryl all the time needing him in the office at Morton to advise on DCs and give second opinions; and never enough 'clean' vets to go out on report cases. The demand for new vets was constant and day by day more of them arrived.

'Call them and they will come.' The phrase jumped at him again from the film 'Field of Dreams'.

'Call them and they will come,' he said it out loud, 'to Fields of Broken Dreams.' It had an ironic ring.

And then a new problem emerged. The number of dead animals to be disposed of became impossible to deal with. Burial was usually prohibited because of objections from the Environment Agency over the pollution of water courses. Burning on pyres was proclaimed the way ahead, and besides it was more macho; a bigger spectacle for the cameras and the eyes of the watching world. A pagan ritual. Cattle layed carefully on their backs atop the coal, feet pointing to the sky. Calves and sheep packed in between to fill the gaps. Soak it all in diesel and then, usually towards dusk, the pyre would be torched, a powerful emotion of medieval triumph rushing through the veins of the onlookers. This was what it must have been like to burn witches thought Steve. Base human instincts stimulated by the ritual of the construction of the fire and then the consumption by flames of the poor sinner tied to the wooden stake in the centre, the crowd cheering, calling out as the flames licked up, singeing the living flesh that blistered and blackened, melting like wax before the pain wracked eyes of the owner.

Yes, thought Steve. Burning the carcasses showed the world that you were doing something. Rooting out the evil disease and committing it to the flames. Like fighting fire with fire. Burial was too tame. Nothing for the telly pundits. No bright orange flame against the black of a night sky, lighting up the eerie shapes of legs and heads, casting dancing shadows in the minds and souls of the viewing public. No black pall of smoke hanging and drifting downwind in the air, a silent messenger for miles around that disaster had struck and could strike again at any one of them. No front page photograph to jump with glaring headlines from the newsstands so that people stared with fascination in their eyes and reached into their pockets for the money to purchase. Yes, burning was macho. Burial was for wimps.

But burning had a problem. Burning caused delay. Choosing a site, ordering the coal and sleepers, building the pyre. It all took time especially with contractors' staff taken straight from the dole. Unmotivated, poor workers who needed constant direction and had no incentive to get the job done.

And so when Steve arrived at Marsh Farm just after midday he found Fernando tired and dispirited, trying to get a fire built. His face was pale, eyes staring with strain, the smile that usually rippled across his face hung loose from his waterproof trousers, trailing in the dust.

'This bloody fire is nowhere near ready,' said Fernando. 'The guys we have working here are very idle people. They cannot use their brains. If they even have brains,' he added. 'You must be on their backs all the time. It is terrible. I feel for Mr and Mrs Thomas the farmers. They are very good people. They are feeding us and making us cups of coffee all day. But it is getting awful here. The sheep were killed two days ago and are beginning to smell very bad.'

Steve walked down the track with him to a large timber framed shed. The smell of putrefaction hung in the air, heavy and rich, constant, unforgiving. Steve felt it catch in his throat momentarily making him wretch. He swallowed, he tasted the stench on his tongue, and then the nausea passed.

He leant against the gate of the shed with Fernando and looked out onto a horizon of dead sheep piled on top of each other, surreal bloated bodies with legs sticking straight out as though inflated with a high pressure line. The skin of their bellies was an array of vivid colour; bright greens and blue, purples and maroon reds. The colours of putrefaction and decay.

'Some of the ones we killed first are starting to fall apart,' said Fernando. 'I suppose with all the wool and stacked like this the carcasses have not cooled quickly.'

'Cooked in their own juices,' said Steve flippantly and regretted the remark. He saw the tears poised on Fernando's lower lids, ready to spill over and down his cheeks.

'It was the lambs that upset me,' said Fernando. 'Three and four week old lambs. So young and lively. Jumping around. Skipping and chasing each other around the pens. I don't mind killing things when it is necessary but it is unnatural with ones so young.' He wiped the moisture from his cheeks. Already his skin had the pale gloss of uncertainty, defeat even.

'We tried to kill them with captive bolts at first but I think their skulls are too soft and there is not enough resistance from their muscle tone. Either the bolt just pushed their head away or if it did penetrate it didn't stun them. As soon as I saw what was happening I stopped it. We used intracardiac Euthatal. It was very slow at first but once we got a system going it went quite quickly. I did not like it though.' He looked at Steve as though pleading for something. Words of comfort.

Steve patted him on the shoulder.

'Don't worry,' he said, 'this won't last forever. I know you will have done your best. That's all any of us can do. We're none of us used to this.' He looked straight at Fernando. 'And what's the alternative? Vaccination? It's not on is it? Too many complications and where would you start? It's not like it's confined to just this area. It's started to pop up all over the place. Devon, suspects in Wales. And Cardington looks as if it's sitting on a time bomb. No, this is all we've got. Got to hit it hard. Kill it out as quickly as we can.'

'Yes I know,' said Fernando. 'It was just that … the lambs.…' He tailed off. 'Disinfecting the damn coal lorries takes too much time too. They come here in a very filthy condition, thick with grease and mud and we have to clean it all away before we can disinfect. I have spoken to Cardington and asked them to tell the contractors they must clean their lorries before they bring them onto farms. But I don't think it will do any good. Look at those lazy bastards now,' he said, pointing to where three young blokes were sitting on a bale of straw a hundred yards away. 'They move half a dozen sleepers and then they need to sit on their lazy arses and have a rest. I must go and make them work.'

'I'll go and see the Thomases. I'll catch you in the bar tonight,' said Steve. 'Don't let it get to you pal,' he added with feeling.

'I am alright, really,' said Fernando and smiled.

The bar was packed that night. More strangers and more familiar faces from other parts of the country. Sonia was there and cheerful, flirting with some of the other vets. Basking in the attention.

'How was your day Steve?' she asked. Friendly and relaxed. Not like Julie had been, thank God.

'It's getting out of hand Steve,' said Jeremy Roberts. 'Here let me get you a drink. Too many carcasses lying and too many animals waiting around for slaughter on Sage Street's confirmation. We need to get in there hard. Three kilometre cull right round Warren Farm; they're all going to get it anyway aren't they? Kill them out now and get them burnt straight away.

'I was talking to another vet today. Told him that if he gets any suspects in his neck of the woods to shoot first and ask questions later. No point hanging around with this. Did you see Ron Steady and the Minister on telly again tonight? Looking very cool and confident. Do you think they know what's happening out here?'

'Probably no idea,' said Steve laughing to hide the panic he felt. 'Probably don't even know where Morton is.'

'They were adamant that it's not an epidemic,' said another vet, overhearing the conversation. 'What about calling the army in to help with the disposal of carcasses?'

'Yeah, it's something I've been discussing with some of the other vets,' said Steve. 'One of them was telling me that the Northumberland Report on the outbreak in '67 recommended bringing them in right at the start. I'll e-mail Sage Street about it tomorrow.'

'Good idea Steve,' cut in Jeremy taking a swig of red wine. 'Rattle a few cages and stir things up a bit. Need to get them moving at

Sage Street. Can't hang around for days while the whole thing just gets worse. Fernando, how did you get on today? Got that fire built yet?'

'Very nearly,' said Fernando sitting down and making room for a couple of young girls following him round like puppies. 'I think we can start loading the carcasses tomorrow. We will need a very big spoon for some of them by then. Or Laddell?'

'Ladle,' said Steve helpfully.

'Yes, that is it. The Thomases are such nice people. So understanding.'

Steve went to his room early. He was not in the mood for small talk and he wanted to phone Neil. Discuss with him the problems of carcasses lying. Plus some other things too. When he stood up to say good-night he saw Sonia watching him. He felt so tempted. So in need of physical comfort. And physical comfort soothed his mind. Dopamine, the pleasure drug. His reserves were low and they needed to be replenished or at least be set dancing. He stifled the thought lest he act on impulse and regret it.

'Good-night all,' he said, and headed for the lift. Once in his room he phoned Neil.

'What's going on over there?' he asked.

'It's not looking good Stevie lad,' said Neil. 'We've had four confirmed cases hear today. It's spreading out north and south of Cardington Bay and heading west. It's going to be a long haul.'

'How's it spreading?' asked Steve.

'Seems to be all traced back to Donchester mart so far. Movement of sheep or personnel from the market. Plenty of drovers in the market who've got their own farms or work on other people's farms. You get a couple of infected sheep in a pen, breathing out virus all over the wool of other sheep. People handle the sheep; get it on their hands, underneath their finger nails and carry it back to their own farms. Other sheep inhale the virus from the wool and after incubating it for a few days they go down with it too. Simple stuff really. It's not rocket science you know.'

'We've got problems here with carcasses lying. They're going rotten even in this cold weather,' said Steve.

'Aye it's started to happen over here too. We can't keep up with it.'

'What about getting the army in to help? A lot of people over here are asking about it.'

'It's an option. Put it in a report to Graham and see what happens. I might need you over here in a day or two. If we keep getting more cases than Morton I'm not going to keep on top of them. Colin Hunt seems to have lost the plot a bit and his boss Des Quiet seems to be doing just that, keeping in the background. He's a vet from Sage Street and I'm not even sure what his role is meant to be: doesn't seem to be doing anything useful, just turns up out of the blue, skulks around a bit and then disappears again without having said anything.'

'I know what you mean,' laughed Steve. 'He's been over here a couple of times this week. Sharp suit, polished shoes, smart briefcase, all the trappings of someone in power but I've not heard him utter a word of sense yet. The only useful thing I've seen him do is make a cup of coffee.'

'Right, keep in touch Steve lad. And don't forget you're a veterinary surgeon. There's a danger if we do forget,.. for all of us.'

Steve wasn't sure what Neil meant.

He turned on the ten o'clock news. The Foot and Mouth outbreak occupied the first twenty minutes with graphic pictures of cattle carcasses being loaded onto half built pyres and others of pyres already lit and burning. Pictures from helicopters; pictures from far away; pictures from close to; the public it seemed could not get enough of it.

Spokesman after spokesman had an opinion of their own to impart; the Farmers Club president more vociferous than ever that the disease must be stamped out with no detrimental financial consequences to his members. Representatives of tourism organisations were beginning to raise the spectre of what was happening to Britain's image abroad, particularly in America where it seemed the average American thought the whole of England was engulfed in flames.

The Minister for Rural affairs looked calm, even complacent as he spoke of 'Bearing down on the disease to first isolate it and then eradicate it.'

And finally Ron Steady. Pompous and self-assured he confirmed that everything was under control; his staff working hard and effectively to contain the outbreak. There was no crisis. No epidemic. The policy was clear and unambiguous with no need to change. He was in charge and steering a steady course with land in sight ahead. If he had but known then that is was merely a mirage on the horizon thrown up by the storms and winds that as yet lay unseen, it is unlikely he would have worn such a confident smile on his lips.

Chapter 32

Steve's report winged its way down the phone lines first thing the next day. He copied it to Colin Hunt, Neil, and Beryl. Looking back he could only smile at its timidity and tone of diplomacy.

'On some farms carcasses are beginning to putrefy whilst awaiting incineration. Could consideration be given to the use of small army teams to help with pyre construction to speed up the process?' it read.

Apologetic in its tone. **'.. small army teams...'** as if it were a heresy to suggest that The Veterinary Service could not cope. He had become a Ministry man he thought to himself. His apprenticeship was over. No longer the plain speaking shit stirrer who left no one in doubt of his views when he first joined. Now he was hiding behind carefully constructed sentences, weasel words, covering his back with the best of them.

'Small army teams..' could mean anything you wanted. From two or three brawny squaddies to half a bloody regiment. He had done enough. Overstepped the mark really. Passed on enough information to those above to exonerate himself of responsibility. His view was there in black and white. Let them act on it or otherwise. He had enough to do with trying to work out the epidemiology of how it was passing from farm to farm and come up with an idea for stopping it. Even in that he felt he was acting out a part. Foot and Mouth was as old a plague as time. Everyone knew how it spread. Movement of live animals and fomites; people, machinery, dung, milk; and in the wind. Okay, birds could probably spread it on occasions and the odd hedgehog, (impaled on the tyres of a passing lorry and later flung into the face of a surprised cow), might have taken it from one farm to another somewhere in the distant past. But live animals and fomites were the enemy. As Neil had said the previous night, 'It's not rocket science.'

It was true that this Pan-Asia strain was more virulent than many of the other strains. But the principle of transmission was the same, and it behaved in the same way as all the others. It was not a mystery virus and the world was full of examples of how it had been controlled in the past. Stamping out by slaughter, and/or vaccination.

With the e-mail gone, Steve went to find Beryl. Jeremy Roberts was there with her, waving his arms around, his moustache flapping up and down on his schoolboy face.

'We need more ammunition out at Peabody Farm. The slaughterers have got another four hundred sheep to get through and they've only got 150 rounds left. I said I'd take some out to them now. We can't hold this up, the farmer is distraught enough.'

He grabbed a box of a thousand rounds from the pile on Beryl's desk. And then grabbed another.

'Better take two,' he gushed, 'you never know what might be just round the corner. Oh hi Steve. How did you get on with Sage Street? Things are getting worse still. How many report cases today Beryl? Cardington are sending over a couple more clean vets for us but apparently they've got even more report cases than us.' He rocked backwards and forwards on his toes as he spoke, his eyes bright and cheerful with excitement.

'Still, can't stop. Got to take this little lot out to Peabody Farm and supervise the slaughter.' He made a grab in passing for a third box of cartridges but Beryl had anticipated his move and was too quick for him.

'No you don't,' she said. 'We need to keep some of these for emergencies, we don't know when we're getting any more. The suppliers have already run out of disinfectant so it'll probably be cartridges next. Just take the one box Jeremy. If the slaughterers can't kill four hundred sheep with over a thousand cartridges then we need to change the slaughterers. Don't you think?' she added with a note of good natured sarcasm.

Jeremy sheepishly handed back one of the boxes. Like a child handing a stolen chocolate bar back to its mother.

'Right, must dash. See you later Steve,' and he was off.

'He's a nutter isn't he,' said Steve.

'Oh yes,' said Beryl good naturedly. 'I was at college with him. He was a nutter then too.'

'But a nice nutter,' Steve added.

'Oh yes,' Beryl agreed and Steve saw a light flicker deep in her eyes, a match half struck and then extinguished.

'Hi Willie,' said Steve. 'What are you up to?'

'Fernando and I are off to Cardington in a few minutes. Seemingly a big beef farm over there gone down with it and we're to take charge of slaughter and disposal seeing as we're so experienced like.'

'How's Morag? And the kids?'

'Fine, fine. Not even missing me yet. I can't believe it's nearly two weeks since we got down here.'

'Nor can I,' Steve agreed. 'And I think we're going to be here a while yet,' he added.

'Right, you look after yourself you big English twat,' said Willie. 'No doubt we'll be seeing you shortly.'

'I think so,' said Steve. 'Beryl, I'm off to John Saunders' place; they're killing sheep there today and I want to have a look at some of the lesions and assess the possible DCs. Is he a pedigree breeder or something?'

'Yes,' said Beryl in her slow way. 'He's a good farmer and keeps good records. I don't think you'll have any trouble there. Now,… who's in charge of the slaughter?' she spoke her thoughts aloud. 'I think it's that young lad who arrived yesterday. Nice lad but a bit wet behind the ears. You'd better get going, it'll take you an hour to get there.'

Steve went out to the car park, the cold cutting through his clothing and settling on his exposed face and hands like the touch of death. His car was at the far end, it was too congested round by the back door with everyone trying to cleanse and disinfect clothing and equipment in tiny rooms that were designed for the relaxed pace of peacetime. This whole place is probably swimming in virus thought Steve. How the hell could you organise it to keep it clean, the infrastructure just isn't there. He shook his head. There were some things within his power to change and some things that were not. He stuck his hands in his pocket, they were already frozen, blue and purple, the skin dried and cracking from the effects of water and disinfectant.

The two foot long gash in the hood of his Austin Healey could only have been done with a knife. Clean and smooth, a single swift stroke; probably trying to steal the radio and been disturbed. Yes, that was it, the radio, and then he thought of Paul and the razor blade in the letter. His finger had only just healed, he stroked the smooth scar with his other hand, still sensitive to the touch.

He looked around, felt the thud of his heart and the hairs on his neck tighten, expecting to see a murderer crouching behind a wall, watching him, waiting his chance. All he saw were people going backwards and forwards to their cars, nothing sinister. Perhaps it was a coincidence. His imagination getting the better of him. A feeling of nausea; of loneliness and desertion swept through him like a rushing river swollen by a flood, as memories that he'd thought were long since dead danced and sparkled.

He took some tape from the boot and taped the inside of the hood and then the outside too. It would keep out the rain and the worst of the wind until he could get a new one. He headed south and turned right towards the Pennines. He knew the area well from when he'd lived and farmed not far away all those years ago.

He bought a ram from a farm close to where he was passing now. A good ram lamb to use on his ewes. Their ewes he corrected himself. Rachel was an equal part of it. Just as interested as he was; just as fired up by the prospects that lay ahead. He smiled to himself. He could look back now with less distress. With warmth and pleasure even. They had been good times back then. Great and happy times until it had all gone wrong. All gone wrong, he thought to himself. For him at least. Rachel had taken it all in her stride, a great exciting adventure, a ride at the fair with all the thrills and none of the spills. Well she was in control. It was bound to be smooth for her. Smooth and exciting with no bottomless pit of snakes and monsters to crawl from. Just walking off into the sunset with her new love without bothering to look behind.

Yes it had been easy for her. She had suffered no loneliness. He had been the one left to pick up the pieces of his life. To travel down to London with everything he possessed packed into two large bags. Climbing aboard the National Express bus with next to no money and a throbbing pain so deep inside his chest that he thought it would split open and that he would die on a bus to nowhere surrounded by strangers.

Sitting on the bus and waving to a couple of friends as it pulled out of the bus station, he had seen in their faces the wasted five years of his life. Five years when he had taken the wrong turn, left the path that he had dreamed was his destiny and headed out into a wilderness with no map and a travelling companion whose heart was not steadfast and true.

And when they had reached the pass; when the mountain had become too hard and steep to climb; when the wind had howled and the driving rain had forced them to take shelter they had met another man. A stranger who had the eyes of a snake and the tongue of a butterfly that entranced and fluttered delicately from one beautiful flower to another; stopping to sip the sweet nectar of each but always looking for what the flower could give it by way of nourishment.

And Rachel had learned from the stranger that there was another way. Another route that they could take that was not so hard and she had told Steve that she could not carry on to the summit. So Steve told her that he could not go on without her. That he would gladly abandon the quest and go the way that she would choose because he could not live but with her by his side.

But she had told him that there was no room for him on her chosen path. That she would go accompanied by the stranger and that he must make his own way from the mountain but to keep in touch. And she left him there, clinging to the rock face not knowing whether to go ahead or turn back down the path or to leap into the abyss and down into the rushing brown river that lay below.

And so he took a bus to London and he marvelled now that he had never again found his way back. Never again found a companion that he would trust with his heart. And now, fifteen years on it was too late.

It was snowing now and the big Healey was sliding around the corners and he slowed down. He was calm and composed. There was a long haul ahead, that much he knew. He had to stay calm. Had to pace himself. Already there were those he could see had overdone things. Fifteen and sixteen hour days. Too much and unsustainable. He braked carefully as a car skidded a hundred yards ahead of him. His Healey was not good in the snow. Rear wheel drive and too much power. Too long and too light. Moved like a wriggling snake when there was ice about.

He found his way to John Sanders' farm and looked across to where the killing was already underway beneath the showers of snow and a gusting easterly wind. In the corner of a field 250 Swaledale ewes milled and bleated. No shelter for man nor beast he thought as he pulled into the entrance of the farm track and came to a halt. He pulled on a thick woollen jumper and then a paper boiler suit, his limbs stiffened and stuck out from his body, held rigid by the thick layers of clothes to keep out the cold. With difficulty he pulled on waterproof trousers and jacket, his hands blue and numb again.

Living at the farm had taught him about the cold. Before that he had not understood how people became lost in snowstorms and died of cold and exposure. He'd never believed it until the winter storms at the farm. Winter storms when they cuddled together inside their house, only venturing out to fetch more coal and wood for the fire that blazed and kept them warm. And the dash from the front door of the house to the door of the byre with wind and white powder stinging their eyes and cheeks so that they could see nothing about them, only trace their hand along the rough stone wall of the house to keep their sense of direction. Then he knew how the snow could kill. How it could disorientate you and lose you and leave you to freeze and die.

Yes he knew the power of the snow and he knew the beauty too. Of stepping out into crisp virgin snow on a still calm day of frost and sun with blue skies reflected blue in the snow so that sky and land were one. And walking hand in hand with Rachel and the dogs leaping and chasing and throwing themselves down into the drifts as they snuffled nose and face and white crystals hanging from their mouths in grinning welcome.

Yes he knew the snow. Knew the power and the passion it held and evoked. Like love. Beautiful and evocative. Cleansing and refreshing. And with the power to destroy a man. Destroy a man and freeze his heart to ice. Freeze it to a solid mass that beat with a pulse so weak and feeble that the blood flowed like cold treacle and he died slow and silent for lack of nourishment and its suffocating grip.

He walked down the track to the yard and then across the field to where he could see them working. A horror film before his eyes. Gratuitous violence with the blessing of the State. The slaughterers were young and rough, uneducated and without culture. They were using the green garden canes that you buy at garden centres for staking plants as pithing rods to make sure that the sheep were dead. But instead of removing the canes they had left them or broken them off so that the sheep carcasses lay strewn around with irregular lengths of green stick protruding at odd angles from the hole in their head, bent over and frayed with blood and brain tissue dripping from them onto the snow covered grass. The deathly look in the pale yellow glazed eyes, accentuated by the grizzly canes that gave them the look of slaughtered unicorns.

It was plainly obscene, the rough and ready probing with a jagged piece of wood, searching out the brain tissue that gave life so that it could be disrupted and destroyed. Like a surgeon in medieval times roughly hewing away at diseased tissue whilst the patient was held down to the operating table and given a piece of padded wood against which to bite his pain. Like the executioner, hooded and gloved, cutting into the living abdomen of the condemned man lashed to the table to draw out the entrails and display them to the gaping crowd of cheering onlookers.

His flesh tingled with uneasy questions. This was not how it was meant to be. He searched around the faces of all those present for signs of distress or disbelief and saw none.

'I'm Steve Turner from the Ministry,' he said. 'I'm in the epidemiology team. Looking at how the disease is spreading.'

'John Sanders,' said a man. 'These are my sheep,' he nodded at the pile of corpses and the pen of live sheep awaiting the slaughterer's bolt.

'I'm Cameron Davies,' said a young lad who'd been checking the corpses for signs of life. 'Practicing vet from Yorkshire.'

'Hi,' said Steve. 'Is this your first IP?'

'Yes,' said Cameron, 'I arrived in Morton yesterday and was told to come out here this morning for 10.00 a.m. We're still waiting for straw and coal to be delivered to make the fire. We should be finished with the slaughter in another hour.'

Steve nodded trying to keep the look of distaste off his face. It was all about respect for the animals he thought to himself. Respecting them as animate objects instead of treating them as waste material. He knew it didn't matter to the animals what happened to them once they were unconscious and unfeeling. But it matters to us he thought. It matters to us as human beings. It's about our humanity. Lose that he thought, and we lose everything. He wanted to tell them to remove the green sticks. To lay the sheep out in rows without the grotesque spectacle of the green canes bursting from their broken heads like some parasitic plant that had seeded in their brain. If he had been in charge of the slaughter he would have made it plain at the start that there was to be respect. But he had not been and now it was irrelevant to those already employed in the gruesome work. To say something now would be to condemn their own sense of judgement and propriety. He stayed silent.

Whilst the slaughter continued he busied himself with examining mouths and feet. The disease had been confirmed at the lab from samples taken a few days previously and already there was nothing to see. This was the great problem with sheep. Too often they showed few signs, mild and transient. They were up against it he thought. Trying to track the movements of a disease barely visible would not be easy.

Bending to examine the sheep was killing his back too. It ached just above his pelvis at the base of his spine. He was not used to physical work now and he was not as supple as he once was.

One afternoon he carried five tons of barley and soya in 50 kilo bags about thirty metres to a mobile grain mill and then carried the milled and mixed feed all the way back again. He had done it by himself, lifting the bags with ease and working non-stop until the job was done. When Rachel returned from work that evening she had thrilled to the feat and rubbed his shoulders for him in the bath before leading him to bed.

Compared to then he was a wreck. Not to look at but underneath the outer skin and within. The only comfort was that age did it to you and it was happening to all those around him too, at a faster rate in many cases. It was a small comfort.

He glanced up to watch the men at their work. He winced at the sight of them poring over a sheep's head, trying to insert the green cane into the hole in the skull, twiddling it around and then forcing it in with brute strength, screwing it round as if clearing a blocked drain, the sheep's legs kicking and thrusting as the slaughterer screwed the cane in harder until it snapped to leave a jagged edge.

'It'll come out its fucking arse, if you screw it any harder,' said one man laughing.

'Aye, y'er fucking right,' said the cane screwer and he moved on to the next one.

If the Public saw what we were doing, thought Steve. Doing in their name. He shivered and it was not with cold. He'd always thought that slaughter was the right way to tackle the problem. He still did. Short term pain for long term gain. Getting on top of the thing quickly was to everyone's advantage. But this was the reality of what that meant. The practicalities of carrying it out. You couldn't just kill animals and dispose of them with a magic wand. You had to gather them up; confine them; slaughter them; and then burn or bury them. And all that added up to a messy business. Blood and guts; shit and brains all over the place. A messy, dirty business. You had to believe in it to get it done. You had to believe wholeheartedly that the end was just.

Only then could you tolerate the bleating of the sheep and the bellowing of the cattle. The clicks and thuds and clatters; the gentle passive sinking of wool against wool; the swearing and laughter of the slaughterers; the tears and desperate eyes of the farmers as they watched their stock reduced to garbage. It was a strange philosophy thought Steve. Someday, somebody somewhere, would have to explain and account for all that was done.

By mid afternoon he had finished his work and the snow had stopped falling. They had cakes and coffee in John's kitchen. The coal and kindling would arrive the next day so Cameron went to spray the carcasses with disinfectant and cover them with a tarpaulin against the crows.

Steve drove slowly back to Morton enjoying the snow clad landscape and the grey sky that promised more snow to come. He turned on the radio to catch the four o'clock news.

'Nigel Brawn the Minister for Rural Affairs said earlier today that he was confident that the Foot and Mouth outbreak was under control and dismissed the allegation that there was an epidemic. He also said that the stories of carcasses being left to rot on farms prior to disposal were greatly exaggerated. The Government Principal Veterinary Officer, Ron Steady, echoed the Minister's words and said that he was confident the disease would be confined and quickly eliminated by his staff.

'In another development there have been several more confirmed outbreaks of the disease in Devon on farms with links to a sheep dealer who transported sheep from the north of England prior to the livestock movement ban. Ministry officials have placed several more farms under restriction and the slaughter of livestock on these farms is already underway...'

Steve's head was fuzzy. He looked around the fields on either side of the road. There were sheep everywhere in this part of the country as soon as you left the fertile arable plain. Swaledales on the hills, mules on the lower ground. It would not be easy to stop the thing now that the sheep flock was infected. He thought about what he would do if he were Ron Steady. Perhaps they should be slaughtering out everything within three kilometres of an IP. Hit it really hard to cut down on the risks of virus spread. Or ring vaccination. Vaccinate a wide strip of animals around an IP to stop the disease getting out. Easy to do if you had a single outbreak but they seemed to be popping up all over the place. Where would you start to ring vaccinate?

Each solution raised more questions. Questions that Steve did not know the answers to. Over and over he turned the possibilities, trying to understand the consequences of each. A pit of serpents, grabbing at each wriggling tail and trying to follow it to its head whilst it writhed amidst a mass of overlaid and tangled bodies. He tussled and teased at it but each time he found an answer another possibility reared up at him that needed to be deflected and disarmed. He arrived back at Morton with a searing headache that threatened to burst out through his forehead in a rush of blood, cerebral fluid and nervous tissue spilling down his face with his brown eyes glazed and staring.

He went to see Beryl in her office. She sat at her desk in the eye of the storm, a tiny patch of calm with the winds of chaos revolving around her yet leaving her untouched.

'We've had another couple of infected farms today,' she said, 'but Cardington are having it worse. Neil's been on the phone today. He wants you over there first thing tomorrow morning to give him a hand for a day or two.'

'I thought he would,' said Steve. 'I suppose I should move to a hotel over there.'

'No, don't do that,' said Beryl. 'We want an epidemiologist over here. Just go over each day for a couple of days, it's only an hour or so. You can't just leave us.' Her smile was genuine and Steve was touched.

A figure that Steve recognised passed the door and he shuddered.

'Was that Conrad?' he asked Beryl.

'Yes. Do you know him?'

'Sort of,' said Steve, his heart quickening and a tight sharp knot twisting at his stomach. 'When did he arrive?'

'He was here first thing this morning when I came in.'

Steve thought about the hood of his Healey. It couldn't be coincidence. Surely. His mouth went dry, a metallic taste, like chrome or copper. He swallowed but there was no saliva, his tongue stuck to the sides of his mouth at the back, his throat tight in a laryngeal spasm that made it hard to breathe. He forced a cough and felt his airway open again.

Thank God he was going to Cardington. He would get his reports up to date and set off from the hotel at just after seven the next morning. With a bit of luck he might be able to move over there permanently. He was flattered by Beryl's wish to keep him in Morton but in spite of all his misgivings, if the disease situation was worse in

Cardington, that was where he wanted to be. And besides, that was where Willie and Fernando were. At Cardington he knew that he would be amongst friends.

Chapter 33

'Come in Steve lad,' Neil greeted him with obvious pleasure. It was nearly eight thirty in the morning. Steve had travelled from east to west on the main trunk road. The fire at Warren Farm was still smouldering grey as he went past and he could see the thick black smoke from another pyre lit the previous day. Then it had been all clear until he'd reached the motorway and then more smoke had appeared in the distance. Like towns sacked in the Middle Ages he thought. Burnt and pillaged, the residents killed or taken away as slaves or concubines. He'd found the Cardington Animal Health Office with no trouble. Parking was almost impossible.

The big open plan office had two or three times the number of people compared to Morton. This was where all Morton's work was allocated. All under the direction of the man in charge, Colin Hunt.

It was the phones ringing that struck him first. That and the number of people answering them and sat at the computer screens that filled the office like a Wall Street trader's dealing room. That's just what it is, thought Steve. A trading room in death instead of shares. 'You cynical bastard,' he muttered under his breath.

'How's it going Neil?' Steve asked.

'Not good. Disease is spreading out north and south of Cardington Bay. Even more worrying is that it's started to go due south down this valley here,' he pointed to the map. 'It's got into the dairy herds and we don't quite know how. That's your job for the next couple of days,' he laughed, 'to find out. I've got to go to Sage Street tomorrow to see Graham. I'll be back the next day. Get your things moved over here; Accommodation will book you into a hotel. It's down to the two of us Steve, there's no one else.'

'Give me a run down on the epidemiology to date will you? We've had trouble getting maps sent over to Morton and there's no one there to draw them by hand. Communications are shite.'

'Aye lad and no better here either. I'm working in virtual isolation myself, reporting to Graham at Sage Street and Hunt's doing his own thing. Just trying to get the initial vet report for each IP copied to us is a bloody nightmare. JENNIFER,' he bellowed. 'Where's the latest IP map? Someone from mapping brought it up yesterday evening.'

Jenny, red haired with a tiny upturned nose sprang into action. 'Here you are,' she said, spreading it out on the table. 'There were three more yesterday in our area including another down to the south here. A big dairy herd I think.'

'That's where I want you to go today,' said Neil. 'Try and find out how it's got there.' He was deadly serious, dark rings round his eyes, fixing Steve with an owl-like stare. 'If you can do that you can maybe save the dairy industry up here. If you can't…. it's that bloody serious.'

'You can rely on me,' joked Steve. He smiled at Jenny and she smiled back.

'Have we got a preliminary report for this place yet?' asked Steve.

'You're joking,' said Neil. 'Just go out there and see what you can find out. Give me a call later if you come up with anything. And I'll see you when I get back from London.'

Steve went back into the main office. Sammy was there.

'Steve,' she squealed.

'Sammy.'

They hugged each other.

'When did you come across here?' Steve asked. 'We're keeping such odd hours and the days don't seem to mean anything anymore.'

'Three days ago. Oh Steve, I'm so glad you're here. Get booked into The King's Head. Willie and Fernando are there and a lot of good vets too. Speak to Doug in Accommodation. Tell him I sent you.' She winked.

'Got them eating out of your hand already eh? I'm back in Morton tonight but I'll organise The King's Head for tomorrow.'

'No, get your gear sent over from the hotel with the courier van. You don't want to drive all the way back over there and then back here again. No arguing,' she said putting her hands to her ears. 'Go and see Doug….. now!'

Steve grinned. 'Yes mum,' he said.

The Accommodation portacabin was in the car park; Broadwich relived. Doug was a bright young bloke from Birmingham who sounded as if he sold second hand cars for a living. Just the sort of hustler you need on this job, thought Steve. He booked The King's Head for an indefinite stay.

'I'll organise your personal gear from Morton too,' said Doug.

As easy as that thought Steve and then he bumped into Julie. Her face reddened on seeing him, hot to the touch, inside and out, her pupils dilated.

'Julie,' he said, 'how are you?' He tried to be friendly. To put her at ease.

'Okay Steve,' she said, 'I, I'm okay. I didn't know you were here. I was across at Morton yesterday and they told me you were…' she stopped in mid sentence. 'It doesn't matter. Nothing matters. It's nothing. Forget it.' Tears welled in her eyes and she looked away.

Steve put his hand on her shoulder to comfort her but she pushed it away and spun round.

'Don't touch me you bastard,' she snapped. 'Don't you dare to touch me you filthy bastard,' her voice was raised and Doug and a couple of others had stopped to watch what was going on.

'Julie,' said Steve. 'That's not fair, I..'

'Not fair,' she was shouting. 'I'll tell you what's not fair. Using me like you did. That's not fair. I hate you, you bastard. I hate you. Don't ever touch me again.'

Steve stood looking round the cabin at the eyes on him. He wanted to tell them all the truth. Tell them what had happened in his life and why he was the way that he was. That he'd broken no promises. That he hadn't led her on. That she'd led herself on. Read more into it than there was. Stifled him and tried to control him. But there wasn't time to tell them everything and what's more it was none of their fucking business anyway. He went out of the door and pulled it quietly shut behind him.

He didn't need that. Not just at this moment. Life was tough enough just now. Stupid bitch he thought. Stupid fucking bitch. His hands and lips were trembling, the blood rushing in his brain; fight or flight. He was angry. He felt like going back inside and shouting at her. He remembered how he had shouted at Rachel one morning as he climbed out of bed.

'What do you think you're fucking playing at Rachel?' he shouted and he threw a mug against the bedroom wall with all his force so that it gouged a piece out of the plaster and the mug broke into a hundred pieces. 'What are you fucking playing at? Do you know? Do you?' he screamed at her.

She lay there with the covers up to her throat, whimpering like a puppy separated from its mother, unable to look him in the eyes.

'I don't know Steve,' she said. 'It's just something I have to do. It's something so strong inside me that I just know it's right. Something as strong as this couldn't be wrong.'

He shouted and screamed at her again and she pulled the covers up over her head so that there was nothing of her for him to see. He dressed and picked up the pieces of mug and went out with the dogs up the field. Ten minutes later he saw her driving up the road to the gate at the top of the hill.

The sharp vivid nature of the vision stabbed at him now. Even after fifteen years the scars were keen and raw, easily reopened. Such a fragile thing human emotion. He caught the movement of a drop of water passing in front of his body. He realised that he was crying. 'Stupid fucking bitch,' he whispered. He wasn't sure if he meant Julie or Rachel.

It was after lunch when he arrived at Spottiswood Farm. There were half a dozen other cars at the gate. 'Another bloody party', he sighed.

There was no good time to do the job he now needed to do. For the sake of disease control it was the sooner the better after diagnosis to pick up any leads whilst they were still fresh in the farmer's mind. It was useful to be there at slaughter too so you could examine the mouths and feet; look for the oldest lesions and decide what percentage of the stock were affected. That way you had an idea of how long the disease had been there and where it could have spread to.

He walked into the yard and recognised Adrian Pope, a Veterinary Officer from the south of England. He had been in Cardington from the start and already had a number of large IPs under his belt. His confidence had grown with each of them, like a prize fighter with some good wins to his name. Now he had a supervisory role, a point of contact and troubleshooter for several IPs, each controlled by a vet. If they had any doubts or problems they came to him and he would solve them. He set newly appointed vets off on their first killing job and the girl beside him was the one for Spottiswood.

'Hi Steve,' he said. 'God you've got an easy job.' He was deadly serious.

How do you know how easy my job is, thought Steve. He felt the blood moving up his neck and had to try harder than he'd expected to control the pitch of his voice.

'We all have our difficulties,' he said, trying to take the sting from Adrian's remark but he felt angry. Who the fuck was Adrian to say that he had an easy job. He was suddenly wounded and resentful, a dangerous beast.

'This is Sue,' said Adrian, oblivious to the offence caused. 'They've just finishing valuing the sheep and are starting on the dairy cows. All bloody pedigrees so it's a case of individual valuations; looking at the milking records; the breeding record; you know the score. It's an all day and probably half the night job. This is Sue's first IP so I'll hang around until the slaughter gets underway. I've got Tam and Bob coming to do the slaughter. Good lads. I've done a few IPs with them. Do you know them?'

Steve shook his head.

'You were at Warren Farm weren't you? Bad case of neglect I heard. Still it was only a small slaughter wasn't it? Five or six hundred? A few days ago we were slaughtering out a farm with 2000 cattle. Had three or four slaughter teams on the go. Finished about two in the morning. Great bit of work too. And now we're getting vets on the phone with a couple of hundred bullocks to kill whinging that they haven't got the facilities or they don't know what to do. It's so bloody simple.'

Steve cringed. It was simple to Adrian. Or perhaps Adrian was simple. Perhaps there was no difference. He was an inflated balloon, growing in importance with every click of the captive bolt and every clatter of the hooves on concrete. Black and white, no shades of grey or blurring round the edges. I'd like to stick a pin in him, thought Steve. To see if he'd go pop or whether he'd just whizz around in the air for a bit before coming back to earth like a used condom and about as much use.

'This is the farmer, Dick Tindall,' said Adrian as more people joined them. 'And the valuers from the auction mart.'

'What do you need from me?' Dick asked. 'I'll not be free to speak to you until the valuers have finished, but the dairyman's here. He can help out now if that's any use. He knows as much about the thing as I do.'

'That'd be good,' said Steve. 'If he can sit down with me and have a chat first and then I'll take a look round. And if I need anything else I'll see you when you're free.'

The farm office was freezing cold and filthy. Cow shit and paperwork mixed to produce a mass of off-white paper with brown and green stains spread liberally across the surface. Mouse droppings and flecks of dried cow dung were scattered across the concrete floor, cobwebs filled the corners and hung from lampshades like forgotten party streamers. Half used bottles of antibiotic sat on a dust laden shelf, a filthy greasy syringe with needle attached beside them. An array of other medicines too, the sort of things that should only be administered by a vet, not supplied to order for the farmer to use whenever he saw fit. In another life, at another time, Steve would have pointed out that all these things should be locked away in a cupboard.

But in the space of some two weeks the world had changed and there was now only one objective. Everything else was consigned to the back burner or the rubbish heap. In times of war, trivia was ignored and there could be no doubt in the minds of anyone in the front line that war was now what it was. And his job in that war was to get at the truth. To ask the questions, hear the answers, and ask the question again and again until he was satisfied that he had the whole truth. The whys and wherefores behind the bald facts were of no concern to him. The virus was no respecter of good intentions. The farmer sat in the witness box and he was the inquisitor. It was a challenge. A mental challenge that he tried to exercise with tact and sensitivity, recognising that on every farm he visited there was a story of human suffering, barely hidden behind the etiquette of non-acquaintance, just waiting to be poured out.

He saw it in the moisture in their eyes and the wide pupils that focused on a distant object instead of on his face. He heard it in the words and phrases they used, the tone and inflection of their voice. Saw it in the way they pulled on their boots and took up their stick; the way they called to their dog, opened and fastened a gate; the way they drank their coffee and ate a biscuit.

He became expert at reading the signs and his own expressions and mannerisms evolved to cope with them. Expression and mannerisms that he prayed were heartfelt and not just Ministry written stage managed platitudes. A smile in the right place; a pause for silence; a change of tack; a hand on the shoulder; trying to show that he at least understood their pain even if he did not feel it himself. He hoped that people might feel better for his visit rather than worse.

And he knew too that **veterinary** risk assessment was the key to preventing the spread of disease without slaughtering countless animals unnecessarily. Without risk assessment, Stamping out by slaughter could proceed uncontrolled until there were no animals left. That was why his job and the job of all the other vets involved was so important. Take that away and you didn't need vets at all. Take that away and it would be reduced to butchery.

He spent two hours talking with the dairyman and then they went outside to look at the first case. The black and white Holstein cow was lying alone in a straw-bedded pen, her eyes sunken, head stretched out, thick gelatinous saliva dripping from her mouth. She had calved two weeks previously, stressful times, her resistance low. 'The only thing I would say,' the dairyman was apologetic, 'is that the smoke from the pyre at Little Framston came right up the valley there,' he pointed, 'and hung around for hours. That was a week ago and the cubicle shed is the nearest building to it. Can the smoke carry the virus?'

Steve wasn't sure. He knew what the official line was: 'That the heat of the fire is such that all virus will be destroyed.'

But who could really know what might happen in the thermals and updrafts before the heat had built up. The science was imperfect. How could it be otherwise? How could experiments be done to cover every conceivable variable in temperature, humidity, wind speed and virus load? Computer models could help but they were only as good as the data they were based on. It was impossible to know for certain.

He answered with the official line but not too adamantly. He was too honest for that.

'If you're finished with me I'll go and see how the valuation's going.'

'No problem,' said Steve. 'Thanks for your help. I'll come and get you if I need anything else. And I'll have a chat with Dick when he's free.'

Steve made his way around the sheds making a plan of the buildings and the type of stock in each one. He had time on his hands now. Time to think and consider. The late afternoon was dull, a curlew called in the distance, a haunting piping call that rekindled a rash of memories. He noticed a couple of blokes in the yard, swinging captive bolts and he went over and introduced himself.

'I'm Tam and this is Bob,' replied one of them. 'Adrian's got us here to slaughter the stock. He told us to get cracking on the sheep in the shed over there. They'll be finished valuing the cattle in an hour.'

Alarm bells ringing in his head; thoughts racing of impending catastrophe. The slaughter should be supervised by a vet but he, Steve Turner, was not there to do it. He had another remit. But Adrian had been at plenty of slaughters. He knew the score. He had experience.

'Where is Adrian?' he asked.

'He and that little vet, Sue her name; they've gone down the field to find a burning site. Told us to get on with the job. Can't wait around any longer. Cracking bloke is Adrian. Fucking good bloke. Leaves you to get on with things without sticking his great fucking nose in. Knows we're the professionals and lets us do it.'

I bet thought Steve. 'I need to have a look at the sheep so I'll come along,' he said.

He saw the two men exchange glances. 'Aye well,' said Tam. 'As you like.'

Whilst Steve set about catching and examining lame sheep, Bob and Tam wasted no time. They filled the main passageway with sheep and waded in with the captive bolts. By the time Steve realised what was going on there was a mass of live sheep overlain by the carcasses of others whilst the slaughterers walked across the sea of twitching writhing fleeces.

'Sto-o-o-p.' Steve shouted above the bleating and cursing. 'This is no good, there're too many in there. We'll have to pull the dead ones back so that you can get to those beneath them. Put your bolts down and let's do this properly.'

'Aye, right enough,' said Tam 'Just pass that pistol first Bob, there's a fucking great tup under here.'

Had Adrian authorised the use of free bullets? thought Steve. He didn't know. Frantically he hunted round for somewhere to hide. A ricochet was unlikely but people got killed every year in even less likely circumstances. He pulled a couple of straw bales between him and Tam and tried to crouch in the gloom behind them. With his layers of warm clothes and protective clothing he was like a wooden man, unbending, unyielding. He tried to crouch to make himself small, curled in a ball but it was impossible and all he could do was get on his hands and knees and hide his head behind the bales. Like a fool, he thought. Like a great big Ministry ostrich burying its head in the fucking sand in the hope that nothing would see it.

The retort from the gun echoed loud and clear and he felt no pain. This is fucking ridiculous, he thought. I can't believe I'm on my hands and knees with my head hidden behind a straw bale in fear of my fucking life.

'Tam,' he called without lifting his head. 'Stop shooting now, it's too dangerous.' He waited a few seconds and cautiously lifted his head. The two men were looking at him with undisguised contempt.

'These tups have awful hard heads,' said Tam. 'The live bullet will kill them stone dead.'

'While I'm here live ammunition is banned,' said Steve. 'Use a Cow Puncher and pith them. It might take longer but it's safer.'

'If that's the way you want it,' said Bob, reluctance thick in his voice. 'You wouldn't have liked what was happening the night before last. We had some right fucking cowboys with us. There was a group of 25 Limmy heifers, completely fucking off their heads with snot and steam coming out their fucking noses and arses. There were these two young guys from Cardington, call themselves slaughterers, straight off the Social more like. They were taking pot shots at them as they ran along the race, fucking bullets flying everywhere. Then you know what one of the cunts wanted me to do. He was going to lie behind a water trough and get me to chase the beasts up and he was going to drop them as they ran past. Not fucking likely I said. It was fucking dark like too with a shit shagging little electric light to work with. Now THAT was fucking dangerous. Even Adrian said so.'

Steve wiped the sweat off his face. His stomach was knotted. Someone would end up dead before this was over.

Tam put the pistol back in its case and Steve climbed over into the passageway.

'These are all done,' said Bob. 'Let's get another penful out.'

'Just hang on,' said Steve. He was shouting. 'They're stacked two and three deep in here. We're going to pull them out and make sure they're all dead because I'm bloody sure they're not.'

Bob and Tam started to pull the dead sheep away and throw them into the pen they'd come from.

'There're two still breathing here,' said Steve. 'Get them shot again please.'

Tam did as he was bid.

'And look, there're three here that haven't been shot at all. This is no bloody good lads. The job's got to be done properly, it's only fair on the animals.' And if the press got wind of it, he thought, they would have a fucking field day.

'Aye, you're right Steve,' said Tam, suddenly mindful of the possibility of losing the most lucrative contract of his entire life, and he popped the sheep that was looking up at him from the heap of fleeces surrounding it. It never moved and its yellow eyes continued staring straight ahead in death.

The slaughterers worked more carefully now that Steve was watching. And with the sheep nearly finished, Adrian appeared with Dick.

'Getting some experience at the sharp end?' Adrian asked Steve. 'You'll not have any problems with these two guys.'

Steve said nothing. Twat, he thought.

'I can speak to you now,' said Dick. 'In fact, once the sheep are done why don't you all come to the office before starting the cattle. Jan is making a heap of bacon rolls and pots of tea. Come and have something to eat.'

It was dark outside now. Damp and cold with the wind racing round the yard rattling gates and loose pieces of roofing tin. Steve hurried to the office with Dick, the smell of grilled bacon raising his spirits, evoking memories of cold mornings back at the farm, the grease on his chin, the burnt smokey taste at the back of his throat. The office looked no cleaner or tidier in the pale artificial light from the shadeless bulb that swayed to and fro in the breeze. A tin tray on the table piled with grease soaked rolls, thick loops of bacon jutting out and spilling clear liquid grease onto the tray, congealing white. Two huge metal teapots, steam drifting out of their curved spouts stood at the ready, a dozen cracked and tea stained mugs beside them.

'Help yourself,' said Dick, 'whilst it's still all warm.'

Steve hadn't eaten since seven that morning and it was now six thirty in the evening. He wiped his hands on some paper towels and, taking a roll from the tray, closed his mouth tight around it.

The warm salty grease and pale smoke swept around his mouth and up into his nasal passages. It sat there, dancing lightly across the pleasure centres in his brain and he felt the Dopamine kick in as a sense of well-being flowed through his tired body and mind. He cupped his hands round the mug of tea that Dick passed across to him, caressing it as a pretty woman.

'Thanks,' he said. 'This bacon roll is just,..... wonderful.'

'Have another,' said Dick. 'There's plenty there and Jan can make more if need be.'

'How did the valuation go?' asked Steve.

'Okay,' he said. 'It looks a lot on paper but I think it's fair. There's some good cows out there. A lifetime's work and more.'

'I can imagine,' Steve said and he took another bacon roll.

The sound of approaching voices and Tam and Bob, Adrian, Sue and the dairyman joined them. The auctioneers were away already; their work done, their pay cheque secured.

'Ah, bacon butties,' said Adrian with relish. He was revelling in the campaign thought Steve.

'Tam and Bob will have these cows finished by eleven tonight,' said Adrian with enthusiasm. 'Sue will get the fire organised for tomorrow and then we can start thinking about the preliminary cleansing and disinfection. This is wonderful bacon. Any sugar for the tea?'

Steve stayed silent. Sometimes it was good just to observe. See how everyone reacted to each other. A psychologist's dream to follow someone around and see the range of emotions that surfaced or were stifled; bent and shaped with the to and fro of events that a couple of weeks ago were unimagined. Adrian's phone rang.

'Adrian Pope,' he said raising his eyebrows to ensure the whole group were listening. 'Yes I know where you are. What's the problem? ... Yes. Yes. I know.... Right. The slaughterers should have been there an hour ago... Well slaughter the three cows that are clinically affected and we'll get the slaughterers there first thing tomorrow if they say they can't come now... Well use Euthatal... Yes, it's pretty bloody simple... You are a vet aren't you? Well just get on and do it. Okay. Okay? Good. Keep in touch. Yes. See you later.' He beamed around at the rest of the group.

'Bloody vets from practice,' he said. 'Present company excepted,' he said to Sue. 'Can't just get on and use their brains. It's all so bloody simple. They seem to want their hands held all the time.'

His attitude was beginning to irritate Steve. This wasn't easy for anybody he thought. At least not anybody who was thinking about what was happening rather than just getting stuck in and following orders. He poured himself some more tea and took a third bacon roll.

'I've only got a few questions to ask you Dick,' he said. 'It might take half an hour.'

'Right,' said Tam to Bob. 'Let's get started on these cows.' He stuffed his pockets full of cartridges.

Everybody else left leaving Steve and Dick alone.

'Are you alright Dick?' asked Steve.

'Yes. Stupid really,' he said, wiping moisture from his eyes with the back of his hand. 'They're all going to be killed in the end anyway. It's just that it seems, well, so final if you know what I mean.'

Steve nodded. He knew exactly what Dick meant. He remembered once seeing a cat catch a sparrow. Trivial, but to the sparrow it was so, so final. That was it. It would never be there again. It was gone; finished. Yes he knew exactly what Dick meant.

It didn't take long to get the answers to his questions.

'Thanks for your help,' he said. 'I shouldn't need to bother you again. I hope the fire gets sorted out tomorrow and everything's cleared quickly.' The sentiment was genuine enough but it had a hollow, dishonest ring to it. Both of them knew it, but they were prepared to pretend for the sake of each other.

'Thanks,' said Dick, and he sounded grateful.

Steve went round to the cubicle shed to see how they were getting on slaughtering the cows. It unnerved him to admit it but he had already developed a fascination with seeing the animals killed. Part of it he could explain by a sense of disbelief and the need to confirm again that it was really happening. But there was a deeper, baser, primeval instinct at work too. A ritualistic, sacrificial instinct. A fascination with being present at the moment when life was changed into death before his eyes without the need to imagine. This is the fascination that spawns ritual sacrifice, he thought. Humanity's thirst for public executions. The experience was shocking but it was a need embedded deep in the psyche of what it was to be human. It was not a noble feeling.

He found Adrian and Sue standing just inside the shed door. In the dim light he could see a crush of black and white bodies, Tam and Bob moving slowly amongst them; a clang of kicking legs against metal barriers; the scraping of hooves on slippery concrete; the thrashing of animals in the throes of death.

'This is where we have to turn a blind eye,' said Adrian to Steve; not sheepishly enough for Steve's liking.

As his eyes became accustomed to the dark he could see the problem immediately. Too many cattle had been crowded into part of the collecting yard and packed tight together at the start. It seemed to have occurred to no one that a cow flat out on the floor took up more room than one standing on all four legs. Now with half the pen of animals stunned or killed, lying and writhing on the floor amidst the blood and piss and shit, the other half, still alive, tripped and sprawled on the carcasses of their herd mates, struggling to find floor space on which to stand.

'They're too bloody tight,' said Steve. 'There're too many in the pen.'

'It's the quickest way of getting the job done,' said Adrian unrepentant.

Steve walked up the feed passageway to stand opposite the pen. It was a scene from the film Caligula. All that was missing was an insane Emperor.

'Can we open that gate and let some out?' he called to Bob.

'No, there's too much pressure on it now, you can't undo the chain.'

Steve could see that what Bob said was true. The cows were now jammed so tight, the ones by the gate were having to lean outwards at an angle, forcing the gates to bow and tightening the chain that kept them closed. Every now and then the frantic kicking of a dying beast would spook the others and they made wild leaps onto the heap of bodies, hooves and legs becoming jammed between the bodies of those already fallen, sometimes with heads and necks flexed at peculiar angles, their weight pinning them to where they balanced precariously on the heap, eyes rolling and bawling with tongues protruded, nostrils flared and flecked with blood and mucus.

'Shoot that one; and that one there,' called Steve, trying to salvage some decency from the whole disastrous business. 'Pith that one next to you Tam,' he called, 'it's still breathing and there's a live one standing on top of it.'

Tam and Bob moved around the pen like apes on a rocky hillside, leaping from rib cage to rib cage, pithing rods in one hand, captive bolts in the other, hands and faces streaked with blood and brain tissue.

God help us thought Steve as he looked at the scene. It was a battlefield from the Middle Ages. Dead and dying animals moaned and thrashed; the few still left to be shot sprawled precariously on top, some sitting unnaturally like dogs, others upended, squashed tight, unable to move.

'There's one here broken its leg,' said Steve pointing to the beast just a few feet away which lay trapped and twisted amidst a pile of bodies, its uppermost front leg flexing and flapping as though there were another joint between its knee and fetlock as it struggled to rise before lying exhausted and still once more.

'It's not been shot yet,' said Steve. 'Tam, put it out of its misery.'

Tam obliged and pithed it immediately setting up a chain reaction of kicking and head throwing that spread out through the group like the ripples on a pond. A mobile phone rang outside the pen and Bob climbed over the gates to answer it.

'It's your wife Tam,' he called. 'She wants to know what time you'll be home and should she keep your supper warm.'

Tam glanced at his watch. 'Tell her it'll be after midnight and not to wait up for me. And tell her to put that little baby doll nightie on for when I get home,' he laughed.

Steve looked across at him and saw a man at ease with himself. A man whose hands and face and clothing were covered in blood and pieces of brain, standing atop a pile of writhing and groaning beasts who stared with unblinking eyes and unthinking minds. In the dim light they were in Mordor. With Trolls and Orcs and Ogres and strange magic with death and destruction at its heart. And amidst all this carnage and debauchery he saw a man who was thinking of his wife dressed in a baby doll nightie awaiting his return. He wondered what Tam's wife would make of it all if she could just for a moment see what was happening.

Then at last it was over. Everything in the pen was shot and pithed. Again the silence. Eerie and disturbing. Broken occasionally by brief reflex kicking or the reflex slapping of a head against another corpse. Nothing breathed. Clouds of steam rose from carcasses like London smog. Steve could smell the smell of death. Something he had not believed or imagined. He could smell it in the air. On his clothes and on his hands. At the back of his throat. It was the smell of blood mixed with dung. The scent of cream white brain tissue mixed with the sweet sickly smell of urine. A smell that clung to everything it touched. That penetrated and made him feel light headed and nauseous. And ashamed. Ashamed that he was a part of what had gone on in front of his own eyes.

'That's that pen finished then,' said Adrian cheerfully.

'They were too crowded,' said Steve, fighting to keep his voice steady. It's not your problem he told himself. You're epidemiology. You're trying to put the brakes on this fucking disease. Welfare at slaughter is up to the likes of Adrian and Sue. You can't do everything.

'I recommend that you only put thirty cows in a pen that size next time Bob,' said Steve. 'Fifty is too many.'

'Aye, you're right enough,' said Bob.

Steve checked his watch. It was a quarter to eight.

'Right,' he said to Adrian and Sue. 'I'm going to go and get this report written. Thanks for your help, I'll see you later. Good luck with getting the fire built tomorrow,' he said to Sue, and tried to sound more cheerful than he felt.

'Bloody part time epidemiologists,' said Adrian, and he was only half joking.

Just do your own job properly, thought Steve. He walked to his car and disinfected as best he could in the cold and rain. His Healey burst welcomingly into life and he felt a damp patch on the seat seep through to his skin where the slash in the hood had leaked. Bastard, he thought. It's that bloody bastard Conrad.

He was shaking with emotion as he drove down the road towards the motorway. His mind was feverish, threads of thoughts found and lost again. Thoughts of Rachel; of Paul's murder; of how Foot and Mouth had reached the farm he'd just left. He thought of life and love and what he would do when this was all over. If it was ever over.

'What am I going to do?' he said out loud. 'What am I going to do with the rest of my life?'

He pulled into the hotel car park and locked the car. He ran through the rain into reception. Fernando, Willie, Sammy and some others were sitting through in the bar.

'Have you eaten yet?' he called through.

'Steve,' said Sammy. 'Where have you been today? You've got blood and shit on your face.'

'I'll tell you later.'

'We are going to eat in here tonight,' said Fernando. 'We will wait for you if you like.'

'I'll be twenty minutes. A quick shower and I'm down.'

He leapt up the stairs and crashed into a young girl. A girl with long, sleek chestnut hair that bounced in curls and waves and ended halfway between her shoulders and her breasts. Her skin was the colour of pale olive oil and her eyes were a mix of green and orange. A leopard. Yes, she was a leopard, he thought.

'I'm sorry,' he said. He saw the startled look on her face, the slight flush of embarrassment in her skin and eyes. 'Are you alright?'

'Yes, I am fine,' she said staring straight at him. At the blood and shit splashed across his face. He saw a glimmer of amusement but it was gone in an instant along with the girl as she made her way down the stairs.

Steve watched her go. Black cotton jeans that fitted snug over her hips and buttocks, a pale mauve cotton T-shirt that highlighted the colour of her bare arms and hair. And she smelt of sea air. Sea air with a hint of vanilla. He went to his room, put all his filthy clothes into a black bin liner, and then he took a scalding hot shower and washed away the pain and obscenity of the day he had just seen.

Chapter 34

He felt better now he was clean and warm. He dressed in jeans and trainers and a Calvin Klein T-shirt. It was cold outside but the hotel was warm, stifling. He had already turned off the radiators in his room. He preferred a cold bedroom. Even sleeping alone he preferred the air around him to be cold.

He went downstairs to the bar, desperate for a pint to soothe away the taste of the day. He wondered where the girl was. He had been thinking of her in the shower. He guessed she was about twenty five. And foreign. Perhaps Spanish from her accent.

He turned the corner into the bar and there she was. She was sitting talking to Sammy.

'Steve, have you met Francesca? She's a vet from Italy. She arrived yesterday.'

Francesca looked at him and he saw again the faint suggestion of amusement in her feline face.

241

'Hello Steve,' she said. 'I think perhaps we have met already on the stairs. At least it was someone very like you but with their hair stuck out like this,' she motioned, 'and on their face some…'

'Yeah, that was me,' said Steve. She was taking the piss. 'Can I get anyone a drink?'

'Red wine please Steve,' said Sammy passing her empty glass to him.

'Fernando?' said Steve, ignoring Francesca deliberately but watching her carefully from the corner of his eye. It would not be cool to dribble and fawn over her and ignore his real friends.

'Thanks. I will take a dry white wine,' he said.

'A pint of lager, big man,' said Willie without waiting to be asked. Steve grinned. When all the world was going mad, some things remained constant. Thank God for Willie, he thought.

'Francesca,' said Steve fixing her now with a gaze that dared her to look away. 'How about you?'

She regarded him unblinking, her pupils large and black, the green and orange irises narrow but brilliant. The whites of her eyes were pure white, no blood vessels to be seen, clear and milky with black eyelashes that curled upwards with no trace of mascara. Her eyebrows, thick, dark and crescent shaped, almost meeting in the middle, her skin clear, unblemished, with a dash of olive oil.

'A glass of water please. Straight from the tap is fine. Your water here is very good,' she added. Serious and thoughtful.

Steve turned away and went to the bar. His mouth was dry and narrow, his stomach filled with butterflies, flitting from side to side, settling for a moment as though on some delicate flower and then dancing and flapping. The feeling of them rose up in his chest and throat, his mind alive and working fast. She had the grace and power of a leopardess and she was beautiful. Quite beautiful. As beautiful as anyone he had ever seen. And her beauty was of the simplest kind. No makeup. No pretentious language or chic clothes. Just simple cotton and nature's blessing. Not for many years had he felt excitement like he felt now.

He took the drinks over, the whole room crowded with Ministry staff and he had to fight his way through. Good old Sammy, thought Steve. Trust her to lay claim to Francesca and keep her out of the way of the jackals that would be circling. Instead bring her to the attention of the Alpha wolf. He laughed to himself at the comparison. An Alpha wolf in sheep's clothing. Or perhaps he reconsidered, just a sheep.

'Shall we go through to the restaurant?' said Fernando. 'There are some spare tables I think.'

They followed him through, the smell of the sea and vanilla filling Steve's head, his skin tingling, stomach knotted. He could not take his eyes from her backside. It was the perfect shape, rounded and full, but narrow and pert. With a little luck and the skill of experience he secured the seat opposite her. Eye contact was the key to her heart. If he could look into her eyes at the right moment, he would see into her soul. Look past the green and orange, through the black hole into the abyss that was her mind and emotion. If he could but look deep inside he could find out all that he needed to know. It had worked so often in the past and his own eyes he knew were hypnotic.

'How can you have such tiny eyes yet such big eyes?' he remembered. He could control people with his eyes. That was why he was sitting opposite her.

'What have you been up to today Willie?' he asked.

'You should have seen the farm I was at. What a fucking mess. They shot the cows five days ago in the cubicles. They're so blown up now they can't get them out. Jammed in tight. And the field in front of the house where they've finally built the fire is like something out of The Somme. They've had this huge heavy machinery running up and down it so many times there are wheel ruts three feet deep. It is fucking shocking.

'Then the contractors went and dug up the mains water pipe when they were building the fire and yesterday they knocked the overhead power cables down. It's lucky no one was killed. So they have no water or mains electricity in the farmhouse.'

'What's the farmer saying to it all?' Steve asked.

'They've had enough and rightly so. The mess we've left there is a fucking disgrace. Colin Hunt wants me to try and sort it out. It's the bloody vet who's to blame for letting it get like that in the first place. This is the fucking pits isn't it?'

'Yes,' said Steve. 'It is and it's going to get worse. How many new cases were there today? Anyone know?'

'Three in Cardington,' said Sammy. 'Six countrywide. Were you out today Francesca?'

'Yes, I was. I went to a report case in a cow near Woodford. But it was not FMD. The animal was limping and it had a wound on the coronary band. The farmer was very worried but it was nothing. All the other stock were very healthy.'

Steve looked at her. She was stunning. Self assured but not over-confident, with a measured tone in her Latin accent. And smelling of the sea and vanilla. The urge to cry when he looked at her was very strong.

'What is your job?' she asked Steve. Direct and with a gentle tone. Wanting to know but not forcing the issue. She looked directly at him. She's trying to see into my soul too, he thought.

'I'm in epidemiology,' he said. He could not bring himself to say 'I'm an epidemiologist.' He didn't use the right words, wasn't familiar with the statistics or the computer programmes. What he did was observe and consider the facts. Look at the possibilities and weigh up what was important and likely. Vets were doing the same thing a hundred years ago to work out how diseases spread and how they could be controlled. Before computers had been thought of. There was too much emphasis today on modern technology, he thought. Too many people looking at the data and analysing the detail without regard for the big picture.

'How long are you here for?' he asked her. He saw Sammy raise an eyebrow and a smile flickered across her lips. She cocked her head on one side to hear the answer.

'I can stay for a few months. My husband is writing up his Doctorate in Rome and needs peace and quiet. He suggested I come here. It is a good experience for me and he can work and work without interference. It is a good arrangement. Don't you think?'

Sammy saw the disappointment on his face. The rigid smile and the slightest change of colour in his cheeks, the eyes that ceased to shine, the creases stiff on his forehead. She giggled to herself. It was just as well he couldn't have everything his own way. He might get above himself and that would spoil him she thought.

Steve did not hear anything beyond the words 'My husband.' He had scanned her hands earlier to confirm that there were no rings. A good Catholic Italian would surely wear a wedding ring if she were married. He had concluded that she was single. Not necessarily unattached, but single nonetheless. Already he had begun to map out his plan of seduction. Skilfully and stealthily he was going to woo her.

'My husband.' At the sound of the words his mouth had gone dry. Instantly and completely, sealing his lips tight shut. He could not speak, the arrow had penetrated deep into his chest, piercing a heart that was still scarred.

Everything inside was squeezed, a room with the sides moving inwards, tight and tighter as he tried to keep the walls apart with his outstretched arms and legs. He held them, straining every muscle and sinew and he held them and he thought he had won. Then the water had begun to enter. Creeping in at first, lapping his feet and ankles, a trickle from some crack that opened and widened until it became a gush and the water crept up to his knees, his waist, rising to his shoulders and then his chin so that he had to tilt his head backwards to keep his nose and mouth in the tiny air space above his head. He was drowning, drowning, his arms ached, his heart was trying to beat, feeble and frail, his chest fighting the weight of the water to let him breathe.

For days and months back then it had felt like he was drowning and he had wanted to give up. To stop swimming in a freezing ocean with no land in sight; tired and not knowing in which direction to strike out. Day after day he had pulled against the water, not knowing if he were moving or merely standing still. Once or twice he had put his arms by his side, let the water cover his head, prayed that he would sleep peacefully beneath the waves and never wake.

But a tiny seed inside him, the kernel of the struggle to survive had resisted. 'Don't give up,' it had said. 'Be strong for the two of you, that is your destiny.'

'I need to talk to you Steve,' Rachel said. She spoke the words with a voice he knew of old. A voice that meant something awful was on her lips. Awful for him. Not for her. He had heard that voice before. A voice of earnest detached sympathy. The tone of a friend commiserating at another friend's loss.

'Come here Steve,' she said and she held his body close to hers, her hands pressing into his shoulders, her head turned sideways, her cheek resting on his chest. They were in the living room at the farm, the blazing fire burning the backs of his legs through his jeans but he did not dare to move away. Late January, a windy rainswept night that rattled the slates and the windows and was black with lack of stars or moon.

She wept against him. Sobbed and sobbed. He felt the wetness of her tears on his skin as they seeped through his shirt. He had held her tight. Not known what to say or do; just held her and rocked her, wondering what she would say.

'Hold me Steve,' she said. 'I love you so much. I do love you Steve,' through the sobs and the shaking of her body.

He knew that. He knew she loved him as he loved her. He had no doubts. The last few months had been hard. That much he knew. All their money spent on the mortgage and feeding the livestock. Ten pounds a week left over for food. It was pitiful. She had taken it badly. She wanted to buy good food and good wine, the little things in life that she enjoyed. And deserved. Of course she deserved them. She worked hard. Always had. And now at thirty she didn't want to live on stewed pig hocks and swedes.

He smiled as he remembered an argument a few days previously. He'd bought a big, fat, smoked pig's hock for 30 pence. A thrilling find and she had refused to eat it.

'If we have to live on pig's hocks and swedes for the next five years so that we can keep this farm then that's what we'll do,' he screamed at her. It was a challenge with the prospect of ultimate achievement. Pain followed by the euphoria of self satisfaction. It would be their journey to the South Pole. Who could enjoy living in temperatures of minus 30 Centigrade whilst seeing their toes and fingers blacken and fall away as they dragged the heavy sledge across ice and snow in howling gales and driving snow. Eating butter and dried meat, shivering in tents as they tried to boil a kettle to make soup to warm themselves. No one could enjoy that hardship and deprivation. It was the challenge. For the prize of achievement when they came through the other side and could look back on what they had achieved. It was a paradox. Looking forwards to a time when he could look back with pleasure. And in between, hardship.

But that was not Rachel's style. She wanted it in the present, the here and now.

'Well I don't want to live on pig hocks and swedes,' she screamed back and the tears flooded down her cheeks and she took the dogs up on the fells and he thought it was nothing more than an argument over a fat pig's hock.

'Tell me,' he said gently. 'Tell me what it is,' he said and he placed his hands on her hair, intertwining his fingers with her thick curls, scenting the faint smell of cows about her, with pride.

She pulled him to her and tilted her head so that her chin nestled against his neck and her mouth brushed his ear.

'I was in my office this afternoon by myself,' she said. 'and this student came in and said I looked as if I needed someone to talk to and did I want to. So I said "Okay" and he just talked to me Steve. About how I felt and he told me about his life too. He's a sad person Steve but he said that things didn't have to be like that. He's intelligent too. Things just haven't gone his way in life.'

Steve patted her on the back. With relief. It wasn't frightening like he'd feared. He'd feared she was going to tell him something terrifying. Like she was having a breakdown or leaving him. He sighed with relief. Naïve uncomprehending relief born of misplaced trust and loyalty. Perhaps if he had stamped on it hard then; recognised the signs and taken her away for a rest then perhaps it would have been different.

But the pressure was on him too. The room with the moving walls and the water flooding in was already a reality in his mind. Keeping himself afloat was already his main concern. He felt a sense of relief that a friendly lad was on hand to lend a willing ear. Someone who Rachel could confide in and who could help her through a difficult emotional time. It was probably just what they both needed.

'Don't worry,' he said. 'Talk to this guy if it helps. There's no harm in that.'

Rachel continued sobbing. 'I love you so much Steve,' she said. 'Promise me you'll always be my friend.'

'Of course I will,' he said. 'You're my best friend.'

'Don't you think it is a good idea?' Francesca was saying. 'Is it a good idea for me to come here?'

Steve looked at her. She was staring straight into his eyes like a cat watching a bird. Direct and unblinking, concentration etched on her face. She was looking at his soul.

'Yes. Yes, it's a very good idea,' he said, flustered by the memories her words had brought back, more vividly than for many years. 'What are we going to eat?' He changed the subject to hide his pain and disappointment.

Sammy read the moment.

'I'm going to have the trout poached in white wine,' she said. 'It sounds delicious. What about you Fernando?' She was jovial; it was the evening after all and she thought Steve was exaggerating about Foot and Mouth. She didn't think things would get worse. She'd watched the news earlier and everyone sounded confident. Movement restrictions were in place and they would soon have the infected farms slaughtered. After that it was just a question of disinfecting and restocking. A couple of months at most. Then it would be back to normal.

'I will have the lamb cutlets with broccoli and potatoes,' he said to the waitress who stood, pencil and notepad ready.

'What would you like Francesca?' Steve asked her, composed now, the discomfort passed.

She glanced at the menu again. 'I would like the fillet of steak in red wine, al sangue. How do you say this in English? Uncooked?'

'Rare?' suggested Steve and Fernando nodded.

'In Spanish we say poco hecho,' said Fernando. 'You say rare?'

'Yeah,' Steve replied. 'Rare, or blue if you want it very rare.'

'Blue then,' said Francesca in excitement. 'A blue fillet steak.'

'I'll have the same please,' said Steve. 'And what about wine?'

Fernando took over. 'Do you have Spanish wine?' he asked and the waitress handed him the wine list.

'Yes this one here is very good wine. It is from the region where I come from. Would you like to try it?'

There was a chorus of approval.

'I'll just order my meal myself then shall I?' said Willie in a voice of mock offence. 'I'll have the sirloin steak. Well done and with a dirty great big plate of chips. And don't bother about the little green salady bits,' he added.

Sammy and Steve laughed.

'The healthy Scottish option again,' Steve said.

'And another pint of lager while you're there,' said Willie draining his glass. 'You can keep your fancy bloody Spanish wine.'

'Sarah is coming up to work here next week,' said Fernando. 'She is my girlfriend,' he said to Francesca.

Francesca smiled at him.

'And how about your wife Steve?' said Francesca looking straight at him again. 'Where is she?'

Sammy winced on Steve's behalf but noted that he showed no emotion or reaction.

I wonder where she is, he thought. All those years passed and he had no idea.

'If you do this I can never see you or speak to you again,' he said to Rachel. Partly in threat at the time. Trying to turn her head from the direction she was taking like pulling sideways on the bit of a bolting horse

rather than heaving straight back on its mouth. To guide it and lure it back into control rather than to fight it head on. But Rachel's head was not for turning. She was not the turning kind, least of all in the face of idle threats. He knew that but he was desperate. Desperate enough to cut his arm off if he thought it would work. But she would have just seen him as more pathetic than he already was.

He hadn't seen or spoken to her since. No that's not true he thought. She phoned him soon after he'd gone to London to work. He'd been consulting and a receptionist he hardly knew came and said that there was a call for him, from Rachel. His heart had leapt; his stomach had churned and caught in his throat; a feeling he remembered from waiting for exam results; eager anticipation with uncertain dread drifting in the background like death.

He picked up the phone, pulse racing, pounding in expectation. She was going to ask him to come back. She was going to say she'd made a mistake. Please forgive me Steve she would say; please come home.

Forgive her? He would welcome her back with open arms. Clutch her to his breast and stroke her hair as she sobbed in his arms. A mistake. A simple mistake under the pressure they'd borne. Marriages could be stronger if they came through this sort of thing. No longer taking each other for granted; appreciating each other for what they both brought to the partnership.

'Rachel,' he said, 'How are you?'

'Fine. Fine,' she said. 'I've been to the farm today and got the cattle away. The Estate Agent has had a few people interested but nothing definite. The sheep look well,' she added.

'Are you sure you want to go through with all this?' he asked. A drowning man clutching for the bank, the overhanging branch, the blade of grass floating by. Chasing after rainbows and moonbeams. He felt sick at himself for asking.

'I've never been so sure of anything in my life,' Rachel said, excitement lifting her voice. 'I just know…'

It was what he should have expected. The final turn of the screw.

'Right. Okay,' he interrupted, 'I've got to go now. See you.' He hung up and the tears just came. They welled up in his eyes and poured down his cheeks onto the office floor and the receptionist looked at him and did not know what to say or do.

'The fucking sheep look well,' he said to himself. 'The fucking sheep look well.' His whole life had collapsed and she was telling him about

the fucking sheep. Who the fuck cares he thought . He didn't care if they were lying dead all over the fucking hill. It didn't matter anymore. It was all pointless now. Hopeless and pointless, his dream broken into a million little pieces. Irretrievable. Unrecoverable. Five years of his fucking life just wasted and blown away.

'I'm not married,' he said to Francesca. 'I suppose I'm not the marrying kind.' He avoided looking at Sammy.

'So what kind are you?' she asked. There was no prying tone, no hint of poking fun. A genuine question that required a genuine answer.

Yes, what kind am I, thought Steve. Twenty years ago he knew the answer to that question. Not now though. Somewhere along the way he had lost himself and had been too scared to look again for fear of what he might find. He looked at Sammy. She was looking at him waiting to hear the answer. She liked this Francesca. This girl from Italy with the face of an angel who asked the most simple and honest questions without malice or self gratification. Questions that she Sammy would have loved to have the courage to ask.

'You don't want to know,' said Steve slowly and smiled at her. 'I'm a selfish bastard with a classic car and no dependants. And that's all I'm telling you.'

'And is your classic car good company?' asked Francesca leaning forward so that he could smell the sea and the vanilla.

He didn't answer her. He simply shrugged, pulled a face and took another drink of his pint.

'Let's hope they bring the food soon,' he said. 'I'm starving.'

Francesca knew that her line of questioning was at an end. She turned to Fernando.

'Tell me about your girlfriend,' she said. 'Is she very beautiful?'

'Yes, very,' said Fernando, his big eyes rolling. 'He is very beautiful and very nice.' No one bothered to correct him. 'You will meet him next week.'

The food and wine arrived. The steak was as blue as he'd seen and Steve watched delighted as Francesca sliced into the blood red meat on her plate, relishing the pink juices that oozed from the cut surface. She's a red blooded Latin alright he thought and as though hearing his thoughts she looked up suddenly and her eyes joined with his. He saw in them Rachel and Julie and Sonia, all with evil intent on their face. And all of them were laughing.

Chapter 35

'Sage Street want answers Stevie lad,' said Neil. 'They want to know how this thing is spreading. Is it all in the sheep and just spilling over into the cattle or are we missing something. Sage Street think we are.'

He had been at Cardington for a week and it was blacker still. More than three weeks after the initial discovery of the infection at the abattoir there had been nearly 250 cases countrywide. There was a shortage of manpower, equipment, and more importantly, leadership.

Those on the front line were working with little sleep, under conditions of severe deprivation and stress. There were heaps of rotten, stinking carcasses lying around the countryside, and in places the air was thick with acrid smoke and the smell of burning hair and flesh caught in the mouths and throats of people as they went to work or did their shopping.

The media were in raptures. Every news bulletin carried pictures of burning pyres; of carcasses being loaded onto stacks of straw and coal; carcasses falling apart with putrefaction; and graphic descriptions of the stench of rotting meat hanging over the farms.

'Colin Hunt has called a temporary halt to all slaughtering until we can dispose of the carcasses that are already lying,' said Fernando as he joined Neil and Steve.

'That's bloody stupid,' said Neil, a look of frustration on his face. 'We've got to get infected animals killed straight away or we'll never get a hold of this thing. Steve, you get out to that dairy farm up by the coast. It was slaughtered out five days ago but I want to know how it got that far away from the nearest case. Check on milk tankers, feed deliveries; itinerant farm workers: why am I telling you all this? You know the bloody score. Just get out there and find out what's going on. We're missing something, that's for certain. I'm going to try and talk some sense into Colin.'

'Hi, I'm Sandy,' said a guy of about Steve's age with an Australian accent. 'I hear you're doing the epidemiology. How's it going?'

'Hi, I'm Steve,' he said, shaking Sandy's hand. 'It's going a bit slow to be honest. The whole bloody thing's out of control but no one up top seems to have realised yet. When did you arrive?'

'Oh me and another dozen blokes got here yesterday. We're here for a month. Do you guys need a hand in epidemiology? I've got a fair bit of experience and I've brought some useful programs on a lap top.'

Steve was defensive. It was up to Neil. He was at the bottom of the heap. He didn't know how these foreign vets fitted in or how they were to be managed.

'You'll need to speak to Neil. He's in with Colin Hunt at the moment.'

'How do you reckon it's spreading? Have you done any mapping of the IPs against time to see the progression of the outbreaks geographically? That's something I could do for you.'

Steve sighed wearily. He assumed that Sage Street were doing something like that but there was no feedback from them if they were. He knew that what he was doing on a daily basis was a complete waste of time, simply documenting the disease's progression. They were making no headway in its control; bogged down in the minutiae instead of looking at the big picture. He had to believe that someone in Sage Street was doing that, coming up with an overall strategy for the outbreak's control. He wasn't even sure of the lines of communication in order to try to find out.

'I've got to go to a farm now,' said Steve, anxious to get away. The pale taste of inadequacy flooded pink with embarrassment at the lack of leadership and control. How could this be happening? he thought. Where were the DVAs and the Regional leaders? They should be there at Cardington, leading from the front, overseeing operations with clear decisive instructions. They should be giving daily briefings so that everyone knew what was going on; explanations of the overall strategy; directing operations and making policy decisions. Instead they were skulking in corridors or dimly lit rooms; sitting in corners during meetings that they should have chaired; acting like impartial observers as though on some training exercise; leaving it up to the front line and junior ranks to discuss and debate policy in a power starved vacuum with no clear objectives or guidance on the way forward.

Give the PVO his due, thought Steve. He was at least on the telly every day, putting his views forward even if they were so complacent as to be laughable to those who knew what was happening out in the field. There was no epidemic said Ron Steady. Everything was still under control he said as the public was served up yet another portion of burning or rotten carcasses; yet another farmer breaking down in tears in front of the cameras; even the occasional long range shot of slaughtermen at their grizzly business. The Minister too was well satisfied that all that needed to be done was being done. The army were most certainly not needed at this stage of the game.

It took Steve an hour to reach the farm. The farmhouse was set back two hundred yards from the public road, nestling into a small dip in the land at the end of a track. There was cow shit all over the road opposite the track, some of it dried hard, some of it still moist beneath a dried out crust. He left his car and after walking a few yards he came across a plastic tub of disinfectant, now the colour and consistency of slurry. Where was the bloody disease security here? he thought. There should be someone at the road end.

It was a clear sunstreaked day with a cold tingle in the air. There were birds singing; mid March. Spring, though not yet here, was perhaps on its way. He saw some primroses in bloom in the hedgerow, pale yellow, delicate, they lifted his spirits. The farm passed out of sight as he went down into a valley bottom and then he was over a bridge across a small stream and up the other side and the farm stood fifty yards ahead.

The strange shapes of black and white cows stacked up on each side of the track stretched out before him. One on top of the other, they came into sharper focus as he approached. No smell he thought and was grateful at least for that. The carcasses were bloated. Legs stuck stiffly out, the skin stretched taut with subcutaneous gas trapped beneath. Udders and teats blown up like inflated four fingered rubber gloves, bright green and blue and rich red and purple, as if sprayed on like obscene graffiti from a can of vivid paint.

Why no smell? he thought and as he drew level the stench caught him in the mouth making him wretch, the gentle breeze at his back had wafted the scent of decay away from him and towards the house.

He walked the corridor of corpses that rose above him on both sides. Fluid drained from the nasal passages of heads hung low, blood and green rumenal contents, liquified brains dripping from the bolt holes in their foreheads, the ground beneath them a soup of liquid waste.

A group of crows flew up from where they had been picking at the orifices; eyes pecked out, vulvas and anuses torn and innards pulled out by the powerful stabbing beaks that had strewn them in coils of dull green and grey purple across the backs and bellies of the cattle. The crows flew off in the direction of a distant wood, crops full to bursting, coarse caws of satiated delight to each other. They would be back later before sunset for another feed, such bountiful pickings previously unheard of at this time of year when usually the odd weakly lamb was a rare treat.

Steve felt the smell in the air. A heavy, pressurising mist, clinging to his hands and face, to his hair and neck. He stopped to take it all in. A moment of silent contemplation. Britain in the new millennium, he thought. No wonder the Americans are staying away if this is what they see on their TVs. Suddenly he knew he was a part of something big. History in the making. Something that was bigger than the whole of the Veterinary Service; bigger than farming itself. He was the tiniest of pieces in the puzzle but on his skill and judgement he could perhaps make a difference. It occurred to him that in years to come people would ask: 'And what did you do in the Great Foot and Mouth Epidemic of 2001?'

Further along the line sheep were piled on top of the cattle. Tongues swollen and protruding in silent bleating protest, bellies full of dead lambs that had not felt the rasping, reassuring lick of their mother's tongues. And further still, round the corner of the farm sheds lay the calves, their skins already beginning to dry and shrivel as the soft tissues liquified and poured their fluid out onto the ground where a trickle ran down into a concrete walled yard to form a scum laced, stinking, grey pink reservoir. Steve held his breath and hurried to the farmhouse. He knocked on the door.

Mr Towers opened it.

'Another Ministry man?' he quipped. 'I thought we'd had them all by now.'

Steve explained why he was there.

'Come on in then son. No point standing outside in all that stink.'

Mrs Towers was in the kitchen with two of her sons at the kitchen table.

'I'm so sorry about all that mess outside,' Steve said. It was all he could think of to say, his body burning hot with embarrassment. How could he ignore what he'd just seen and smelt. How could he pretend that outside the door there were not tons of rotting stinking corpses. How could he pretend that this was just another normal day in the spring farming calendar that showed pictures of cuddly lambs and proud ewes in knee length grass with the sun on their backs. 'It's some bloody mess,' he said. 'I'm sorry you've got to live here with that.'

'Do you think you're getting on top of it then?' asked one of the sons.

'Do you want the official answer or what I think?' Steve asked.

'Are they different like?' asked Mr Towers senior, a gleam in his eyes.

'Well you've seen the news. Officially it's all under control.' He paused, uncertain of how much to say. 'Personally I think we're in a bloody mess and no one really knows how to get us out of it. There could be worse to come in my view.'

Mrs Towers put a cup of coffee in front of him and some home baking.

'Eat that son,' she smiled. 'And help yourself to milk. It's the first milk I've had to buy in all my married life.'

'It's those damn crows spreading it,' said Mr Towers. 'You'll have seen them on your way down here. Dozens of them on the carcasses sometimes and then flying off to God knows where. I've been at them with my shotgun a couple of times but they're soon back. Waste of time really.'

'It's possible,' said Steve, but once the carcasses are sprayed with disinfectant there shouldn't be any virus on the surface of them. I don't think it's a big risk.'

'Well who's meant to spray them then? These ones were never sprayed, just dumped where you saw them and then left. And that was five days ago and still no word of when we're going to get them burnt. And that pompous bastard on the telly says it's all under control. He should get his arse down here and see how we're having to live. He'd soon change his mind on whether it was under control or not. What do you say lad?'

'It's not his fault dad,' said one of the sons. 'He can't alter things.'

'Another thing we were upset about,' said the other son; he glanced round at the rest of the family as though seeking permission to continue. 'The slaughtermen were pretty rough. They were just laying into this and that, shouting and laughing without giving it much thought. They didn't really care about the animals, or us for that matter, just kept boasting about where they were going to go on holiday with all the bloody money they were making.'

'Aye I might as well tell you lad,' Mr Towers said. 'I went outside about nine o'clock the night of the killing. I couldn't settle. I couldn't believe it had really happened. Do you know what I mean?'

Steve thought back to Rachel. 'I know exactly what you mean,' he said gently.

'I wanted to check for myself. To make sure I hadn't imagined it. I put all the outside lights on and went round that corner, where you've just walked in from, and there were four ewes and a bullock standing there, heads down, blood running out of their noses and from that bloody hole in their heads. They were walking, slowly, like dead things, or drunks, as though they didn't know what was going on or that they were really alive.' His eyes were watering and Steve knew that he was going to cry.

'Don't dad,' said one of the sons,' forget it now, it's not important. It's happened and it's done with.'

'Aye it is important,' said the old man wiping his eyes. 'The public should know what's being done in their name. These things shouldn't be covered up. That's how men needlessly lose their lives in wars.'

Steve waited a few seconds, his head fuzzy, a ripping ache inside it like it would burst. He had known that this sort of thing would happen. People became careless, blasé about the killing business. He tried to think of something appropriate to say. He stayed silent.

'They'd recovered you see,' said Mr Towers. 'Not completely of course. Just been stunned, and there they were just standing amongst all the death and mayhem, their heads down almost on the ground, their eyes glazed and staring, their tongues hanging out. They couldn't really walk, just staggered a bit but they were conscious enough to know that I was there because they turned their heads towards me and looked at me as much as to say "See what you have done to us. You and all your kind," and I tell you it was enough to make me believe in the Devil because he was there looking at me, through their eyes.

'I turned straight round and went and got my shotgun to put them out of their misery. And you know what, each of them came right up to me and just stood there in front of me as though they were asking me to do it. As though they understood that I could take their pain away for them. That's not right is it?' He was pleading with Steve.

'No it's not right,' said Steve firmly. 'It's not right at all. There's no excuse and I can only apologise that it's happened. What was the vet doing while the slaughter was going on?'

'Oh he was just a waste of space. A nice enough lad but he didn't seem to know what he was meant to be doing. Spent most of the time on his mobile phone, half of it to his girlfriend I think. Cheerful sort of lad but bloody hopeless.'

'I'm very sorry,' Steve repeated, he could feel the anger inside him sloshing around like a pan of water coming to the boil. 'Most of the vets I've had dealings with have been excellent. Most of them have tried hard to make sure things have been done properly. What's happened here isn't acceptable. I'll speak to the person in charge of the slaughter teams when I get back to the office and he can give this guy a bollocking. You've enough to put up with without that sort of hassle.'

'Now lad,' said Mr Towers, changing the subject abruptly. 'What else do you need to know?'

The smell made him wretch as soon as he opened the door to leave. Mrs Towers smiled at him.

'Don't you worry about us,' she said. 'Once this lot is burnt we'll soon have this mess cleared up. There's a lot of others worse off than us. People who are under restrictions and can't move stock home for lambing and no prospect of any money coming in either. At least we'll have the compensation when it arrives. And the vet who was here said that he thinks Jim and the two boys can be taken on to clean and disinfect the place. Don't be too hard on that young vet. I don't think the poor lad really knew what he was meant to do. It's a bit of a shock to us all isn't it?'

Steve smiled at her, 'We won't be too hard on him,' he promised. 'I just want to make sure it doesn't happen again.' He touched her on the arm. 'Thanks for coffee and cakes,' he said. 'Good luck.'

He ran the gauntlet of the rotting carcasses again, the breeze blowing the stink straight into his nostrils. Some people were so stoical, he thought. No wailing and gnashing of teeth for them. It happened; they accepted it, and then got on with it. Mrs Towers was right of course. The poor young vet probably didn't know what he was meant to do. Probably arrived one day and sent out to an IP the next with no training in the procedures and the current instructions. It was bad enough for full time staff, he wasn't sure himself what current policy was. It was Swine Fever relived, only tenfold.

But not checking animals were dead was unacceptable. A single mistake was bad enough. But five of them was bloody negligence. If vets weren't there to safeguard the welfare of the animals then what were they there for?

He passed the patch of primroses again. He didn't feel quite so jolly. His mobile rang and he fished it out of his pocket. It was Neil.

'Bad news,' he said. 'There's an infected farm ten miles further south from where you are now. Confirmed this morning on clinical grounds. A small milking herd, several cows salivating and half a dozen pigs on the place. The vet says that they're infected too. I want you to go out there now and see if she's right. A foreign girl, Francesca Capotti or something like that. She sounded competent on the phone but if she's right this has jumped. Jumped a long way and I don't want us making any mistakes. Sage Street have confirmed it on clinical grounds but I want your opinion. I've persuaded Colin we've got to kill it out straightaway. Someone's trying to organise a slaughter team now.'

'No problem Neil,' said Steve, the familiar tingling and rush of emotion in the pit of his stomach. 'It'll be a pleasure,' he finished, unable to keep the excitement from his voice.

'Do you know this Francesca?' Neil asked, detecting the note of interest.

'Only in passing. She's a big fat hairy woman. Not your sort at all Neil.'

Neil laughed. 'Don't hang about there too long,' he said. 'I want reports on these two visits tonight for Sage Street. Graham is under pressure to give some answers and we don't seem to be able to come up with any yet. One of the PVO's babes, bossy cow, Sally Pringle, you might remember her from Broadwich; well she thinks we're missing something again. I told him to send her up to give us a hand if she's so bloody good. He says he might just do that.'

'Okay Neil, I'll be as quick as I can.'

He disinfected and checked his map. It would only take twenty minutes to get there. He stood to the side as a tractor towing a muck-spreader passed by on the road. It was filthy, and muck had fallen off all along the lane. What a bloody idiot thought Steve as he set off behind it. There's me going to all the trouble of disinfecting and this bloody guy drives along with shit all over the place.

Three miles down the road he came to a crossroads with a tiny white washed cottage on one corner. There were six goats milling around on the wide verges and wandering along the road nibbling at the hedges. Steve stopped his car. What the hell are they doing out, he thought. He wound down his window and called to the half open stable door of the cottage.

'Hello,' he shouted. 'Hello?'

A woman in her fifties came to the door. She looked harassed.

'Hello,' Steve repeated. 'My name's Steve Turner, I'm a Veterinary Officer with The Ministry. Are these your goats?'

The woman looked at his car, doubt in her mind. She nodded.

'Don't you know there's Foot and Mouth in the area?' he said aggressively. 'These goats should be shut in, not allowed to wander the roads. You know they'll be slaughtered if they get it,' he said.

The woman broke down in tears. 'I know,' she said. 'I just can't keep them in. They jump the fences or push their way through them. I've tried so hard but they just keep breaking out. I don't know what to do.'

Steve bit his tongue, annoyed that he'd been so harsh. The whole area was under stress and suffering. Not just commercial farmers, but smallholders too. Hotels and B and Bs. It was like the whole community was under siege.

'Look,' he said. 'I'm sorry to shout at you but it is important. You've got to keep them in. They could pick up the disease and spread it by wandering up and down the road. I'm not going to take any action now; but sort something out will you?'

'Yes,' said the woman. 'I promise I will. I'll get someone to come and help me.' She dabbed at her eyes with tissue paper. 'I'll feed them now. That will bring them home.'

Steve drove off. His brain was fizzing with the possibilities. How the disease was spreading and what other options there were for control. He kept returning to vaccination. Sure there were problems. The vaccines weren't 100% effective but they were bloody good. And people said they could mask the disease and perhaps leave it to resurface in the future. But he kept returning to the fact that mainland Europe had relied on it and half the rest of the world still did. The options spun round and round and slipped away like sand through outstretched fingers. A man could go mad trying to work out what was best. Some men probably would go mad, he thought.

What tormented him most was that he didn't know what he would do if he were in charge. That was the intellectual exercise that was troubling him. What would he do if the decision were his to make. If he did not know that, then he could not know if what they were doing now was right.

He swerved to the side as another tractor and trailer came down the narrow lane, feed sacks bouncing around in the back, mud and dung spraying off the tractor wheels as it passed. Another mile and a quad bike passed, wheels and mudguards thick with mud, a sheepdog crouched in a box on the back. The evidence was all around him; slowly, slowly it began to filter along the connections in his brain; chasing up dead ends and cul-de-sacs where it stagnated and lay thick like sludge, before moving again into the main stream from where a picture could begin to form.

It was just after one in the afternoon when he pulled off the road onto the edge of a concrete yard. This was the farm alright, there were a couple of cars already there. He climbed out and stretched his legs.

'Hello,' said the Latin voice he remembered so well. 'You have come very quickly.'

He turned to find her dressed in a navy blue paper boiler suit, her chestnut hair drawn up in a ragged bun on her head.

'You're the one with shit on your face today,' he said and he reached forward and wiped a wet messy lump from her cheek.

She smiled. 'So this is your girlfriend,' she said touching the shiny blue wing of the Healey 3000. 'It is very pretty. But cold. And hard. This will not keep you warm at night, no?'

She is amazing, he thought. She speaks openly about the most sensuous things yet with no sense of sexual provocation. She says it because she thinks and feels it. Not for effect.

'What's the story here?' asked Steve.

'The farmer, Mr Barrie, said that he found two cows with saliva this morning and they had no milk. When I arrived I checked their temperatures and they both have a fever. They also have tongue vesicles, not ruptured. There are other cows too with a little foam on their nuzzles.'

'Muzzles,' said Steve.

'Yes, muzzles,' Francesca said.

'So it's started in the dairy cows then?'

'I do not think so,' she replied. 'There are six fat pigs here too and I have examined them. They all have older lesions on their feet and noses. Mr Barrie said that they were off their food a few days ago but seemed to get better. I think that they are the first cases.'

Steve put on a paper suit and waterproofs and disinfected himself again before entering the farm.

'This is Mr Barrie,' said Francesca as a man in overalls came round the corner. 'Mr Barrie, this is Steve. He is an epidemiologist.'

Steve did not correct her.

'Hello Mr Barrie,' he said as he shook the farmer's hand. 'Francesca has told me a little about what's happened. I'll need to ask you a few questions but I'd like to see the pigs and cows first if that's okay.'

'Aye we can arrange that. Very switched on young lady this,' he pointed at Francesca. She had him eating out of her hand, Steve thought and he winked at her. She lowered her eyes in mock embarrassment.

'Have you got a pig snare?' Steve asked her.

'Yes. It is by their pen. They are not so big. Easy to catch.'

The pen next to the lane. There was a short metal gate that opened onto the yard and opposite it was a stable door that looked out onto the lane. The top half was open.

Steve took the snare that Francesca offered him and quickly slipped it over the upper jaw of one of the pigs. They were well grown baconers, probably 80-90 kg liveweight, strong enough, but easy to control. The squealing started as soon as the noose tightened and he handed the handle to the farmer. 'If you could hold that tight please Mr Barrie,' he said.

Francesca and Steve bent down either side of the pig's head.

'Look, here on the snout,' she said.

Even above the smell of pigs he caught the scent of the sea and vanilla. He stared hard at her, his chest hurting with the pulse of emotions that grabbed at his heart and stomach.

'Can you see?' she asked.

But he could not hear her. All he could see was the smoothness of her skin and the fullness of her lips, the line of her neck and how the chestnut hair slowly fell forwards from the bun on her head. The lashes on her upper eyelids, deepest brown and upward curling, quivering with each blink of her eyes. He was overwhelmed by her. Shocked and distrustful of his feelings. He wanted to hold her in his arms and make love to her there on the straw, gently and carefully.

She looked across the pig's head and caught the look in his eyes. Her own eyes melted into his and he saw the wonder and fear in them at what she knew she had unleashed in him. But he saw no anger or resentment. Just a flame that danced and sparkled red and orange against a black background.

'We can talk later,' she whispered. 'For now we have the pigs and the cows.'

'Er, yeah. Okay,' he said, not believing what he'd heard. He looked closely at where she was pointing, a typical healing lesion on the pig's snout; five days old. He carefully lifted the animal's lips and there were more lesions on the mucosa of the gums. He touched a front foot around the coronary band, red and swollen with necrotic skin hanging down and the hoof just starting to separate.

'Looks pretty conclusive to me,' he said.

Francesca smiled, her eyebrows curved and prominent, each hair delicately orientated in the same line like the tail feathers of an exotic bird. Again the aroma of vanilla, gentle, wafting, intoxicating above the smell of pigs.

'I'll check the others too,' said Steve and slipped the noose off the pig's snout and the squealing stopped. All the pigs were the same save for one whose lesions were a few days older.

'The first case?' Francesca asked, and Steve nodded.

'Almost certainly. If there are no older ones in the cattle.'

'I think there aren't,' she replied. And Mr Barrie only noticed the cows sick this morning. I have the sick ones separated for you to look at them. There is a caroosh.'

'Crush,' said Steve.

'Crush,' she repeated, the whites of her eyes dewy moist with excitement, the origin of which he dare not believe.

The lesions on the tongues and inside the lips of both cows were typical one day old lesions. Large raised vesicles, a couple of them bursting as Steve grabbed the tongue, the surface layer stripping away in his hand.

'I'm sure you're right,' Steve said to Francesca. 'Started in the pigs and then spread to the cows. Any movement of people or equipment to or from other premises? In other words, how has it got here?'

'None,' she said with confidence. 'Mr Barrie is the only person who works the farm and he has no other premises. I don't know how it has got here. There are no other places close I think.'

The structure of her sentences, spoken in a soft, sultry voice, like syrup mixed with wood smoke. Already he loved her. Already he would die for her like he would have died for Rachel. A hundred times over. A million times over. Why was she married? He wanted to scream out loud with pain.

Life was cruel to him. To take Rachel from him and now to tease him with Francesca. His head was muzzy again. The stress of Foot and Mouth and now Francesca. He could have done without her being there. Fuck Rachel, he thought. Fuck women. Fuck the lot of them.

'Have you heard if a slaughter team is organised?' he asked her.

'No, but Cardington said they would try to get one here this afternoon. I think it is important with this farm being so far from other cases that we kill them soon.'

'Very important,' he said. 'I've got plenty of Euthatal in the car. I'll phone Cardington to see what's happening and I'll kill the pigs and those two cows now. That'll reduce the environmental contamination in the short term at least.'

The guy at Cardington was having a bad day. Eight new infected farms in the area already that morning and he was losing track of what was going on; what was needed. A new heap of vets had arrived and no one was taking charge of them and now Steve Turner was demanding that he get a slaughter team out to a farm that had only been declared an IP a few hours previously when there were others already waiting in a queue that was getting longer by the hour. The problem was that he knew Steve was right. This was an outbreak in clean country and it needed stamping on straight away. He looked at the list of IPs in front of him. They were going to need more slaughter teams if this kept up. Another few days and they would be well behind.

He scanned down his list. The slaughter team at Little Ham Farm would soon be finished. He could send them to Browns Farm instead of High Fell.

'Okay Steve,' he said. 'I'll get someone there this afternoon. Frank and Bert. A couple of good blokes. I can't promise what time.'

'Ah, I know them well,' laughed Steve. 'Meanwhile I'll get the clinical cases killed. Thanks a lot.' He turned to Francesca. 'That's good. Frank and Bert are coming later to slaughter out here. They're good lads so long as you make it plain what you want.'

'You are a man of influence too, I see,' she teased and could not help laughing out loud at him. 'I will go and tell Mr Barrie.'

'I'll get the Euthatal and some syringes and needles and meet you at the pigs,' he said.

Mr Barrie disappeared to the house. He knew all the cows by name, their mothers and grandmothers, sisters and daughters. The news that the slaughterers were coming overwhelmed him leaving him tearful and red eyed.

Steve had never in his life euthanased a big pig with Euthatal but his experience at Broadwich gave him confidence. Francesca held the first three pigs while he showed her how to find the right anterior vena cava and injected 50 ml of 20% pentobarbitone straight into the vein. Each pig collapsed off the needle in a few seconds. Francesca was impressed. Then he held the others so that she could try. She was quick and dextrous, thrusting the needle home with confidence.

'It is very quick and humane,' she said.

'Why are you really here?' Steve asked.

Tears flooded her eyes and fell like rain into the straw. 'How do you know?' she said. 'How do you know?'

'Because I can see into your mind,' he said. 'Through your eyes. You are so open. So transparent. I thought you were lying the other night at dinner. And now I know you were.'

He caught the teardrops that ran down the olive skin with the back of his hand, gently brushing them away.

'Do you want to tell me?' he waited. He would not ask again.

'I love Carlo, my husband,' she said. 'But he loves me too much. He protects me, stifles me. I am not allowed to get a job. He will provide all we need he says. He treats me like a delicate ornament, a flower that must be protected from the wind and rain. His love overpowers me. It is as though I am not truly alive; not able to be myself to test the limits of my knowledge and skill.

'Inside my heart, it breaks every day,' she said, patting her chest with her clenched fist. 'Life is there to be lived, not to be protected from. It is there to be tested and the limits explored with the disappointments of failure and the excitements of success. Carlo will not let me live, to be myself. To fall down and to pick myself up again; to triumph and achieve. That is why I am here Steve. To live a little; to test my skill; to have the satisfaction, here, in my heart, that I am a good vet. That is what I told Carlo when I left. And I told him that I would come back once I had achieved that. Can you understand this?'

Steve looked at her and wiped more tears from her face. Yes he understood. Reflexly he leaned forwards and kissed her on the forehead. The smell of vanilla filled his nostrils, he wanted to hold her tighter than he had held anyone ever before. To pull her to him and protect her. To love her and cherish her. And for the first time she seemed flustered. Gently she removed his hand from her cheek and placed it slowly and definitely by his side.

'Thank you,' she said, 'I am alright now. Lets us get on with the cows.'

Steve followed her to the crush. He showed her the routine he used for slaughtering cows with BSE; 10 ml of 2% Rompun intramuscularly; let them out of the crush and leave them in peace for fifteen minutes. By that time they were lying down, well sedated and with a rope halter on their head it was simple to inject 100 ml of Euthatal into their jugular vein. Simple and effective; quiet and trouble free with no trauma to cow or vet.

They had not long finished when Mr Barrie reappeared.

'Might as well see the job through,' he said. 'I want to make sure it's done right and that cows are treated wit' respect they deserve.'

'These ones went very peacefully Mr Barrie,' said Steve. 'The pigs too.'

'Did they lad?' he said. 'Did they really?'

'I promise you,' said Steve.

It was another three hours before he left the farm. He had been through all the paperwork with Mr Barrie before Frank and Bert and the valuer arrived. He'd explained to Francesca all the possible slaughter scenarios and what he thought she should look out for and how to instruct the slaughterers in what she wanted.

'If you ask these two nicely,' he told her, 'they'll do whatever you ask.' And so would I, he thought.

Francesca followed him to the car.

'Steve,' she said as he climbed into his car, 'please don't tell anyone.'

He put his finger to his lips and smiled at her.

'And thank you for understanding,' she said.

Tears flowed down his cheeks as he drove back to Cardington.

The same tears that had flowed and burnt his skin as he drove away from his farm. He remembered the last time he had seen Rachel. They had met in a pub car park to exchange something, he couldn't remember what. Keys perhaps. He couldn't understand it now, but at the time it had been of the greatest significance. Like a scene near the end of a film when all the little bits fall into place and a line is drawn underneath it.

Yes that was it. It was the drawing of the line that had been important. They had arranged to meet and they each knew that it was for the last time. Anything left to be said; any doubts or misunderstandings had to be said then. He was going to London the next day.

It was a warm summer's evening in early June. The fields were full of thriving lambs, the hedges green and studded with delicately coloured wild flowers. He had arrived first. He had sat in the car and waited. Excitedly. Anticipating that something might happen. That something might change. This was the final test. All that was to pass would now pass. From this point they would cross a threshold.

He had tried to think of something new to say. Something new and persuasive. Something that would touch her, move her, like nothing before. But his heart was empty. There were no words that had not been offered a dozen times. In a dozen different ways and voices. In tones and shades; with tender patience and threatening power. His mind was ravelled and worn; a man waiting for the gallows; dreading, yet wishing it were all over.

When she arrived he knew that there was something different about her. She climbed out of the car, bare legged, a simple cotton skirt to mid-thigh, a cotton T-shirt. He could tell from the tone of her skin and the light in her eye. His naivety had sustained him the last few weeks; his trust in her still unshakeable; a belief in her loyalty and sense of fair play. He could laugh at it now. Laugh at himself the way others must have laughed at him back then.

She had crossed the car park with a self assured stride. A gentle swinging of her arms, shoulders square set, head held high. A smile, no, a smirk, on her face. He climbed out of his car and stood facing her. He looked in her eyes and she could not hold the gaze; she looked away, to the side. And then he knew. Knew as sure as it is possible to know anything.

'You've slept with Patrick, haven't you,' he said. It was not a question.

She looked to left and right, the smirk on her face fixed solid, unable to say the words.

'You have,' he persisted.

'Don't even ask Steve,' she said. In exasperation.

He glanced at the fingers of her left hand. The wedding ring and the solitaire diamond were gone. As if they'd never existed.

Discarded already, he thought. Or sold.

He wished he had turned and walked away. Turned with pride and self belief and walked back to his car without a second glance. Perhaps if he had done that the intervening years would have been different. Perhaps if he had held himself together he would have moved on with dignity and the sense of new beginning. But he did not walk away. Instead he walked towards her and buried his face in her neck and wept. Sobbed and wept like a child that had lost its mother. His body shook and he put his hands on her back to hold her to him, in desperation; in a final desperate act of humiliation that he had regretted and not forgiven.

She showed no emotion save perhaps the faint whiff of contempt. She stood inanimate whilst his tears bathed her neck until eventually she removed his hands from her shoulders like someone removing the paws of a dog that had jumped up at them.

'Take care of yourself Steve,' she said, as at the end of a journey to a stranger met on a train. And she was gone.

No fading picture, no poignant music or the role of credits. No mad dash for the exit. This was real life, not the movies. The film hadn't ended, it had broken down. It would not finish until it was repaired. And no one knew how.

He took the wrong road on his way back to Cardington. It took him towards Kenilborough and in the distance he saw palls of black smoke, to the left and to the right. Three, four, five even; separate clouds. As he came closer to the town he could see that the smoke was all around, across the road like a desert storm, pale grey with smuts that landed on the windscreen of his car. The acrid smell of burning flesh wafted in through the windows and the hole in the hood, filling his sinuses and nasal passages, bringing on again the hot bitter taste of nausea. Not with physical revulsion but with mental anguish of uncertainty of when it would all end. This was primeval Britain, a throw back to the dark days of prehistory when man could have known no better. He drove into the High Street, smoke hung between the buildings like fog, the stench visible as people did their shopping and took their kids and dogs for walks. Their tolerance astounded him. This was a war zone.

A war zone without an army. The danger lay within, he thought. Indifference, indecision; the tolerance of a community of its own misgovernment.

What would I do? he thought. What would I do if it were my call?

I would bring the army in to help. Of that I have no doubt.

But would I vaccinate? Would vaccination be to admit defeat? Would it make things worse? Could anything be worse than this? he thought as he looked at the smoke choked street that reflected an eerie afternoon light and he switched on his windscreen wipers to clear the smuts.

This was no good, he thought. Over three weeks in and they'd slaughtered nearly 200,000 animals. There were piles of rotting corpses everywhere and it was getting worse by the day. They could not carry on like this. Something had to change.

He left the town and its stinking smoke and headed south, passing two more pyres on the way whose smoke wafted up and over the hill and lay like a blanket of doom in the floor of the next valley. Would they be the next farms to go down with the disease, he wondered. Were the pyres spreading it?

When he reached Cardington, he found Neil in less than jovial mood.

'I've got to go to Sage Street again tomorrow,' he said. 'Graham's copping it from the PVO who's copping it from the Minister. Why don't we know how this thing is spreading to the dairy herds? Ron Steady's coming up here to address the local Farmers Club in two days time. That's Monday. I want some bloody answers by then.

'Now tomorrow I want you to head back over to the east. There's a new hot spot developing around Todley. Close to an important constituency. We've got to stop it. Colin Hunt wanted you to go down to Devon but I've told him I need you here. This is where it's all going tits up.'

'Why don't they open a new disease control centre at Morton?' said Steve. 'It would make more sense.'

'Course it would,' said Neil, 'but Hunt, or maybe his boss Des Quiet, won't have it. Says there's no one capable of taking charge over there. Load of fucking crap of course. Ivory Towers and all that.

'Anyway, how did you get on today? Any the wiser?'

'Perhaps,' said Steve. I'm still thinking about it, but yes, perhaps I am getting an idea. Let me think about it overnight. When are you back?'

'Tomorrow evening. I'll be into the office the next morning, Monday. Get your reports written and straight down to Graham tonight.'

Steve made his way back to his hotel. It was 6.30 in the evening and he'd had enough. He would write the reports in his room. Not that they would help anyone. There were too many outbreaks for even report cases to be seen the next day so he knew no one was going to follow up his tracing requests. They were still a long way from that stage. What they needed was an overview of what was happening. Someone had to take a step back and say, this is what we need to do to stop the number of cases increasing. Once that had happened, then they could start to follow up each case and hunt out the virus wherever it might be. And since nobody else seemed to be doing it, he figured that it might just as well be him.

Chapter 36

He did not see Francesca in the bar that evening. Sammy was there, Willie and Fernando too. A bunch of Aussies bad mouthing the Ministry's organisational skills, and a couple of Americans who thought the Gulf War was alive and well in Cardington.

'You've got to hit this thing with all the firepower you've got,' drawled a man from the Lone Star State, looking like a Texas Ranger minus the Stetson and six shooter. 'It ain't no good holding back. You gotta cream the whole darn area; get ahead of the game before it gets ahead of you.'

Sandy Oz was more circumspect. 'What do you think Steve? You've been in since the start. What do you think we should do?'

Steve sat and thought for a minute.

'Well first of all, I think it's out of control,' he said.

Sandy smiled, not with glee but with professional sympathy. 'I think you're right,' he said.

'I also think that we need the army in to help with disposal. We can't cope and the contractors that have been brought in are milking the system for all it's worth.'

'Aye, fucking right they are,' Willie called out. 'I had a row with one today. I was at Stick Hill and they were out there building a fire. They had that much earth moving machinery that was moving that much earth it was like they were laying out the foundations for a new airport. There's this little fat Twat in charge and I asked him what the fuck he thought he was doing.' Willie took a long drink from his pint of lager. 'And do you know what he told me?' He waited for a few seconds. 'That it was none of my fucking business. So I phoned the office and spoke to that curly heeded vet chappy whatever he's called. And he told me it was none of my fucking business as well. So I just let him get on with it. No point busting my own arse over something if nobody else cares. The fucking money going to waste though is something else. And who's going to ever want to land a plane between all those hills?' he joked. 'I'm just glad I'm not paying for it all.'

'You are though indirectly,' said Sandy. 'It's taxpayer's money paying for all this after all.'

'And how is the European connection today?' Sammy teased. 'I hear you went to her aid today. I hope you maintained a strictly professional relationship and behaved yourself Mr Turner,' she smiled.

'Of course,' said Steve. 'And I always behave myself.'

'Today I was killing small lambs,' said Fernando. 'Newborn lambs. It was terrible. We were pulling them from their mothers and then killing them. There is something wrong with that.'

Steve patted him on the arm. Writing his own reports earlier, despair had settled on him too. The news bulletins had promised more of the same. What else could they promise? Not much, he thought.

He glanced across to the other side of the bar. Oh shit, he thought. Julie was there and she looked drunk. And she was talking to Conrad. Steve hadn't known he was staying there too. Sammy saw the change of expression in his face and followed his gaze.

'Well, well,' she giggled. 'There soon won't be room in this hotel for all your lady friends. Sonia moved in this morning too. Drafted over from Morton because there are so many outbreaks here.'

Steve groaned. He couldn't believe this was happening to him. Sonia he could handle, she at least was rational. But Julie. There had been a change in her since they had split up. As though she had become obsessed with him.

The abuse she'd given him when he'd arrived had been bloody embarrassing. And what was she doing talking to Conrad. She had used to find him repulsive. A cold wind tingled in his spine. He thought of the letter, the hood of his Healey, and Paul. Jesus Christ he was forgetting about Paul. They all were. And no one caught yet.

Conrad had been questioned by the police at the time but had been released. No evidence he supposed but there was no evidence against anyone it seemed. They could be sitting just a few yards from Paul's killer and not even know about it. Any one of them could be next.

Steve felt the hotness in his throat and ice cold in the pit of his stomach; red creeping inside his chest and into his neck and up around his throat. Julie was laughing with Conrad, throwing her head back and touching his arm with her hand. God she was like Rachel, he thought. In looks and mannerisms. He knew why he'd fancied her. She glanced in his direction, feeling his gaze on her like a warm blanket all around. He saw a coldness, a hard edge in her eyes, her face more lined than he'd remembered. She whispered something to Conrad who looked across at him and then back at Julie and they both laughed.

Steve looked at his watch. It was 9.30 p.m. It was early but he was going to bed anyway. He'd had enough of this bloody business. The Foot and Mouth; and Paul; and the things that were happening to him. He would make an early start tomorrow. Head over to Todley and visit the four latest outbreaks there. It was probably a waste of time but he was a small cog in a huge machine. He just had to do what he was told.

'I'm off to bed,' he said trying to sound cheerful. 'Early start in the morning.'

Sammy looked at him. It was not like Steve to leave the bar so early. She saw the strained edges of his mouth, the slight puffiness around his eyes. Suddenly she was worried for him. It had never occurred to her that he might suffer from stress. He wasn't that sort of bloke. But there it was, written on his face for all but the blind to see.

Sammy stood. 'I think I'll go to my bed too,' she said. She caught Steve on the stairs.

'Steve,' she called. 'Steve.'

He half turned at her voice, the tears already streaking his cheeks, his eyes red and blinking.

'Come and have a coffee in my room,' Sammy said. She put her arm round him and kissed him on the cheek. 'Come on.'

He offered no resistance, just let her guide him down the corridor as she fished her key out of her pocket with her one free hand. She took him in and he slumped into one of the chairs.

'Tea or coffee?' she asked. Uncertain. 'What's the problem Steve?' she asked. 'What's the real problem? It's not just Foot and Mouth is it?'

Sammy the soothsayer. Sammy the one with the power to look behind the mask and the outward signs, he thought. He wished she were twenty years younger.

'No of course it's not,' he sobbed. Unashamed. He had long ago lost the fear of crying in front of people. For a year he'd cried in front of everyone he'd talked to for more than a few minutes. Always about the same thing. Always whilst telling them the same old story. 'No, the Foot and Mouth is just the last straw. It's fucking awful isn't it?'

'Of course it is,' said Sammy. 'I've seen hard headed farmers breaking down in tears. I've seen children trying to hide their pet lambs from the slaughterers, in the house, in wardrobes. Yesterday a woman refused to let us on her place. Her sheep were considered DCs because a farmer had delivered her a load of logs four days before disease was confirmed on his farm. We had to get the police to restrain her so that we could go in and kill her ten Jacob sheep; all with names. She was standing sobbing and screaming at us the whole while; calling us murderers and begging us not to do it. Of course it's awful. But what else can we do?'

'I don't know,' he said. 'I keep thinking of vaccination. Plenty of other countries use it. Some as routine. Others in the face of an outbreak. Maybe we should go down that route. Now before it's too late.'

'What else?' said Sammy. 'What else is bothering you?'

'Paul's murder,' said Steve. 'I'm scared Sammy. You know about that letter I had and then the hood of my car. I can't believe they're not connected.'

'Did you tell the police about the hood?' Sammy asked.

Steve shook his head.

'Well I would,' said Sammy. 'It's probably nothing, a coincidence, but they might as well know about it. No one knows the motive for Paul's murder but it's probably something personal from his past;

nothing to do with the Ministry. He just happened to be working for us when whoever it was caught up with him.

'What else?' she said.

He said nothing for a few minutes. He wiped the tears away with a tissue from a box on Sammy's dressing table. He felt foolish. He was starting to relax now. Everything was coming back into focus; back into perspective. He sipped the coffee that Sammy placed in his hands.

'What else?' she demanded an answer. She would not be put off by silence.

'It's that Italian girl, Francesca. I...' he hesitated, not certain what Sammy's reaction would be. 'I've only known her a couple of days, spoken to her for a few hours. It's stupid. I know it is but I can't help it.'

'Can't help what?' said Sammy making light of it though she knew what was coming. 'What is it you can't help Steve?' she repeated.

'I love her,' he said simply. 'I can't explain it but I love her.'

'She's married,' said Sammy.

'I know. But I love her and I can't help that. For sixteen years, ever since Rachel and I split up I've been chasing women and had a string of superficial relationships with them. For sixteen years I've been ditching girls that I could have fallen in love with and every time I've refused because I didn't want the same thing to happen again. And now in the middle of a bloody, fucking crisis I've never seen the like of before, I've fallen in love with the most beautiful girl I've ever seen and she's fucking married. What is fucking wrong with me Sammy?' he shouted at her.

She looked at him steadily. She felt her own heart might break in two. She had never seen him like this before. Steve. Always so in control. Always so distant and detached from his girlfriends. Not unkind to them but hardly every mother's idea of the perfect son-in-law.

'So what are you going to do?' she asked.

'What can I do?' he said. 'It's a complete fucking mess Sammy. I can't believe it's happening, everything all at once like this. My brain is bursting. My heart is bursting. I'm full of emotions that are flying around inside me like I'm some spotty faced adolescent.

'Oh Sammy,' he said. 'She is beautiful, isn't she?'

'She is,' Sammy agreed. 'And she's married.'

He finished his coffee. He felt calmer. Not happier, but calmer.

'Thanks for coffee Sammy,' he said and kissed her on the cheek.

'Steve,' she said. 'You've got a whole new life ahead of you when this over. Don't forget that. The sixteen years you talk of are behind you.' She squeezed his arm. 'Goodnight.'

Several hours later he lay awake in his bed. Sleep was impossible.

He was back at the farm lying in bed with Rachel asleep at his side. She had come home that evening and told him she had spent the afternoon at the beach with Patrick. He'd met her in the corridor and asked her if she'd wanted to talk again. They had slipped out of college together, the lecturer and the student and driven to the sea. She'd sat on the beach holding his hand with her head on his shoulder.

'He said he just wants to help me Steve. Wants what's best for me. He's a good man. A sad man.'

'Don't do this Rachel,' he said. 'For God's sake don't do this or we'll lose everything.'

'I love you Steve,' she said. 'I love you so much. Take me to bed and make love to me. Please Steve. Please.

She clung to him and her whole body was shaking.

'I do love you Steve. I do. I do. I promise.'

Now she was asleep, peaceful, her lips turned gently upwards in a smile, her nostrils flaring softly with each exhaled breath. Steve swore she could see him through her closed eyes; the smile was for herself while he wept silently, his mind tormented by the vision of her naked on the sand, entwined with Patrick, writhing and moving like the swell of a mighty ocean.

He wanted to go outside and run through the night. Run up onto the fell in the moonlight, run through the horrors of the dark until the morning sun came again and the shadows of pain and uncertainty were driven underground. He had thought she was mentally ill, a breakdown, or worse. It had all been misplaced ... on his part.

Now sixteen years on he was lying in bed reliving it again. A knocking at the door, he looked at his watch; just gone one in the morning.

'Rachel?' he said. He did not know why.

'Rachel? Who's Rachel? It's me, Julie.'

She was drunk, the words slurred.

'Let me in Steve. Let me in. I love you. I know you're there. I know you want me. You do want me... don't you?'

Her voice was pleading and she began to hammer on the door.

'Look Julie,' he said through the closed door, trying to sound calm and in control. 'Go to bed. I'm not going to open the door. You're being silly.'

'Silly?' She screamed it and banged harder on the door. 'You used me and I'm going to get you. You wait and see. I'm going to hurt you like you've hurt me.'

Steve got back into bed and pulled the quilt tight over his head. He couldn't stand this for much longer. Something had to happen to put an end to it. He thought of happier days and wished himself to sleep.

Chapter 37

On the east side of the Pennines, Todley is as miserable a place as you are ever likely to find, even on a sunny day. Grey buildings with peeling paintwork stained with diesel fumes from the lorries that rumble past just a few feet from front doors and bedroom windows. Grey men and women who have taken early retirement or redundancy or never worked at all; smoking cheap cigarettes as they walk along the narrow pavement, the creases and stubble on their face making them look ten years older than they really are. In early spring with a penetrating drizzle, the stench of burning animals and the corners of fields stacked with dead sheep, it had nothing to recommend it.

Steve arrived at Whiteleas Farm a little after ten in the morning. Tommy from Morton was there, big smile on his round ruddy face, the sleeves of his paper suit pushed almost up to his elbows to reveal hairy well muscled forearms that easily hoisted the dead sheep into the bucket of a telescopic loader.

'How's it going old fella?' he greeted Steve. 'Come to give us a hand have you?'

'Have you got a fire built already?' Steve asked.

'No, not here old boy; we're going to bury them. The Environment Agency said it's alright so we've dug a bloody great hole and away we go. It's a damn sight easier.' He smiled as he heaved the last sheep carcass into the bucket and waited for the next pen load.

They were being shot twenty at a time. Nice and steady; not over excited, no rush or shouting; just steady, constant work. Steve helped toss the next batch into the bucket, thorns stuck in the fleece pricked his fingers, the now familiar sagging weight of dead animals, poorly balanced for lifting. He followed the loader down the field to the mounds of rich brown earth, the damp scent reminding him of planting spuds. They'd had great spuds at the farm. Great white oval things, some of them a pound in weight, their skins rubbing off with your fingertips, lightly boiled with fresh mint and served hot with salted butter.

The bucket lowered to the ground and one of the contractors punctured and slashed each belly with a sharp knife like a billhook to help with decomposition and prevent the carcass filling up with gas and literally rising up out of the ground. And then the bucket tilted.

The sound of dead sheep falling twenty feet onto other dead sheep is a dull, hollow thud mixed with squelching and the occasional hiss of gas. The pit was packed solid with their white fleeces and mottled brown faces, huge bellies swollen with full term lambs that Steve assumed would die from suffocation within a few minutes of the ewes own death.

He left the edge of the pit and went to talk with the farmer who was bringing a bunch of ewes with one and two day old lambs in from the field.

'This was the field it all started in,' he said. It's only a mile from the abattoir where they had those pigs infected near the start of the thing. Probably came from there on the wind I'd say. We've got sheep at three other places too. Been taking food to them from here every day. I suppose they'll have to go too?'

Steve nodded. Classic DCs. Shared personnel, machinery and food supply. Too risky to ignore them.

'I came out here yesterday and half the ewes in this field, fifteen or twenty of them were either lying down or hobbling on all four feet,' said the farmer. 'Some I could catch by walking up to them. Usually they'd be off and away but these were bloody sick and in pain with their feet. Off their food, miserable looking. No milk for the lambs either. I found some of the lambs dead too,' he said.

'Nice girl came out yesterday. Sonia her name. Lovely lass, bright and really interested. Post mortemed some of the lambs, showed me the funny stripes on the heart where the virus damaged it she said. Took some blood samples and the hearts as well for the lab. But no doubt about what it was, she said.'

Steve cursed to himself. He couldn't get away from these bloody women and everyone always had a nice word to say for them. He looked around the field at the ewes. Some could hardly walk and a couple lay down repeatedly, finally refusing to move at all. Steve examined the mouth of one of them. No doubt about the diagnosis he thought. He helped the farmer lift her into a box on the back of the four wheeler. She lay motionless, head down, and they put her twin lambs in beside her.

'People say it's just like the flu. They should come and see these sheep,' the farmer said.

Near the gate the field was thick and wet with mud. Some of the weaker lambs slipped and sprawled in wheel ruts, lost their mothers and bleated plaintive and pitiful. Steve picked a couple up in his arms and the farmer did the same. They carried them through the gate as a wren started to sing in a gorse bush next to the gatepost. They set the lambs down on the grass and they struggled to find their mothers, tails wagging, skipping and jumping. In twenty minutes they would all be dead and in a bloody great hole. The sweaty feeling of nausea made him breathe deep and slow to clear the taste of death from his throat. It's getting to be too much he thought.

An hour later and he was on the road again to an infected farm five miles distant. He overtook a farmer carrying a few bales of hay on a filthy four wheeler, mud spraying up from the wheels and mudguards, all over the road. The ideas that had started to form were at last coming together and it was becoming increasingly difficult to ignore the obvious. He had to get a handle on it, write it down and send it off to Sage Street.

The next farm was down a long private road. He stopped and looked at his notes. Sheep again. This farmer had two more properties, and beyond the farm further down the track was another farm owned by someone else.

'Where's the disease security?' he said out loud to himself again.

He was angry with everyone; with everything. No one at the road end. A pathetic mat of straw; a filthy footbath and a knapsack sprayer lying on its side. Where was the policeman? Where were the Ministry officials? Where was anyone to prevent unnecessary visitors entering and leaving; licensing on and off only those that were essential and only then after a full and thorough disinfection? Here there was nothing. Sweet fuck all, he thought; save for a sign designed 30 years ago; something from the past, a museum exhibit. People didn't obey signs anymore. People laughed at signs: ripped them down and screwed them up or shot at them with air rifles or crossbows.

He phoned Cardington on his mobile. Surely they would agree that this was unacceptable. Somebody somewhere must do something. He tried the main number but it rang out unanswered. He tried another number,.. engaged. He rang the mobile of Keith Brewer the guy in charge of IPs: 'The Vodaphone you are calling may be switched off, please ..' he hung up.

The trouble was that everyone was so under pressure with new report cases there was nobody to answer the phones. He knew what it was like. No time to think, no time to consider what might be best. People demanding decisions on things you knew nothing about. No wonder they all had their fucking mobiles switched off.

The blackness of powerless despair stirred deep in his abdomen, a seed germinating, pushing upwards into his stomach, the stinging rancid bile, yellow and foaming, burning with sharp vinegar pain in a sliced finger. It was an old friend he knew well. A friend he had coaxed and tried to mollify for many weeks, many years before. A hollowed out feeling, like a perfect-to-look-at soufflé only seconds from collapse. A feeling that caused nausea and loss of appetite, sleeplessness and physical pain; self loathing and denigration. Yes the signs he recognised from long ago. But now he was in a position to respond. To fight back and say, 'This is what I can do.'

He knew that what he was doing now was a waste of time. Like trying to find out how one soldier on the battlefield had died whilst the battle raged all around. What was needed was a strategy to turn the tide against the enemy, a strategy to win the battle.

'Fuck I'm not doing any more of this today,' he said out loud.

He turned the Healey around and headed back to the main trunk road. And then he put his foot to the floor, seventy, eighty, the roar from the engine sent pulses of energy round his body, his mouth dry, a smile sat on his lips. He sounded the horn; again; and again. 'Fuck you bitch,' he shouted out. 'Fuck you.'

He lost count of the filthy tractors and trailers, Land Rovers and farm pick-ups that he passed on the road. Now that he knew, now that he was certain, they jumped out at him from every farm gate, every field entrance, every minor road. None so blind as those that can't or won't see he thought to himself. Can't see the wood for the trees. The clichés sang out to him, egging him on, the car drifting sideways round corners, back end snaking as the power was piled on again.

Tell tale wisps of smoke on distant hills; a pile of rotting sheep in the corner of a field; the empty fields stretching out to left and right; all told him that the killing was alive and well. He had to get back. Get back to Cardington to write a report that would put a stop to it. No time to spare he thought. 'No time to spare' he said. 'No time to lose.'

There again a farmer pulling out onto the road having just fed some sheep. There too. And another towing a trailer full of silage, mud and dung flying off the tractor wheels. All around the evidence was plain to see. Farmers going about their business as if they didn't have a care in the world.

It was mid-afternoon when he pulled into the Cardington office car park. He ran up the stairs and into the main office, a huge rectangle packed with desks and chairs, computer screens and phones. And dozens of people. People with sheets of paper and files stacked in front of them, working with narrowed eyes and sweating faces, pushing back their chairs, rising to deliver a file to another station; a noisy hush of murmured comments and exchanged glances with phones ringing unanswered, building like an orchestra but with no conductor and no end to the performance in sight.

Down two sides, smaller offices led off from the main room, one for Licensing; others for Infected Premises; Health and Safety; and Epidemiology. Epidemiology, slotted into the smallest room of all, a sign perhaps of the esteem in which the discipline and those that worked in it were held.

Groups of vets were milling around in corners, talking noisily, some with frustration, voices raised to shouting. A couple of Ministry vets that Steve knew were trying to keep order. Trying to get them organised, explain what was happening and what was needed. A strategy built on sand, Steve thought. Moving and changing with the ebb and flow of the tide.

The warm pink glow of embarrassment embraced him, his shirt collar tightening as though he were choking. Veterinary Officer Keith Brewer scurried by, sweat dripping from the end of his nose. He did not notice Steve. His face fixed straight ahead, defying anyone to deflect him from his path.

'Keith,' Steve called after him. 'Keith, what's going on?'

'It's madness here,' said Keith. 'We've already had 12 cases confirmed today and there's been 30 report cases. The system's collapsed. If we ever had a system,' he added. Colin Hunt's sitting in his office talking to Sage Street the whole time. There're new vets arriving every hour and no one in charge of them. We need more VOs but there're none to be had. Devon apparently is drowning in a sea of rotting carcasses and South Wales is starting to look a bit sick.'

'And what are our illustrious leaders saying to it all?' asked Steve.

'What can they say? They're doing their best I guess. They'll be under a lot of political pressure too.'

'You're far too kind to them,' said Steve.

'Colin Hunt's giving a briefing at 5.30 this evening. We might learn something then. Look, I've got to go. Trying to organise slaughter teams is getting impossible.' He wiped the sweat out of his eyes, his temple pulsating, his eyes bulging.

Steve hurried to his office, avoiding eye contact with everyone. Jenny was there sorting files.

'Hi Steve,' she said. 'You're back earlier than I expected.'

'Yeah, well, I didn't do all that Neil asked me to,' he said, the thick note of guilt in his voice. 'I just had a flash of inspiration and I wanted to get a report to Colin and Graham tonight before Ron Steady comes up here tomorrow. Would you have time to type it for me please if I write it now?'

'Of course. What else is there for a single girl to do on a Sunday evening in Cardington?' she joked.

'Don't let anyone in to see me,' Steve said. 'I'm not here; okay?'

'Okay,' she laughed.

It took him an hour to write. And once Jenny had typed it he read it through again.

GENERAL OBSERVATIONS ON THE FMD OUTBREAK AROUND CARDINGTON

1. New outbreaks of FMD are continuing in spite of a ban on the movement of all susceptible livestock.

2. This leads us to focus on vehicular and personnel movements as the main means of spread.

3. A large number of farms (perhaps the majority), have stock on outlying land; sometimes two, three, or even more properties. These premises may be anything from a few hundred yards to over ten miles distance from the main holding, with three or four miles being common.

4. Most of the outlying stock are visited on a daily or every other day basis by the owner/stockman to feed/inspect them. The number of individual journeys made by farmers each day will add up to many hundreds, perhaps thousands. I believe that these movements are by far the commonest agriculture related movements in the area.

5. Most of these movements are made in farm vehicles such as tractors, farm pick-ups, Land Rovers, quad bikes etc. These vehicles are mostly undisinfected other than a drive over a disinfectant straw mat (usually severely soiled). Many of the vehicles are filthy on the outside and in the cab.

6. I believe that there is the opportunity for spread of infection and cross contamination of one farm vehicle by another as farmers criss-cross each others tracks on their way to their respective holdings. This would account for Infected Premises appearing in geographically related clusters in which the Premises are not contiguous to each other.

7. The above theory is impossible to prove but farmers should be alerted to this risk by a prominent media campaign giving appropriate advice on biosecurity and how to limit the spread of disease by this means.

Steve Turner MRCVS, Epidemiology

Yes that was it. He was certain. There could be no other explanation.

'Would you e-mail that to Graham please Jenny, and put a copy in Neil's tray. I'll take a copy to Colin now.'

He knocked on Colin Hunt's closed door.

'Yes,' was the gruff response.

Steve went in.

'What do you want?' Colin Hunt said. 'I'm very busy.'

Charming, thought Steve. So this is the new management style so beloved of IiP is it? He felt like saying 'Bollocks' and turning round and walking straight out again.

'I've written a short memo to you about how I think the disease is spreading and what I think we need to do to stop it. I've sent Graham Thompson a copy too.'

'Leave it on the desk and I'll look at it later.'

Steve stood and waited. He had expected Hunt to read it and then quiz him on it. Query and probe his ideas. Test its validity from a veterinary standpoint. Force him to defend it. That was what he had expected. He stood his ground. Perhaps Hunt was thinking. Perhaps he was going to ask Steve how he saw the whole disease picture and where he thought things were going wrong. A discussion between two vets as equals, an exchange of information. Yes he was looking up at Steve, he was going to test Steve's theory with some incisive questions of his own.

'Is that all?' he asked.

Steve felt he was Bigwig standing before The Chief Rabbit in Watership Down. Yes that was it, it was perfect. Hunt was The Chief Rabbit.

'Err, y-yes,' he said, almost adding 'Sir' on the end. 'Yes, that's err, all.'

He went out. 'Yes that's all,' he said to himself. 'Only the biggest fucking breakthrough since this fucking disease broke out and yes, that's all. You twat, Hunt. You wanker. You stupid fucking twatty wanker.'

'Something I said?' said a young vet standing next to him.

Steve laughed. 'Nothing personal. How long have you been here?'

'Arrived today. I'm staying at The King's Head. Many of us there?'

'Dozens of us. We've sort of taken the place over. There's a swimming pool, sauna, and gym; not that I've had a chance to use any of them yet. Probably see you there tonight.'

Steve looked at his watch. It was nearly five. He went to get a cup of tea before Hunt's briefing. He could hardly wait to hear what gems he had up his sleeve.

Adrian Pope was in the tea room.

'Hi Steve,' he said in the easy manner of a man who was confident and comfortable with himself. 'Why can't people just get on and do what they're supposed to instead of wanting their hands held all the time? Vets who just won't make a decision on the bloody farm about the simplest damn thing and are constantly moaning about what the Ministry is or isn't doing. Some European bastard just upped and left today. Said it was madness. Cocky little shit. Said he was off to do real veterinary work somewhere else instead of carrying on with the butchery. Good riddance I say. If he can't hack it, we don't want him.'

Steve nodded but he did not agree. He was coming to the conclusion that there was more grey around than black and white and that terrible things were being done without question. The instructions said do this, and so it was.

'Each to their own Adrian,' he said idly. He didn't want to lay bare the confusion and sour taste of disloyalty that he felt in the pit of his stomach. If only he knew what he would do if he were in charge. Not necessarily what was best because that would be judged in hindsight. But if he were put in charge tomorrow, what would he do? He couldn't yet see clearly through the fog and steam. The misted pane of a bathroom window, pale grey distorted. He didn't know where truth was. Or honour.

He drank his tea alone. To think. Thinking was the thing that would beat this. Thinking and understanding. He hoped that those in charge were doing plenty of both.

The large open plan office was filled to bursting when Steve went back upstairs. It was nearly 5.30 and there was an atmosphere, a buzz, an energy about the place; a cinema audience at the premier of a long awaited film hoping for a glimpse of the stars as they arrived. With difficulty, he squeezed through to near the front. Eager faces of all ages stared back at him; young graduates only a few months out of vet school; old craggy faced stalwarts in which still glowed the fires of 1967. Each had an opinion on what should be done. Criticism of the Ministry's current handling of the outbreak was on everyone's lips.

The Chief Rabbit crept rather than strode from his office to the front of the crowd. He was pale and tired, lines around his mouth, darker patches of skin around his eyes. He was suffering too.

'Ladies and Gentlemen,' he said. His voice flat and cheerless. 'Thank you all for coming. As you know Ron Steady the PVO is coming here tomorrow. He'll be meeting farmer's representatives in the morning and is planning to address us here at 2.30 tomorrow afternoon.

'You don't need me to tell you that we have a difficult job on our hands. We are now up to 14 confirmed farms in this area today and there will be more. We are currently unable to get to all report cases on the same day and some are not being seen until the third day after the initial telephone contact. That is due to a lack of resources and in particular a lack of clean vets. We're trying to improve this situation. We're appealing in the media for vets and as you are aware the rates of pay for temporary vets have been increased substantially. There are another eight vets due to arrive from the USA tomorrow and the European Union will be providing some too.

'Carcass disposal has become increasingly difficult due to the number of cases. We are trying to get more rendering capability to reduce the number of pyres being built as these are holding us up in many cases. The difficulty too is in ensuring that the lorries available for hauling the carcasses are genuinely leak proof. There are of course problems……..'

It was a blur. A deep fog with no clarity and Hunt was no guiding light.

'…. Thank you all for your patience. Are there any questions?'

'What about using the army to help with disposals?' called out a young vet 'Wouldn't that be a sensible approach?'

'It's been looked at but has been dismissed for now. Private contractors are the preferred option'

'What about the problem of DCs?' said an older guy. 'Wouldn't it be better if the vet on the ground could make the decision on whether a neighbouring farm should be classed as a DC?'

'Sage Street are very keen that all DCs should be approved by them. If you think a neighbour should be classed as a DC because there is nose to nose contact over a boundary fence with animals on an infected farm then you must make the case to the field epidemiologist here who will then make the case to Sage Street.'

'But this all takes too long,' the questioner responded. 'If we can see stock grazing the other side of the fence then we should be able to make the decision there and then. Surely that makes sense? We obviously can't go and inspect them because we're already dirty. But we've got a good idea of the risks from seeing the situation on the ground.'

'What I would say,' said Hunt, 'is that you should try to make an assessment of whether there is clinical FMD in the animals in neighbouring fields by inspecting them over the hedge. That way if you do suspect they're already infected you would flag it up for a priority visit.'

Steve winced at what Colin Hunt was suggesting. The next question was as predictable as it was embarrassing.

'Are you seriously suggesting that we should try to diagnose FMD through binoculars?' said another vet, laughing with undisguised ridicule. 'Is that what you're suggesting?'

'No of course not,' snapped back Colin Hunt.

'Well what are you saying then?' the guy persisted. It was a fair question.

'I'm just saying that you may be able to get an idea of trouble. If there are a lot of salivating cattle or a lot of lame sheep then you have a good idea that there may be something amiss.'

The questioner did not press the case further, merely shook his head.

'If that's all then, thank you,' said Hunt, and he retired passively to his room, closing the door quietly and very deliberately behind him.

Chapter 38

Steve went to the pool alone that evening. He avoided even Sammy and Willie. He clung to the side immersed in the water to his chin. Thinking and planning. The door of the sauna opened and Francesca stepped out. She was wearing a blue, one piece swimming costume. The design was simple and elegant, discrete, girl-like. Beads of sweat glistened on her olive skin, smooth and shining. Her hair stuck to the sweat on her face and neck. She walked with the grace of the leopard, lithe, sure-footed, a light touch. She glanced around the pool, caught sight of Steve. Her smile of recognition made his mouth go dry, his stomach fluttered with memories of adolescence.

'Hi,' he said, his voice squeaky and effeminate.

'Hi' she said. 'How are you tonight?'

'I'm fine,' he lied. He knew he was in love with this girl. Small talk was inappropriate, a waste of time. He wanted to cry with pain and injustice. He could not hold her. Could not tell her.

'I have thought about our conversation two days ago,' she said. 'I have never spoken like that before to anyone. Not to my family. Not to my best friends. And you are a stranger. Why did I tell you this? I keep asking myself and I find I have no answer. Not an answer I can accept anyway. And you understood how I felt. I have never met a person who could understand how I feel. Why do you understand? Why you, Steve, with the big fast car and the old girlfriends crying outside your door? Why do you understand?' she shouted.

He did not answer her. Could not answer her. He could not lie to her. He could not tell her the truth. She was sitting in the pool now just a few feet from him, her eyes blazing hot with life and energy, passion in their core. He shrugged his shoulders. Shrugged his shoulders and stayed silent.

'Tell me,' she said. Tell me what is inside your head. Tell me what is so special about you,' she was demanding.

He told her everything.

About how he had asked to meet Patrick and how he had pleaded with him to leave Rachel alone. Pleaded that she was his; a part of him as much as his arm or leg. About how Rachel had decided she needed space to think and had gone to stay with her parents for a few days and had disappeared on the train journey home to be with Patrick.

He told her about the nights he had spent alone at the farm, feeding the animals and lambing the ewes whilst Rachel stayed he knew not where. How he had talked with her on the phone. Pleaded with her not to do this. Pleaded that he loved her more than he loved his own life and the lives of all his friends and family.

He had visited the doctor and persuaded Rachel to visit too. He had thought she was ill. He told her how they had spoken on the phone one night and that Rachel told him she was coming back to the farm the next morning because they needed to talk. It was the College holiday and Patrick was away working. Besides, she said he was peripheral to their problem. Only the two of them could sort that out.

She arrived the next morning at six o'clock. Waking him by shouting up at the window.

'I couldn't sleep,' she called. 'I couldn't wait to get started, so here I am.'

He looked down at her, the smile spread across her face, a face that was a pale dream of what he remembered. Darkness on the skin around her eyes, a she-devil waiting to suck the life blood from him. She ran to the big shed to see the lambs, ruffled the cat's ears. She kissed him on the cheek as acquaintances would kiss, her hand fleetingly on his wrist, the touch of restraint rather than affection.

That evening they sat by the fire and she looked long and deep into the flames. They flickered in the blueness of her eyes, orange fingers curling up to consume his own reflection when she glanced across at him. There was a new confident look in her face. A look of self satisfaction that glowed from within, shining like a star. And he saw too, many things different from the previous five years. Indifference instead of love; pity instead of respect; betrayal instead of loyalty.

She sat silent and at peace. If he had not known better he would have said she were high on drugs. Drugs that stupefied and left her at the mercy of her emotions.

'You don't have to own a farm,' she said as though speaking to someone in another room. 'You don't need possessions. It's not what you do in life but how you do it. I could be happy working on the checkouts at Sainsburys.'

He did not understand. He did not know how to respond.

'I just hope that when this is all over we'll still be friends,' she said.

And then he knew how it would all end. At that moment he saw the future and understood why she was there. This was her olive branch to their friends and family. So that everyone would say that dear Rachel was trying her best to make it work; giving it a second try; not simply throwing in the towel. If it all went wrong dear Rachel should appear guiltless.

He remembered looking across and seeing defiance in those black pupils. The flames of the fire burnt from within too, not mere reflections of those in the grate. She was there in body but her spirit was elsewhere, flying with the birds, soaring in distant lands.

'If you want we can sell everything and go on another trip somewhere,' he said. 'Buy a Land Rover, drive to India. Drive anywhere. I don't care where we go. I just want you. To be with you. I love you.'

'Don't say that,' Rachel said. 'Just don't say that Steve.'

She looked in the fire and sang to herself. 'I believe when I fall in love this time it will be forever.' She sang it over and over. To herself but so that he could hear. She had a gentle smile on her face. A smile that said I know what I am doing. A smile that said you can't stop me, I can do whatever I want.

The next day they had driven to the nearest town for lunch. They hadn't been out together for months. No money to pay for it. The overdraft near its limit, no income from the sheep for another five months.

'This must be really hurting you Steve Turner,' she said over lunch. She smirked, gratuitous and cruel. They had got into debt together because that was what their dream required. He had been prepared to live on potatoes and swedes and cheap meat if that was what the dream demanded. He had known it and was prepared for it. He could not have known that she was not.

It spilled out of him like lava from a long dormant volcano. He told her of the night Patrick had phoned the house and he, Steve, had answered it. Patrick had coolly asked to speak to Rachel, unabashed that he was speaking to her husband. Steve had wanted to shout and scream at him, 'Fuck off. Leave her alone.' But he was afraid. Afraid of driving her deeper into his arms. He called her in from the byre where she was feeding the dogs and sat himself in the lounge close to the fire to warm the icy cold inside him that flicked and flickered up his spine, freezing his blood so that his fingers turned blue at the tips.

He watched her across the room in the dim light, talking excitely, her eyes shining with the light of youthful love, the light she used to have for him and which had been missing these past months. Her talk was rapid, he caught snatches of it, a sordid voyeur eavesdropping on the murmurings of young lovers.

'…. you don't half give me a hard time…' she simpered '.. missing you too..'

He was a stranger in his own house. Unwanted. Out of place.

She hung up. Her countenance changed to the drooping dark grey face of the last few weeks.

'He's doing fine,' she said as though Steve would be as pleased to hear from him as she. 'They're working him hard but he's doing fine. I can't *do this Steve,' she said. 'I'm going to go and stay with Carrie. I'll come up here whenever it's necessary to help with the animals. I can't stay here. It's not right.'*

A knife, sharp and bright embedded in his gut. A bayonet thrust in and up with force and then the final twist; the wicked gut tearing twist.

'I've never loved you,' she said. Spat it out like a cobra's poison, sharp and direct, no time to duck or dodge. It hit him straight in the face, absorbed through his eyes and mouth; through his skin; the sound ringing in his ears; spreading through his body and mind, weakening every muscle; every nerve; his self belief and self worth turning to dust and blowing in the wind.

'I've never loved you,' she repeated, driving the steel home with contempt. 'I know that now.'

He said nothing. His voice had dried and withered. He felt everything inside him shrinking, shrinking to a spec of nothingness.

'I'm going now,' she said, and went out of the room. He heard her climb the stairs, rummaging in the bedroom above, packing her bag. She came down.

'I'll take the dogs with me,' she said. 'It's less for you to do. You can phone me to organise feeding the animals when you're working away. She went out into the chill of the night and closed the door. He heard the car engine start, the crackle of wheels on gravel, and she was gone. Like his hopes. His dreams. Nothing left.

He could not cry anymore. He had cried in the last few weeks until his eyes were red and swollen and the tears came no more. There was nothing left to cry. He tried to think ahead. A brick wall, a hundred feet high and ten feet thick.

He could remember climbing the stairs, going to the spare room where the shotgun lay. The shotgun they'd borrowed when a fox killed one of their lambs. Feeling and admiring the smooth grey of the barrels, the rich brown of the stock. He slid two cartridges into the barrels, closed the gun and sat on the bottom stair opposite the front door. He cocked the hammers and placed the end of the barrels in his mouth. He hoped that it would be Rachel that found him. He hoped it were she that found him slumped and stiff with his blood and brains spattered across the walls and ceiling of the entrance hall. He closed his eyes and he could see her opening the door, the gasp of pain and shock on her face at the grizzly scene before her.

And then another entered the hallway. It was Patrick. He looked at Rachel and laughed. She laughed too. Hysterically with glee. They stepped over his body giggling, avoiding the pool of congealed black blood and the soft pieces of creamy brain stuck to the stairs and hand rail. Then he heard them making love wildly and noisily on the bed. On his bed that was a wedding present to them both.

The vision saved his life. He did not know if he had placed his fingers on the trigger but now he thought instead of his friends and family. Of his mother and father, and of his brothers and sisters. He would not do this to them. He lay the gun down at his side and gently released the hammers.

He spent the next week alone. Food, a slice of toast. He had no hunger. He fed the sheep and the heifers and lambed the ewes. But there was no excitement or pride. No desire for a good lambing. There was no joy.

The following weekend he was working for a veterinary practice and staying with friends. He left the farm at midday on Friday. He would not return until Monday morning. Rachel would go there to stay and care for the animals.

When his work was done on the Sunday he told his friends he was going back to the farm. He arrived as dark was falling. The faintest wisp of smoke from the chimney, a light yellow glow from the lounge window. He pulled into the yard in front of the house. There were no other cars. He opened the house door, the dogs leapt up in greeting. He patted them and fussed them. He'd missed them too. Like he'd missed Rachel.

He went into the lounge, the fire flickering low. He switched the generator on and the lights came up to the thud thud of the Lister engine by the side of the house. He put the tin kettle on the two burner gas stove and went to make up the fire.

The bubble wrap packet of contraceptive pills on the mantelpiece sent a burst of adrenaline into his blood that made his legs shake and his heart pound. He put a hand on the wall, a sickly taste caught in his mouth. He swallowed it back down, burning his throat and making his eyes water, misty opaque, through a glass bottle.

He picked up the packet, five tablets gone. He breathed deeply; early days yet he thought. A drowning man reaching for dry land, a tumbling man pawing at the air, hoping to catch a hold of something that would save him. A blade of grass, an overhanging twig.

He made up the fire and turned the generator off. He moved his car to the back of the house. He would sit in the darkness and wait. Wait and see what the night would bring. He fell asleep. Not a sleep of rest, but a sleep of demons and goblins that leapt at him from the shadows with bony fingers clutching at him, clawing at his face and arms for a touch and perhaps a taste of his bare flesh.

He was woken by the dogs whining, the sound of a tail slapping against the leg of a table, the bright lights of a car pulling up in front of the house. The sound of giggling, the key turned in the lock and still he sat in the dark and waited, his pulse racing in excitement and fear.

'Hello,' he said as they opened the door to the room. 'Just popped in for coffee?'

'Steve's here,' Rachel said. 'Get in the car Patrick.'

A scurrying of footsteps, a car door slammed.

'Why are you here tonight?' Rachel demanded. 'You were coming back tomorrow.'

'Yes, and I'm so sorry to have spoilt your plans,' he shouted. 'And what is this?' he asked, holding the packet of contraceptives in his hand. 'Well?' he shouted, his mouth twitching at the corners as he stared at her.

She made a grab for them and he snatched them away and threw them in the fire.

'You fucking bitch Rachel,' he screamed. 'You promised. You fucking promised you would never bring him here. You fucking promised.'

'You shouldn't have come,' she said. 'We've just been out for a drink, that's all.'

He grabbed at her. She was strong but he was stronger still. He spun her round and threw her face down on the settee and with the palm of his hand spanked her on the backside, three, four, five times; using all his force.

'You bitch. You fucking bitch. You fucking whore,' he screamed. And then he ran outside.

He pulled open the passenger door and grabbed Patrick by the arm. 'You fucking bastard. How dare you come to my home you fucking bastard.' He was pulling at his arm, trying to pull him from the car but Patrick had jammed his legs against the door frame and was pulling back with all his strength. Steve let go of his arm and grabbed him by the hair, two handfuls, pulling and ripping until he forced him out of the car and into the cold night air of late spring.

'I'll break your fucking neck you little cunt,' he screamed and raised his fist to smash it in his face.

'Stop it Steve,' Rachel grabbed his arm. 'Stop it, leave him alone. This is stupid.'

He let go. Patrick jumped back into the car and locked the door.

Rachel relaxed her hold and they stood facing each other. Sweat was pouring from his face, saliva leaked from the corner of his mouth. Rachel's face red, defiant. He knew that in spite of their six years together she would have shot him before Patrick.

'I'm going,' she said. 'Now. Don't try to stop me.'

She unlocked the driver's door. Steve walked to the front of the car and looked through the windscreen at Patrick cringing in the passenger seat. His eyes were open wide, he was nursing the back of his head where Steve had had a hold of his hair. He glanced about him and saw the axe leaning against the generator shed. He thought to pick it up and smash it through the windscreen. Smash it through the windscreen and then climb onto the bonnet and smash it through the fucking roof. He was mad, frenzied and then in a second it all stopped. He was calm again, the engine roared and he stood to one side as Rachel drove away, the engine screaming as the car laboured up the hill. The lights stopped moving at the top and Patrick got out to open the gate, and then it was away and the whine disappeared into the night to be replaced by the eerie drumming of a snipe, high above him. He went back inside and locked the door. He put the fireguard up and went to bed.

The next morning he fed the animals for the last time. He packed his clothes into two hold-alls and a couple of bin bags. He looked around at the cardboard boxes of books and ornaments. Files and old letters, photographs, the flotsam of the time they had spent together. He sorted out a few things and loaded them into his car. He locked the door and stood on the front doorstep to take a last look at the view that had been his joy and inspiration for the last two and a half years. A curlew called and glided into the rushes by the stream in front of him. He ushered the dogs into the car. He would drop them at a friend's and Rachel could collect them from there.

He drove slowly up the hill and through the gateway. As he latched it shut he took a final look down onto the little house that had been his home. Tears would not come and he knew that he would never return. He would see Rachel only once more, in the car park of a pub to exchange some keys. His life would be forever changed.

There was silence. A calm, gentle silence like after a heavy fall of snow. He looked at Francesca and she looked at him.

'Now I understand,' she said.

'And now I love you,' he replied.

Chapter 39

Colin Hunt was talking to Des Quiet when Steve went to see him.
Des took up a position in the corner of the room, crossing his legs
in the way that a woman would, his neat pin-stripe suit blending in
with the shadows from the curtains.

'Yes?' said Hunt as he looked up from his desk.

The Veterinary Service was a hierarchy. The culture of superiority
and subordinacy went deep and though Steve despised it he had
learnt to live by the rules. Now though there was a crisis. The rules
could go to bollocks.

'I was wondering what you'd thought about that memo I gave you
yesterday? About how I think FMD is spreading?' Steve asked.

Colin Hunt looked at him with the soulful eyes of a Bassett
hound. He bowed his head, placed his left hand on the side of his
face, lowered his eyelids and gave a heavy sigh. He spoke slowly,
deliberately, with no attempt to hide the contempt in his voice.

'Do you seriously expect me to believe that this is what is
happening?'

'Well I think it's very plausible,' said Steve. 'Livestock movements
are at a standstill so we're only left with windborne infection and
fomites. And farmer movements are by far the commonest source of
potentially infected vehicles on the road. And the dirtiest,' he added.
'How else could the infection be spreading?'

Hunt sighed. 'If what you say is true then diseases like BVD and
IBR would be on every farm in the country.' He picked at a lettuce
leaf on his desk and Steve took that to mean that the conversation
was at an end.

Steve glanced across to Des Quiet, looking for support. Surely
he would see the validity of what Steve had said. Des sat slowly
nodding his head like a toy dog on the parcel shelf of a car but said
nothing. Slowly his head came to rest and he blended again into the
background like a chameleon recovering from a fright.

'Can you make sure the PVO gets a copy of this later today please,'
said Steve. It was his parting shot. There was nothing else to say.
He left the office with the empty ache of nausea, and bumped into
Fernando in the corridor.

'What is wrong?' said Fernando. 'You look sad.'

Steve told him.

'Of course you are right,' said Fernando. 'It is obvious now that you say it. What else can it be? Aliens?' His eyes rolled wide and white and Steve laughed aloud.

'You're a great lad Fernando,' he said. 'How is Sarah?'

Fernando smiled. 'She arrived yesterday,... and she is lovely,' he said. 'Will you be here for the PVO's visit this afternoon? I plan to be but I'm not sure I will be back in time.'

'I wouldn't miss it for the world,' said Steve.

He went to find Neil. He needed to talk. This is how it feels to go insane, he thought. Hot and cold pressure in his head; a tap full on damned back, pressing against the sides, expanding, forcing; a tightness in the chest, jabbing pain, breathing fast. He had never had a panic attack but he new that he was there, on the edge. Balanced on the rim. He concentrated on his breathing, slowed it down, deep and slow, cleared his head; walked calmly through the mayhem that was the ringing of phones, the rustling of paper; the squeaks and grunts of the printers, fast footsteps on cheap carpet; the shouting and sweating of the office; mobiles singing to church organ music; the William Tell Overture; tinny tunes befitting a tinny society that was more spin than substance.

Someone called his name and he ignored it. Now intent only on getting to the fresh air, to the real world that now seemed so distant. He let FMD slip through his mind. He thought of Francesca. He thought of nothing other than Francesca. Her eyes, her lips, her smile, the fall of her hair, her skin soft and clear, the tender curve of her breasts, the gradual sweep of her waist, the flat abdomen in front, the rounded buttocks behind, the long thigh and calf, smooth and muscular but not strung with tendons like a violin bow, the skin taut and without blemish. Her smile and laughter, the tears on her cheeks; the pain in her eyes. Both comfort and torment to him. Untouchable. Out of reach. Not his to love.

When he had told her yesterday in the pool she had looked away. Not with anger. There was no anger. She had looked away with chastity and modesty, and he thought sadness too. She had looked away for a full minute but when she had looked back she was smiling. Smiling and breathing deeply and she touched his cheek the way he had touched hers to wipe away the tears. Then she climbed out of the pool and went to get dressed.

He reached the street and sat on the wall. He was thinking too of the farmers and how they could be told of what was happening. Colin Hunt should be on the television ramming home the message: 'Don't leave the farm unless you have to; disinfect your boots and tractors, and four wheelers.' It should be shouted from the roof tops not consigned to a file that would gather dust and be seen by no one.

A young bloke came and sat down next to him.

'Are you Steve Turner the epidemiologist?' he was aggressive.

'Yes,..' said Steve cautiously.

'I'm a vet from practice.' Abrupt and self confident. 'I want to know why you've recommended that Elm Farm over at South Ralston is to be slaughtered as a Dangerous Contact. It's a bit bloody harsh isn't it?' Arrogance oozed from his skin like slime on a slug.

Steve could not remember the case. He had dealt with dozens in the last week. Names and faces had merged like paint on an artist's palette, everything a dull muddy grey, nondescript.

'I don't remember,' he said.

'Well you bloody well should shouldn't you?' the guy continued. 'It's all the man's dairy cows you're talking about slaughtering. You bloody well should remember. There's another farm between Elm Farm and the IP, and apparently that's not a DC. Why not? It's not bloody fair is it?'

It all came back to him. Now he remembered the case clearly. He lost his temper.

'How long have you been here?' he asked bluntly.

'Three days,' said the man.

'Well I've been here for over three weeks without a day off yet so don't fucking come in here and start telling me what we should or shouldn't be doing. I'll tell you why it's a fucking DC; it's because the farmer's son milks his dad's cows and was also a relief milker at the IP the day before disease was confirmed there. That's why it's a fucking DC.' He was shouting and other people in the street were looking at him.

'These aren't easy decisions to make you know. I don't make them fucking lightly. I weigh everything up, agonise over it and then do my best. So don't come greasing in here and tell me what I should be fucking doing.' He was trembling, shoulders shaking and he could feel tears running down his face. He was forever crying these days, he thought. He cuffed his face to wipe the tears away. The other vet looked shocked, and embarrassed.

'I'm sorry,' he mumbled. 'I hadn't realised.'

Steve's anger faded, smoke dispersing in a breeze.

'I'm sorry too,' he said. 'It's just that, it's not easy and I'm absolutely fucked. Lots of other people in the same boat. It's a bloody mess.'

The guy went away.

'Pressure getting to you is it?' said Julie standing behind him. He turned to find her laughing. 'Trying to get a little bit of Italian now are we?' She was teasing but not in jest.

'You're a sick bastard Turner,' she said. 'You need to watch out or you'll get what's coming to you.' It was a threat, plain and simple. After all that had happened it chilled his spine and made his mouth go dry. Dullness in the void of his chest. He walked away. He did not want another row. Least of all with Julie.

And then Sammy was by his side. She slipped her arm into his.

'Let's go and get a coffee,' she said.

They walked along arm in arm and found a café with the smell of fresh coffee wafting onto the street.

'This is getting worse isn't it?' she said.

'Which bit?' Steve said. 'Foot and Mouth, or Steve Turner's emotional state?'

'I think probably I mean both,' she replied.

'Well what do you think we should do about Foot and Mouth? I'm coming round to the idea of vaccinating but I'm still not certain what I would do if I were in charge. If it were up to me what would I decide? I don't know and that's what's bothering me.'

'You could kiss goodbye to the export trade for the next few years if we do vaccinate,' said Sammy. 'And where would you start? And what would you vaccinate? Just cattle? Cattle and pigs? Everything susceptible? It's a minefield.'

'But where's the leadership and the scientific debate?' Steve persisted. 'Who's considering these things? I've no idea if they're even being considered. There's no..., no communication from up top other than on procedures and they're usually so confusing that everyone just does their own thing anyway. And when I think of the awful consequences that this policy is having on animal and human welfare; the misery and suffering and how much this slaughter policy is starting to cost, I'm beginning to think it can't be justified. Not on the strength of safeguarding a few hundred million pounds a year in export revenue. And look at what it's doing to the tourist industry and the environment. The whole thing's barbaric isn't it?'

Sammy looked at him.

'Let's see what Ron Steady says this afternoon,' she said. 'We might get more guidance then.' She paused. 'And what about your love life? Do you want to tell Auntie Sammy all about it?'

Steve laughed. 'There's nothing to tell. For once in a long while I don't have one. I told Francesca I loved her, if that's what you mean.'

Sammy frowned. 'Was that wise?' she said. 'Bearing in mind that she's married. Or fair even?'

'All's fair in love and war Sammy,' he said.

'Do you believe that?' Sammy asked.

'Yes,' he lied. It was convenient to believe it now.

'You surprise me Steve,' Sammy said, and there was disappointment in her voice. 'I always thought,.... well, I suppose I thought you were more honourable than that.'

He was disappointed in himself. Sammy was a best friend. She and Willie and perhaps now Fernando. He didn't want her disapproval. He tasted the bitter taint of shame.

'Something as strong as this can't be wrong,' Rachel's words sang in the background, taunting him, confronting him.

'You can't help what you feel,' he told her. 'But you don't have to act on it. You can let it pass; let it go; let it fade away to nothing.'

But she was not that kind. Not of that style. Hers was the present. The future would take care of itself.

They sat for a couple of hours in the café. Sammy was 'dirty', nothing pressing to drag her away. She was worried about Steve. She had never seen him so confused, so.... weighed down. She knew that they all felt a bit like that, apart from the few who seemed to thrive on it, even relish the challenge of what was to be achieved. Of course some of them were not the brightest folk. Unquestioning, following their 'orders', hoping to be noticed; a good step forward for their career. She knew that Steve questioned everything to the point of annoyance. Not because he was indecisive, far from it. When the time came, he would make a decision but he would review it in the light of new knowledge and expectations. He could probably drive a woman quite mad, she thought.

This girl Francesca had got under his skin. In all the years she'd known him she had never known him to get involved. To her knowledge he had always been honest with his girlfriends, not pretended to care for them more than he did. And he'd always treated them with a superficial kindness even if it were obvious that they were accessories, something for Steve Turner's pleasure and enjoyment. Like books borrowed from a library, read and enjoyed to a greater or lesser extent, and then returned, undamaged but perhaps a tiny bit more soiled; before another was checked out.

Francesca was different. Something that had more depth and which would endure. She smiled to herself. It was a fascinating scenario unfolding before her eyes. She wished it didn't involve her old and dear friend.

'Take a day off,' she told him as they made their way back to the Animal Health Office. 'Colin Hunt has told everyone that they must take off at least one day a week. You're not indispensable you know. We'll cope without you.'

Steve laughed. 'You're right. I'll ask Neil if I can have Wednesday off.' He kissed her on the cheek. 'I'll go and see him now.'

'Steve, where have you been lad? I've been looking for you. The shit has hit the fan again. We've got a new IP fifteen miles from the nearest case. No idea how it got there. Go and see what you can find will you?'

'What stock are affected?' said Steve, trying to lift his spirits with a display of enthusiasm.

'Started in pigs and now showing in the cattle and sheep. A bit like that one you were at the other day, Browns Farm wasn't it?'

Steve nodded.

'I'll go later this afternoon. I want to hear what Ron Steady has to say first. See what those up top are thinking about the whole thing.' He paused. 'And could I have Wednesday off this week please Neil? I've not had a day off in the last three weeks and I'm shagged.'

'Aye, of course you can. And what about this memo on how you think it's spreading? Seems feasible to me. What did Hunt say?'

'He belittled me and dismissed it out of hand. He thinks I'm a fucking nutter.'

'Well we all know that,' said Neil. 'But your memo seems to be on the right track. Look, here's the preliminary report from the vet at this farm I was telling you about. Nothing in it to go on. You'll just have to do some sniffing around and come up with a convincing story for Sage Street. They're starting to think we're incompetent up here.'

'Why so long?' Steve laughed.

Keith came through the door, beads of sweat on his face.

'Twenty new infected farms today already,' he said, 'we can't cope. There're dead animals all over the place; animals awaiting slaughter; sheep lambing away from home with no shelter or attention; and now one of the big milk powder producers is threatening to sue us if we light the pyre that has taken three days to build and is half a mile down wind of them. They're afraid it'll taint the milk powder. I don't know what to do.

'And did you see the news again last night? The same thing is happening in Devon and the Minister still calmly saying that everything is under control and that there is no crisis. What planet is he on? He should come up here for a few hours.'

He turned and went out again without waiting for an answer. Steve glanced at Neil but they said nothing.

At 2.30 that afternoon the office was packed with standing room only. An air of nervous anticipation and expectancy. An expectancy that the PVO was going to announce new measures that would put everything right. A policy statement, an understanding and recognition that things were not going well and that a change of direction was needed. And recognition that more logistical assistance was needed in the form of the army.

Steve's eyes moved around the room studying the faces. Everything you needed to know was there to see. In their eyes and mouths, the lines, the tiny movements, the colour of their skin. There was someone suppressing anger, a glint of red on their cheeks, a darker purple tinge across their brow. Over there the look of helplessness and depression; hollow lines on the face, a dirty grey colour. A Spanish girl to his left, her hair shining bronze, laughing good naturedly with the old retired vet with the greasy grey hair and milk bottle glasses in thick black plastic frames. An American vet; overweight and wearing a baseball cap bearing the legend IDAHO, chewing noisily on gum and explaining in a loud voice what would be done if this were The States.

A mass of young men and women, administrators, young and self possessed; working tirelessly at their computers and spreadsheets, exhausted by the long hours but determined to do their part with the added bonus of a swollen bank account that promised future package holidays to Ibiza and beyond. They were shielded from the horrors of what was happening on farm; the stench and filth, the noise and tears of animals and people. Long hours of intense concentration were the devils that flew in their mind's eye.

Steve saw Sammy near the front and Willie too, putting on a brave smile. The lines on his brow told a different story. He was missing Morag and the kids but he dare not go home for a couple of days off. Morag's brother had a farm and the children were always going over to stay or help out. He dare not risk the infection spreading so far north, regardless of how improbable it might be.

The disease instilled paranoia in everyone it brushed against. A paranoia that virus particles were everywhere; in a person's hair; their car; on their pens and notepads; hiding in the turnups of their trousers. Beneath their finger nails and on the soles of their shoes.

Steve caught Willie's eye and winked. He made a face. And then a hush spread from the far end of the room and the crowd parted like the Red Sea to reveal Colin Hunt creeping through, followed closely by Ron Steady, Des Quiet, and a young girl dressed in a skirt and dark jacket.

Colin Hunt addressed the crowd.

'Thank you all for coming. Today has been the worst day to date for new outbreaks. We have a backlog on report cases, slaughterings, and disposals. I'm very grateful to you all for all the hard work you've been putting in and I would urge you all to take off one day a week. You're no good to me if you work yourself into the ground.' He stopped and waited for the murmurs to die down.

'The PVO is with us for a short while this afternoon. He's been meeting with farmer's leaders and other industry representatives this morning and has very kindly made the time to address us now. I don't think I want to say any more so I will just hand over to him now. Ron.'

Ron Steady stepped forward, no hint of uncertainty in his face or voice as he began to speak with the buoyant, jacket flapping air of an old music hall 'Cheeky Chappie.'

'There's been a lot of criticism of our handling of this outbreak. Let me just say that in the '67 outbreak, a total of nearly 450,000 animals were slaughtered over a seven month period. In this outbreak, in under four weeks, we've slaughtered about 300,000 animals. Now I don't think that's bad going and it certainly doesn't imply to me that we can't cope.'

'So that's his measure of success is it?' said Steve to a vet by his side. 'How many animals we've killed in what period of time.'

'The problem we're having is that disease is hiding in the sheep and then spilling over into the cattle. The sheep are often asymptomatic and the farmers aren't recognising it. Only when their cattle become infected do they call us in. The problem we need to crack is how to detect it early in the sheep and stop it in its tracks.'

Steve looked puzzled. Who says that's what is happening? he thought. In nearly all the farms he'd been on after the first two weeks there was no connection with any sheep from the market that originally disseminated the disease. Now it was cattle or in some cases pigs that were the first animals to be affected on a farm. Why did the PVO think the problem was the sheep? he thought.

'.... and people keep on asking me if we have a Plan B. Well,..' he paused waiting for the penny to drop before continuing, 'let me tell you all here and now, that there is no Plan B. This is it. This is the policy that we're continuing with.' He was jaunty, ebullient, confident in his delivery.

'Others seem to want to bring in the army,... guns blazing,' he opened his arms to emphasise the point, jocular now as though there could be no madder idea on God's earth. A few sycophants nodded their heads approvingly.

'And can I just say how grateful the Minister is to you all for the hard work you've been putting in. It really is most appreciated and he asked me to pass on his sincerest thanks. Now I think I may have time for one or two questions?' he looked across at the young girl and she nodded. She must be his PA, Steve thought.

'It would be helpful if there could be more decision making at a local level,' said a vet. 'Too often there are delays whilst Sage Street decides what's to be done and it slows everything down, from slaughter right through to disposal. Can we have more power to make our own decisions?'

'It's always a problem getting the balance between local and central decision making. We think we have that balance about right. Any local difficulties should be taken up with your line manager.'

Colin Hunt nodded approval and Ron pointed to another raised hand.

'I'm concerned about the welfare problems that a complete standstill on animal movements is causing. Surely we should be able to look at each of these cases on its merits. I mean, stopping the movement of a flock of ewes that are due to lamb from what now looks like a ploughed filed to a field ankle high in grass because they would have to cross a minor public road. Well it doesn't make sense does it?'

'Our control strategy relies on a complete cessation of animal movements. We can have no exceptions or the whole process could be opened up to abuse.'

Steve knew then that they were going nowhere. He had hoped to be told that all options had been considered and that now they were going on the offensive rather than rely on a reactive policy. He had hoped to hear about plans for a mass vaccination campaign, a campaign whose details were being finalised and which would then be given the highest priority. Instead they had been told that all was going well. That it would simply be more of the same.

The Young PA was looking agitated, glancing at her watch. The PVO noticed and called over to her.

'How are we doing for time? Where have I got to be next and when?' He bounced from foot to foot, enjoying the attention and sense of celebrity. Colin Hunt and Des Quiet simpered, rubbing their hands together in gentle ingratiation and delight at the honour the PVO had bestowed on them with his presence.

'I think we'd better call a halt there,' Hunt cut in. 'I'm sure you'd all like to join me in thanking Ron for giving us that roundup of the current situation and for clarifying exactly where we're going in this outbreak.'

'Where we're going,' muttered Steve to the girl next to him, 'is to fucking Armageddon.' He was shocked by the complacency. Shocked by the lack of a coherent contingency plan. Shocked by the lack of appreciation of what was happening on the ground, out there on the farms. Shocked by the complete misreading of the epidemiological signs.

He had to get to speak to him. Give him a copy of his memo and ask him face to face under what circumstances they would vaccinate. He pushed through the crowd trying to see where the PVO had gone. He checked Colin Hunt's office. It was empty. He went down another corridor towards an office that Des Quiet sometimes used.

The door was slightly ajar and he could hear raised voices as though an argument was taking place. He listened.

'It was a long time ago,' he heard Ron Steady say. 'I was young for God's sake. I didn't know what I wanted. I ...' Steve couldn't catch the last bit of the sentence. 'How was I to know it would turn out the way it did?'

'But you lied to me. You let me down. And so badly. That's what I couldn't cope with. You lied to me and then you deserted me.'

It was a familiar voice. Steve strained his ears to listen.

'I swore I'd get even with you some day. Make you pay for what you did to me. Do you know that? Well I've never forgotten, don't think I have. Every day I've thought of how you used me and dumped me when the going got too hot. Every day I've thought of how to get back at you. I still do,' she said.

'Don't be ridiculous,' Ron said, his voice raised. 'I didn't use you. You seduced me in the first place and then it was, well it was mutual. I just wasn't going to throw away ten years of marriage to keep seeing you. When my wife found out she gave me the choice, you or her. With the kids to think of there was no choice. So it was hard, but that was how it was. In another life, another time, it might have been different.'

'Hard?' The voice screamed. 'Not for you. It was hard for me. I had to go through with the abortion, not you. You just sent me the money and told me to bloody well get on with it. Not a phone call or a letter to find out how I was. How I was coping. It was like the cheque was enough. You'd done your bit. Money would solve the problem. You were buying me off: and back then I was too naïve to realise.

'Best for everyone you said. But you didn't care what was best for me. I should have had the baby. Dragged you through the courts, forced you to recognise it as your own and make you pay for its upkeep for the rest of your life. That's what I should have done. Instead I let you off the hook. Let you carry on with your star studded career unhindered by a silly girl with a baby on her hip who demanded recognition and attention.

'Well you've made it in your career haven't you? You've made it right to the bloody top, chatting to the Minister, calling him by his first name no doubt. Yes Nigel. No Nigel. Three bags full Nigel.' She was scathing.

'Now look at me,' she was screaming. 'What have I got? Forty five and scraping a living doing locums. No career, no family. Not much self respect either. That's what you've done to me.'

A numbness in Steve's chest and a tightening in his throat at recognition of the voice. It was Sonia. Shouting and ranting at the PVO who was clearly more than just an old friend. So Sonia had been his bit on the side, his floozy, his muse. The sly old bugger, he thought. I bet he never expected to see her when he set off up here today. He giggled.

'... and I'm sorry that's the way you see it. There's no point in me trying to explain anything more. Now if you'll excuse me I have another meeting to attend. We're very grateful to you for helping out along with all the other vets.'

'Don't patronise me you bastard,' Sonia said and Steve heard the whip crack sound of a hand against loose flesh. Who's hit who, he thought.

'I hope that makes you feel better,' Ron said. 'Now I must go. Goodbye.'

Steve turned and fled down the corridor. He was no longer in the mood to tackle the PVO about farmers' movements and he suspected that Ron Steady would not be overly interested either. He was intrigued by the conversation that had passed and had a glow of amusement that such a pillar of the Civil Service and the Veterinary Profession had this neatly stashed away in the past. Outward appearances were misleading. They always said it was the quiet ones but he'd never believed that philosophy.

Beneath the glow was another emotion. Hiding and tucked away but growing like a germinating seed grows in the spring. It was fear, as irrational as it was powerful. Sonia's voice had been the voice of evil, curled and forked like that of a cornered snake, tasting the air with poisoned fangs bared ready to fight. He had not heard that in her voice before. Sure there had been strength and passion, anger too when he had split with her. But never a suggestion of menace or malice such as he had heard now. He shivered, cold inside, despite the heat of the office.

Her voice was sinister, he thought. There had been determination and resolution when she said she would get even. And undiminished by the years, fresh as the day her lover told her it was all over between them. As fresh as the day she had received and cashed his cheque or woken in the hospital and been told that the deed was done.

Steve could imagine it all. A young professional woman, alone and just starting her career after years of hard work and study. The choice of single motherhood, constant battling through the courts, juggling career and child without support. All that or unfettered freedom. It was not surprising the path she'd chosen. Then why so bitter? Perhaps there was more than he had gleaned from the few minutes conversation he'd overheard. He was glad to be rid of her. Too many hang-ups and a liar too.

He went to the disinfection room, picked up the clothes he'd left to dry the previous evening and headed for Midvalley Farm, which, like Browns Farm, was on the roadside. There were already several cars there and Ministry signs and plastic tape fluttered in the breeze like bunting. Steve could see a Television van parked further down the lane, the big satellite dish pointing skywards to beam the pictures to the rest of the world so that from the comfort of their living rooms, cup of tea in hand, all were able to witness the carnival of unfolding tragedy.

It was a dirty farm with broken and dilapidated buildings, large patches of mud and dirty water, scrap metal and rusted rolls of wire scattered in heaps and leant against buildings. The concrete yard was potholed with pieces of broken concrete strewn around and slurry filling the holes. The economics of farming had not been good for a while. Foot and Mouth was the death knell for many though perversely it was seen as the lifeline for others, a means of getting out of the industry with cash in hand for the first time in many years. In the last few days livestock valuations had begun to creep up with rumours of auctioneers phoning round farms with guarantees to give the best valuations if their services were requested. A happy client now might put business their way in the future.

So for some farmers, the diagnosis of Foot and Mouth meant a secure financial future with the option to retire gracefully and perhaps even sell most of their land to a neighbour. Just as with Swine Fever, the ones suffering most financial hardship were those under movement restrictions who were now having to feed animals that were no longer gaining in value.

Steve walked into the yard. Two men in white boiler suits came towards him. He recognised one as a young vet and the other was an auctioneer he'd met a week earlier.

'Hello Steve,' the auctioneer said. 'I've finished the valuation. This disease doesn't seem to want to stop does it?'

'You're right there,' Steve said. 'What's the story here?' he said to the vet.

'There're three sows with litters in that straw yard next to the road. Two of the sows went lame about a week ago and then seemed to recover. Then some of the piglets went lame, with eruptions on the snout too, and yesterday the farmer noticed cattle in the shed across the way drooling. It's absolutely classic FMD.'

Steve nodded. The nightmare was continuing and the pressure thing inside his head was getting worse. He wanted to leave the farm now and never come back. Everything was telling him to run away, heart and mind, feelings and senses. The smell of burning meat; the taste of pigs in his throat; putrefaction and decay clinging to his hands and clothes. Lambs bleating, the rolling eyed bellowing of cows; the high pitched squeals of snared pigs; the innocent click of the captive bolt; the swearing and laughter of men; the dull thud and clatter and hooves; the naked silence at the end of the day. The sight of rich red blood turning dark and sticky; creamy brain mixed with green rumen contents, froth from the nose; pale steam rising, milk dripping from a full udder. And tears on faces; dark around the eyes, lips trembling; children wide eyed, disbelieving.

'Run,' said the voice, 'run away from all this killing. This was not how it was meant to be.'

He wanted to run. He wanted to run as far and as fast as he could. Run away and not stop running until he had reached a sea of turquoise with white sand and coconut palms where girls with coffee skins and bright bikinis lay on the hot sand and dipped their toes in the surf. He promised himself that once this was over he would go to that place. And as he stood and watched the slaughterers begin their grizzly work yet again, he realised that time could not come soon enough.

Chapter 40

He lay in his bed late on Wednesday morning. His first day off since it had all started. He did not go down for breakfast at his usual time. He didn't want to meet people and talk about Foot and

Mouth. He didn't know what was right and he was tired of his mind wandering in circles.

Sky News was full of it. The newspapers too. Commentators from all walks of life had something to say on the matter. Everybody had an opinion on it. Bishops gave their views; business leaders chipped in; travel agents and sports personalities too. Each had the solution at their finger tips. Only the veterinary profession was silent, a stiff upper lip solidly behind the Government's policy. The Minister was peddling the phrase 'bearing down on the disease' with a slow gravity designed to demonstrate that he had the measure of the crisis.

Steve lay with his head under the blanket listening to it all on the television. He would go to the pool, he thought. Sit in the sauna and the jacuzzi. Wander into town, have lunch at a delicatessen, read a newspaper at leisure.

He walked into the dining room at 9.30 a.m. It was empty, the breakfast buffet glowing brightly at one end. He helped himself to sausage, bacon, black pudding and mushrooms; fried tomatoes, toast and two fried eggs. A pot of freshly made breakfast tea. He sat at a table looking out towards the hills. He could not stop thinking of what was going on out there. Even as he sat eating his hearty breakfast there was death and mayhem, havoc and pitiful sadness. All around, unseen. But there.

He looked around the empty dining room, shafts of early spring sunshine lighting the carpets and table with silver. He wished he were a dog. To curl up in the sun on the carpet under the table he was sat at. Curl up like a dog that had no one to please but itself and no thoughts of anything other than its next meal or next walk. A release from all responsibility. A release from all the pain and the suffering. He ate his breakfast and drank his tea.

There was no one in the pool when he arrived. It was too small for real swimming, more for floating and loafing in. He was happy with that. He lowered himself off the side, the water cool and invigorating. He floated out to the centre. The painted palms on the walls and the sun loungers gave an air of splendour that he was happy to enjoy. He moved to the side and clung to the rail, arms outstretched, looking across to the door of the sauna. Everything was still and silent. His mind began to relax. To think of things more gentle on the mind and spirit. Things that sat more easily on the soul.

Francesca came through the changing room door wearing a different swimsuit to last time. She smiled immediately when she saw it was Steve. A smile of warmth and, he dared think, affection.

'Always in the pool we meet,' she said. 'What is at work here? Are you following me?'

He laughed. 'I was here first,' he said. 'And I'm pleased to see you.'

She neither blushed nor brushed away the remark. She smiled and slipped into the water beside him with the elegance of a tiny dolphin. She ducked her head under the water, her dark hair floated like an anemone, the ends whispering against his upper arms and sending tingling bursts of electricity through his body. He wanted to hold her. To caress her. Make love to her. His head was spinning, running away from him with fantasies too beautiful to describe. He had to take control. Too much too soon and everything could be lost.

'You have a day off today?' she asked resurfacing. 'And why do you sit here all alone when there will be many others who would like your company?'

She was teasing him again. She was always teasing him. But there was no mischief or malice in her eyes. They were open and clear; honest in her feelings. He saw affection in them. Affection and interest; a hint of wonderment and respect too.

'I wanted to be alone,' he said, and regretted it.

She turned and swam to the other side.

'Not from you,' he called. 'Not alone from you.' He had offended her. He had not meant it. But when she turned she was laughing.

'Am I far enough away now?' she teased again.

His body wept with the pain that she was married.

He swam across to join her.

'You're off today as well?' he said and she nodded. 'A lucky coincidence. I'm going to drive down the coast, away from all this killing. The sun's out. I'll put the hood down. Will you come with me? We can have lunch somewhere.'

It sounded fumbled, ill conceived, spoken with dull witted clumsiness. He waited for her rejection.

'I would like that,' she said. 'Shall we try the sauna and then the pool again and then go?'

The intimacy and heat of the sauna he found almost too much to bear. Her body glowed with perfect droplets of salt laced sweat, a few strands of her hair stuck to her cheek. He could taste her in his throat, a scented lick of salt, laced with the subtlest hint of musk. Her legs well muscled, firm and smooth like a baby's skin. Her breasts sitting comfortable, unsupported, understated in their beauty. Her face, the nose and mouth, the eyes, the set of her cheek, they had an angel's grace and humility. If heaven existed he thought, it was there before his eyes, sitting only feet away from him. Tempting him, encouraging him, and dashing his hopes away again. Ecstasy and despair mixed like water and oil.

The sun was warm on their faces as they left the hotel park. The hood was folded away and the roar from the engine and exhaust mingled with the rush of wind as they headed west for the coast. There was no need for conversation. The car and the sun said everything as the miles passed and the palls of smoke were left hanging in the air far behind.

They came at last to the sea, white topped waves rolling in from the Atlantic, a deserted beach. They walked along it side by side. Steve took her hand and her fingers closed tight around his, soft, elegant fingers of gentle brown, dry and warm, disappearing in his closed palm.

They sat together on the sand, her head against his shoulder, his arms cupped around her waist, face buried in the feel and scent of her hair.

'I love you so much,' he whispered to her. She smiled and looked a little sad, placing a finger against his lips as if to quiet him.

'It makes no sense,' she said and a tear spilled out of the corner of her eye, creeping down her cheek to leave it streaked and damp.

He kissed where it had stopped. Tasting the salt and the softness of her. She placed her hand to cup his cheek and he wished that the world could be stopped forever at that moment so that he could live the rest of life with that feeling inside him. He felt his own tears flowing too. Not only from his eyes but from deep inside where they had been waiting for so long. He held her tight and they disappeared into her hair, raising the scent from her like a shower of rain on the earth.

They watched the sea ebb and flow and a little dog ran along the edge of the water chasing the gulls and oystercatchers that were feeding on the sand.

'It is hard to understand this life of ours,' she said. 'It is hard to understand our destiny. Do you believe in destiny Steve? Do you believe in a greater purpose? A greater thing than we understand here on earth. Do you?' she was insistent. 'Do you Steve? Tell me.'

'Do you mean God?' he asked

'Perhaps,' she said.

'I don't know. When my wife left me I prayed to God every night to bring her back to me. Nothing happened and I cursed God. I don't know what I think now.'

They went back to the car and drove along the coast road until they reached a small town with a hotel and restaurant with a crowded car park. The tables in the restaurant were set with white tablecloths and bright silver cutlery, glasses shining like starlight on winter's frost. The other diners looking up from their meals confirmed Steve's opinion of Francesca's beauty. It showed in their faces; in the slight intake of breath; the overlong, indiscreet stare.

A waitress met them and guided them to a table for two away from prying eyes in a corner by the window that gave a view of the town square.

'A special occasion?' she ventured. Innocent and unassuming.

'Yes,' said Steve immediately, 'a very special occasion. I'm just about to ask this girl to marry me.'

The waitress smiled. 'I hope she says yes.'

Steve sat down avoiding Francesca's gaze. It had come out suddenly, without him giving thought to the consequences. He almost, but not quite, regretted having said it.

'Why did you say that?' asked Francesca. Her voice was steady, no hint of annoyance.

'Because it's true, he said. 'Will you marry me? Please.' He looked straight at her, unblinking with earnest expectation.

She returned his gaze, laughing.

'I'm married,' she replied simply. 'You know I am. I can't marry you. And besides,' she added as an afterthought, 'I don't even know you.'

'Of course you know me,' Steve laughed. 'You know me better than people I've known for years know me.'

'That was my excuse,' she said. You know why I can't marry you. Now, what shall we eat?' she said picking up the menu. 'I am very hungry, and how do you say? This is my treat.'

'No, I'm paying,' Steve protested. 'I asked you to come to dinner.'

'And you asked me to marry you. It is not every day that a girl is asked to marry someone. No Steve, this is my treat.'

He gave in. He was relieved she hadn't stormed out and demanded to be taken home. She had every right to. He looked at her over the menu. She was magnificent. He had never met a girl like her.

She ordered mussels in white wine for starters and Steve had fresh oysters. Sea bass with ginger on a bed of wild rocket salad and sweet potatoes with parsley butter followed for both of them. The fish was bright silver and fresh tasting, flaking easily off the bones and a moistness that reminded him of the fish he and Rachel had barbecued in Mexico.

They ordered a bottle of Pinot Grigio to accompany it, crisp and smoky green, ice cold with a hint of bitter pear and lemon zest. They talked to each other of their families and their childhoods. Of holidays and of places they had visited. Of food and of their heart's desires. For nearly three hours Foot and Mouth was forgotten.

When the coffee cups were empty Francesca glanced at her watch. 'A very Italian lunch,' she said. 'We do not like to rush our food. For us it is a ritual. A very important ritual. It is what holds the family together down the generations.' She lowered her eyes, not in shame or remorse but in wistful reflection.

Steve understood and knew he was the cause of her distress. He reached out across the table with both hands and taking hold of hers in his he gave them a squeeze.

'I'll always remember this meal,' he said. 'Whatever happens I will never forget you and I will love you forever whilst there is breath in my body and my heart still beats. It is a love that I have never felt before, an unselfish love whose only reward is your own happiness. I give you my heart and my mind, and I give you my soul. I entrust you with all three because I know that they will be safe in your own heart. Whatever happens in this life will not change what I know and feel about you. You will be with me forever.'

He leaned across the table and kissed her gently and fleetingly on the lips. She did not draw away but held his hands in her own and stroked the back of them with her thumbs.

The waitress came and gave them the bill and Francesca went over to the desk to pay.

'Did she say yes?' the waitress asked Steve, her eyes expectant. 'She did say yes, didn't she?'

'Not in so many words,' he said. 'There are complications. You see, she's already married.'

'Yes I can see that would make things difficult,' the waitress nodded wisely. 'Still, that might all fall through mightn't it?' she added hopefully.

'I wish I had your faith,' Steve laughed. 'We'll have to wait and see.'

They drove home with the hood up, the sun had gone and a cold drizzle was blowing all around. Francesca rested her head on Steve's shoulder, he drove slowly, wanting to prolong the time with her. It was nearly eight o'clock when they reached the hotel. They walked in past the door to the bar, already there was a mass of Ministry folk settling in for the night. They collected their keys from reception and made their way upstairs. Francesca's room was on the first floor and Steve walked along the corridor with her.

'Thank you for today,' he said. The happiest day of my life. Ever.' He emphasised the word.

Her hand was on the door handle, she turned the key and pushed the door ajar. She turned to him and there was a silence. He could see that she was thinking. She smiled. She seemed to have decided what to say and do. He caught the slight movement of her head that was a prelude to her saying something and he instantly brought his finger up to her lips to stop her.

He bent forward and kissed her, very gently, on the lips, lingering for a second and then drawing away. She motioned to him to enter the room but he held her shoulders in his hands and his eyes went dewy moist. He kissed her on the cheek and squeezed her shoulders with his fingers.

'Sleep well,' he whispered. 'Sleep well and thank you,' and he walked along the corridor and up the stairs to his room without looking back.

Chapter 41

'Hi Steve, did you get that list of farms that have pigs on them?' Keith Brewer asked as soon as he walked into the Animal Health Office.

'What list?' Steve said. 'I must be going round the twist. I don't

312

even remember asking for one.'

'No, that attractive woman did. Sonia isn't it? She came and asked me for a list of all farms with pigs. She said that you'd asked her to get it for you.'

'Oh yes, I remember,' Steve said. 'I'll get it from her later. Thanks anyway. How were things yesterday? I had a day off.'

'Another disaster. Twenty five more infected farms. We don't seem to be getting on top of it. The whole Kibble valley looks like it's going down with it. Dairy after dairy. At least we're getting more carcasses away to rendering now but there's still a huge backlog. We're slaughtering tens of thousands of animals a day countrywide at the moment. It's popping up everywhere.'

Steve went to find Neil.

'How's it going?' he asked.

'Badly,' said Neil, deadpan. 'Not only are we losing control over this side of the country but things are getting bad over at Morton too.' He pointed at the map. 'There's a cluster out of control around Springholm. Get over there today and see what you can find out. See if there're any dodgy dealers or feed merchants about. People moving stock that shouldn't be moving stock.

'Jenny's got six files for you, the latest farms that we've got any details about. Take your pick and see what you can come up with.'

'What are Sage Street saying to it all?'

'They're struggling. There's a lot of political pressure on them to get results. There's an election coming up this spring and word is that the Prime Minister wants this cleared up before announcing the date. Veterinary science might be going out of the window. But we're not going to let it go out of the window,' he added with a gleam of rebellion in his eyes. 'Now get out there and do some veterinary work.'

Steve laughed and Jenny smiled at him as she handed him the files. 'Good luck,' she said.

Sonia was in the store room when Steve went in to fetch more overalls

'Hi Sonia,' he said trying to be cheerful and natural. 'Anything exciting happening?'

'Just the usual,' she said. 'I'm off to another report case. Seems like there are plenty coming through still.'

'Did you ask Keith for a list of pig premises yesterday? Only he seems to think that I asked you to get it for me.'

Sonia's face twitched. Almost imperceptible, fleeting, and her neck pinkened ever so slightly.

'I don't know why he thought that,' she said, her voice defensive at first but quickly returning to its normal pitch. 'I asked him because I thought it would be useful to see where the pig herds were so that if they were near any infected farms we could keep them under surveillance. I think I said I was going to discuss the idea with you. Perhaps that's where the confusion was.'

'Perhaps,' said Steve. He was watching her closely. He now knew her to be a skilful liar. 'And what did it tell you? This list.'

'I've not really had a chance to look at it yet,' she answered brightly. 'Maybe we could take a look at it together. How about this evening at the hotel. I've got some wine in my room. Why don't you come round about nine this evening and we can have a look together.' Her voice had changed. She was pleading.

'I won't be back till late,' said Steve. 'I'm away over to Springholm. No. If you come up with anything, let me or Neil know. Right, I must go. Cheers now.'

He felt uncomfortable. He thought he'd known this girl and it was obvious now he didn't. She had a mean possessive streak. He shook his head. What with her and Julie, he didn't half pick them. It wasn't just Foot and Mouth that was a bloody mess.

On a grey day Springholm looks like the end of the world. Surrounded by stark bare farmland, sour and damp, fit only for grazing hardy Swaledale and Blackface sheep. Field after field of grey green grass Steve passed. Field after empty field that lay silent, devoid even of bird song as though they recognised that something strange had happened here. Strange and evil too. Something that was against the natural order of things. Something carried out by man.

He imagined that battlefields could be like this. Towns that had been ethnically cleansed too. Stark, eerie, silent. The smell of burning flesh. People staying in their homes, trying to pretend that nothing had happened. Hoping that time would change the truth of what had passed. Time dulling the memory, bending it away from unpleasant recollections towards more palatable mouthfuls. Truth though, thought Steve doesn't change. Truth is a constant. It is only a person's perception of truth that changes. That is what should be challenged.

He came to the entrance to Woodlands Farm and pulled off the road. He found the file and read the notes. In big red letters he read;

'Mrs Ruddock's husband died a few days ago.'

It was stark and to the point. It hit him right in the guts, savage and unequivocal. He opened the car door and was sick onto the earth, retching, retching; the weeks of emotion spewing out onto the soil.

'Shit,' he said to himself. 'Shit, fucking shit.' This lady has just lost her husband and then Foot and Mouth strikes. How shit can life be? How fucking shit can life be? he thought.

He drove a few yards forward to get rid of the sight and smell of vomit. He breathed in and out slowly and steadily, forcing himself to stay calm. He wanted to turn the car around and head for home. Leave the whole fucking thing and head for home with his foot flat to the floor. Call into Willie and Morag's. Have a beer and a laugh. A joke with Willie's kids. He wanted everything to be back the way it was before Foot and Mouth. Everyone just plodding along in the same old way. No excitements or surprises. A steady, unfulfilling existence. An existence which he now knew had gone forever.

He walked up the drive to the farmhouse, a man going to the gallows. He could not imagine the reception he would get from a woman whose husband had died and whose animals had been killed in such a short space of time. He knocked at the door, a sound of chair legs scraping on a stone floor; the opening door; a young girl of twenty, eyes rimmed red, tear streaked cheeks, clear pale blue eyes.

'I'm Steve Turner, a Veterinary Officer with the Ministry,' he began. 'I'm really sorry about what's happened in the last couple of weeks.' He felt his own eyes wet and pink.

'Come in,' said the girl. 'Mum's in the kitchen.' She led the way.

At the kitchen table sat a middle aged woman, long grey streaked hair. It must have been deep brown, thought Steve. Large eyes, grey and proud, pink tinged now, dark skin around the eye sockets. Wide mouth with firm sensuous lips, that parted in a smile when he said 'Mrs Ruddock?'

'Yes,' she said, 'come in. Would you like some tea or coffee?'

'I'd love a cup of tea please,' he said. 'I am so sorry at what's happened.'

She smiled with genuine gratitude for his remark. 'You'll need to ask me some more questions I suppose. Go ahead, I'll do my best to answer them. I don't want others to have to go through this. The young vet we had here to help, Mitch, Mitchell Ford, was absolutely marvellous. The slaughterers were a bit rough but Mitch just told them how he wanted the job done and he put up with no nonsense. Cardington wanted to burn them but Mitch said there was an excellent burial site and he had the hole dug and everything under the ground the same day. He was wonderful. He made the whole thing so much better than it might otherwise have been.'

'Daddy would have been pleased with the way it was all done,' said the girl. 'I'm glad he didn't have to see it though. He'd been so ill. It was right for him not to go through all this too.'

She put her hand on her mother's shoulder. Steve wanted to embrace them both. To tell them to hang in there and that it would all pass.

The phone rang and Steve saw the moisture glistening on Mrs Ruddock's cheeks as she listened and then spoke.

'Yes, ten thirty at the church so you'll need to be here at ten. No, I hadn't thought of that but there's someone here now. I'll ask him.' She turned to Steve her face quivering with emotion.

'Will the funeral cars be able to drive up and collect us the day after tomorrow?' she asked. 'If not we can walk to the end of the lane.'

Steve swallowed. There was nothing in the instructions to prepare you for this, he thought. He looked at the pleading eyes on both the faces turned towards him. Pleading with expectant hope, no hostility or resentment.

'I'll make sure they can,' said Steve. I'll make sure that the lane and yard are disinfected tomorrow so that nothing goes wrong. I promise you.'

Relief lit their faces. Gratitude he could see in the glint from the pink stained whites of their eyes. He would do anything to ease their suffering.

Mrs Ruddock put the phone down.

'This is very difficult for me,' she said. 'So soon after Jack's death. But I want to help all I can. This is a dreadful business and I don't want others to suffer it. Please, ask whatever you need to know. Afterwards, Sal,' she nodded towards her daughter, 'can take you round the sheds and show you where the cattle were that first went down with it.'

'Now, do you want more tea?'

Steve accepted gratefully. Admiration burned inside him for this woman's resolve not to let personal tragedy stand in the way of defeating this disease. And it was then, whilst his emotions were off guard and his mind was open to difficult and unpalatable truths that it struck him that the likes of Mrs Ruddock were being let down. Sold down the river by a policy that now had a life of its own; a snowball gathering size and pace down a mountainside; ever bigger and faster; ever more difficult to stop.

'Stamping out' had become a mantra. Like the chant of 'four legs good, two legs bad,' in Animal Farm. Only those at the top could change it. Those on the ground, in the frontline, the sacrificial sheep; they could only follow orders. It came to him in a blinding flash.

VACCINATE. VACCINATE. VACCINATE. All it required was a change of mindset. An acceptance that enough was enough. We could beat the virus on our own terms, at our leisure by damping down its production and removing the pool of susceptible animals. Sure he didn't understand the science intimately but he knew enough to know that no other country in the world had controlled an outbreak of this size purely with a slaughter policy.

Stamping out would work. He didn't question that. It would work because in the worst case scenario there would be no animals left. But it was brutal, barbaric and hugely stressful to animals and humans alike. In a small outbreak it was wholly justified. Kill the infected animals before they could infect others and the disease was controlled. He had no argument against that. But in the face of the outbreak they were into it was looking increasingly like madness to him. They were already over the half million mark for animals slaughtered. Where would it stop?

It was clear to him now that the ethical and moral response was to vaccinate. Starting in those areas where the disease was rampant and gradually working outwards until clinical cases ceased. The animals could be revaccinated at the recommended intervals and any future outbreaks of clinical disease could be dealt with in a controlled, rational, eradication campaign by reverting to Stamping out. He would bet a year's salary that the disease could be eradicated within months using that policy. It was simple. It was humane

Okay, slaughtermen would stop earning upwards of a thousand pounds a day and the export of a few hundred million pounds worth of lamb would be put on hold for a few months longer. But the benefits would be that the country could return to normal; the tourist trade could be reinvigorated; and the Government would be applauded internationally for its humanity and common sense.

The whole future control strategy was worked out there in Mrs Ruddock's kitchen. The grand plan that would save The Nation's heritage, reputation and humanity. When he left the kitchen to go and view the buildings with Sal he shook Mrs Ruddock vigorously by the hand. She could have no idea of the plans that had been formulated in his head as he sat opposite her and diligently recorded the answers to his questions.

Sal took him round the buildings. He wanted to tell her that he knew how she felt. The raw terrible sickness. The disbelief, the empty hollows inside. They would stay with her, sharp and real for many months. But as time passed they would begin to dull, the brightness would disappear and the pain would be less keen. He wanted to tell her these things but there was too much happening inside his own head. Too much of Foot and Mouth, of Francesca, of Sonia now too. He had not enjoyed their meeting earlier that day. There had been a bitter edge to her voice.

Sal walked down the lane a little way with him when he left. He wanted to hug her but instead he shook her hand.

'I hope everything goes well at the funeral,' he said. 'The pain will get better. I've been through it too.'

She smiled and her tears flowed freely. He squeezed her shoulder and went on alone. A feeling of humility overwhelmed him. The quiet unassuming dignity of Mrs Ruddock and her daughter in the face of indescribable bad luck had touched a part of him he had not known existed. As he walked to his car the tears streamed down his own cheeks. Everywhere was grey. Trees without leaves. Fields without stock.

A car came towards him as he disinfected his boots. It stopped and a young cheerful lad jumped out. He was chirpy and he bounced when he moved. He had short cut hair, an easy smile.

'Mitchell Ford, Temporary Veterinary Inspector,' he said holding out his hand. 'Call me Mitch. You are?'

'Steve Turner, Veterinary Officer. I'm working in epidemiology. I've just been in to see Mrs Ruddock.' He wiped the tears out of his eyes with a flush of embarrassment.

'You're an epidemiologist? Brilliant. What do you think about how it's all going?'

'It's a bloody disaster,' said Steve unguardedly. 'The whole bloody thing. No one up top seems to be organising the job.'

'Just what I thought. By the way, did you hear on the radio, the army's been called in? The Minister announced it an hour ago. Detachments moving in to Cardington and Devon straight away. Coming to provide logistical support; organising the slaughter and disposal, that sort of thing. Good idea I think.'

'Thank God for that,' said Steve. 'Thank God someone's seen sense.'

'And something else interesting. There's a couple of scientists been interviewed who have some mathematical model that has predicted what will happen if we carry on the way we're going. Half the animals in the country slaughtered by the end of the year. They say we've got to change policy. A radical change apparently.'

'What's the PVO saying to it?' asked Steve. He was intrigued.

'They didn't mention him,' said Mitch.

'Mr Ruddock's funeral is the day after tomorrow,' said Steve. 'I've promised Mrs Ruddock we'll have this lane and her yard disinfected so that the funeral cars can get up there.'

'I'm already on to that,' said Mitch. 'The disinfecting wagon should be here in half an hour. That's why I'm here. To supervise and check it's done properly.'

'Are you working out of Morton?' Steve asked. 'I'm heading there today to see Beryl.'

'Yeah, started ten days ago. It's turning into a hectic place. Look I might phone sometime to run a few ideas past you. Good to meet you.' He held out his hand again.

An up front no nonsense sort of bloke, thought Steve as he headed to the next farm on his list. His mobile rang. It was Beryl.

'You must be psychic,' he said. 'I was just telling Mitchell Ford I was coming to see you later today.'

'Oh you met our Mitch did you?' Beryl drawled. 'A bright sort of spark isn't he. Just needs a bit of restraint, that's all, otherwise he'd have most of the north of England slaughtered out.'

'What's this I hear about some new announcements from the Minister?'

'Well I only know what I heard on the radio a few minutes ago. A

319

couple of Gurus have popped their heads up with some revolutionary ideas and apparently the policy they're proposing is going to be carried through. The Prime Minister himself is going to take charge. I think he's afraid the whole mess is going to scupper his election chances.'

'What is the new policy?' Steve asked. 'Are we going to vaccinate?' Perhaps the nightmare was going to come to an end.

'I don't know,' said Beryl. 'We'll probably be the last ones to know. Anyway I'm glad you're coming in. We're needing some input from an epidemiologist. One of our American colleagues has a problem up the Hamble Valley. He's not sure which properties should be classified as DCs. There's a problem with the boundary fences and sheep escaping. What time will you be here?'

'I'll visit this one farm on the way so,.. about five I reckon.'

'I'll put the kettle on then,' said Beryl and hung up.

She was so laid back. So calm and unflusterable. What an asset to the Ministry, thought Steve. She was the sort of VO that deserved reward and who would probably never get it. He shrugged and thought about what the new policy could be. Maybe at last someone was seeing sense. Someone high up had perhaps realised that the killing machine couldn't carry on the way it was going. 'Thank God,' he murmured. 'Thank God.'

It was well past five p.m. when Steve made it into Morton Animal Health Office. The light a sombre grey twilight of east coast drizzle and North Sea winds. He went in through the back entrance, past the tiny disinfection room that was jammed with waterproof clothing hung out to dry in the damp cold atmosphere of a shower room. Past the lab where a man was frantically packaging and labelling samples for the courier to collect, and into the main office where a few harassed men and women were answering phones and taking notes.

Steve slipped through unnoticed and knocked at Beryl's door. Beryl and Nancy, another vet that Steve knew well were in the room together drinking coffee.

'Our epidemiologist returneth,' said Beryl smiling.

'Hello Steve,' said Nancy smiling even more broadly. 'You didn't expect to find me here did you? Into my second week and already feeling it.'

He kissed them both on the cheek. The feeling of coming home took him back to Christmases past. Nancy went out and reappeared with a cup of coffee for him.

'You don't take sugar do you?' she asked.

'No,' replied Steve, 'and thanks auntie.'

She cuffed him round the head. What a pair of women he thought. What a pair of stars.

'Victor the American has been to a farm up the Hamble Valley,' Beryl said pointing to it on the map. 'Disease in sheep and cattle, at least ten days old he says. There are two neighbours with stock in adjoining fields that we're taking as DCs. The problem is the other two neighbours who say they've had no stock next to the boundary fence. Victor doesn't believe them. What do you think?'

What did Steve think? He didn't know what to bloody think. He'd never been near the fucking place and he was being asked to decide whether a man's stock lived or died. On the basis of no known facts. He might as well throw a dice or flip a fucking coin.

He looked at Beryl and shrugged. 'It's simple really. If there's been the possibility of nose to nose contact then they go as DCs. If there hasn't been then they don't need to. Now whether or not the farmers are telling the truth is a different matter and one that I don't see any possibility of resolving in a rational, fact based manner. Hunches like Victor's can often be right but they can also be wrong. But not having been there I don't even have a hunch.'

He thought a while. 'What about putting a restriction notice on them and getting a clean vet to go back every couple of days to inspect the stock? That's the sensible thing to do isn't it?'

'I suppose you're right,' she conceded. 'The trouble is we're short of clean vets and we're likely to get shorter if it carries on like this. I'll just have to see what Victor says when he comes back in.'

'I'm sorry,' said Steve, 'but he's the guy on the ground. I just haven't got the time to visit all these places. There're only Neil and me for how many Infected Premises in this area now? Two hundred odd? Plus all the DCs. And you wouldn't believe what's happening on some farms with revolvers and rifles. I had to instruct a vet the other day that he was not under any circumstances to allow slaughtermen to use a rifle to kill a sheep that had escaped and was on the nearby village cricket field. You can just see the fucking headlines now can't you. "Gun toting Ministry official terrorises local village." Or how about, "Hit for Six," or, "Bowled Over".' He laughed. 'It doesn't bear thinking about.'

'We had a bad one yesterday,' said Nancy. 'A bull escaped from a pen during slaughter on a DC and ran down the field to a river and swam across to join up with the neighbouring farmer's heifers. We had to get a whole new team of clean people to try and get it back and it was going berserk trying to serve the heifers and getting more and more stirred up. Eventually we called a police marksman to drop it in the field and cart it away dead.

'And now of course the farmer's furious in case the bull's infected his bloody heifers. We've stuck a restriction notice on him and we'll just have to keep going back for the next few weeks. What else can we do?'

'Nothing,' said Steve. 'You can only do your best.'

'Are you going to stay here and help us now?' Beryl asked.

'I can't,' said Steve, 'Neil's snowed under in Cardington. He phoned me earlier to say he's going to London this evening for a meeting tomorrow. He wants me in the office until he gets back. Maybe it's something to do with this new policy. I hope they're going to vaccinate.'

'Do you?' said Beryl. 'But where would you start? Or stop for that matter?'

'I'd start in the hot spot areas and work my way out until there were no more clinical cases. That's what I'd do. Now I'm certain of it I feel a lot better.'

He looked around in expectation of dissenting voices but they stared back as though they had received a revelation. It occurred to him that it might just be the case that those in charge didn't dare promote the idea in case it were seen as an admission of defeat.

Steve arrived back at his hotel late that evening. Julie was in reception with Conrad and she ignored him when he said hello to her. Why is she going out with Conrad? he thought. The receptionist handed him his key and an envelope with his name, handwritten, on the front. He opened it.

Steve,
Please come and see me when you arrive. I am in my room.
Francesca.

He ran up the stairs, his heart racing. The shortness and directness of the note meant something was wrong. Did Julie have anything to do with it? he wondered. She had avoided his gaze downstairs. He knocked on Francesca's door.

'Yes, who is there?' He heard her voice and relaxed. He was getting things out of proportion.

'It's me. Steve.' His voice cracked with emotion, his pulse rapid, pounding.

He heard the door being unlocked. She'd locked the door. Was she frightened? It opened slowly and he saw her face, anxious like a fawn emerging from the safety of the trees. Satisfied it was really him she threw the door open and flung her arms around him. Sobbing.

'Steve, Steve,' she cried. 'I am so glad to see you.' She held him tight and he lifted his arms to cuddle her to him, feeling the warmth of her young body against his; the softness of her hair against his chin, the faintest smell of musk and vanilla in his nostrils. He stroked her hair gently, felt her body quiver in his arms and the dampness of her tears on his neck.

'It's okay,' he said. 'I'm here. You're alright.' He guided her back into the room and closed the door.

He held her close for several minutes and she sobbed and twitched in his arms.

'Tell me what it is,' he said. 'Tell me what the matter is.' He held her away from him to look at her. She was beautiful. Beautiful. He kissed her. Kissed her on the mouth and the neck and held her away again.

'What's the matter? What's happened?'

'Tonight when I came out of the office the car park was dark,' she said. 'I am not afraid of the dark. It does not bother me. Only in one's mind is the dark to be feared. But when I reached my car I smelt something. Like a solvent, like paint. And I looked at my car and there was blue paint all over the roof and the side. Like it was thrown on, not put on with a brush, but splashed on like from a tin or bucket. I was very angry. I thought that some naughty boys have done this to me. How do you call them, hooli... hooli..'

'Hooligans,' said Steve, smiling at her accent, her indignation.

'Yes, hooligans. Naughty boys who have nothing better to do.' She was animated. 'And I thought, what should I do? So I went back inside and got paper towels and dried it off as best I could and I went to the office and told Colin Hunt and he said he would telephone the police. But I said "No, there is no need, it is just silly children," and I went back out.'

'And I unlocked the car and tried to open it and,...' she started to cry again. 'Someone had hidden razor blades behind the door handle and I cut my fingers so.' She wiped the tears away. 'Who would do such a thing Steve? Why would they do it?'

He shivered, the snows of winter stirring inside him. It was following him. Just when it went to the back of his mind it appeared again. He was the centre of it. First Paul's murder. Then the letter. His car roof. And now Francesca. It was all to do with him. He was the object. He felt sick at what could happen to her. He could not lose her. Not when he had just found her. He held her wrists and looked at her hands. The right one was bandaged, a dark red smear seeping through.

'Is it bad?' he asked. 'Are you badly hurt?'

'No it is nothing. Not even stitches,' she tried to smile. 'Just that I am scared. I do not know why they have done this. Why they have done it to me.'

'Have you told the police?' Steve said.

'Yes, I went back in with my hand bleeding and Colin Hunt called them. He insisted I went to hospital too but they just bandaged it. Colin was very kind to me. And so were the police. They said I was just unlucky. A random attack. It could have been anyone. I hope they are right. Do you think they are? Please tell me Steve?'

He told her all that he knew. About Paul's murder and the letter he'd received, and about his car.

'No I don't think it's random. I think it's because of me. I think they're trying to get at me.'

'But who? Who hates you Steve? And why?'

He thought about it. Conrad? Julie? Sonia? They all had reason to dislike him. But physical intimidation? Murder? Surely none of them had feelings that strong.

'I don't know who could hate me enough to do this,' he said. 'But I'll go and see the police tomorrow. And you? What are you going to do?'

She turned away but not before he had seen the tears glistening in her eyes again.

'I am going back to Italy tomorrow,' she said.

'NO.' He shouted. 'You can't. I mean you mustn't. You mustn't go. I love you. I love you more than I loved Rachel. A hundred times more. You can't leave now. You can't. I won't let you.'

She smiled. 'I am only going for the weekend. I must go and see my husband. We have much to talk about.'

Steve looked at her. 'And you'll come back?' he said. Doubt filled his voice.

'On Monday. I promise.'

'Are you going to tell him about me?' he spoke quietly, unsure of why he was asking or what the answer would be.

'I have to,' she replied softly. 'I'm going to tell him that I love you.'

Chapter 42

She would be gone by now. Her plane was leaving the airport at 7.30 a.m. and it was now eight o'clock. He had lain awake most of the night thinking of her. She had reached out and touched him without trying. That was why she was so irresistible. He had fallen in love with her without encouragement. He hadn't been able to help himself. The complications were huge and as he lay there he knew how Carlo would feel.

He would hope that it would pass. He would hope that Francesca would stay loyal to him. He would live the sleepless nights and the pain in his guts. His would be the lack of appetite, the dull aching hurt that he could not ease or take away. Carlo's would be the pain and Steve's would be the joy. It did not sit comfortably with him.

Steve sat with Willie and Sammy at breakfast. He was quiet. Sombre. And so was Willie. Nearly four weeks had passed since he'd seen Morag and the kids. It was too long. The spark had gone from his wit. His mood was reflective. Fernando and Sarah joined them. Happy together. Sandy came across too.

'How's it going Steve?' he asked. He was not the stereotypical loud Aussie. He was thoughtful. A listener too.

'It's terrible and getting worse,' Steve said. 'I'm convinced we should vaccinate. I'm convinced there's too much movement of farmers and their vehicles with a huge potential for spread. I've put my views on the risks of farmer movements in writing to Colin Hunt but he thinks I'm mad. I'm not mad am I?'

'Of course you're not,' said Sandy. 'You're right. And I agree that the time's come to vaccinate. The management here stinks. It's appalling.

325

You guys aren't managed, you're treated like shit. You're not mad at all, but the management is so far up the next one up the line that they don't know what's going on beneath them.'

'They don't fucking care either,' said Willie. 'They don't care what's going on down here.'

'The election's the thing at the moment,' said Sammy. 'That's what it's all about now. We'll have to see what comes of this new initiative. What the details are. I don't know much about these two epidemiological groups, the ones with their computer models, but they seem to have the ear of the Prime Minister. The news was adamant last night that there was to be a change of policy and there wasn't sight or sound of the PVO.'

'No doubt we'll hear when we go in,' Steve said. He had forgotten about the new policy. When he left the table Sammy followed him and spoke as they climbed the stairs.

'What are you playing at with Francesca?' she asked. There was annoyance in her voice, her face was taut. 'Are you sure what you're doing is wise, or fair?'

'Fair to who?' he asked.

'To her. To her husband. Maybe even to you Steve. You've been through this you tell me. Doesn't that make you stop and think?' She was lecturing him.

'I don't need this sort of advice Sammy,' Steve said. 'I'm a grown up and so is Francesca. They're our lives, not yours. It's none of your business.' He regretted saying it. Regretted the pale moist sadness he saw in her eyes. Regretted the silent turn of her body as she headed for her room.

'Sammy,' he called after her. 'Sammy, I didn't mean to...' he stopped. What was the fucking point. It wasn't any of her business. He could do what he fucking liked.

There was more movement than usual outside the office when he arrived. There were army Land Rovers and men in camouflage kit everywhere. The car park had been cordoned off with fluorescent tape and a complex of portacabins had been installed overnight. There was a buzz about the place that lifted his spirits. Something was happening at long last. Someone was taking things seriously. An air of professionalism exuded from the men simply in the way they walked and held themselves. This was what they had been lacking. An air of purpose and professionalism.

He reached the main office just as Colin Hunt was preparing to speak.

'We're very pleased to welcome Brigadier Batchworth and his troops to the Disease Control Centre,' he began, looking anything but pleased. 'You are all no doubt aware that it was announced yesterday that a shift in policy was imminent. I am now able to give you some more details of that.

'From today onwards and retrospectively going back ten days, all susceptible animals on premises contiguous to an infected farm are to be slaughtered automatically as Dangerous Contacts.'

There was a murmuring around the room. A mix of approval from some quarters, dismay from others.

'How is contiguous defined?' someone called out.

'If any land belonging to a neighbouring farm abuts any land that is part of an infected farm then it is contiguous,' replied Colin Hunt.

'What if the cattle are in a shed a mile away and there are arable fields in between?'

'If the arable fields abut the land of the infected farm then it is contiguous,' said Hunt with the air of one who is losing their patience.

The murmurings of dissenters increased.

'What is the reasoning behind this change of policy?' one of the vets asked.

'The Prime Minister has taken personal control of the FMD eradication effort and his advisers have been using mathematical models to predict the effects of certain control strategies. The policy that has been arrived at is that all animals on an infected farm must be slaughtered within 24 hours of diagnosis and all animals on contiguous premises within 48 hours. That is now our target and mission and Brigadier Batchworth and his men are here to ensure that the target is met.

'In addition there is to be a policy of a cull of all sheep on farms within a three kilometre radius of an infected farm, and in this area a further voluntary slaughter of any sheep in an attempt to reduce the likelihood of a farm's cattle succumbing to infection. Part of Brigadier Batchworth's remit is to identify and commission a cull site for sheep.

Steve's mouth had gone dry and red anger grew inside him. There was to be more slaughter, not less. They were turning the screw harder rather than reconsidering their approach. Vaccination appeared to have been dismissed.

'Can you assure us that a contingency plan has been drawn up for the use of vaccination?' he asked Colin Hunt.

The Chief Rabbit looked at him with the world weary eyes of the punch drunk boxer. 'Yes,' he said, 'a plan has been prepared and is ready to be implemented should it be considered necessary.'

'That's that dealt with then,' Willie whispered to Steve.

'The other important piece of news,' went on Colin Hunt, 'is that a great deal more rendering capacity has been secured and rendering will now be considered the preferred method of disposal for carcasses. The army will take over the organisation of disposals and will begin working to clear the backlog still lying on farms. It is hoped...'

Steve had heard enough. He eased his way through the crowd to his office and sat down at his desk. He could not believe what was happening. They had already slaughtered hundreds of thousands of animals and they were now going to step it up some more: increase the rate and widen the cull. Was no one in power prepared to stand up and say, NO?

His phone rang. It was a farmer out near the coast. Out in the middle of the whole damn catastrophe. All his neighbours had lost their stock two weeks ago. He wanted to know if his cows were on the list to be culled. It was the waiting that was the worst thing he said. Waiting and not knowing. Every time the phone rang he wondered if it was the Ministry phoning to give him the news. He would like to know so that he could prepare one way or the other.

'Do you want your stock taken?' Steve asked.

'No I don't,' the farmer said. 'They're my life, I want to keep them.'

'I'll find out what the story is and phone you back,' Steve said.

He checked where the farm was on the map, close to the sea with no living stock near it. He went to IP section and with casual enquiries managed to ascertain that Hoggs Farm was not on the DC list. He phoned the farmer back.

'Look,' Steve said. 'I can't guarantee that no one's going to phone you and tell you that your cattle need slaughtering but at the present time there is no intention to take them. If you want to keep them then my unofficial advice is to keep your head down and say nothing about them to anybody. Keep an eye on them and phone us immediately if you see any signs of disease. Otherwise stay quiet and stay put. Does that make any sense to you?'

'Aye, it does lad. And thank you.'

My good turn for the day thought Steve. Christ this new policy was the fucking pits. Where was the veterinary science in it all? What were they saying at Sage Street? A loss of confidence in Ron Steady perhaps. There was no other logical explanation. Maybe Neil would be able to throw some light on it when he returned.

He spent the day writing his meaningless reports. Documenting again the progress of the disease; writing a tiny bit of history to an agreed format. Sage Street still seemed to be running with the theory that it was silent disease in the sheep from Donchester market that was spreading it to cattle. But he knew that all the farms he was now visiting had no history of contact with sheep from Donchester, not even a tenuous one. He was more certain than ever that his theory on spread by the movement of vehicles and personnel was the correct one. But how to convince those above him was the problem.

It was late in the afternoon when Sammy came to see him. 'Steve, I'm sorry about this morning. You're right, it is none of my business.' She hesitated, not sure whether to go on.

He ran to her and hugged her tight. 'I'm sorry,' he said. 'You're one of the most important people in the world to me. That's why what you said hurt so much. I can't explain everything Sammy. I don't understand it all myself. But this thing I feel is so strong. It can't be wrong.' Rachel's words of long ago echoed from his mouth.

He held her by the shoulders away from him so that he could see her face. They were both crying. 'In another life Sammy,' Steve said, 'I would have met and married you.'

'Perhaps in the next one,' she laughed. 'Who knows what may happen there.'

They hugged each other and Steve kissed her on the neck. 'What's going to become of us all?' he said. 'I can't believe what we're being asked to do now. What are our leaders saying to it all?'

'Where are our leaders?' Sammy asked. 'We don't even know who they are after today's announcement. Seems like the PM himself is pulling the strings now.'

'A good question,' said Neil standing in the doorway with an amused and interested expression on his face. 'So this is what you get up to when I'm away. Smooching with the other staff. I don't know

Turner, you do seem to have the knack for it, that's for sure.'

'Hi Neil,' Sammy laughed. 'Just an old lady getting her daily dose of love and comfort. Nothing sinister.' She wiped her eyes. 'I'll leave you two high powered epidemiologists to it then. See you later.'

Neil looked serious. There was a darkness around his eyes that Steve had not seen before.

'Well? How did you get on?' Steve asked.

'The shit has hit the fan,' said Neil. 'Ron was threatening to resign but has been persuaded to do otherwise. The PM has taken charge and has put the control strategy in the hands of a couple of computer literate epidemiologists who have dreamt up this contiguous cull policy. It's a numbers crunching game. Killing by numbers. There's to be no veterinary risk assessment on the ground; just get in there and slaughter the contiguous premises within 48 hours.'

'It's fucking madness,' said Steve. 'We'll end up emptying the north of England of animals if we carry this through. Why doesn't Ron stand up and say NO if he doesn't agree with it? Most of us would back him wouldn't we?'

'Aye, but his hands are tied. He's got to dance to the politician's tune and this is the tune they're playing. The PM can't see further than the election. That's what he's got at the back of his mind. There's not a lot Ron can do about that.'

'Well if he doesn't agree with it he should resign,' said Steve. 'And he should make it clear to all the media why he's resigned. Then let the mathematical modellers answer the questions. What data are they using to set up their model? Sage Street still thinks it's a sheep to cattle infection. How can you use a model if you don't even know how it's spreading?'

'Don't ask me,' said Neil. 'This is going to cause trouble, believe me.'

'And what are the farmers' leaders saying.'

'Hah! They're using a new term now. The Stakeholders. There's some committee been convened to oversee the whole thing and anybody with any sort of interest in the outcome or the means of influencing it is being called a Stakeholder. What's the committee called? PYTHON. That's it.'

'As in Monty?' said Steve with no attempt to disguise his contempt for the name.

'Aye that's about it.'

'They'll probably make a film of the whole event. Armageddon 3 starring John Cleese as the PVO. There's no Plan B,' said Steve laughing and walking round the room like the Minister for Silly Walks.

'Yeah, you've got the picture. The farmers' leaders are dead set against vaccination and won't have anything to do with it. They want the thing slaughtered out and are demanding that the government puts in the money and resources to make it happen.'

'I bet,' said Steve, his voice grating with cynicism. 'They know the country's overstocked with cattle, and especially sheep. This is a great way of reducing sheep numbers at the same time as putting stacks of money in their members' pockets. A nice golden handshake to retire on and a slimmer fitter industry at the end of it with higher lamb prices. All paid for at public expense and with no thought for moral or ethical issues.

'I know I'm cynical but why else would they be so dead set against vaccination? Only because it would put a stop to all the compensation payments and a farmer's animals would be worth even less. They're not thinking about human or animal welfare that's for sure. I can't help thinking that the Farmers Club spokesman, Len Hill, is just full of bluster, hot air and wind. What gives him the right to veto vaccination and hold the rest of the country to ransom?'

'And the other thing,' said Neil, 'as if all that isn't enough. There's going to be another category of slaughter. As well as IPs and DCs we're going to create SOSs; Slaughter on Suspicion. If the vet on the farm can't rule out FMD, then he's to take samples but the whole farm is to be slaughtered immediately.'

'Without waiting for the results?' Steve asked.

'That's right. If the lab results are negative then the contiguous farms are okay. If they're positive then all the contiguous go as DCs.'

'What's the point of sending a vet there in the first place?' said Steve. 'What's the point of using vets at all? We can't make any judgements on what constitutes a DC based on veterinary risk assessment. Everything gets killed. It's just a blanket clearance of stock from an area without rhyme or reason. It'll work, of course it will,... eventually. But at what cost? How many millions of animals are going to die in, let's face it, pretty unpleasant circumstances. It's all very well saying the vets will safeguard their welfare but I've already seen some grim things. Now with everyone trying to meet the time targets set by people in offices, by bloody administrators with no idea of what's really happening on farm, it's only going to get worse. We're in danger of losing our fucking humanity here, descending into Barbarism.'

Neil looked at him, surprised at his strength of feeling. He didn't agree completely but he knew there was truth in it. But surely, he thought, the killing wouldn't extend to millions. Someone would pull the plug before they reached that stage. Surely. Wouldn't they?

'Aye well Steve,' he said, 'there's not much we can do about it other than keep putting our reports in and making the point about what we think should happen. That way, when the enquiry comes, everyone will know that it wasn't the likes of you and me that was driving the thing in the direction it's going.'

Steve nodded. Neil was probably right about there being little he could do. But he must try. He must try and canvass support amongst the other vets for a vaccination program before it was too late.

He drove to the hotel that evening deep in thought. He kept coming back to PYTHON. The humour was magnificent, the irony just perfect. And SOS too. He giggled, hysterically. 'Slaughter on Suspicion,' he murmured to himself. 'More like fucking Shoot on Sight.'

Chapter 43

It started straight away. People with stock on contiguous premises with no signs of disease grew used to the sound of heavy machinery, captive bolts and the carnage and mayhem of battle. People who for weeks had hardly left their farms, refused entry to postman and feed merchants, child minders, grannies and grandpas; now found that it had all been in vain and that nothing could stop the knock at the door; the click clatter on the concrete; the blood and shit and piss amidst the bellowing and the bleating, and the fallen bodies and the kicking and writhing limbs.

No heed was paid to protestation. The instructions were clear. Their stock must go. Most accepted meekly if bitterly. A few relished the arrival of the compensation cheque in the post and even fewer barricaded their farm entrances and refused to co-operate. Then the police were called to force an entry so that the slaughterers and the men from the Ministry could begin their grizzly work. One woman locked her pet sheep and goats into the house with her but the men came regardless and slaughtered them whilst she was kept talking in another room. In its madness, Britain had become a Police State.

For Steve, the week-end was full of mind-numbing grief, soul searching and uncertainty. As a veterinary surgeon he was appalled at what he saw and heard. Everything was now measured in terms of the efficiency of killing and disposal. The battle that the British Government had fought with its European partners to force then to accept that animals were Sentient Beings seemed now to be forgotten, consigned for the sake of expediency to the scrap heap. Now they had become commodities; weights and numbers; live animals or carcasses; the difference was the firing of a captive bolt, the rattling of a plastic or metal rod inside the skull and the passage of a few seconds.

Everybody became focused on their own tiny bit of work without an understanding or appreciation of the whole. People began to measure their success by how quickly they had killed the animals from the time of diagnosis. Whether it had been done humanely with minimum effect on the farmers, their families and the other staff involved had been pushed to the bottom of the list.

New faces in dark shiny suits had appeared in the office. Senior administrators with sheaves of paper and silk ties, clean shaven, and who smelt of Calvin Klein instead of muck and disinfectant. They were Grade 4 and 5 Civil Servants, part of the growing army of the PM's cronies, put in place to ensure that his bidding was done. They commandeered the larger offices and they had young, mainly female assistants that fetched and carried, and typed for them. They had a necessarily narrow view of things. Their job was to ensure that the resources were there and correctly managed to reach the targets that had been set. The consequences of their actions were for others to consider.

The Brigadier was not one to be moved from his mission either. He was close to retirement and this was his swan song. He had quickly identified a site for the sheep cull, a deserted airfield in the north of the county. It had good access and was far from residential areas.

On Sunday March 25th, Colin Hunt gave another briefing to explain how the sheep cull would work.

'There will be a number of slaughter teams, including trained army slaughterers, who will be based at the cull site. Sheep will be transported live to the site where temporary holding pens with races will be erected. Slaughter will proceed at the rate of twenty thousand per day and the carcasses will be disposed of in large rectangular pits dug out of the airfield.'

'Like extermination camps,' said Steve to Willie. 'The sheep will be told that they're going on a package holiday and will be singing "Summer Holiday" on their way to the airfield.' He wondered if his own judgement was going.

He went for lunch with Willie who drove them down the motorway, passing empty fields with palls of smoke in the distance. Steve saw a group of ewes and lambs in the deserted landscape and began to cry. The tears flowed like a torrent and his face trembled and his mouth twitched and he was unashamed. Willie patted his leg.

'Don't worry,' he said. 'It'll be alright.'

'I was just thinking,' said Steve, his voice thick and cracking between his sobs. 'I was just thinking that the next time I see them they might all be lying dead in a pile,... on top of one another.,' He forced the words out amidst a sob and hysterical laughter.

They pulled off the motorway at a service station called The Golden Fleece. There was a fire burning in an old oil drum on some waste ground behind it, tended by a youth wearing a boiler suit.

'Shall I ask him if he's got room for a couple of sheep on there?' Steve giggled.

'Aye,' said Willie laughing. 'Then we could rename this place The Charred Fleece.'

Thank God they could laugh about it. Despite the ugliness and the waste; the barbarity and lack of respect for life; the single minded striving for the one desired goal. Despite all those dark emotions and dark deeds, and cruel thoughts and self righteous attitudes, a black humour rose to the top, like froth on a pint of beer, cream in a liqueur coffee; scum on top of a slurry tank. A black humour that was hilarious to those involved, and sick to those that weren't.

'What's happening with you and Francesca?' Willie asked. The question came from nowhere.

'She's in Italy,' Steve said. 'She's coming back tomorrow.'

'Are you going to do the right thing?' Willie asked.

Not you as well thought Steve. He was sure Willie and Sammy had been talking. Bound to have been. Why shouldn't they?

'It's not easy,' said Steve defensively. 'I love her so much.'

Willie looked at him. 'Aye maybe,' he said, but there was doubt in his voice. 'But if I heard someone was trying to steal Morag, I'd break their fucking neck. Wouldn't you?'

Steve thought how in the intervening years he'd often wished he'd broken Patrick's fucking neck. Time and again he'd wished he'd punched his teeth out and broken his nose. It would have been easier to live with then.

'I don't want to talk about it Willie,' said Steve. 'You and Sammy are my best friends. All I can ask is that you trust me. And forgive me if that's how you feel about it. Anyway isn't it about time you went home to Morag and all those kids of yours. They'll have forgotten what you look like. It's four weeks now isn't it? Or more? I forget what day it is even.'

'Yeah, you're right, but I feel as though I should finish the job now. You know. I've started, so I'll finish.'

'You don't need to,' said Steve. 'This will go on for weeks yet. Months probably. Get home and look after them all. Give them a few treats. You can come back to this.' If you really want to, he thought. 'It'll still be here in weeks to come.'

'You're right,' Willie repeated. 'I'll give it another couple of weeks and then I'll start making noises. To be honest I'm fucking shit scared of taking anything back up the road with me. I couldn't live with myself if I did. This thing gets to you, doesn't it?'

It was Steve's turn to pat Willie's leg. 'Don't let it,' he said. 'Think of Morag and the children. That's what's important to you. Not all this fucking mess.'

Later that evening Steve and about twenty others met up for a meal. There were more new faces, some vets lured by the increased salary of £250 per day though it was small beer compared to what the slaughterers, the valuers, the contractors, and the digger and lorry drivers were getting. He listened in to a conversation further up the table where a vet was telling them about a slaughterman who had stumbled and shot himself in the belly with his captive bolt.

'He was screaming, "I've shot myself, I've shot myself,"' she giggled. 'So we told him to get his boiler suit off and he lifted up this dirty old T-shirt to reveal the hugest, fattest, belly you've ever seen, great folds of white lard just hanging down and bouncing up and down. He didn't dare look at what he'd done so we got him sitting down and leaning back against some straw bales and then I started searching through all the rolls of fat to find out where he'd been shot. And do you know, all we could find was a tiny bright red circular mark where the bolt had hit. I suppose it had been engulfed in all the fat and never penetrated the skin, just bounced, like off a blancmange. When we told him he started laughing and the farmer was laughing and we were all laughing.'

Steve smiled. He liked this woman. She was scatty and hare-brained but she was upfront and honest and without malice.

On another table was a group of older guys reminiscing about '67. Bluster would have enjoyed it here, thought Steve. Funny, he'd hardly thought of him in the last four weeks and they'd had no contact from him by phone to see how they were getting on. Presumably too busy organising things up north in case the disease spread. Probably didn't care how they were getting on either. Just glad to have them out of his hair.

Towards the far end of the table others were competing with each other as to who had the best contacts. This one could get a slaughter team on farm within thirty minutes at the touch of a mobile phone button. The one opposite had at his command a shepherd with mobile sheep pens and a couple of sheepdogs for difficult handling jobs. The one next to him knew who to phone to divert lorries to pick up carcasses for rendering, jumping the queue if necessary. Each had a pride in their ability. Each self satisfied with the job they were doing and, Steve admitted, doing very well. But he couldn't help but wonder. Wonder if any of them were thinking about what was happening in the big picture. Just like the suits in the main office they were preoccupied with the targets and the deadlines and the minutiae. He wondered if any of them were thinking about where they were all headed and what the final outcome might be.

Pints of beer and glasses of wine were disappearing with enthusiasm but he could not get into the frame of mind to join them. Was it Francesca or was it Foot and Mouth that was bothering him? He didn't know but he knew he had to get away from this crowd of people. They were overpowering him. Polluting his thoughts and feelings. It seemed there were too few others that felt as he felt. His mind was confused. Like an autumn butterfly dancing from one spent flower to the next, searching for sweet nectar with disappointment.

He slipped away from the table unnoticed save by one who was watching him unseen from the far corner of the restaurant. He set out to walk to his hotel, it was barely a mile and it was only a little after nine. He wanted the walk. Hoped it would clear his mind and focus his thoughts. He now knew what he would do if he were in charge but he wasn't. He knew his options were not great. He had no power. It was that which frustrated him. The lack of power. The inability to exert influence and shape policy. It was the feeling he'd had when Rachel left him. A feeling of mental impotence. Neurological castration.

He walked along the pavement, not hurrying, not dawdling. Francesca should arrive tomorrow but he was terrified she wouldn't return. A cold sweat dampened his palms and neck. If she didn't return he would go and find her. He would not let her go.

'Patrick says he means to get me,' Rachel said it with unashamed pride. Taunting him. Teasing him. She could have added 'And Rachel means to let him get her,' but it would have spoiled the effect, removed the tease. Better to have him dangling, childlike in a baby bouncer; babbling and gurgling rubbish, wide-eyed and hopeful.

Did he mean to get Francesca? Yes he did. At all costs? At all costs. At any cost. His stomach churned at the thought of her. With tenderness. With lust. With love. He always thought of her. He had known her less than two weeks and now he always thought of her. The chemistry was there. Constant and pressing. Feeding the flames so that they burned and raged. Uncontrolled. Uncontrollable.

A cold chill from deep inside made him turn around. There was no one behind him on his side but across the street a figure was walking. Unhurried. The same pace as himself. The street was poorly lit, he couldn't make out if it was man or woman. And now they stopped to look in a shop window. The coldness came again, he shivered uncomfortably. The hairs on his neck pricked up like the scruff of a dog disturbed in the quiet of the night. His pulse quickened as tiny spurts of adrenaline rushed into his blood, his breathing faster and deeper, a tingling in his hands and toes.

He walked on quickening his pace. He tried to watch the figure without turning his head. It had left the shop front and appeared to be matching his speed. A car went past but apart from that the road was deserted. A sleepy Sunday night in a sleepy market town caught up in violence and destruction. A tiny seed of disquiet was germinating within. Too many nasty things happening with him at the centre. His mind was wandering, his pulse beat harder and his mouth went dry. He tried to swallow but there was no saliva. He moved his mouth and tongue around searching for moisture, the sides of his throat stuck together impeding the flow of air.

'Who killed Paul?' said a voice inside him.

This is stupid, he told himself. There is nothing happening. The person over there is out on their own business. I'll prove it. I'll turn left at the next street and let them go on by. He brightened up, his breathing slowed. He was pleased with his speed of thought. Always a practical solution to his worries.

That was one of Rachel's criticisms too. He had looked for practical solutions to emotional needs.

'You have no empathy,' she said. 'All I want is a friendly word of support when I need one. Not a lecture on time management or the importance of sticking to a budget.'

He understood now. Time and age had shown him the way, in part at least. If only she had given him the time. Given him the time to grow and develop and understand her wants and needs. He shrugged. Perhaps that was why he had changed. Because she'd left him. Perhaps he would never have changed stuck up on that farm in the hills with only the birds and the animals for company. He wondered what it would be like now. What he would be like now if she'd never left. Would they have succeeded in their dreams? Would their sheep be winning at the shows and selling for thousands of pounds. That had been the plan. That had been the goal. But in their plans and goals they had forgotten to care. Forgotten to care for each other. And perhaps it would all have been right if Patrick hadn't come along. Perhaps they would have had a tiny warning, something less serious that would have made them take notice and make the changes that would have saved them. But the words haunted him still.

'I've never loved you Steve,' she said. 'I know that now.'

He smiled. She said whatever suited at the time. Whatever would justify her want and desire. He remembered her words in the letters he had burnt. Opening her heart to him, laying her cards on the table, telling him she loved him. Knowing that he would not resist; could not resist her charms.

He remembered the phone calls she'd made whenever she was upset. His dashes in the car to be by her side after her car crashes; when she was crushed by the falling horse; when she was upset after a failed case.

'I've never loved you.'

That was the sentence he remembered above all others. The one that he would never forget, that would make him smile. The sentence that exposed her as a fraud. Because whatever the truth there had been a fraud, either at the start or at the end. At one point, and he could never be certain at which, she had been lying. And he did not know which lie was the more wicked. Which lie was the more calculated; the one designed to do the most harm; to cause the most hurt. In the end he supposed it didn't matter.

He turned left down the first road he came to. It was darker than he'd expected, leafless branches overhanging the pavements, cars parked bumper to bumper. The idea came from nowhere and he ducked through a gateway into a front garden protected by a thick *Leylandii* hedge. He pressed his face up against the foliage at the corner that looked back to the main road. It was thirty yards away and now that his eyes had adjusted to the gloom he could see it clearly.

The figure that interested him came into focus. It was coming across the road, making towards where he was hiding. Now real fear settled on him. Clawed at him and caressed him, stroking his sweating skin; running an icy finger down the nape of his neck to his shoulders; driving in deep between his shoulder blades, a stiletto searching out his heart.

'Remember Paul,' said the voice. 'Remember Paul.'

The person was following him, hurrying now and looking around as though confused. His own heart was thumping in his ears. The figure was only twenty, fifteen, ten yards away. Steve held his breath, biting the inside of his cheeks, afraid of crying out involuntarily. Five yards away, he recognised the shuffling, hunched gait, the angular face and beady eyes of Conrad, the lopsided grin, more furtive than he remembered. He was level with Steve now; he must see him; smell the fear that was on him; and then he was passed.

Steve breathed deep and slow, trying to get a rhythm, to calm his heart and his head. The bushes were thick, he would never be discovered if he stayed silent and still. Why was Conrad following him? he wondered. He felt his knees trembling and his chest gave small involuntary twitches. Nerves he thought. He remembered his fear of the dark as a little boy. A fear that had never left him though he could control it now. He tried to relax, to take control of his emotions and then suddenly he was aware of another figure coming down the street towards his hiding place. A shorter, more upright figure, striding confident and elegant. It was Julie.

So she was in this with Conrad, he thought. Whatever it was. The two of them were following him. What were they planning to do? Fear wafted over him again. Paul's death. Conrad creeping around the Broadwich car park. Julie's vow to get even with him. He held his breath as Julie approached. She was staring directly at him, their eyes locked on each others; he dare not blink lest he give the game away. He knew now how a hare felt with a dog sniffing round where it lay, holding fast yet wondering whether to leap up and run.

'Don't move. Don't move,' he said to himself silently. 'Don't move. Don't make a sound. Stay calm. They can't see you. They won't see you.' He smelt a gentle scent of perfume and she was gone.

He dare not move. Could not move. His legs weak and helpless. Gently he let himself squat down and then sit down on the damp grass. He had no idea where they were. Whether they had gone on or were standing just yards away or searching gardens for him. He didn't doubt that he was more than a physical match for Conrad; probably both of them together if it came to the crunch. But who could know what they were planning; what weapons they might be carrying. Paul had been a strong young guy too but he had been murdered. Caught unawares and unsuspecting. Dead within a few seconds, without a struggle.

Well he, Steve Turner was aware of what was happening. He wouldn't be taken by surprise. He heard footsteps returning towards him, muffled excited voices.

'He must have run as soon as he turned up here,' Conrad said. 'I'm still not sure he knew I was following him though.'

'He knew alright,' Julie said. 'He's tricky, that's for sure. We'll get him though. Bide our time and we'll get him.'

They stopped on the other side of the hedge not a few yards from where he sat.

'It's a pity it's come to this,' Conrad said. 'I thought he seemed a decent bloke at first.'

'Believe me,' he heard Julie's voice, edged with a bitterness he had heard before, 'I know him better than you. And that good bloke act he puts on is just that, an act. No, we can't just let this pass, we've got to carry on and do something. One way or another, Steve Turner has to be stopped.'

Chapter 44

'So you want me to devise a plan to stop the spread of FMD in the area around Springholm?' said Steve.

'That's about the measure of it. The instructions come from on high. Something to do with an election coming up,' Neil winced as he said it.

'No problem,' Steve said. 'I know what's going on there as well as anyone. You'll have it by lunchtime.'

He was thankful to be doing something he considered useful. Thankful that he could use his brain and apply sound veterinary principles to the problem instead of fatuous conjecture.

As he saw it there were three issues to tackle. The movement of animals. The spread of virus in fomites by the movement of inanimate objects like vehicles, clothing, feed, equipment. And wind borne spread. The movement of animals was already banned. Illegal movement could still take place but without 24 hour surveillance of all farms it would be impossible to stop. Wind borne spread? Well that was in the lap of the Gods.

The big problem was the fomites. Too many farmers moving around with filthy vehicles and no attempts to cleanse or disinfect. Sure he knew Colin Hunt didn't buy the idea. It was a week past since he'd tried to discuss his memo with Hunt and nothing had changed. Now he was being given a second platform on which to plead his case.

The plan he came up with was to draw a ring around each cluster of cases and call that the Infected Zone. Farmers inside the zone would not be allowed to take vehicles and equipment out of it unless they could prove they had been cleansed and disinfected. In that way the virus would be contained and be prevented from jumping to other farms many miles away. Routes out of the zone would need to be policed to enforce the rules. There were huge implications for manpower but so there were in killing all the stock on contiguous premises. And Steve's plan was based on good veterinary science and humanity.

He showed his plan to Neil. 'What do you think?' he asked.

'It makes sense,' Neil said after he'd considered for a few minutes. 'Send it to Colin and Graham and see what they say.'

'I'll do better than that. I'll send it to Graham and take it to Colin.'

'Good luck,' said Neil.

The door to Colin Hunt's office was closed. Steve knocked.

'Yes?' The familiar monotone of tiresome forbearance drifted through the flimsy wood.

Steve opened the door and entered The Chief Rabbit's burrow. Des Quiet was there too, sitting, suited, in the corner of the room. Always in the corner, thought Steve. He looked pale and drawn, and appeared as though trying to shrink into the furniture; to disappear into the padding; to pretend he wasn't there in the hope that it would all pass him by, leaving him untouched and with nothing unpleasant smelling stuck to him. In that way, when it was all over he could rise again phoenix-like from the ashes. Reborn and revitalised. Untainted by the unfortunate turn of events that were unfolding.

For now though he acted simply as an observer, keeping to the periphery, as though this were some sort of training exercise. Perhaps offer a light hearted comment from time to time, or a restraining influence in the face of over excited decision making. But always detached from the situation, as though it wasn't really anything to do with him. After all he had his monthly returns to worry about. Paper and figures to keep the computers and those above him happy. He had more than enough to keep him going.

Steve did not understand. He wanted to see Des Quiet taking control. Leading and inspiring the troops, thumping the table; advising the army on what was or wasn't needed. Finger on the pulse and all that. Showing that there was someone in control and in charge. That was what he was paid for wasn't it?

'Hello Steve,' Des Quiet said.

'Yes?' said Colin Hunt. 'What is it?'

You need to go on a 'Human Relationships' course, thought Steve. That, and 'Effective Staff Management'. And while you're about it you might as well do a 'Motivating your Workforce' and 'How to get the best out of your Staff' course. And 'Fixing Priorities' too. Oh you've already been on them all and have the certificates to prove it. Which just shows what a waste of time they all are doesn't it? He looked straight at Colin Hunt.

'Neil asked me to come up with a plan for halting the spread of FMD around Springholm. I've brought you my thoughts on it.' He handed the report to Colin Hunt and a spare copy to Des Quiet. The two of them read it in silence. Every now and then Des Quiet nodded his head up and down. Not necessarily in agreement, thought Steve, more in the manner of the nodding dog again.

Colin Hunt finally put the document on the desk in front of him, leaned back in his chair, removed his glasses and rubbed his eyes. Des Quiet continued nodding wordlessly. What does it all mean? thought Steve. What are they thinking? What do they plan to do? There was an uncomfortable silence. A silence in which Steve felt his enthusiasm drain out of him. Like water disappearing out of the bath. The sap oozing from the axe marks in an ancient tree. The breath leaving a dying man.

'What do you think?' he wanted to say. Wanted them to treat it as a serious proposition. Examine its merits and its pitfalls. Use it as a starting point and discuss how it might be improved. How it could be practically applied. It was a genuine proposal, he thought. The French and Dutch had done similar things in their outbreaks. The Irish too. The police and army mounting road blocks. Boxing in the infection until it was considered safe to do otherwise. If they could do it so could we, he thought. Providing the foresight was there to recognise the need and the commitment to bring it about and make it work.

'Do you seriously believe that anyone is likely to countenance this course of action?' Colin Hunt was scathing, speaking slowly, deliberately choosing his words to demonstrate his superior education and intellect. 'Have you considered the practicalities of what you are suggesting? The implications for manpower? The effect on the everyday lives of the men, women and children that live within this so-called Infected Zone?' Scathing and belittling. Not the tone of a man who considered he was speaking to someone who was his veterinary equal or anything like.

And that was what pissed Steve off more than anything. All those fuckers in positions of authority had no more veterinary knowledge, qualifications or expertise than the lowliest Veterinary Officer, the newest recruit. But they couldn't see that. Couldn't see that a vet was a vet was a vet, whether he was the PVO, a DVA, or just a plain Veterinary Officer. There were good, bad and indifferent in all ranks but the considered veterinary opinion of any one of them was as valid as the veterinary opinion of the Principal Vet. And deserved to be treated as such. To be debated and considered with credence. Not to be dismissed as the ideas of a fool, an imbecile, a maverick.

Des Quiet's head was nodding vigorously but he kept his mouth firmly shut. He was not to be drawn to give an opinion. Far too risky to go out on a limb like that before he knew which way was the lie of the land. He would nod to everything and agree to nothing. It was the ultimate survival strategy and so far it had worked to perfection.

'The effect on the everyday lives of the men, women, and children,' Steve repeated it to himself under his breath. Did Colin Hunt have any concept of the effect on the men, women, and children of seeing their animals systematically destroyed by rough looking men in paper boiler suits? The effect of the piles of rotting carcasses they saw each and every day on their way to work and school? The effect of the stench of putrefaction? The smell of burning hair and flesh? The empty desolate fields devoid of life? The clouding of the sky with smoke and cinders that caught in their nose and throat and left a grey black deposit on their cars and their clothes hung out to dry? And that with the increased killing that was planned the whole thing could only get worse.

Where had he been for the last few weeks? What was going on inside his head? Did he know what was happening out there? Steve shook his head. Of course he fucking didn't. And worst of all, seemed not to fucking care.

'So you're not going to pursue the idea?' Steve ventured. 'Not even going to look at the possibilities of how it might be implemented?'

Colin Hunt sighed with irritation. His time was being wasted. Important time that he could be using to complete his daily returns to send to Sage Street.

'Well thank you for your thoughts,' he said glancing across at Des Quiet.

Steve turned and went out. As he closed the door he could hear Colin Hunt whining to Des Quiet. 'This is the kind of rubbish that I have to contend with every day.'

He did not hear Des Quiet's reply but he assumed, beyond all reasonable doubt, that he would be nodding.

'How did you get on?' Neil asked.

'How do you think?' Steve smiled. 'Colin Hunt thinks I'm a complete twat and Des Quiet is still in hiding. I'm wasting my time.'

'I've got a visit for you anyway,' said Neil. 'Right over on the east coast, south of Morton. It's a long way to drive but Beryl wants some input from us. It's a clean area again. A few pigs and masses of sheep and cattle. Been there a while according to the vet, Jan Jeffries. You should have a bit of fun anyway.'

Steve laughed. Jan was young, single, and foul mouthed. He was happy to go and meet up with her, they hadn't spoken in weeks.

He reached the farm in mid-afternoon and when he saw Jan he was shocked. She was pale and haggard as though she had aged five years in less than five weeks.

'Are you okay Jan?' he asked .

'Hi Steve. Yeah I'm fine. This is fucking shit isn't it? It gets fucking worse. The sheep here are riddled with it. The farmer was treating them for fucking foot rot. When the cattle went down with it he started to think twice.'

'And pigs? He's got pigs hasn't he?'

'Yeah, riddled with it too. Feet sloughing off. There's only three sows and a boar. Rare breeds. Spotty things. He'd been treating those with Terramycin spray. I think he's lost it a bit. Split up with his wife a while back and I don't think his heart's in it now. What the fuck is happening at Cardington? I hear there are fucking squaddies everywhere.'

'There are. You should get yourself over for a night out,' he teased.

'Too fucking knackered to bother about it,' she smiled, and she looked young again. 'The other problem is that the guy next door is a bit of a dealer. Apparently he's got sheep all over the fucking place. The ones next door will definitely have to go as contiguous. The others? Well I guess it's your call.'

'Marvellous,' said Steve. 'We'll run out of animals to kill if we carry on at this rate. Show me where the pigs are will you? No let me guess,' he said suddenly, 'in a pen right next to the road.'

'How did you know? Don't tell me you're psychic?'

'A lucky guess,' he replied but the germ of an idea was forming. Not clearly. Not clear at all. Almost impossible really. Outside the realms of rational consideration. But there were coincidences. Coincidences that kept happening and which left him looking for a common link to unlock the puzzle. Maybe he was being fanciful. Imagination getting the better of him. Maybe he was looking for something that didn't exist. But he had an idea and if he could just get some space and time in which to get his brain working clearly and rationally again he could develop that idea.

It was just like Jan said. The pigs were hobbling lame, reluctant to stand. They were in a straw pen just five metres off the road that passed the farm and the coincidence was too great to ignore. Somehow or other the pigs were becoming infected because they were close to the road. He had seen it on four farms now. In all cases it was the pigs that were infected first. And in all cases the pigs were next to the road.

What was the means of spread? Infected spray from a passing lorry? Infected dung thrown off the wheels? But why always the pigs and not the cattle that were also close to the road? Cattle were more susceptible to aerosol infection. Pigs were relatively resistant.

'What are you thinking Steve?' Jan asked.

'Nothing,' he said. 'Just turning things over in my mind. Preoccupations of a middle aged man,' he laughed.

He stayed to help get the slaughter underway. The sheep had started lambing five days previously and there were already a hundred lambs between a few minutes and five days old. The ewes were big strong halfbreds, all inside on straw. Those not yet lambed were gathered in groups of fifty whilst those with lambs were shut in individual pens to help the mother/lamb bonding.

'If you slaughter the ewes that have already lambed, Jan and I can inject the lambs whilst you carry on with the others,' Steve said.

'Good idea,' said one of the slaughterers.

The first pen held a ewe and twins. They 'popped' the ewe in a couple of seconds and head shot the two lambs before Steve realised what was happening. The bolt had penetrated the skull but not stunned them and they stood swaying on their feet bleating.

'I'll try again,' one of the slaughters said but Steve was alert now.

'Stop, the skull's too soft,' he said. 'Don't shoot the lambs. I'll kill them by injection.'

He quickly drew up some Euthatal and put the two lambs down by injecting into their hearts. And then he followed the slaughterers down the line of pens, laying each dead lamb gently on its side, unable to stomach piling them in a heap. It was dismal and soul destroying and he thought of Francesca to see him through; of her smiling face and hearing her voice and stroking her hair and neck and the feel of her shoulders and the scent of her skin. Thinking of her helped him through it all; he closed his mind to what he was doing, mechanical and detached.

The slaughterers moved on to the main pens and roped in an agricultural student from Australia to stand between them and insert a fresh cartridge into each captive bolt as the spent round was ejected. They were working fast now, the farmer and shepherd holding hurdles across the width of the pen to keep the sheep tight and the slaughterers moving forward, shooting the sheep one at a time and then offering up their captive bolts to the student who soon became deft at slipping another cartridge into the chamber.

I wonder what her parents would think if they could see her now, thought Steve. I bet they never imagined she'd be involved with something like this when they waved her off at the airport.

'Not too fast,' called Steve. 'We don't want anybody hurt.' He thought of having to phone Australia and tell a pair of distraught parents what had happened to their daughter. That he was very sorry.

He helped Jan check that the first pen of sheep were all dead and then walked around the shed again, thinking. He came across a couple of tiny pens they'd missed, each with a ewe and lamb in. 'I may as well kill the lambs,' he said aloud, shocked by the detached, even callous tone in his voice. This was what happened. This was how the atrocities in the world came about. 'May as well,' without a second thought. No questions asked. Policy is policy and we must do what our superiors tell us. I am not responsible for my actions. I am just following orders. Lambs or babies. In other circumstances there might be no difference.

Yes it was easy to duck responsibility. Not my decision. The instructions were clear and I did not think to question them. Did not

347

want to draw attention to myself. Did not want to rock the boat. Did not want to be seen to be letting the team down. Did not want to rebel. Preferred the safer option.

Dissent was not easy. Especially not if it were a lone voice. A voice that was calling against the crowd like a fish swimming against the tide. Canute tried to turn back the tide and he was seen for the fool he was. It did not do to emulate Canute.

But what of the little boy in the crowd? The one who stood near the front and stared in wonder at the procession amidst the oohs and aahs of the townsfolk. Unblinkered by protocol, untainted by self importance and self deception he spoke the plain and simple truth, 'The Emperor isn't wearing any clothes.'

And once it was spoken the whole world could see and they saw through their own idiocy and complicity in the illusion and they pointed and laughed instead. Who was the Emperor here thought Steve. Who was calling the tune? And was there one or were there many? It was too difficult to unravel. A sea of hidden agendas and backroom deals. And now that the policy was set, so brutal and exacting in its execution it could not be turned without a loss of face or the sour taste of criticism that it had been the wrong policy from the start. To turn back would be an admission of wrong and a betrayal of those who had already suffered at its hand.

No. Stopping it now would not be easy. It would require a change of personnel right at the top; a change from those that had staked their political and professional careers and reputations on its success. For them there was no turning back. They must pursue the policy to its bitter end and if necessary seek safety in the phrase, 'With the benefit of hindsight.'

'Of course it is easy to be wise after the event,' they would say, 'but we were acting on the best scientific evidence and advice at the time.' It had been said in the past over BSE and it would be said in the future over Foot and Mouth.

Steve had no doubts about that. And he had no doubts that in the great scheme of things, what he was doing was wrong. Even as he injected the lambs and lay them gently on the straw in the pen. And then immediately he realised his mistake in the detail too as the ewes began to paw at the lifeless forms with their forelegs; push at the warm yet motionless carcasses with their muzzles and make plaintive bleating noises as they tried to bring life back into the bodies of their offspring. It was heart wrenching, emotionally charged; the pawing more frantic, moving the tiny body across the straw, pushing it with their nose, bleating and pleading with it to stand and jump and answer with a call.

He had not realised. Not anticipated the ewes' simple grasp of life and death in their offspring. Having seen so many stand unperturbed as those around them were slaughtered. Unmoved. Uncaring. Unafraid of anything other than the noise and scent of man, oblivious to the finality of the mechanical bolt. Yet here and now in front of him he saw the understanding born of recent labour; an instinctive understanding of the thread of life beating within her newborn offspring; and he saw the destruction of an equilibrium by his hasty and thoughtless action.

Quickly, as though to absolve himself he drew up more Euthatal into a 50 ml syringe and catching each ewe in turn he injected the barbiturate into their jugular veins so that their pain and sorrow were extinguished. And then he cried. Cried and sobbed for all the wicked things he had ever done in his life. Through ignorance and devilment as a boy; through lack of self belief and self esteem as an adolescent; and through lack of pity and compassion and through arrogance and the desire for power as an adult. He sat in the dimly lit shed with his hand on the back of a dead ewe and cried for the sins of the world that were his and for those that were not. He wept for the Jews and the Moslems that had been killed and who were killing each other. He wept for the Hutus and Tutsis of Rwanda and for the Christians and Moslems in Nigeria and Indonesia. He wept with despair, lack of hope, the inevitability that the world would always be this way.

Tears fell onto the fleece of the ewe, droplets that collected on the wool like dew; droplets of sea salt spray, tinged with blood and anger and pain. The pressure in his head, thudding with each pulse from his heart, despair and confusion; hatred for the part he was playing yet unsure of what he should do.

'Steve? Are you okay?' Jan was speaking to him.

He looked up at her, tears streaking his cheeks, eyes red, lids swollen.

'Yeah I'm fine,' he smiled and stood up. 'How's it going back there?'

'Alright. We'll be through the sheep in another hour.' She began to cry. 'Where's it all going to end? Does anybody know?'

'They don't know and they don't fucking care,' said Steve. 'We need to vaccinate. That would put an end to this, stop all this fucking madness.'

It hit him straight between the eyes like a religious experience, a revelation. Decide to vaccinate and all this madness stops. Immediately. End of story. The slaughterers can pack up and go home. Start vaccinating on premises contiguous to IPs and work your way out from there. Within a few days the number of new IPs would be down to virtually zero. If they could provide the resources to slaughter and dispose of the number of animals they were now talking about then they could provide them to vaccinate. **IF** the powers that be could be persuaded that that was the right thing to do. Suddenly he felt empowered. Empowered with a knowledge and a conviction that his way was the way ahead. All he had to do was to convince those at the top.

'Do you need me here any longer?' he asked Jan.

'No,' she wiped her eyes and Steve gave her a gentle hug. 'You get going, it's a long drive back to Cardington. I'm going to call a halt once we've finished the sheep. It's dark already, too dangerous to start on the cows. We'll get cracking with them at first light. We'll still meet the 24 hour target. More or less anyway,' she grinned.

He gave her another hug. 'Don't worry,' he said. 'We'll look back on this in a year's time..,' he tailed off. With affection? With calm appraisal? More like with dread in the dark of early morning nightmares, he thought.

He drove slowly to Cardington. He was tired, his reactions dulled by physical and mental exhaustion. The lights of oncoming cars blinded him, the bright orange flames of burning pyres lit up the dark March sky like beacons from a bygone age. Why are the public tolerating this? he thought. Why aren't they demonstrating against the brutality and the futility? Where are the RSPCA? Where are the animal rights people? He had little time for either but he couldn't understand why they weren't complaining. It was as though there was a conspiracy of silence. A conspiracy born out of the obscene need not to be found guilty of backing the wrong policy.

It was 9.30 when he finally reached the hotel. His body flushed warm, tingling with anticipation and excitement, butterflies dancing in his stomach, emotions of adolescence long since forgotten; of college days; of his time with Rachel before they were married. The lights of the hotel welcomed him. Like Christmas. A familiar feel and smell in the air. Cold like snow, the scent of Christmas trees; of family returning home.

He ran to the reception desk, the high spirits of youth and new love. The desire to see her, to touch her, to speak with her, from deep inside him flowed to the surface; honey rising from the cut comb, intensely sweet and blossom scented.

'Francesca Capotti?' he asked. 'Is she back yet?' The receptionist raised an eyebrow good naturedly, noting the unrestrained excitement in his voice, prepared herself to give him the news.

'She phoned earlier today to cancel her room. Something had come up and she couldn't make it. I am sorry,' she added with a tenderness she thought had long since left her.

'No that's alright,' said Steve. 'It's not a problem. All for the best I'm sure.' He took his key and headed for his room. Once inside he locked the door and undressed. He did not bother to shower. Did not bother to clean his teeth. He curled up in the bed, pulled the covers over him and cried noiselessly until his whole body ached with the effort. And then he fell asleep.

Chapter 45

Within two days the sheep cull was underway. Holding pens, races and undercover killing facilities were quickly installed and the sheep wagons began the task of transporting truck load after truck load of ewes and lambs to the killing site.

A few vets expressed their concern about the welfare implications of transporting ewes with newborn lambs but they were dismissed as troublemakers who were unable to appreciate the bigger picture. Farmers clamoured for a place in the queue, the scent of compensation money in their nostrils, too good an opportunity for many to miss. Others misguidedly believed that they would save their cattle by getting rid of their sheep. The theory that it was sheep spreading the disease to cattle was too good for the authorities to let drop. Too convenient an excuse for all concerned for the failure to get the disease under control. Perhaps they were even foolish enough to believe it themselves. All things were possible in the present climate thought Steve.

He stayed peripheral to the sheep cull. Hearing the gossip and rumours was enough. The ewes that lambed on the journey to the cull site; the lambs that were trampled underfoot in the lorries and arrived dead or with broken legs and chests; the sound of bleating sheep as ewes and lambs tried in vain to find each other at journey's end; the teams of slaughterers working twelve and fourteen hour days; the teams of vets injecting lambs in a conveyor belt system of death, the like of which had never before been seen in history. At its height there were twenty thousand sheep a day being transported to the site, slaughtered, and tipped into huge rectangular pits cut deep into the soil for mass burial.

The Brigadier was the model of efficiency. A man with a mission and who meant for that mission to be completed in the shortest time with the minimum of hold up. A man who took **NO** as a challenge to his authority and who could turn a No into a Yes.

News bulletins had changed too. Ron Steady was no longer to be seen or heard, and Steve joked with anyone that would listen that he was locked in a padded room with his mouth taped shut until it was prudent to wheel him out again. The scientific advisers were now required to give their thoughts and comments and in response to any criticism of the draconian measures implemented, gravely referred to their mathematical models and a set of three magical graphs that showed the catastrophic outcomes if their recommendations were not followed to the letter. They were all insistent that vaccination would not help.

The Minister for Rural Affairs was still 'isolating, bearing down and eradicating,' and the Prime Minister was popping up everywhere with a concerned and steadfast look on his face. The stakeholders were all powerful with an apparent veto on every aspect of policy. And it was that that worried Steve the most. Their only interest was the economic effects of the disease on their members. They had no concern with the wider economic implications, the effects on human and animal welfare or on the environment. Their responsibility was limited, their power absolute.

Informed debate on the new policy began to appear in the broadsheet newspapers, 'the hapless Principal Veterinary Officer' said one. Everyone in the country had an opinion of sorts as to what should be done, from virologists, through organic farmers, to members of the clergy. But wherever official comment appeared, the spin and focus was against vaccination. 'Would not help eradicate the disease'; 'Would not reduce the number of animals of slaughtered'; 'Would pose more questions than it answered.'

Why then thought Steve did the rest of the world rely so heavily on vaccination as a means of control. Why was an emergency stock of vaccine held by the European Union for use in just such a scenario as the one they were now experiencing? Why had Europe used vaccination throughout the eighties? Why in the face of the most destructive outbreak of Foot and Mouth that the world had ever seen did Britain consider itself capable of a unique response? It was this last question that he put to people time and time again. And the one for which he would never get a satisfactory answer.

And all the time he thought of Francesca. She was with him always, her spirit and humanity touching everything he did. And everything he thought and said and did was for her too. He wanted her to be proud of him. That was what he wanted more than anything. Her pride and respect for him. That was where the pain from Rachel had been worst. Her lack of respect. He knew why Francesca had not returned. Knew why and understood. He did not believe it was the end.

On Friday March 30th, Steve drove across to Morton once again. Beryl and Nancy were under pressure, the number of cases mounting and they desperately needed advice on where the campaign was headed. He arrived at midday at the same time as two other VOs from Cardington. Rumour and innuendo was that Morton was to be opened as a Disease Control Centre in its own right. In the words of one VO 'Colin Hunt has decided to cut Morton loose.'

'Yes' said Steve with no attempt to disguise the contempt in his voice, 'before it drags Cardington under too.' He was angry. Blood red angry. Weeks of indifference to Morton's needs from both Colin Hunt and Des Quiet. Beryl, Nancy and Tommy had with the help and commitment and dogged hard work of the rest of the staff managed to keep Morton afloat. The centre had been shamefully understaffed and under resourced. Neglected both in terms of practical and moral support. Nominally led from Cardington, but left to its own devices to either sink or swim. That it had swum for so long was a credit to all those that had contributed.

When Steve walked into Beryl's office the toll exacted was there before his eyes. The pale, tissue paper faces of Beryl and Nancy looked back at him, still smiling and cheerful, no hint of defeat in their eyes but a tired gentle distance that spoke of lost sleep and painful mental anguish.

'Hi,' he said, immediately ashamed of his own preoccupations and misgivings. Whilst he was bitching and soul searching and worrying about what should be done, these people were getting on and doing it. And how? For fifteen or sixteen hours a day. Answering queries on the phone. Directing vets and slaughterers. Making decisions on DCs, and for the last few days helping the army and the administrators who had parachuted in to take over the administrative and logistical running of the show. A show that had struggled on for days and weeks with the minimum of help and complaint, now expanded to three or four times the size because that was what was deemed necessary to cope with the workload.

Tommy came in to join them, smiling as ever, the furrows on his forehead deeper and paler than Steve remembered. Steve looked at the three of them standing in a line. The three wise monkeys, he thought. The Ministry had to be proud of these people. They deserved a fucking medal. But when all was said and done he had no doubt that it would be the likes of Colin Hunt and Des Quiet that received the pats on the back. They and the PVO and anybody else who had managed to avoid any of the shit sticking to them.

The anger bubbled in him, hot and fomenting. Molten lava flowing close to the surface, eager to erupt and shower those around it with fire and wrath. He knew he was being unreasonable, condemning those in authority without giving them a fair hearing. But he kept coming back to the same thing. It was their complacency. Their lack of leadership. Their reluctance to stand up and put themselves on the line. He thought of the old battles in history and the legendary warriors of long ago. Of Roman Commanders and Trojan kings. Alexander the Great and William Wallace. Great leaders who had led by example. Great leaders who put themselves in the front line to lead and inspire their troops. Exposing themselves to the risks as well as the glories. Leaders such as that would not have skulked in shadows in tents or in the corners of rooms. They would not have dismissed their Captains ideas as worthless or puerile. They would have discussed, considered, decided and then led. Their men would and did follow them to the ends of the earth and back. Endured hardship and suffering because their leaders endured it too and they believed in the cause.

And amidst all his anger he felt sympathy too, because he could see that those at the top were as lost as anybody.

'It's nice to have our epidemiologist back,' drawled Beryl.

Steve winced with embarrassment. For all the good I've done, he thought. Not much to show for it. Cases going up and none of his suggestions or ideas acted on. He was just a messenger or a gatherer of information.

'It's nice to be back amongst people with a bit of sense,' he said. He smiled at them.

Nancy smiled back, a pale lazy smile of relief. Her eyes kept closing, sleep not far away in spite of being standing. 'I'm going home for a few weeks tomorrow,' she said. 'To see the family.' Her relief was palpable.

Steve hugged her and kissed her on the cheek. He seemed to be kissing everybody these days, keeping him in touch with the important things in life. Human warmth. Human emotion. Love and compassion. There was little enough of it around just now.

'You deserve it,' he said. 'You all deserve a break. You all deserve bloody medals.'

'Ah stop bullshitting us old fella,' said Tommy, his big face smiling like a donut. It's bloody Hunt that'll get the medal,' he was laughing good naturedly. No bitterness. Open good humour. There was no political manoeuvring with Tommy. What you saw was what you got.

'How are the army settling in?' Steve asked.

'Very well,' said Beryl. 'They've commandeered all the other spurs in the building. Shoved the Social Security lot out somewhere else. They just came and told them and did it. No discussion, no argument. The Social Security manager made some pretence at complaining but old "Army bollocks" just bundled him out of the door with the rest of them.' Her face quivered with mirth. It was Monty Python to her too.

There was a knock at the door and a man came in.

'Steve,' said Beryl, 'this is the guy who was up the Hamble Valley. I spoke to you about the problem there last week.'

'Hi.' Steve shook his hand. 'I remember. It was a problem with DCs wasn't it? Did you get it sorted out?'

'I sure did,' said the man in a deliberate southern States accent. 'When I headed into that valley at the start of the week there were sheep and cattle on every hillside you looked. When I left it at the end of the week,' he paused, waiting for the tension to build, 'there weren't left nothing moving. Cleared the whole darn thing out. That's the way it should be done if you want to beat this thing.' He spoke with conviction, belief, a man at ease with the work he was doing.

And how many more valleys were to be cleared out of their stock? thought Steve. Of course it would work but where would it stop?

'Anyway, just stopped by to say ma farewells. I'm flying home tomorrow. I've done ma four weeks and I'm just about beat out.' He held out his hand and shook hands with everyone. 'Good luck to yerall.'

He went out whistling. You had to admire his fortitude. His self confidence.

'I think we'll be seeing a lot of Americans before this is over,' said Beryl. 'It's a bit like the war isn't it. They'll be handing out chocolate and nylons next.'

'What do you want me to do?' asked Steve.

'Sort out some of these DCs,' said Nancy. 'We've got sheep on some common land infected. And feral sheep in the forest. We don't know what's contiguous, what's a DC by virtue of shared personnel or equipment. In fact we don't know very much at all.' Her eyes blinked closed, the lines on her face deepened and she swayed ever so gently. Steve caught hold of her arm and sat her in a chair. She looked as if she was going to faint.

'Leave it with me,' he said. 'Give me the files and the names of the vets involved and I'll come up with something.' It was the least he could do for them, these brave uncomplaining souls who had worked themselves into the ground.

'I've got the day off tomorrow too,' said Beryl. 'I think Keith Brewer's coming over today to stand in for me.'

'Yeah, I've seen him around already,' said Steve, the warning bells suddenly ringing, red lights flashing bright and clear. Beryl and Nancy off on the same day. It could all collapse. He could see it now. Black on white. Nothing grey or uncertain. Could nobody else see it too? Thank God he had his own work to do. But what of Keith?

Mitchell Ford walked past the door and seeing Steve turned and came in.

'Steve,' he said raising a hand and pointing a finger, 'good to have you on board. I've set up a special unit with one of the army Captains here to create a rapid reaction force for DCs. We're just about to give a presentation to the Commanding Officer and the Admin guy who's in charge here. Will you come along and see what you think of it?'

Steve was taken by surprise, trying to work out who was in charge of Mitch and on whose say so the rapid reaction unit had been convened. Already he was fascinated by the dynamics and the tensions at play here. Who was commanding who and who was co-ordinating it all? He knew another DVA, Daniel Barnes, had arrived a few days ago to take charge of the new Control Centre. But where he sat in relation to the admin group and the army was anybody's guess. It was a huge machine pulling in a host of different directions. He didn't know who was steering it or in what direction it was going.

'I'll be along in ten minutes,' said Steve. He was enthralled.

'Excellent,' said Mitch, 'I'll go and tell the Captain.' Steve was convinced the thought of saluting crossed Mitch's mind.

'That's our Mitch,' said Beryl with a gleam of amusement on her face. 'Daniel Barnes doesn't know what to make of him. He's a law unto himself but the army have taken him to their bosom and given him Most Favoured Adviser status.'

'But why isn't Daniel or Des Quiet advising the army?' Steve said. The question was obvious but no one had yet asked it. The answer was even more elusive.

'I don't know,' said Beryl. 'Des Quiet just appears, wanders around and then goes away again. I've no idea why he's not there explaining policy to the army and telling them what he wants doing. I don't know if he knows what he wants doing. That might be the problem.'

'I'll go and listen to what Mitch has to say anyway. It can't be worse than most of the shite I've heard so far.'

He walked down the corridor towards Spur 3, a sixties style building, straight lines and lots of glass in metal frames. No imagination. Nothing tasteful. Soon be ready for abandonment and demolishment. Typical of the era, he thought. Soldiers everywhere, camouflage clothing, black boots, walking purposefully. Electricians and phone engineers pulling panels off the wall, feeding wires this way and that, pliers stuck in back pockets, polished crack-arsed builder's bottoms smiling up at him; glint of money in shining eyes everywhere he looked.

He followed the arrows to Spur 3, came to a room with a large sign on the door. Intelligent Disease Control Rapid Reaction Force. He knocked.

'Come in.'

Pushing the door wide he entered a world he had only previously seen at the cinema. A world of army personnel and maps on walls with coloured markers and grids and people saluting and pacing the floor and voices in clipped tones and military speak; short sentences spat from the mouth; maximum impact, minimum discourse.

'Steve,' Mitch jumped forward, 'this is Captain Andy Triggs.'

'Glad to meet you Sir,' said the Captain clicking his heels. 'Mitch has told me all about you. You're just the guy we need on this team to make it really work.' He shook Steve's hand.

A boy thought Steve. The Captain is a boy. Early twenties, dark haired, dark eyed. Clean shaven. The earnestness of youth, bouncing and bubbling. The gleam of adventure in his eyes, of challenges to be conquered not yet met. I was like him once, thought Steve.

'We'd like to give you our presentation,' said Mitch as though auditioning for a play or selling computer software.

'I'd like to see it,' said Steve, not certain what to make of the two of them.

Mitch weighed straight in.

'At present the virus is well ahead of us, jumping from farm to farm, moving all the time, popping up where we least expect. Resources are limiting our response and slowing us down. We chase it here,' he tapped the map on the wall, 'it moves to over here. What we're lacking is a clear strategic response so that we can get ahead of the thing. That's where the Intelligent Disease Control Rapid Reaction Force comes into play. The map reference of each new IP is passed to us here and plotted on this map. Then our team here, that's me, Andy, and you Steve if you'll join us, evaluates the data and draws up a list of priority IPs and DCs that need taking out. We then direct the valuers, slaughterers and clean up teams to the priority farms so that we get them and their contiguous premises slaughtered out without delay.' He spoke without notes, eloquent and direct, certain of his ground and with the self confidence born of doubtless simplicity.

The phrase 'often wrong but never in doubt,' floated across Steve's mind, not with malice or sarcasm but with a warm admiration for the lad's enthusiasm and efforts. Here was a guy who was not afraid to stand up and speak out. To give his views honestly and forthrightly. To defend them and to be shot down in flames if necessary. He was not to be found skulking under a stone or hiding in the corners.

Mitch finished with a flourish, painting a doomsday scenario of what would happen if the idea wasn't followed and then handed over to Captain Andy whose timing at the takeover was divine perfection. Either they had rehearsed intensely, thought Steve, or they were just a natural phenomenon. Captain Andy spoke of the virus as though it were an enemy army. He tapped an area on the map with a short cane:

'And if it pops up here,' he barked, 'we flood the area immediately and take out all the animals in the premises around it. Any other possible DCs are rapidly evaluated by our close knit unit, to which your input is vital,' he waved his baton at Steve, 'and these are prioritised as the next properties to be taken out.' He clicked his heels and standing shoulder to shoulder with Mitch looked Steve straight in the eyes.

Steve was impressed. These guys had obviously grasped the important basic points of a Stamping out policy and they had worked it up into a practical applicable art with some science thrown in. It made more sense than much of what was currently finding its way down the modems and fax machines.

'Well, what do you think Sir?' Captain Andy asked. 'Will you join the team? The input of an epidemiologist is essential to this.'

Would he join the team? Steve thought about the question. In the current climate anything was possible. No one knew who was working for who, chains of command were blurred or non-existent. He could probably have said yes and no one would have known or cared until he was well dug in, with the ear of the military and administrative high command. If by then he was doing a good job they were hardly going to stop him were they?

What an opportunity. To have his own personal unit and run the epidemiology side of it the way he wanted, plus the power to shape the policy. It was an enviable prospect; he would be a mercenary with all the pleasures and attendant risks that that involved. In a few brief moments he had to decide whether to throw in his lot with Mitch and Captain Andy and risk the consequences, or pull back and go with the Ministry.

In the end it was no contest. If he had believed in the overall policy then he would have gone with it and left the Ministry to pick up the pieces. But he didn't agree and already something else was forming in his mind. Something that he couldn't ignore.

'I can help you unofficially as much as you like and I will,' he said. 'I think your ideas for implementing the overall policy are great. My problem is that I don't agree with the policy.' He shrugged and gave a little smile. 'I think we should vaccinate.'

'I see,' said the Captain. 'Maybe you should speak to the Colonel. If there's to be a change in policy it needs to come from the top.'

'I'm happy to speak to him,' said Steve, 'but a change in policy won't come from the likes of me. It'll come from far higher up the tree. That's where King Kong will be.'

The Colonel was summoned anyway. Younger than Steve, intelligent and as earnest as Captain Andy.

'You just tell us what you want and I'll get it for you,' he said to Steve. 'I've got all the resources I need and more. Do you need another computer? Any more transport? I can get you a helicopter if you need one.'

'It's not really up to me,' said Steve. He was defensive, put on the spot. It was bloody Des Quiet who should be talking to the Colonel, not him. He should be the Ministry man in charge.

'I can't believe how little power is delegated down to you guys,' said the Colonel. 'I give my infantrymen more scope for decision making than you guys get.' It was an observation, not a criticism. An observation with a liberal sprinkling of surprise that professionals were given so little freedom to exercise their professional judgement.

Steve squirmed with embarrassment. Embarrassment that he worked for this bloody shower and by association was implicated in the whole damn mess. Not even a mess, he thought. A shambles. A debacle. Not too strong a sentiment. He turned away unable to look the Colonel in the eye. He was ashamed, tarnished by the whole damn bunch. Soiled goods that had been tested and found to be wanting.

'I'll speak to Daniel the DVA,' he said. 'I'll see if he wants anything else.' He was mumbling as he backed out of the door. He headed to the safety of the office he'd commandeered and began the job of looking through the files on the common land known as Midmoor Moss. And within minutes he knew that the case of Midmoor Moss would, more than anything that had gone before, test his resolve to the limit.

Chapter 46

Saturday. The last Saturday in March. The shit had hit the fan. Big brown gobs of it. Wet green streaks of it. Beryl and Nancy weren't there. Everything was in confusion. Telephones rang red hot, unanswered. Men with short haircuts in green and brown camouflage; black boots laced above the ankles. Walking fast, the corridors shrieking with activity. An orchestra without a conductor. Everyone with a tune to play. Some the same. Some different. No one to co-ordinate the sound. A harsh unpleasant sound. Unproductive; disharmony. People playing louder, trying to take the lead, to drown out the music of others. A free for all, the music painful to the ears. We need a conductor. A leader to guide us on our way. To show us the way with vision and rational commitment. Is that too much to ask for?

'Is that too much to ask for?' Steve said it out aloud to himself. He had phoned all the farmers who had sheep on Midmoor Moss. Hefted sheep. Sheep that had learnt their piece of moor from their mothers back through tens of generations and hundreds of years. Learnt the patch of moor that was their own and from where they rarely strayed though no fences prevented it. They knew where the springs and the sweetest grasses were to be found, the shelter from wind and snow. Hardy hill breeds like Dalesbred, Swaledale and Rough Fell. They were a part of the nation's heritage. They and the men and women that farmed them. Tradition and landscape handed down over the centuries and in safe hands for the generations ahead. And now, in the space of two hours and eleven phone calls Steve had arranged the slaughter of all of them the following day.

FMD confirmed in one of the hefts of sheep on the moor. Eleven other farms had hefts on the moor and all had their farms on the lower ground surrounding the moor. The contiguous cull policy meant that all eleven properties were to be depopulated. A gentle, easy to say word. It disguised and sanitised the truth of what was to happen.

Many of the farmers had been reluctant to agree. Steve had persuaded them to comply. He had followed the policy. 'All for the greater good,' he had said. 'We need to be certain of stopping the spread here so that others might not suffer.'

Emotional blackmail. Not lies but clichés. Clichés to support the policy that had been decided upon. Clichés in which he did not believe but that he spoke anyway. He felt disgust at himself.

If only Francesca were there. He could talk to her. Explain the problems. She would comfort him. Steady his thoughts. Give him the focus and the strength to do what he knew was right. Killing the fell sheep was like destroying works of art. It was like ransacking the pyramids for financial gain. Selling the family silver for short term profit. The economic argument for not vaccinating was becoming more bankrupt by the day.

He wrote a memo to Graham Thompson that he copied to Colin Hunt. A memo in which he pleaded the case of the fell sheep. Pointed out their unique, irreplaceable value. Their social value in securing farmers to pieces of land that were difficult to manage and which had been shaped by the sheep's presence.

'We may come to regret the action we are proposing to take,' the memo said. 'I believe that we should leave the fell sheep untouched and vaccinate all the cattle on the farms that surround the moor.'

He e-mailed it to Graham and Colin, and Neil. Then he went to find Tommy. A tall man in a suit and tie stopped him in the corridor.

'I'm Brad Thomas, Grade 5 administrator. Are you Steve Turner the epidemiologist?' he asked.

Steve cringed again at the title. 'I'm working in epidemiology,' he said. 'And yes, I'm Steve Turner.'

'Can I see you for a few minutes?'

Steve followed him to his office.

'I've only been here a couple of days and it's clear to me that there is no co-ordination of effort. The army are doing one thing, we in the Ministry another. Permanent vets have one view, temporary vets are making up their own rules. We have to get a grip on what is going on because at the moment it is chaos. I should like to hear your view on the matter.'

Steve looked at him suspiciously. Brad held his gaze, did not look away, his eyes shining and clear. Why are you asking for my view, thought Steve. No one in authority in the Ministry asks the views of those lower down. He chose his words carefully and spoke with a measured tone.

'You won't like my view,' he said slowly. 'I now believe we should vaccinate. The whole thing is getting out of hand; out of control like a runaway train. Slaughter will work. Eventually. I don't know when but it will work. But the losses are too great. Economic, social, animal welfare, human welfare. Our own humanity is at stake. We're descending into Barbarism.'

'What about this guy Mitch and his idea of intelligent disease control?'

Steve smiled. Good old Mitch, he thought. Rattling cages and rocking boats.

'I have a lot of time for Mitch,' said Steve. 'He's thought about the problem and he's doing something about it. I suspect he's not really a Ministry man,' he smiled.

Brad smiled back. 'No I think that's safe to say. He's already ruffled a few feathers. But what about the idea he's hatched with Captain Triggs? Will it work?'

'It's a good idea,' said Steve. 'Our resources are limited and this seems a good way of prioritising the work that needs doing. If you agree with the policy behind it,' he added. 'And I don't. I think we'll regret what we're doing. As I've said already, I think vaccination is the way forward. A lot of people would disagree with me but there's a good few out there who would agree.'

'There's a meeting in the main ops room at 2.30. That's in five minutes. Come and see what everybody else is saying.'

Steve followed Brad down the corridor. It seemed that everybody was heading in the same direction. Daniel was up ahead with Des Quiet, the two talking secretly to each other. The ops room was crowded with soldiers, the now familiar men in suits, vets from practice, Ministry vets. On one wall was a huge map of the area, coloured pins stuck in for the IPs and 3 Km circles neatly drawn around them. Brad Thomas strode to the front and called the meeting to order.

'Thank you all for coming. I just wanted to get you all together to try and keep you in the picture as to what is going on and also to get your views on some of the key issues. As you are probably aware, I am now in charge of the administrative side of things and Colonel Thompkins here is charged with delivering the logistics side of the equation. You're well aware of the change of policy with regard to the slaughter of livestock on contiguous premises and I want to make sure that you're all aware of how this is going to be implemented.'

Steve caught Brad's eye.

'Yes Steve?'

'The problem as I see it is that the disease isn't spreading out in a nice orderly fashion from an infected farm to surrounding farms and then on to other contiguous farms. If it were it would be relatively straightforward to slaughter out around an IP and put an immediate halt to it. But it's not behaving like that. It's cropping up three, five, even ten kilometres away from the nearest IP. It's behaving in a more random fashion and as such we've no way of predicting where the next infected farm is going to occur. That's the problem. And slaughtering out all the stock on contiguous premises isn't going to stop it doing that.'

'What if we draw a straight line fifteen kilometres to the north west of the most westerly IP and another fifteen kilometres to the south west and then start slaughtering all the sheep to the east of those lines working our way across to the east coast? A sort of pincer movement. If we do that we're bound to get rid of it aren't we? Especially if it's hiding in the sheep,' Brad said.

Steve waited for Daniel or Des Quiet to answer him but they remained silent. Is no one in a senior position in the Veterinary Service going to take charge here? thought Steve. He waited patiently but no one said a word.

'Eventually that would work,' said Steve, unable to bear the silence any longer. 'But you'll end up slaughtering hundreds of thousand of animals. And there's still no guarantee that it won't break out on the other side of the line that you've drawn. You could end up slaughtering all the sheep across a wide band of the whole of the north of England.

'And,' he went on, cautiously now because he knew that his own ideas had already been rubbished and discounted, 'the disease is no longer being spread by subclinical infection in the sheep as far as I can see. It's a cattle to cattle infection now and I'm convinced that the main problem is the movement of farmers and their vehicles. That's what's spreading the virus. That's why it's so difficult to know where it's going to appear next. I think that we should be concentrating more on getting that message across.'

Other ideas began to be thrown into the ring. Almost all of them required an increase in the rate and numbers of animals to be slaughtered. Every vet through to every admin person above the grade of junior clerk had an opinion to offer on the matter. Ideas were expanded with animated sweeps of the arm across the map in front of them, in a demonstration of how this or that pincer movement would take out the enemy before it could do damage somewhere else. Only Daniel and Des remained silent.

What's going on here? thought Steve. Why is everybody but those who should have an opinion giving it so freely? Why are Des and Daniel saying nothing? He giggled hysterically. PYTHON was alive and well, and living in Morton. He half expected the toilet cleaner to be brought out to the front and to be gently coaxed to give her thoughts on the matter. Why not? They may as well have a full house. He spoke up again.

'This is the problem,' Steve said . 'The whole thing is MADNESS. Where is it all going to end? We need to start vaccinating. Change to that control policy and this whole mad thing that is happening before our eyes, stops. Stops NOW. IMMEDIATELY.'

The Colonel looked shocked. Daniel and Des Quiet frowned the frowns of the dispossessed. Steve said no more. It was a case of pushing shit up hill. He thought of Francesca, turned around and left the room.

Half an hour later, Tommy came to find him.

'Steve, we're having a vet's meeting now. Have you time to come along?'

He nodded. Thank God something was happening within The Service. Embarrassment was starting to take hold of his life. Embarrassment and disgust.

There were twelve people in the room, a jury of sorts. A small room tucked away at one corner of a large open plan office with tables and chairs scattered about and people carrying computers in and out and mobile phones ringing. And Angus MacSporran was there and appeared to be about to chair the meeting. Why wasn't Des in the chair instead of sitting in the corner as unobtrusively as possible? Once more playing the role of the calm detached observer. How is this happening? thought Steve as Angus began to lay the law down on protocols of administration. The importance of ensuring that telephone enquiries were dealt with effectively and that files were properly minuted.

'Caesar fiddled whilst Rome burned.' 'The violinist played on.' 'Like rearranging the deck chairs on the Titanic,' thought Steve.

PYTHON rules. This is PYTHON. PYTHON lives. Steve looked across at Des Quiet, expecting him to tear off his facemask to reveal himself as John Cleese. For God's sake wake up to what's happening Steve wanted to shout at him as Des Quiet nodded his head with increasing frequency like an over wound metronome.

'This Report form needs revising as well,' continued Angus.

'Actually that's a very good point,' said Des Quiet suddenly coming to life as he recognised something on which he felt capable of passing comment.

Steve wanted to scream 'It's not a very good point. It's a fucking lousy point. The form's a disaster, but changing the form isn't going to help us beat this thing. This is a fucking charade; a waste of fucking time. If you don't know that already you're a bigger fool than I thought.'

'There's been a bit of trouble this morning,' said Tommy, a nervous smile on his face. 'Two live sheep were emptied into the mass burial pit at Apsley when the lorry dumped the carcasses. They must have recovered during the journey, see. It's not bloody good enough you know. If the press get hold of stuff like that.'

Des Quiet's nodding increased in speed and intensity. Was he agreeing or expressing displeasure? Shock? Horror?

'Did you hear what happened at Apsley village hall the other night?' someone else chipped in. 'They were having a meeting to try and organise a protest against the mass burial site we're using up there and they had to...' she started to giggle hysterically, 'they had to abandon it because the hall was filling with smoke from one of the nearby pyres.' Her eyes streamed with tears, her shoulders rocked up and down. Steve joined in, grateful for the opportunity to release the tension. Black humour; essential humour. Saving humour. The best. And it was the only thing of any good that came out of the meeting.

Back in his office, Steve phoned Graham at Sage Street.

'Did you get my memo about the fell sheep Graham?' he asked. 'I'm right aren't I? We can't carry on doing this.'

'It's fine as far as it went,' said Graham. 'But you've spoilt it by being too emotional and not totally objective. The Chief Scientist and the modellers don't believe that fell sheep are worthy of being made a special case.'

'But that's because they don't understand Graham. They don't know anything about farming or animals. Or people for that matter. They're mathematicians, scientists, computer modellers. They're dealing with numbers and theories, not with flesh and blood and guts and gore. They're putting themselves forward as experts and saviours with all their measured tones and careful certainty. They know their recommendations will work. We all know that they'll work. Anyone can tell you that if you kill all the animals on premises contiguous to IPs that the disease will die out. You don't need a sophisticated computer model to work that out, it's common bloody sense. If you kill all the animals the disease will disappear. It's the same with those SOSs. If in doubt, kill it out. You hardly need vets at all now do you? Just send out any old person with a few photos of FMD and a tick box and if they can't rule out FMD then phone the slaughterers. The office girl, the cleaner; the trained chimpanzee. Anybody will do.' He was ranting. Hot and sticky with sweat down his neck, eyes wide and blazing, the sharp anguish of the last few weeks racing to the surface to escape; shaken champagne from an uncorked bottle.

'You're overtired,' Graham soothed. 'Overtired and over emotional. Take a week off. Take a break and then come back.'

'We're all tired,' said Steve. 'But Graham, where will this end? We've killed almost a million animals. If somebody said to me that if we kill another million then that will be the end of it, I'd say go ahead. But there's no guarantee of that is there? We might go to two million, then three, then four million? How many is too many? Especially when there's a vaccine just sitting waiting to be used. It's unethical. Unethical and immoral. Yes Graham, that's exactly what it is, unethical and immoral.'

'Steve,' said Graham, 'you've a great future in The Service when this is all over. The quality of your reports and ideas are really excellent. What we're doing is unpleasant and arguably wrong. But the Prime Minister is in charge. The PVO's hands are tied. We have to go with this thing; see it through. Think about it. Your future is in your hands.'

Steve said no more and hung up. He sat with his head in his hands. He felt the weight and smelt the smell of conspiracy. The whole GVS; the whole veterinary profession; conspiratorial in its complicity. The silence of its leaders an eerie tribute to what was happening. The death and destruction of tens of thousands of animals a day seemingly without a dissenting voice.

Again an understanding of the tragedies of human history pierced him like a shard of glass. The trenches in the First World war; Hitler's concentration camps where the Jews and the gypsies and the mentally ill were degraded and destroyed. The slaughter in Rwanda and more recently in Croatia and Bosnia. All encouraged and permitted by the complicity of silence. By being borne along with the flow and not thinking about what was happening all around or the part played by each person in the whole. That was the great danger. Complicity to be one of the team, one of the crowd. It took courage, even foolishness to stand against the flow and say 'No, this is wrong. This is not the way it should be and if it is then I will take no further part in it.'

He wondered to himself if he had the courage. Wondered if he had the strength of character to stand up and say 'Enough is enough.' And would it make any difference anyway? Why sacrifice his own future if the whole thing continued regardless? A senseless gesture. Worthless and unhelpful to anyone. What would be the point of that?

For how he felt inside.

That was the reason. For peace of mind; self worth; and self respect. To know that he had stood up for what he believed was right and not bowed and bended to the will of his masters through cowardice or lack of self belief. He thought of the fell sheep on Midmoor Moss. He thought of the hill farmers that owned them, sitting at home now awaiting the arrival of the slaughter teams or perhaps out gathering their flocks with their collie dogs beneath the wailing call of the curlews fresh home from their winter on the coastal salt flats. The peace and quiet of Pennine skies soon to be torn and ripped by the bleating of sheep and the wailing of hardy hill men and their wives and children whose generations of work and care would soon be turned to dust and blood that drained into the soil from which it had sprung.

His mobile rang, a name he knew lit up on the tiny screen.

'Sammy. Where are you?'

'I'm in Cardington. It's completely manic over here. More and more cases and more and more people milling around. The Brigadier seems to be in overall charge but no one is completely sure. Colin Hunt hardly comes out of his office. I despair of what is going to happen.'

'Same here,' said Steve.

'But that's not why I phoned. Look Steve, I don't know if I'm doing the right thing but Francesca is back. She booked into the hotel this

368

morning. I didn't know whether to tell you or not. But it's your life, and I know how you feel about her.'

Pounding, leaping. A heart stirred with hope and silk sheet passion, wrapped, entwined in smooth kissed arms and legs with curls of velvet chestnut, scent of salt sea air and vanilla spice; beads of dew drenched glistening oil reflecting light in rainbow tinted hue. The touch of smooth moist skin, strawberries and cream; green tinged wine of smoke and swirling oil, amber lit, reflecting her eyes with sun bright face.

His own body warm and liquid centred, oozing and churning, a bubbling cauldron of melted chocolate, sweet and aromatic, cocoa laced with sleep and pleasure.

She was come. He knew she would. Did not believe she had lied to him and betrayed his trust after all he'd said and she had understood. He knew she would return but never dared to think of when; so soon and now he was not there to welcome and comfort her. Alone and lonesome. He spoke.

'I'm coming across tonight Sammy. I'm finished here. There's nothing left.'

Sammy didn't understand. 'What do you mean?'

'Thanks for phoning Sammy,' he said. 'I'll probably see you later. Don't tell Francesca. I'll surprise her.'

He rang off and looked around the office. He closed his file. It was nearly 6.00 p.m. One of the army Corporals rushed into the room, tears streaming down his face, his mobile phone in his hand.

'It's Mrs Dawson from Windy Knoll Farm, Midmoor Moss,' he said through red faced tears. 'She's threatening to kill herself if we insist on culling her sheep. What do I say to her?'

Armageddon had arrived. It was all around them. Pain and suffering. Fire and blood. Steve could imagine the scene up on the lonely hilltops. A simple farmhouse, with stoned walled sheep pens. A thousand Swaledale ewes gathered with black faces and grey noses, a few weeks off the lambing, heavy bellied and wired fleeces. The bleating in the cool spring air, the pasture not yet greening to nourish the unborn lambs that would soon be jumping and racing across the distant hills. The work of many lives through hundreds of years gathered in the pens in front of her. The valuer writing figures in columns as though money were the answer, a sugar sweet inducement to make the medicine more palatable.

He didn't need this. There was enough stress without the thought of human blood on his hands. His body numbed by it, his head hurt by it. He'd never met or spoken to Mrs Dawson but he couldn't bear the thought of her killing herself. Nothing was worth that. Certainly not the salvage of a few hundred million pounds of export earnings.

He looked at the Corporal. A big muscular bloke in his late twenties. Camouflage battle dress and shiny black ankle boots. And tears dripping from his face like a tropical storm; red rimmed eyes. A man trained to fight and kill reduced to this by a tiny virus that couldn't be seen. No, thought Steve. Not by a virus. By our response to it. The virus wasn't killing tens of thousands of animals every day. The virus wasn't destroying the work of generations and leaving the carcasses to rot in their owner's backyard or creating dense smoked pyres with the smell of burning flesh. Nor was it causing the release of who knew what in terms of BSE prions into the environment as the brains and spinal cords of the shot cattle liquified and spilled out into the yards and into the slurry that would soon be spread on the grazing land.

No, the virus was responsible for none of these things. That responsibility lay with the policy makers. And now Mrs Dawson was threatening to kill herself.

Steve took the Corporal's phone and motioned to him to sit down.

'Mrs Dawson,' he said. 'I'm Steve Turner, one of the vets. I spoke to your husband earlier today. Can I explain to you why we need to do this?'

The words were almost too painful to say, barbed hooks that caught in his throat, in the roof of his mouth, tearing at his lips as they passed like barbed wire or the trailing fronds of brambles.

'The sheep,' she said. 'They're our life.' He heard the screaming sobs above the words. 'My father left them to me when he died. His father left them to him. They know the moor. We can't replace them. If you kill them you kill me. You townies, you don't understand,' she was screaming.

You townies, thought Steve, and smiled to himself. He knew Midmoor Moss. It was but an hour's drive from where he and Rachel had had their farm. They would drive there every few weeks with their dogs to chase hares. He thought of the dogs, a bitter sweet thought. In the end he had let them down. Abandoned them to Rachel because he had been unable to cope.

'Mrs Dawson,' he said, his voice breaking with fear. 'I understand. I know Midmoor Moss. I lived not far from there many years ago. I understand about hefted sheep. It's a horrible thing to have happened. It's a horrible thing to have to do...'

'Then why can't we wait and see if they get the disease?' she sobbed. 'Why can't we keep them isolated? Keep us isolated. Why can't we do that?'

Why not indeed, thought Steve. Why not do as she suggested? Because that was not the policy. The policy was clear. Kill everything on contiguous premises. There was no ambiguity. No room for veterinary judgement. No room for common sense.

Pain pierced his body. The pain of deception and lies. The pain of lack of time and energy to fight this thing. To stand in its path and turn back the tide that ran ever faster, ever stronger. Could he stand up to it? Did he have the strength and stamina to fight against it?

'Mrs Dawson,' he said, his voice rushing on before his mind could check it. 'I'm on your side, believe me. I agree with what you're saying. We'll postpone the slaughter for now. I'll send an e-mail to head office explaining the problem and advising that we quarantine and blood test the sheep later. I can't guarantee that they'll agree, but it's the best that I can do. Please, please, don't do anything silly in the meantime. Do you understand what I'm saying?'

'Yes,' she sobbed. 'Thank you, thank you,' her voice floated away into the mist that surrounded him.

Steve looked at the Corporal. 'Tell your men to hold off on the slaughter of all the flocks on Midmoor Moss. I'll e-mail Sage Street now.'

'Yes Sir,' said the Corporal. He was smiling.

Steve left the office at 7.00 p.m. He said goodbye to Daniel, told him he was heading back to Cardington.

'Not another one that can't stand the pace,' Daniel joked. 'I sent poor old Keith back home earlier this afternoon for a week's rest. He was like jelly. We should never have let Beryl and Nancy off together.'

Steve nodded. 'Good luck Daniel,' he said, and shook his hand.

He took the road over the Pennines, heading west. It was dark but dry at least with no sign of freezing. He was about half way to

Cardington and coming up to a sharp bend to the right. He knew it well. Just past here was a farmhouse set back fifty yards or so from the road with farm buildings stretched out for thirty or forty yards along the roadside. Coming in the opposite direction he had frequently seen young fattening pigs snuffling around on the other side of a galvanised gate. Rounding the corner something caught his eye. Parked at the side of the road in the lea of the buildings was a car he recognised. Running from the gate where he'd so often seen the pigs he saw a figure he recognised too. She wore no wellies or protective clothing and she had her head down, furtive and anxious. She did not look like one who was on official business.

Another second and he was past and he pressed the accelerator to get well out ahead of her. He didn't know if she'd seen him, she hadn't looked up, intent on keeping her head down, her face hidden. It was all becoming clear in his mind as to what was going on. The suspicious happenings of the last few weeks were coming together at last. Coming together and forming a picture of deceit, misery and terror. He shivered in spite of the heater whining full on. Not with cold outside but an ice cold within. A chemical cold of emotion, steel sharp; a knife glistening and moving in random cuts, nicking and slicing; a childhood nightmare when there is nowhere to run and nowhere to hide.

The hairs on his neck rippled. His mouth had the dry sour feel of something bitter, like putting alum on a mouth ulcer. He moved his lips and cheeks, tried to get the saliva to flow, his throat dry and stuck; he swallowed, there was nothing there, just an empty space and the bitter metallic taste of fear.

A shot of adrenaline exploded inside him like a firework, a burning flaming firework in the depth of his stomach, spinning and turning, heating and paining the coils of his guts and the folds of his stomach. His liver burning, throbbing, blood red oozing, draining, as the vessels supplying it shut tight and those supplying his heart and lungs opened wide. Fight or flight, he was trapped in the cockpit of his car, he pushed the accelerator hard with fear and excitement, tyres screaming round bends, letting the adrenaline burn.

He didn't know who to tell. He had no proof. All the evidence was circumstantial. Everyone would think he was mad. But it all fitted. Every little piece fitted together to make the clear, unambiguous picture of a cold blooded killer driven by an unshakeable and single minded desire.

Disbelief settled on him. Low cloud, damp and chilling. Touching and caressing every part of him. He couldn't believe it was happening. Not to him. It was the thing of films and plays, books and comics, not of real life. He shivered and shook, gripping the steering wheel tight, not daring to slow down lest she catch up with him. Fear of breaking down on this lonely road with her just behind churned his stomach and tore at his heart. Time and again he looked in the mirror fearing to see the headlights of her car; her shining eyes staring back at him from behind the seats, a syringe and needle in her hand; a vision of loveliness and cruel death; the white teeth with pink tongue thrust between them, streams of blood spilling out through laughing lips and across her chin, spattering the simple white t-shirt stretched across her breasts.

He remembered her unashamed desires and wants; steaming hair plastered to her neck with rain and sweat, steaming with the passion of sexual arousal, muscles taut and firm in pain wracked ecstasy. He saw her arched spine, the weight of her pressing onto him; heard the moans and smelt the wind whipped sea. He placed his hands on either side of her head and tilted her face up to him so that he could look into her eyes.

He glanced in the mirror again and the shock of Rachel looking back at him made him cry out loud. He looked at the road ahead, back at the mirror and she was gone. He was sweating. Cold and greasy sweat. Shivering and shuddering. The whole damn fucking world had gone mad and he was somewhere at the centre with everything spinning round about him. Spinning so fast he couldn't see what was happening out towards the edges. So fast he thought he might lose his grip and spin off into the depths of space or collapse and shrivel like a spent autumn leaf.

He saw the lights of Cardington in the distance and breathed slow and deep. Francesca, Francesca, he thought. Oh my love Francesca, I love you more than I can ever tell you. I love you more than I loved Rachel. I love you more than I have loved anyone or anything in my life before. I will love you forever.

He pulled into the hotel car park. Emotional and mental exhaustion weakened him. He drooped against the steering wheel like a marathon runner at the end of the race, and then with an effort climbed out of his Healey and locked the door. He staggered up the steps of the hotel and went through the swing doors to reception and there she was, sitting facing the door with her chestnut hair falling gently to her shoulders, her eyes smiling and laughing at him as though she had been waiting all evening. And suddenly everything was alright.

He ran to her and as she stood to welcome him he threw his arms around her waist and pulled her to him and kissed her on the neck and smelt the soft delicate scented smell of her and he sobbed into her neck like a child and she linked her arms around his shoulders and from the corner of his tear streaked eyes he saw HER hurrying towards the stairs with a look of determined hate spread across her handsome face.

Chapter 47

He lay in his bed awake and thinking. CNN news at 6.00 a.m. had focused on the cull of livestock and the Chief Scientist had given a measured and polished performance explaining the need to implement his recommendations in full or risk disaster. He had showed the graphs and projections again and the visions of the mathematical modellers had been elevated to that of prophets or the Messiah himself. There was no one in authority with the courage to question the data on which the predictions were based, far less suggest that what was being done was wrong. Ron Steady had disappeared.

Francesca loved him. Her husband Carlo had begged her not to leave him and she had stayed in Italy to try and persuade him to let her go. He had refused and finally she had left. In desperation. To see Steve. To see him and find out if her feelings for him were real. Complete love and sublimation. And their meeting last night had confirmed it. Desperate, unashamed love and happiness. She had wanted him last night but he had taken her to her room and kissed her on the forehead and told her that he would love her forever and then left her. He loved her too much. Loved her beyond sex.

He had gone to bed and he had lain awake all night thinking of Francesca and Paul and Rachel and everything that had happened in his life. He had tried to understand it all and decide what he was to do. He needed some evidence before he went to the police. So far there was only suspicion. He needed to get proof. He would watch and observe and meanwhile tell his suspicions to no one. Not even to Francesca.

He reached the office early. He wanted to speak to Neil about the hefted sheep to see if he was of the same opinion.

'Now then Steve lad,' Neil said when Steve entered his office. 'This memo of yours has created quite a stir. Graham's been asked by the PVO to come up with some ideas on it and apparently PYTHON are saying it's a load of crap and shouldn't be allowed to influence the policy. Quite right lad. Make the buggers think and justify what they're doing. Do you know, I even offered to take one of the modellers to a farm during slaughter to show him what really went on. He refused point blank. Said he didn't want to compromise his objectivity.'

'I can't carry on with this Neil,' Steve said suddenly. 'I don't believe in it and I can't do it. It's too brutal. We're turning into Barbarians. This is Barbarism. We're living it and condoning it. Taking part in it when there's a perfectly good alternative.'

'Vaccination?'

'Yeah. We should vaccinate. Forget our export trade for the next year or two and if necessary subsidise the humane slaughter of excess fatstock. It would be a fuck sight cheaper in monetary terms and I'm not kidding you Neil, I think we're in serious danger of losing our humanity here.'

'Sit down,' said Neil. 'You know the problems of vaccination don't you.'

'Not all the science, but most of it. I know the pitfalls and dangers. But we're the only country in the world that has tried to deal with an outbreak of this size without recourse to vaccination. Surely we're not the only ones who are right? Don't tell me that. You've seen what's happening on farms Neil. You've seen the animal and human suffering and misery. You've seen the incompetence of our leaders, the hours of hard work that everybody on the ground is putting in. The tears of the office staff, half of whom have got friends and family who've lost stock or are going to lose stock. The policy we're pursuing is out of control. No one can put a finger on how many more animals are going to be slaughtered. It's a blank cheque with no one in control or responsible. The PVO seems to have washed his hands of it. Taken a back seat to see where we end up.

'Rascal Ron's mystery tour to hell and back. That's assuming we make it back. We're vets Neil, not butchers and politicians. These are live animals we're talking about, not sacks of spuds or cubic metres of sand. Everyone seems to have forgotten that. The great mantra that the Ministry has been quoting at farmers for years that "economics can't take preference over animal welfare", appears to have been conveniently forgotten. How are we going to recover from this? How are we going to stand up at the end of it and look at ourselves in the mirror in the morning, let alone look another farmer in the face who isn't looking after his sheep properly?

'We've turned our back on the animals Neil. What about the promise we all make on qualifying? "That our constant endeavour will be to safeguard the welfare of animals committed to our care." There was no caveat to that promise. No, "Providing it's economically expedient to do so." Or, "Providing the Ministry doesn't tell me I've got to do otherwise."

'We're letting them down Neil. We're letting ourselves down. We've tried our best but the thing has beaten us. We need to change tack, to fight it in a different way. Not to be blinkered and blinded by the pure scientists and their fucking computer models who wouldn't know a sheep from a cow from a pig and would care even less anyway. We can kill the virus by killing all the animals but we won't have won. It'll be a pyrrhic victory, a victory of our own bloody-minded dogma and our refusal to not just consider the alternative but to grasp it too. And the alternative isn't bad Neil. An alternative that's far more constructive and gentle and less damaging to the environment. Instead of fighting fire with fire we should fight it with an all engulfing rain. A gentle harmless rain that will damp the fire down and stop it spreading. And if any little hot spots re-emerge well we can stamp on them hard.

'But carry on like this and we're heading for oblivion. And may God have mercy on us.'

There was silence. Neil looked at the floor and Jenny wiped tears from her eyes and busied herself sorting files and checking e-mails. Steve slumped into a chair.

'So what are you going to do?' Neil asked gently. 'I agree with a lot of what you've said but the Government aren't going to change course as far as I can see. The PM's thinking of the election. He wants this all hushed up by early June. All we can do is battle on and try and save animals here and there if we get the opportunity.'

'I don't know what I'm going to do,' said Steve as though Neil were no longer there. 'I just know I can't carry on with this. It'll kill me.'

'Look,' said Neil, 'take the day off. Go into Cardington. Get a few beers down your neck and have a think about things. Come back tomorrow and you might feel differently.'

Steve nodded. 'Okay Neil.' He went out, stooped, shuffling, as though his life was being sucked from him.

'Is he right?' asked Jenny.

'Of course he is,' snapped Neil. 'Now let's get back to work.'

Steve stumbled through the main office, his head pointing to the ground ignoring the chaos around him. The army might have arrived but the mayhem was continuing.

He drove into town and found a coffee shop. Bought himself a cappuccino, a newspaper; to relax and think. So much going on and so much of it unclear

His mobile rang. It was Francesca.

'Steve, where are you?' She was happy.

'I'm at a coffee shop in Cardington.' He wished she was there with him.

'I just phoned to say that Sonia has asked me to have lunch with her so I will see you later,' she said.

Cold damp fear. He had forgotten. Too much on his mind. Too much emotion. Sonia, Sonia, he couldn't believe he'd forgotten about her. She was mad. Completely raving bonkers, he knew that now. He'd worked it all out. Completely mad and she was having lunch with Francesca. His Francesca. Don't alarm her, he thought, his hands sweating, his face and neck burning with heat.

Why was Sonia asking Francesca out to lunch? There could be only one reason. He had seen her face last night as she passed them in reception. He'd seen her running to the car. He should have gone to the police this morning. 'Oh God keep her safe,' he said to himself, thinking, thinking of what to do.

'Francesca,' he said, 'where are you?'

'I am in the vets' room at the Animal Health Office. But I am very hungry Mr Steve so you must very quickly say what you have to say to me.' She was teasing him.

'Is Sonia there?' he asked her.

'Yes, she is making coffee. Do you want to speak to her?'

'No, no, that's fine. Can you wait twenty minutes before you go to lunch? I want to ask you something. It can't wait, I'll come back straight away. No, don't tell Sonia you called me. Just delay going to lunch until I get there,' his voice cracked with fear.

'What is wrong Steve?' said Francesca suddenly serious. 'What is the matter? Are you alright Steve?'

'I'm fine. Please don't move. Promise me you won't leave. Wait for me. Don't tell Sonia you've spoken to me. Trust me. Do you trust me?' he was shouting.

'Yes, I do trust you Steve.' Francesca's voice was pale.

'Good, stay where you are. I'll see you soon.'

He was running to his car now breathing hard, cold sweat on his cheeks. He reached the deep blue Healey and jumped in, the throaty roar from the exhaust giving him comfort. He screeched out of the car park, heading for the Animal Health Office, weaving in and out of the traffic on the one way system. His heart was pounding, thumping in his chest and in his ears, his legs were shaking, his breathing fast and shallow. He couldn't lose her now. Not now. Not when he'd just found her. Faster, faster, he sounded his horn, swerving round lorries, he heard the sound of metal against metal behind him.

He heard Rachel's voice in his head: 'Steve, what's happening Sunshine? What's the hurry?'

He wanted to tell her to shut the fuck up. Tell her that he wasn't her Sunshine and to get out of his fucking life for good. He hadn't time or energy for her. She was his past. Francesca was his future. She was his life. Her life was his life. He could not lose her now.

He slowed as he pulled into the car park at the Animal Health Office. Grabbing his notebook he found the number of Cardington Police. He dialled them and told them who he was.

'I know who killed Paul Smythe,' he said. 'A girl called Sonia, Sonia Carlton. She's in the Animal Health Office and I've every reason to believe she's dangerous. I think she wants to harm my girlfriend. Can you come quickly? Please, please. Come quickly. The Animal Health Office, Cardington. I've got to go. I've got to go and protect her.' He threw his mobile down and jumped out of the car.

'You can't leave it there,' someone shouted. 'I need to get out. I'm going on a report case. I've got to get there within an hour to meet the targets.'

'Fuck off,' Steve shouted as he pushed past him and raced into the building and up the stairs to the vets' room. His pulse was missing beats, he felt sick and dizzy, a dream, a nightmare, the lack of sleep, it was his imagination, paranoia. 'Got to get her away from Sonia,' he said to himself. 'I must get her away from Sonia.'

He stopped at the door to the room breathing fast. He tried to control it, to slow it down, got to be calm, he thought. Like hunting a wounded animal. Mustn't panic it, mustn't corner it; don't let it turn at bay, that was when it was at its most dangerous.

He went slowly into the room. It was packed. Lunchtime. People eating sandwiches and reading newspapers, the hustle and bustle of conversation; the rustle of paper, the chink of spoons on china.

He scanned the room, Julie and Conrad together talking, he caught their eye and they went into a huddled whisper. What were they up to? he thought. What was their part in all this? His eyes darted around, searching, searching for Francesca; where was she? Where was she? Surely she hadn't left already.

Towards him, the chestnut hair flowing down her back. The other side of the room. Good. She was there. He dare not call her. He began to inch his way over, halfway there, relief flooding over him and then her eyes; Sonia's eyes staring over Francesca's shoulder at him; fearful eyes; the trapped eyes of a maniac; locked into his own so that they could read each other's thoughts. And in that moment they both knew that the game was up.

Steve made towards her.

'Francesca,' he called. She turned smiling with joy at his voice and then Sonia had her by the arm, twisting it up behind her back tight so that she cried out in pain and from the corner of her eye saw the syringe and hypodermic needle with the clear yellow fluid just inches from her neck.

'Don't come any closer Steve,' Sonia spat it out like a viper, sweat glistening on her forehead, the light of madness gleaming in her eyes.

'If you come any closer I'll stick this Immobilon into her,' Sonia shouted.

The room cleared from around her. People were screaming, chairs kicked over in the rush.

'Keep still,' shouted Steve. 'Keep quiet.' He looked at Francesca. The fear in her face was like a knife in his throat. Sonia, shaking with rage, inched her forward towards the door.

'Sonia, it's over,' Steve said gently, watching her all the time, trying to maintain eye contact.

'Let Francesca go. She's not a part of this. She's done nothing to you.'

'Shut up,' screamed Sonia. 'You can't beat me. Nobody can beat me. Look what happened to Paul. He thought he could beat me and now he's dead.' She laughed. 'And so too will be sweet Francesca if you try to stop me.'

'You killed Paul?' Julie said from a corner of the room. 'You told us you thought Steve had done it. You said you needed our help to trap him. That's why we agreed to help you.'

Sonia laughed again. 'You were so easy to fool,' she said. 'It was as though you wanted it to be Steve. Hell hath no fury like a woman scorned Julie. I knew you'd believe me.'

'Sonia,' Steve said, 'the police are on their way. They'll be here any minute. Put the syringe down and let Francesca go. There's been enough pain. Enough suffering. There's no point in any more.'

'Suffering?' she shouted. 'You don't know the meaning of suffering. None of you do.' She screamed it out looking round the room at the faces watching her. 'Now move away from the door. Move away from the door or I'll kill her,' she screamed again.

Fernando glanced questioningly at Steve. He shook his head, a tiny imperceptible movement. His head was thick with indecision. He had to do the right thing: had to get it right.

'Sonia,' he said, 'just let her go and leave. No one will stop you. Let Francesca come here or if you like I'll swop places with her. She's only been here a few weeks. She knows nothing of all this.'

Sonia raised her syringe hand a fraction. 'Keep back and shut up Steve Turner. I don't care about her. It's you I care about. You're the one that used me. You're the one that must suffer. Just like our high and mighty PVO who used me all those years ago and left me to pick up the pieces. I swore I'd pay him back and bringing Swine Fever and Foot and Mouth back from Asia with me seemed such a simple idea. Simple and devastating.

'Swine Fever was too easy though, all under control within a few months and a pat on the back for everyone into the bargain. This is a different story though isn't it? This will finish him. He'll be out on the streets looking for another job by the time this is at an end.'

'You've been spreading it too haven't you?' he said quietly.

'Deliberately infecting farms.'

'Of course I have. It was so easy. Too easy. Handling all that infected material every day, taking samples. Lamb hearts for the lab. Except they never made it to the lab. They all went into Mr and Mrs Piggie's dinner,' her voice was high, filled with laughter.

'That's why you asked Keith for a list of farms with pigs wasn't it? So you knew where to find them.'

'Quite the detective now aren't we. Steve Turner, failed epidemiologist, now turned detective.' She was closer to the door now. 'Keep back,' she screamed and held the needle closer to Francesca's neck. 'Keep away.'

Francesca had closed her eyes. He lips made tiny movements as though she were praying, her breathing fast and shallow. She was ten feet from Steve. Ten feet from paradise; a few seconds or minutes from paradise lost.

He had to keep Sonia talking. Had to try and calm her down. She was shaking with rage and hate. The police would soon be there. They would know what to do. She couldn't escape. There was a room full of witnesses to her confessions. Just a few more minutes, nobody do anything stupid, please God, please, thought Steve. Stay calm everyone. Stay calm.

'Let Francesca go and get yourself away Sonia,' Steve said. 'We won't follow you, I promise. I'll stand by the door and stop anyone leaving. You can get away if you go now. Go abroad again. Leave her be.'

She was almost at the door, her back to it, facing Steve and the rest of the people in the room, who stared back at her, fascinated by the primeval look on her face; lips and cheeks contorted like a snarling dog. She twisted Francesca's arm tighter, her eyes opened with the pain, black terror sparked across the gap that separated her from Steve. Pleading loving eyes, he saw in them a Bosnian Moslem dragged from her husband to be sent to a house of prostitution; a Jew to be sent to the forced labour camps of the 'Final Solution'. And he understood their despair. The helpless despair when there is no hope. A finality of suffering with no expectation of reprieve. Only this time the expectation was still alive. This time it would be alright. It had to be alright. Calmness and time. Calmness and time.

The door opened and Jason a VO from the Allocations desk came in. 'I need five clean vets straight away for report cases,' he said. He stopped, felt the silence, saw the anguish, the pale shocked look in Francesca's eyes, the syringe raised ready like the executioner's axe, the plunging hand, downwards with force through the skin and into the shoulder muscles.

'She's finished Steve,' Sonia shrieked and she let go her hold on Francesca and was out through the door before anybody could stop her.

Chapter 48

Steve caught Francesca in his arms, pulled the syringe out and held it up to the light. There was a millilitre of Immobilon left in it. He had no idea how much had been injected. It didn't take much, a needle full perhaps.

Francesca was sobbing in his arms.

'It's alright,' he said, 'I'm here. You're okay now, you're okay.' He turned to Jason. 'Do you have Narcan in the safe here?'

'I...., I think so,' Jason said.

'Get it now,' he was shouting. 'Hurry. Bring it all here with some 5 ml syringes and 21 gauge needles. Hurry for fuck's sake. Run.'

'Are you there Steve?' Francesca said, her words pale and indistinct. 'I love you Steve.' She swayed, felt heavy in his arms and he let her sink to the floor and lay her on her side.

'I love you too,' he said. 'You'll be fine. You can't leave me now Francesca. Not when I've just found you. Not now. Not you.' His tears fell onto her clothes and he held her hand tight.

She was sinking. Ebbing and floating away from him on the retreating tide. She was trying to open her eyes but her lids were heavy, her pupils black, constricted like tiny full stops; the end: finis.

'Don't go to sleep my love,' Steve said. He held her hand tight, it was already cold, her breathing slow and deep, a blueing of the skin around her lips and nose.

'Don't sleep Francesca. Please don't sleep.' Tenderly he undid the buttons of her polo shirt from her throat.

'Where the fuck is that Narcan?' he screamed. 'Someone go and tell Jason to hurry up.'

He stroked her forehead, cold and clammy, rolled her onto her back and watched her chest rise and fall, slowly, slowly.

'You'll be okay,' he cried. She could not hear him And all he could hear were the sobs of those around him and feel the touch of Fernando's hand on his shoulder.

Slowly and slow her chest rose and fell, her lips blue like the ocean on a winter's day, her fingers cold and pale. He felt at her wrist for her pulse, irregular and slow with missed beats.

'You must not die,' he wept. 'You must not die,' his face buried in her neck by her ear, his hand on her chest to feel the fall and the rise, the fall and the rise and the fall…

'She has stopped breathing,' said Fernando. 'We must give her CPR.'

Steve tilted her head back and taking a deep breath and holding her mouth closed covered her nose with his mouth, blowing the air into her lungs and watching her chest rise. Twice he did it and then, placing his hands one on top of the other over her breastbone, he gave fifteen firm downward thrusts.

'I've got it,' said Jason, panting into the room, sweat on his face. 'Do you really think you need …' he stopped in mid flow at the sight of the corpse stretched out on the ground in front of him.

Steve grabbed it from him, his hands stiff and shaking.

'Fernando, carry on with CPR. Do you know what to do?'

Fernando nodded and immediately inflated her lungs twice more and gave her chest another fifteen thrusts.

'Please God, please God,' Steve said aloud as he loaded 5 ml of Narcan into a syringe. 'Hold her arm for me,' he shouted at someone. It was Sammy. Dear Sammy with tears in her eyes who turned over the limp arm to expose the deep blue veins beneath the dull blue skin. She squeezed hard above the elbow and Steve fumbling and trembling pushed the needle through the skin, drawing back on the syringe plunger and sighing with relief as the thick, dark, too dark by far, blood, swirled into the syringe.

Sammy released her grip and he injected all five mls of the Narcan into her vein. It was a start at least. A step in the right direction. He looked at his watch: 12.53.

'Keep going Fernando,' he said. 'Don't stop. Don't ever stop. I'll give her some more in a couple of minutes. How much have we got?'

'There're three bottles of ten ml each,' said Jason. He was shaking.

'Has anyone phoned an ambulance?' Steve asked.

'I phoned for one,' said Julie. 'They're on their way. I'm so sorry Steve.'

He squeezed her arm, gently with compassion. She squeezed his hand.

The blue colour in Francesca's face was unchanged. He felt for a pulse. There was nothing. Nothing. Nothing. He wanted to turn and run. Run and run and never stop running; back to the farm; to a pond; to a loaded shotgun; a syringe with clear yellow fluid that held the power over life and death. He wanted to put the responsibility in someone else's hands, let them take over and he would run and wait and the world would turn and then it would be all over.

'Shall I give Fernando a break?' said Sandy Oz, and Steve nodded.

And suddenly he felt calm. He was in charge and he was doing his best and Francesca depended on him. He drew up another 5 ml of Narcan and hit the vein again first time. He injected it and loaded another clean syringe. He sat for a minute and then took Francesca's wrist. A pulse, a pulse. Weak and thin but it was there, beating by itself.

'She's got a pulse,' he said out loud. Keep going with the breathing Sandy but stop the cardiac massage for a while.' He felt for her pulse again, it was stronger and as he injected another 5 ml of Narcan, the blood looked less black.

The pulse was growing more regular too and although her hands were still cold and clammy, the blueness of her lips was less sombre, a paler sky blue instead of the dirty grey blue of the ocean's swell.

'Try letting her breathe herself,' he said to Sandy.

The whole room watched like at the climax to a film; silent and in dread of what was to come. Thirty seconds passed; forty seconds; there was nothing, but the pulse was still strong.

'I think I should give her some more breaths,' said Sandy and then gently, agonisingly, her chest rose, just a touch and then fell again. A few seconds later and again, only higher this time, then down and up again.

'She's breathing,' said Steve and he heard the sound of people weeping.

'Move back. Let them through. Move away.'

Two paramedics in green overalls came across to where Francesca lay on the floor.

'Etorphine overdose,' said Steve. 'A morphine derivative. I've given her 15 ml of Narcan i/v and she's had CPR but she's breathing by herself now.' He was trembling and now the tears came. Huge salt tears streaming down his face. Sobbing and shaking. He clung to Sammy as an oxygen mask was placed over Francesca's nose and mouth, hugging her to him and feeling her arms around his waist.

'It's okay Steve,' she said. 'You've saved her. She's going to be fine. Her colour's better already, nearly pink. You have your whole life ahead of you with her.'

'Does anyone want to come in the ambulance with her?' a paramedic asked.

Steve kissed Sammy and went forward.

'Are you her partner?' the man asked.

'Yes,' said Steve through his tears. 'Yes, I'm her partner.'

He followed the stretcher down the stairs. There were policemen everywhere. They went through the office on the ground floor, past Sonia handcuffed to a policewoman and with two male police officers in attendance. She looked at Steve but showed no emotion. He ignored her. He felt no hate or malice, only pity. An overwhelming pity that it had happened this way.

He climbed into the ambulance and sat beside the stretcher. Francesca was breathing regularly and deeply, her lips a healthy pink, her hands too, and warmer; the cold clammy feel of death had left her. He stroked her hair and she opened her eyes, the pupils still constricted, tiny black dots in orange green irises.

'My love,' he said. 'My love,' and he held her hand and wept and the faintest smile crossed her lips and he felt the love in her finger tips and he thanked God that she had been spared and he wondered if he would ever sleep again.

Chapter 49

Steve returned to the hotel at 10.00 p.m. Sammy and Willie, Fernando and Sarah were there in the bar. There was no joy. No laughter. His smile told them that Francesca was well.

'She'll be in hospital a couple of days,' he said, 'but no permanent harm done. Not physical harm anyway,' he added thoughtfully.

Willie patted him on the back. 'You big English poof,' he said. 'I didn't think you had it in you,' and then he was serious. 'Well done,' he said. 'Sammy told me. You were fucking brilliant.'

Steve smiled. He didn't feel brilliant. Felt like a child that wanted its mother.

Fernando shook his hand. 'It is amazing what you did. I will never forget it.'

Steve patted him on the shoulder. 'Your CPR was pretty good too. And Sandy's. Where is he?'

'He's in the restaurant,' said Sammy. 'How is Francesca feeling?'

'Confused. Still terrified I think. Can't believe what's happened to her.' He began to shake.

'Aye, sit down Steve and I'll get you a pint,' said Willie.

'How did you know that Sonia had killed Paul and spread the disease?' asked Sarah. 'I had no idea, no suspicion even.'

'It was just circumstances,' said Steve, taking a drink from the glass Willie put in his hand. 'Lots of little things that I heard and saw that just kept cropping up and always Sonia's name on them. I suppose what really made me think was when I heard her arguing with Ron Steady and threatening that she'd get even with him. It seems like she had an affair with him years and years ago, got pregnant and he paid for an abortion for her before dumping her. There was a bitterness and hate in her voice. More than just anger. A pathological desire for revenge I would say. And then I kept hearing things that I couldn't explain.'

'Like?' said Sammy.

'Well, a farmer told me that she'd taken lamb's hearts to send to the lab to confirm disease. Why would anyone take lamb's hearts? There're no instructions for that. It didn't make sense. And she asked Keith for a list of all the premises with pigs. She told him I'd asked for it but that was a lie. Why?

'Then I started to notice that when there was an outbreak well away from the main hotspots it followed the same pattern. It always started in pigs that were housed next to the public road.'

'So?' said Willie.

'Well, pigs aren't easy to infect by the respiratory route so it was unlikely to be through virus thrown up by passing traffic. An initial outbreak in pigs is more likely to be through eating infected material.

So it struck me that maybe Sonia was seeking out pig farms with pigs next to the road and was simply throwing infected material into them.'

'Like lamb's hearts,' said Fernando.

'Exactly. Easy to do and unlikely to be caught. Especially if you do it after dark. All the evidence eaten of course.'

'It's easy to put all those things together now,' said Sarah. 'But surely it wasn't enough to tackle her like you did this morning?'

'No, you're right, but coming home last night from Morton I saw her running away from a pig shed by the road, back to her car. It confirmed everything I'd thought. And then when she came in last night when I was in the lobby with Francesca she looked at me with such hate that I just knew that she wanted revenge on me too for packing her in last year. All the horrid things that had happened to me; the letter with the razor blade; the slashed hood of my car; and of course the paint and razor blades on Francesca's car. They all fitted in with the picture I now had of her. And then when Francesca phoned me today to say that Sonia had asked her to lunch I just knew that she was going to do something wicked. That's why I told Francesca to stay put until I got back. I thought she'd be safe.' He stopped and shivered.

'How did you know Sonia killed Paul?' asked Sammy.

'I didn't but it just fitted in. You remember the Swine Fever samples that went missing? I guessed it must have been Sonia that took them to spread the disease down there. I suppose Paul found out somehow. Perhaps he saw her do it or saw them in her car. Who knows, maybe she even told him in a moment of excitement and then regretted it. The evening before he was killed he told me that he had something he wanted to tell me. He looked scared and worried. Maybe he told Sonia he was going to have to report her and that's why she killed him, to cover her tracks. Paul was a nice guy but he was a threat to her. As simple as that.'

'So has Sonia been spreading FMD to all the farms?' said Sarah.

'No,' said Steve, 'there's no need. The farmers are quite good enough at that themselves. Not on purpose of course, but because they've got stock all over the place that needs visiting and feeding and they really don't understand about disinfection. Colin Hunt and Sage Street won't have it of course. They're still banging on about it being silent disease in sheep spilling over into cattle. They don't seem to be worried about the need to explain how it's getting into the sheep.

'No I'm sure Sonia was just giving it a helping hand from time to time as the opportunity presented itself. Spreading it further afield to create confusion and panic amongst us all and then just letting it spread itself.'

'Well she's succeeded as far as the confusion and panic is concerned,' said Willie. 'There's certainly no shortage of that.'

'The stupid thing is that for a long time I thought Julie and Conrad were involved with Paul's death. Just because Conrad looks like a stalker I thought he had to be one. And again I thought the motive was jealousy because I'd gone out with Sonia.'

'What a tangled web we weave,' said Sammy, but she was contemplative.

Hearing their names, Conrad and Julie came over to join them.

'Steve,' Julie said. 'I'm so sorry. For everything. Is Francesca going to be okay?'

'Yeah. Fine, fine,' he said. He smiled and took hold of her hand.

'Sonia told us she was certain that you'd killed Paul and that you were spreading the disease. She convinced us Steve. Convinced us to follow you around and get some hard evidence.'

'We were so stupid,' said Conrad. 'I can't believe it now. We're sorry.' He held out his hand and Steve shook it.

'Sonia took us all in,' he said. 'Thank God it's over now.'

'Yes, thanks God,' said Fernando, 'but Foot and Mouth is not over. We are only just beginning there I think. The problem is still the same. What should we do about it?'

There was silence.

Steve drank his pint and bought a round of drinks for everyone. 'I'm off to bed,' he said shortly. 'I need to think. There's too much going on that I don't agree with. I don't know how to deal with it but by tomorrow I will. I'll see you in the morning.'

Sammy followed him out of the bar and put her arm round his waist. 'Don't be too hard on yourself,' she said. 'You can't change the world you know.'

'No, you're right Sammy,' he said, 'but I don't have to do it if I don't agree with it. None of us do.' He kissed her on the cheek. 'Don't worry, I'm not going to do anything stupid.'

He went to bed but sleep, if it came, was fitful and unnerving.

The visions came and danced in his mind; lambs bleating and babies crying. Machetes and blood, flesh crawling and writhing; the sound of screams and cries, pleading for life. The click of captive bolts, the crash of metal, hollow laughter; the stench of rotting and burning flesh. It was frenzy and thoughtless. A job to be done.

When he had seen enough he felt the hot sourness of nausea, the metal taste at the back of his throat and he made his way to the bathroom to vomit. Then he had a shower before sitting in a chair to read Hemmingway, and at 7.30 a.m. he went to the dining room and ate a huge fried breakfast.

He returned to his room and phoned the hospital and spoke to Francesca for a few minutes. She was to stay there all day and he promised to visit her later. Then he took out a pen and put the following heading at the top of the page.

2nd April 2001
Memorandum to: Ron Steady, PVO
From: S Turner VO, Epidemiology

And then he began.

FOOT AND MOUTH DISEASE CONTROL

1. I have already expressed my opinion verbally that current Foot and Mouth Disease control policy is flawed.

2. I should like to reaffirm my opinion that to continue to rely solely on a Stamping-out policy will be too costly in terms of the number of animals slaughtered and the ill-effects on human health and welfare, both Ministry of Rural Affairs staff and farmers. I believe that the use of vaccine against Foot and Mouth Disease should be sanctioned immediately. It should be used on farms contiguous to IPs instead of the contiguous cull of susceptible stock. Vaccination should then be used on other farms in the infected areas until new cases of the disease cease.

3. I believe that the slaughter policy is now proceeding in an irrational manner without veterinary judgement and without informed consideration of the consequences. I believe it is unethical and immoral.

4. I should like to inform you that from the time of despatch of this memorandum I must withdraw from the FMD eradication campaign on grounds of conscience and I tender my resignation from the Government Veterinary Service forthwith.

5. I have prepared a report for Neil Franks summarising the Epidemiology of the disease outbreak in the area for which I am responsible, and this can be used to brief my replacement.

Steve Turner
Epidemiology

Once he had finished he made himself a cup of tea. Relief and tiredness tinged with the hollow grey of saddest moments. Emotions he knew well in a context long since passed. He thought of Francesca and Rachel and Sonia. Three women that he knew. One he loved; one he had loved; and the other he had merely desired. A breath of wind through the open window stirred his feelings like dried leaves in a gale, changing the picture. There was something missing from his thoughts. Something obvious but lost, like a familiar word or song. He tried to reach it but could not.

He drove to the Animal Health Office and went to see Neil.

'Steve. How are you? What's the news on Francesca? This Sonia girl. Is she round the twist?'

'I think so,' said Steve, 'and Francesca's fine.'

'And you?' asked Jenny.

'I'll be fine,' he said, and smiled at her. 'Neil, I need to speak to you,' he hesitated, looked away and swallowed.

'Right Stevie lad, spit it out 'cos I think I know already what you're going to say.'

Steve looked him straight in the eye. 'I'm very conscious of letting you down. Letting the whole team down. All my colleagues; my friends; the farmers; everyone really. But I can't carry on with this. I don't believe in it and to keep going I think you've got to believe it's right. I don't believe it's right Neil. I think there is another way but I know that I can't change it. I'm going to resign. As of now. I've written the letter and I'd like Jenny to type it for me if she will.

'I'll write a summary report today of where I think we are with the epidemiology in the east and then I'm going to pack my bags and leave. I don't feel happy about it but I know it's what's right for me.'

'What are you going to do about work if you resign?' said Neil. 'I know it's none of my business but have you thought all this through?'

'Yeah, of course,' he said. 'I've thought everything through and I've no idea what I'm going to do. What I do know is that I can't keep doing this. I can't carry on. I have no choice. But I'll be fine. Rest assured. I'll be fine,' he smiled.

Neil smiled back. 'At least you've got the balls to stand up and be counted. That's more than can be said for some of the spineless twats around here.'

'I'm going to the hospital now. To see Francesca. Would you type this please Jenny and I'll come back and sign it?'

'Of course,' she said, her voice choked with tears.

'Thanks. I'll see you later.'

Francesca was sitting up in bed, a drip in her left arm. When she saw Steve her face became like an angel's, the orange and green eyes shining, the pupils now a healthy size of inky blackness, brilliant and dancing with excitement. Her hair, chestnut streaked with auburn tints, her skin clear but uncommonly pale, radiant like an Empress.

Steve kissed her on the forehead. She shivered and pulled the covers around her.

'I thought I'd lost you,' he said. 'I thought I'd lost you forever.'

'Look at what you did to my arm,' she said suddenly, turning her right arm over to reveal a deep blue and purple bruise. 'Call yourself a vet.' She laughed. 'I am joking. Thank you for saving my life.' Her eyes filled with water. 'Oh Steve it was so terrible. I cannot imagine how terrible it was. Was it really terrible?'

'It was the most dreadful thing in my life,' he said. 'But it's over. Everything is over for me now,' he said and he told her what he was going to do.

She looked at him. 'That's why I love you,' she said, 'because you always do what you think is right.'

'Not always,' he said.

She looked at him as though in severe pain, the tears glistening in her eyes. 'I think perhaps always,' she whispered and held his head to her breast.

'Will you come with me when you get out of here?' he said.

'Of course,' she replied. 'I will phone Carlo and tell him. I still love him and he loves me. He will be upset. I am sad for that. I did not want to hurt him like this. I did not plan it. It has happened. I cannot help the way I feel.'

'You can't help the way you feel but you don't have to act on it.'

The words hit him hard, bouncing around his head. The words he had spoken to Rachel had returned to haunt him. He could see Carlo in his mind, pleading and tearful, his self respect discarded in his attempt to keep the wife he loved.

And he felt shame. He, Steve Turner felt shame at what he was doing and he buried his face into Francesca's shoulder to hide the shame from her and he smelt the wonderful smell of her above the sanitised hospital sheets and he wished that the world could end at that moment so that all the complications of the next few weeks could be removed.

'Tomorrow I will come to you,' said Francesca. 'Tomorrow I will be yours. Can you wait for me until then?'

He hid his face in her shoulder and murmured the words just loud enough for her to hear.

'Forever. I will wait for you forever and I will always be with you.'

And knowing without a doubt in his heart what was going to happen, he cried.

Chapter 50

The letter was sent. He was now without a job. He had copied the letter to Colin Hunt, Des Quiet, Graham Thompson and Herbert Bluster. He wondered what Bluster would make of it. Probably choke on his incredulity at the bare faced cheek. Questioning Head Office policy. Refusing to comply. He would love to have been a fly on the wall.

A weight had been lifted from his shoulders. He no longer had to lie to people. No longer had to persuade them to do things he didn't care for. He had one more unpleasant thing to do. In his hotel room he picked up the phone and dialled an Italian number he had got from Personnel.

The phone clicked and a voice said something he did not understand. He hoped Carlo could speak English.

'Is that Carlo Capotti?' he said.

'Yes. Who is speaking please?'

'You don't know me. My name's Steve Turner. I'm a … a friend of Francesca's'

'I do know you. You are the one who is hurting us. How do you think I feel? Francesca is my wife. I love her. Have you not thought on that? No respect for it?'

'Look Carlo. I'm sorry but I love your …, I mean I love Francesca.' It was an easy mistake but it hurt him. Deep down inside it hurt him. It had seemed so natural to say 'your wife' but the word 'your' had been the trigger for the hurt. 'Your' was an admission of theft. An admission of having done something about which to feel guilty. He could not honourably use the word 'your'.

'You love my wife. I love my wife. The whole world loves my wife. How could anyone not love my wife? She is beautiful. The most beautiful woman in the world. But that is nothing to you. She is my wife. Not your wife. She is not yours to have.'

'Francesca doesn't know I've phoned you. I wanted to tell you that I love her and want to look after her. She loves me and wants to be with me. We cannot change the way we feel.'

'And me. Am I to sit here and wait? To sit and see you take her from me. Like watching a man cut off my arm or my leg and do nothing. She is as much a part of me as that. How can I just sit and let it happen. It is too painful. Too terrifying. Too much to bear.'

Steve heard him sobbing. Like a pan of water boiling on the stove, the heat full on. He wanted to turn the gas off. To stop it bubbling over the top and burning with a sharp fizz. But Francesca was his too now. They had crossed the boundary of normal convention. Not physically. But they had said too much to each other. Confided in each other. Declared their interest in each other. An intimacy of deep intent. Of prolonged commitment and interest. Not a whim of physical attraction. That would be easy to resist in comparison.

'I want what is best for Francesca,' Steve said. 'I just want her to be happy.' Words echoed from the past, stored up for his own use, a searing pain in his head and heart, an old familiar pain.

'And me?' said Carlo through tears of fear. 'And my love for Francesca? And her love for me? What is to become of that?'

*'I've never really loved you.' Rachel's words drove into his chest with
the white heat of rage. 'I've never really loved you. I'll always love you. I
didn't know what I was doing. I must have been insane.'*

*Like the shifting sands of a desert; the truth in motion. Yesterday's
reality; tomorrow's fantasy. The cold hard feel of the barrel of a gun, his
mouth embracing it, his hand trembling on the trigger. A battle in his
head between an unsure, painful future and certain merciful oblivion. He
had found the strength. Dragged it up from the love of his friends and his
family and it had kept him alive.*

He thought of Carlo. He wondered if Carlo had such family and
friends who would care for him.

'Francesca is my life. I cannot live without her. Please, please, leave
her alone.'

Steve hung up. There was nothing more to say. Nothing more he
could say. He had hoped to persuade Carlo, and now he was shaking
with emotion and frightening memories. He went to the bathroom
and washed his face, the cold water steadied him; calmed him. Forty
five and still messing up like an adolescent. He shrugged. That was life.
There were no guarantees in life. He lay on his bed and went to sleep.

It was nearly eight at night when he awoke. He changed his clothes
and put on CNN news. A lady contiguous to an infected farm had
barricaded herself into her cottage with three pet goats in her living
room to prevent them being killed. There was no suggestion that
they were infected but policy was policy and The Ministry were
seeking a court order permitting entry to the property to kill them.
No exceptions could be made for individuals. An Englishman's home
was no longer his castle.

He went down to the bar.

'I've resigned,' he told Sammy and Willie. 'Resigned on grounds
of conscience. I wrote to the PVO today and told him my views on
what was going on. I'm going to stay here for another day or two and
then I'm going home.'

He was light headed as though he were a child and tomorrow
was his birthday. The warm sparkling feeling of the end of term or
the receipt of successful exam results. Euphoria that something had
ended. Experience told him the feeling would not last. The hangover
of reality would follow.

'Are you sure you've done the right thing?' Sammy asked. Her face twitched with concern, her eyes narrow, looking into his soul. Disbelief and respect mingled in the face he knew so well and loved. Yes he loved Sammy. She was unusual and he would miss her. He flattered himself that she would miss him.

'I don't have a choice,' he said quietly. 'I can't condone what's being done.'

Willie spoke up. 'Aye you're quite right Steve,' he said. 'I don't understand it all myself but there has to be a better way than this. It's fucking shocking; it's mayhem out there.'

Steve drained his pint. 'Who's for another?' he said and went to the bar. Willie joined him.

'When does Francesca get out of hospital?'

'Tomorrow if all's well.' The look of fear in her eyes was burnt into his soul.

'Any news from the police on Sonia?'

'Nothing I've heard.'

He looked across the room to where Fernando and Sarah sat gazing and smiling at each other. Two people in love with no complications; hopes and expectations on their faces. It lifted his own spirits and he raised his glass to them and decided there and then that he would get unashamedly and completely drunk.

Chapter 51

'Can we go for a drive please Steve?' Francesca said. 'To the restaurant where we had lunch. I would like to go there one more time. Before we leave tomorrow.'

She was pale and troubled. Steve had collected her from the hospital and brought her to the hotel where she had phoned Carlo. A phone call that had lasted an hour.

'I had to persuade him not to come,' she said. 'He must not come. That I could not cope with. The pain is too much. In here,' she patted her chest. 'I don't understand what is happening. I loved him. I still love him. But you are different. It is a different love that I have for you. An exciting love. A dangerous love. Not a safe love. It is the love of swimming underwater in a warm sea to see the fishes. Holding your breath beyond endurance because you cannot bear to resurface and leave behind such a beautiful world. A love you would take risks for. Risk all for. Risk my life for. It scares me. And the pain I am causing Carlo scares me too. Can we go now?'

He opened the car passenger door and clicked it shut behind her. Rain fell; a fine drizzle. Grey as his thoughts. Shades of grey with black and tiny sparks of white. A magpie in the tree, calling in alarm. He searched for a second one, waited, and there it was, in the bushes to the right. He wasn't superstitious. Just cautious.

He drove west with Francesca's head on his shoulder and he kissed her hair every few seconds to reassure him that she was there. The smell of her hair and skin. Vanilla and roses, orange light in her eyes. He felt the slow rhythmic rise and fall of her chest, a rush of euphoria and the empty ache of a lonely grey green ocean that washed upon a rocky shore.

He found no peace. That was what he craved. Peace and fulfilment.

'I feel peaceful inside,' Rachel said, pointing at her chest with closed fingers. The world was collapsing around her and she felt peaceful inside. His own frustration and torment and the serene detachment on Rachel's face taunted and teased him. Sitting in the armchair looking at him with the undisguised interest of a collector in a specimen. That was what he had become. A specimen to be examined and worked on and finally put away as unwanted.

'What are you thinking Francesca?' he said, and they reached the coast where powder grey waves drifted onto the shore and the rain whipped into swirling spray.

She did not reply. Not immediately. She moved her head a little. Working it deeper into his shoulder as a cat might curl in a down pillow; seeking out the warmth and comfort and softness.

'I am thinking that I am lucky to be alive. That I have been given a second chance. That I must use that chance wisely.'

Steve thought of Carlo. When Rachel had left him for Patrick he had wished her dead. Dead, dead, dead. Her death he could have coped with. Living a life without her was cruel but living without her knowing that she was with another was crueller still. He had wished her dead every day at first waking. Patrick too. Would Carlo wish Francesca dead? Was he even now wishing her dead? Praying for a fatal accident that would reduce his own pain?

That was the real pain. Lying alone and wondering where she was and what she was doing. That was pain on pain. A hot knife in the throat, twisting and cutting. A spear in the stomach, hooked and tearing, ripping out his innards like eviscerating a chicken for the oven. In the dead of night seeing her writhing and moaning beneath 'him', her hands clasping his naked back, her fingers gripping his flesh and then thrown backwards to cling to the bed frame, to resist the force of his movements, her head thrown back with slightly parted lips and the sweat on her forehead and the dilated pupils of imminent death and rebirth.

That was the real pain and he knew it so well and knew that it would now be Carlo's and he knew that he would wish Francesca dead and he wanted no one to ever again wish her dead.

'And I am thinking about Carlo too.' She shifted her head again and looked up at him.

'I don't want to go to the restaurant now Steve. It was so perfect the last time. It cannot be so good again and I want nothing taken from that memory. Nothing at all.' She sighed. 'It is too good to lose. Too good to expect the same again. Let us go nowhere near for fear we stumble on it and the memory is changed. Do you understand Steve? Do you Steve?' She was pleading again with him.

He kissed her head and one of his own tears fell onto the chestnut hair and sat, unmoved, quivering like a drop of morning dew on a spider's web, clear and magnificent like a diamond glinting in pale lemon sunlight. He stopped the car where they could look out to sea and he took her face in his hands and kissed her gently, oh so very gently on her lips. And on her eyes and cheeks too; on her forehead; the tip of her nose; her chin; the curve of her neck. Intimate but not passionate. A soft and tender intimacy. He wanted nothing in return but her happiness and he trusted that his own inner peace would stem from there.

'Is this really true?' she said. 'All that has happened, this joy and sadness. Like oil on water, mixed but not joining. Moving like dancers around each other, touching and caressing but never becoming one. What are we to do Steve? What are we to do? Tell me. Tell me, please.' She demanded it of him and her green and orange eyes flashed and burnt molten with strength and energy, pleading with him for an answer that would make everything alright.

'It's all true,' he said. 'Foot and Mouth; Sonia; Paul,; you and me;

Carlo. It's all true and we must all live with the consequences. Some will be easier to live with than others. What is important in all these things is that our consciences are clear. We must be true to ourselves. We must do what we think is right.'

'And that is why I love you, Steve Turner,' she said. 'Because you do what you think is right.'

'Not always,' he whispered.

She looked at him with intense pain in her eyes and he could see at that moment that it was lost.

'I think perhaps always,' she murmured. And she kissed him with sweetness on the lips.

They returned to the hotel in late afternoon. Sammy was sitting in the lounge, reading the paper.

'Francesca,' she called. 'How are you?'

'I am fine,' she said. 'Thanks to everybody I am fine.'

'Have you heard the news on Sonia?' Sammy said to Steve. 'It's even worse than we thought.'

'No, what is it?'

'Well she's confessed everything to the police about spreading the disease and bringing it into the country. During that trip in Asia she was telling us about it seems she collected lymph glands from pigs that had died of both Swine Fever and FMD. She froze them and then brought them back in her luggage on the plane and stored them in her mother's freezer at home. The police have been there and found more bits and pieces still frozen. She infected the pigs in East Anglia with Swine Fever and those at Warren Farm with Foot and Mouth.'

'She planned the whole thing then, right from the start,' said Steve. 'Hard to believe such bitterness could last so long.'

'There's more to it than that,' Sammy said. 'It's a sad story really. She got married years ago but the marriage failed. She couldn't have kids. The abortion was blamed for causing adhesions. Her husband left her because of it and she had a mental breakdown. Spent some time in a psychiatric unit and apparently recovered fully.'

'I feel sad for her,' said Francesca. 'It is a sad, sad story. I do not believe that she is wicked.'

'Maybe not, but look at the harm she's done. Killed Paul. Tried to kill you, and God only knows how many farmers will go under before all this is finished,' said Steve.

'What will happen to her now?' asked Francesca.

'A secure hospital I guess,' said Sammy. 'She'll be given treatment I suppose though whether she'll ever get out again. Who knows?

'And what are you two going to do now?' She smiled at them. Steve was forgiven.

They did not answer. 'I'll see you tomorrow Sammy,' said Steve. 'At breakfast. And I'll tell you then.'

And then he took Francesca in his arms and lifted her off her feet. He carried her up the stairs and she looked into his eyes with wonder, unblinking and unflinching. He carried her into her room and lay her on the bed and took off her shoes for her. And then he lay on the bed facing her, his eyes focused on hers.

They lay together all night unmoving, their hands held tight in each others. They did not sleep. They did not kiss. They did not make love. They did not speak. They stared into each others eyes and they lived a lifetime together. A lifetime in which they had fine and beautiful children with their mother's chestnut hair and their father's eyes. They walked together on beaches of white sand with swaying palms where white surf spray made rainbows against an azure sky. They lived in an Italian farmhouse where they raised sheep and grew grapes for wine and olives for oil, and they loved each other for always. They grew old in peace and their grandchildren came to stay and they told them stories of how they had met and fallen in love. They grew old and their bodies stooped and their skin became cracked with the wind and the sun. But to Steve, Francesca was always the most beautiful woman in the whole world with her shining chestnut hair, now streaked with grey, and he was the man who had shown her such happiness.

At six in the morning as the dawn began to break Francesca spoke.

'I love you Steve and I will always love you. I will never forget you and you will be in my heart and in my dreams, always. But it will be hidden from all others so that no hurt is caused to them by the feelings that I have for you. I know that what we do now is right and may God keep us safe in his hands.'

He kissed her fleetingly, tasting the sleepy saltiness of her lips.

'I love you Francesca. You have shown me that a new life exists for me and your beauty and loveliness have become a part of my heart. I know now that I will love again but the love I have for you will never fade. Be happy. Enjoy your life and bring joy to all those around you.

That is your gift to this world and I would change none of it lest it change the very thing in you which I love.'

He kissed her again on the lips; the cheeks and forehead and then gently on each eyelid. He felt her body sink deeper into the quilt and the slow rhythmic breathing of restful sleep.

'My love, my love,' he said as he closed the bedroom door quietly behind him. He went downstairs to breakfast; he was early, the restaurant empty. He sat at a table and smiled to himself. An hour later he was joined by Sammy.

'And where is Francesca?' Sammy asked, a twinkling smile on her face.

He said nothing and she caught his mood.

'I'm sorry,' she said.

'Don't be,' he replied. 'We all of us know it's the right thing to do. I'm not sad. I feel relief Sammy.'

'What are you going to do then?'

'I'll go home and rest for a while and then I'll decide. It's changed my life Sammy and that's no bad thing. I've been a selfish bastard for years and now I've got the chance to change. And there's something in the back of my mind that I can't quite grasp but I think it's important. I'm got to give myself a chance to find out what it is. I just need the time. I just need the time.' He was weary.

'Steve,' Sammy said. 'If it's any help, I think you're doing the right thing. In all ways.'

'Thanks,' he said, stretching his hand across the table to hold hers before standing and kissing her on the top of her head. 'Cheers,' Sammy he said. 'Say cheers to Willie for me.'

'I will,' she said. 'And good luck Steve.'

He walked out to the car park and over to his car, climbed in and looked in the mirror. He saw Rachel staring back at him; saw the golden curls and the pale blue, tear filled eyes and everything that they had shared together from long ago. He smiled at her, winked, and closed his eyes. When he opened them she was gone.

'Goodbye Rachel,' he said. 'Take care, and good luck.'

He started the engine of his Healey and reversed onto the drive. He drove slowly past the hotel door without looking, eased out onto the main road and pottered along in the traffic until he was out of sight and earshot. Only then did he gun the accelerator and pull out into the fast lane to head north for the life of freedom that now lay ahead.

Postscript

The UK approach

The 2001 United Kingdom Foot and Mouth Epidemic started on 20th February 2001 and the last of 2026 confirmed outbreaks occurred on 30th September 2001. Official figures put the number of animals slaughtered as a result of the control strategy at greater than 6 million. It is also estimated that an additional 3 to 4 million young lambs and calves were slaughtered but not counted. Estimates of the total cost to the country in direct and indirect losses range from six to nine billion pounds Sterling.

Many weeks after Steve Turner suggested that poor hygiene and fomites were the main means of disease spread, Biosecurity became the buzz word of the eradication campaign. Four months after he had suggested designating an Infected Zone as an area that farm vehicles would be prohibited from leaving, the 'Blue Box' concept of restricted areas, (within which farm vehicles had to pass through disinfection stations), was introduced as a means of preventing the spread of disease.

Three Government commissioned enquiries investigated and reported on the epidemic, none of which, to Steve Turner's satisfaction, looked deeply enough or broadly enough into what really happened and why. It appeared that everyone in any position of power to influence the policy and its outcome was entirely blameless.

The alternative approach

In Uruguay an outbreak of Foot and Mouth Disease began on 23rd April 2001. A Stamping out strategy was initiated but this was abandoned on 29th April due to the rapid spread of disease and resistance by local farmers to the policy.

On 5th May systematic vaccination of all the county's 10.6 million cattle was started and this was completed on 6th June. A second round of vaccination was begun on 15th June and completed on 22nd July. Only cattle were vaccinated in spite of large numbers of sheep being present and which grazed alongside the cattle.

A total of 2057 outbreaks occurred, the last one on 21st August.

Total number of animals slaughtered during the outbreak was 6,937 (all during the first week of the outbreak). Total cost of eradication is given as 13.6 million US Dollars, of which 7.5 million US Dollars was spent on vaccine purchase.

Total economic losses as a result of the epidemic were estimated to be upwards of 200 million US Dollars.

The European Union opened its borders to the importation of chilled, deboned meat from Uruguay in November 2001.

Reference: The successful control and eradication of Foot and Mouth Disease epidemics in South America in 2001, P. Sutmoller and R. Casas Olascoaga

Evidence for the Temporary Committee on Foot and Mouth Disease of the European Parliament, Meeting 2 September 2002, Strasbourg. Presented by Dr Paul Sutmoller